Praise for *CLADE*

Short-listed for the 2003 Philip K. Dick Award

"Smart, well-written, and highly imaginative, *Clade* does for cutting-edge biology what *Neuromancer* did for a cyber future. Budz may well have created a new genre: BioPunk."

—Kevin J. Anderson, bestselling author of the Saga of Seven Suns series

"A remarkable book. Scientific, tense, gritty, and thoughtful, *Clade* pulls you into a bioengineered tomorrow that may come startlingly true."

—David Brin, bestselling author of the Uplift series

"An excellent first novel . . . Budz has created an intelligent future that is highly original while evoking the best elements of the dramatic street stories of William Gibson."

—*Denver Post*

"Budz writes poetically, with grand descriptive power. His characters are worriedly and necessarily in one kind or another of trouble. You'll itch and fret for them, moms and brothers and lost kids and all. The very advanced tech surround, though, immerses the reader, and I want another dose."

—*San Diego Union-Tribune*

"*Clade* is a very accomplished first novel—indeed, it's a very accomplished novel full stop. Budz's characters are well drawn, the California setting is vivid, and, without preaching, he makes some strong points about the fragility of our environment . . . a striking debut."

—*Sci Fi Weekly* (A- pick)

"Budz has imagined a world with sufficient texture and resonance to make it not only a rewarding place to explore, but one worth thinking about, and one worth revisiting." —*Locus*

"A fast-paced read animated by an engrossing, nervous energy." —*Booklist*

"*Clade,* a first novel by Mark Budz, demonstrates biotech's story potentials admirably. . . . The book's heart beats with age-old questions of loyalty and betrayal, Information-Age questions of community and choice, and ageless questions of what makes a family." —*Strange Horizons*

"A whopper of a debut . . . if you prefer the hard science of 'Minority Report' and 'The Matrix' to the space opera 'Star Wars,' you're going to love *Clade.*" —*Santa Cruz Sentinel*

Praise for *CRACHE*

"Imagine a collaboration between John Steinbeck and Michael Crichton, written in the overheated style of William Gibson's *Neuromancer.*" —*New York Times Book Review*

"Budz's first book, *Clade,* drew comparisons to William Gibson; his second proves that such claims were far from hyperbole. . . . Budz may be poised to become hard SF's next superstar." —*Publishers Weekly* (starred review)

"Budz imagines some delightfully creative twists in quantum physics, as well as nods to advanced mathematics and biology that will thrill masters in those fields. *Crache* is a novel full of the unexpected, concocted from the brain of someone who really can imagine what it's like to be 'post-everything.'" —*Sci Fi Dimensions*

"Read on, *rockeros. Crache* has novel situations, rounded characters and Big, Big Conflicts." —*San Diego Union-Tribune*

"A fascinating look at Orwellian society." —*Midwest Book Review*

"Budz's second glimpse of the bizarre post-ecocaust world of *Clade* is one of gripping intrigue." —*Booklist*

"Both entertaining and comprehensible... It makes us even more curious about Budz's third novel than we were about this one." —*Locus*

Praise for *IDOLON*

"Postmodern fun... I started the novel on my subway ride home last night, and was utterly engrossed by the time my stop arrived." —Salon.com

"This new book finds Budz still hip, energetic and talented." —SciFi.com

"*Idolon* is a fun, old-fashioned science fiction noir thriller with a well-thought-out premise and up-to-the-minute scientific speculations. Budz is building a name for himself among hard science fiction readers and this new novel should add to his growing reputation." —*BookPage*

"Budz demonstrates a solid talent for balancing his hard-SF speculation with briskly paced storytelling.... [*Idolon*] succeeds as both a noir thriller and an acerbic comment on an image-based culture." —*Locus*

Also by Mark Budz

Clade

Crache

Idolon

TILL HUMAN VOICES WAKE US

MARK BUDZ

BANTAM BOOKS

TILL HUMAN VOICES WAKE US
A Bantam Book / August 2007

Published by Bantam Dell
A Division of Random House, Inc.
New York, New York

This is a work of fiction. Names, characters, places, and incidents either are the product of the author's imagination or are used fictitiously. Any resemblance to actual persons, living or dead, events, or locales is entirely coincidental.

Cover design by Shasti O'Leary Soudant

ISBN 978-0-553-58851-4

Printed in the United States of America
Published simultaneously in Canada

www.bantamdell.com

OPM 10 9 8 7 6 5 4 3 2 1

For Marina

Man's main task in life is to give birth to himself.

—ERICH FROMM

TILL HUMAN VOICES WAKE US

1

Santa Cruz, September 12

The singing was back.

Rudi Lauchman paused on the sidewalk, trying to isolate the precise source of the sound. The voice was soft, melodic. He couldn't make out any words. It was more like humming, vaguely choral.

And not, he felt reasonably sure, coming from inside his head.

He had been hearing the voice around town, off and on, for a week. Close to the Café Pergolesi one day, the library the next. Elusive. More imagined than real.

This time it seemed to be coming from a recessed doorway partly concealed by a juniper bush dotted with small blue-purple berries. A FOR LEASE sign hung in one window of the small office building.

Rudi found himself standing next to it, his hands thrust into his pockets, unable to remember how he got there. He couldn't recall turning onto the walkway, or making his way up the path.

Another lapse.

He shut his eyes. He'd heard the song before, he was sure

of it. Church, possibly. But maybe not. He got confused. Sometimes, voices didn't match faces. He heard one person talking and saw another.

The music could be the accident talking... his old life—before the crash—bleeding into this one.

But this song wasn't the one he was running from. This full-bodied contralto was different from the sinuous soprano that slithered into his head and spoke to him in a flicking, unintelligible whisper, raspy as scales against dry grass.

The singing stopped. Rudi opened his eyes.

"What are you doing here? Peeping on me?" A large woman with a metal cane and a blue knitted cap stood in the doorway. She glared at Rudi with bloodshot eyes before cutting a glance at his hands.

Rudi jerked his hands from his pockets. "I wasn't—"

The woman sniffed. "Why don't you play with yourself someplace else? Before I call the cops."

Rudi adjusted his baseball cap, careful not to disturb the lining. In the doorway behind her, he could make out a shopping cart, blanket, and scuffed black boom box. "I heard you singing. That's all."

The woman leaned forward, her forehead creased by a frown. "What have you got under there? Reynolds Wrap?"

"You've been drinking," Rudi said. His scalp prickled.

The woman chuckled. Her shoulders rocked like two sofa cushions jiggling in an earthquake. "Not enough."

"I've been hearing you a lot. Do you always sing when you're drunk?"

"Singing's cheap. It don't cost nothin'. Which is exactly what I got right now. In case you were wondering."

"Except for a broken heart," he said. "Or an empty soul."

The crease in the woman's brow deepened briefly, then

relaxed, as if overcome by sudden weariness. "You're crazy," she said.

"Rudi." He held out his hand, then snatched it back when it looked like she might whack it with the cane.

"Get a move on. Before you get any wrong ideas." She wavered, eerily insubstantial despite her size. "You hear?"

Rudi tilted his head. Barely audible music from the boom box scratched at the air.

The woman followed his lopsided gaze. "Aretha," she said. " 'This Bitter Earth.' Now, leave me be." She shifted her weight. "My knees are givin' me hell."

"I have a radio show," Rudi said. "I play music sometimes and talk about stuff. I always do one Sunday mornings." He told her the A.M. frequency. "It's for people who can't make it to church."

"I'll be sure to listen. Now get outta here." She waved him on with the cane then hobbled into the shadows of her makeshift cave.

The next morning, at six-thirty, Rudi was transmitting from behind the Safeway on Mission Street.

Radio Baptiste. That was how he thought of himself: baptizing anyone who would listen with radio waves instead of water.

Sitting at the console in the back of the sound van, Rudi's skull felt like a pressure cooker ready to explode. He'd kicked off the hour-long program, *The Rod of God,* with a classic Greg Brown tune, "Lord, I Have Made You a Place in My Heart." It had been a favorite of his before the motorcycle accident, and like everything else associated with his old life he kept it around as a reminder of history not to repeat. From whiskey and bare-naked women, he launched into a rambling sermon that equated faith to the sound of one hand clapping.

"Belief can't be explained," Rudi said, winding down. "You don't have to see the tree to hear the sound it makes when it falls."

That was what he clung to since being released from the Lakeshore Foundation facility in Birmingham. Back in the apartment he'd been renting before the accident, he had found several joss sticks that had once belonged to his sister, a copy of *Zen and the Art of Motorcycle Maintenance*, and a book called *The Blue Cliff Record*, with the Zen koans circled like points on a map he couldn't remember. Linnea. He hadn't thought about her for years. That part of his life was like an old well sitting in the back of his head. One misstep, and he'd fall in. Never see light again.

As usual, he wrapped up with a confessional, beamed out to the world via the dish atop the van.

"My mother knew I was a worthless sinner the day I was born." Rudi cleared his throat. "She said she could tell from the way I whined. I wasn't like my big sister. When I heard that, all I wanted to do was crawl back into the hole that spat me out. Not that she'd ever take me back. According to her, after all the problems I caused her those first nine months, she was glad to get rid of me. Her only regret was she didn't do it sooner."

The words, close to fifteen years old now, still hurt to repeat. But pain, as he'd reminded his listeners many times, could be a blessing. Lance a boil and it would heal.

Exhausted, his face sweaty and his hands shaking, Rudi slumped into the wrinkled bosom of the sleeping bag in the back corner of the van.

He woke two hours later, roused by a heavy-fisted thrombosis of sound. Someone hammering on the back of the van.

His brain felt pureed, Gerber baby food in a cracked jar. Drained, empty of the euphoria that gripped him during a broadcast, he sat up and pressed his fingers to his temples.

Food. That was what he needed.

He checked the time. Just after nine. Maybe the woman he'd met would be at the soup kitchen. Maybe she'd listened to his broadcast. Maybe the radio waves had washed over her like the waves of the River Jordan, leaching the hurt from her heart and the alcohol from her veins.

Rudi opened the back doors to the van and staggered out. The coastal fog was burning off, retreating under an unfocused sun. Mottled patches of melanoma blue shone through the haze. Rudi squinted at himself in the passenger's side mirror. He needed a shave and haircut. He ran his fingers through the lank strands plastered to his forehead, smoothing them into place. His eyes were red-rimmed around glossy black pupils. This morning they seemed to radiate as much light as they let in.

Turning from his reflection, his gaze skittered across the rust-scabbed side of the van. Despite several glossy applications of white enamel spray paint, a school of Jesus Saves fish with crosses for eyes, and a three-foot gash left by Hurricane Anika, the van's corporate logo was still barely visible:

RAD I/O.

The outline of the letters, tintype gray under the patchy paint, resurrected the dusty memory of a Greek bas-relief he'd seen during a fifth-grade field trip to a museum.

Rudi didn't think of the van as stolen. More like borrowed . . . or on temporary loan. He'd refused to hole up with his traveling companions when the hurricane hit and they'd opted to wait for the storm to abate before continuing on to Mobile. After they'd hunkered down in a cable-ready Pascagoula motel, playing it safe, he'd decided to go on without them.

"I'll be back in a day or two," he said before leaving.

"You're crazy." Bethel eyed the low-slung clouds and the apoplectic thrashing of sycamore trees. "You're gonna die."

"If that's God's will."

"Suicide is a sin," Travis had reminded him.

"Not if it's in the service of the Lord," Rudi quipped with blithe, practiced fatalism.

Besides, he suspected they had an ulterior motive for wanting to spend the night in a motel. He didn't want any part of it.

In the days leading up to landfall, the Scion of Adam congregation had decided to dispatch the sound van from Prattville, Alabama, to Mobile and vicinity. The little strip mall church rented the van on weekends to spread the Gospel to people who couldn't make it into town for services. With the storm coming, they wanted to be there on the front lines when it hit.

"Eye of the devil," Bethel had said when the hurricane was still a couple of hundred miles offshore.

"That's right." Jim Odette's head bobbed as if attached to a spring. "People are gonna need hope. They're gonna need to hear the Lord is with them."

"Amen," Marilee Odette echoed. "If things get as bad as they say, we've got a duty to help lift them up."

On the drive down, along I-65, Rudi had been consumed with thoughts of Ezekiel; of dead bones rising up out of the earth, coming together, and putting on flesh. He kept his Bible on the seat next to him, within easy reach, and vowed to do whatever it took to make that happen. People would hear the Scripture, and if their spirit was broken it would be mended. If their bodies were injured, they would be healed. If their hope was spent, it would be replenished.

In retrospect, zeal had gotten the best of him. Proverbs

warned that "pride goeth before destruction." There was too much fury, during the storm and after, to make it to ground zero. But at that point he was on a mission, stopped only when a wind-borne branch slammed into the thin shell of his van. For a second it was déjà vu all over again. He had fishtailed off the asphalt, nearly plunging into a drainage ditch choked with water, clapboard siding, and a chicken coop deposited there by the category four winds.

He blacked out, then. Darkness claimed him, as it had after the motorcycle accident. He didn't remember hitting his head, but he must have. This time around he lost the rest of the day and a night. When he came to and could drive again, the road to Mobile was full of obstacles. In addition to a bone-crushing headache, he was hindered by debris, infrared-sniffing FEMA drones looking for stranded flood victims, and roadblocks. The police and National Guard refused to let anyone but relief and rescue workers into the city. The streets were swamped. Squeezed by the headache, pursued by the mosquito whine of the drones crisscrossing the sky, his vision blurred and finally his resolve.

So he'd gone on, out of the devastation, and kept going. The van was fully insured, covered against all damages including loss. That meant if it disappeared in the storm, if *he* disappeared, both of them could be written off.

He should have stopped, turned around, and gone back, but he didn't. The storm had done something to him, broken some fragile infrastructure. Layers of silt, which had settled under the calm currents of the church, stirred to life. His thoughts became muddy, his purpose less clear.

On the way out of town, he covered the license plates with mud and his head with aluminum foil so the rescue drones wouldn't spot him. Later, he switched the plates with plates from other dead vehicles. By the time he reached the

West Coast, he had as many plates as there were major cities, and then some.

The soup kitchen was run out of the auditorium in a Veterans Memorial building downtown. It opened at six each morning with the aroma of black coffee and oatmeal.

Rudi parked in the bank lot next door, tucked a wrinkled but clean white shirt into his tan corduroys, slipped on his blue polyester suit coat, and went to talk to Sister Daminca, who was ladling out bowls of warm oatmeal for distribution in the makeshift cafeteria.

"I met a woman last night," Rudi said.

"I'm not sure this is a conversation we should be having." Sister Daminca smiled. In jeans and a beige pullover sweater, she didn't fit his image of a nun. She wasn't old enough or plain enough, and she wore makeup—a smidgen of eye shadow and pink lip gloss. Rudi tried not to hold her vanity, or her affiliation, against her. Underneath, she was a decent person.

Rudi picked up a ladle and described the woman. "I was wondering if you knew her."

"Sounds like Irene. But she hasn't been around in a while. Not for a few months. I kind of figured she'd moved on. You know, decided she needed a change of scenery or whatever. How did she look?"

"She threatened me with a cane."

Daminca puckered her lips. "Definitely Irene. Except for the cane. That's not a good sign."

"She'd been drinking."

Daminca's brow wrinkled. "Next time you see her, tell her I said hi."

Rudi nodded, his ladle poised over an empty bowl. "If there is a next time. I don't think we hit it off."

"The fact that she talked to you at all is a miracle. You must have done something right."

Rudi squirmed. He'd always felt more comfortable giving praise than accepting it. "All I did was listen."

"That's all any of us can do. Sometimes that's all it takes. After that it's in God's hands."

"Did you listen to me earlier?" he said.

Daminca looked at him, puzzled. "I'm listening to you now, Rudi."

"I was hoping she'd hear me. You know?"

"Sometimes it doesn't look like a person is listening, when they really are."

She spoke the words gingerly, careful to explain herself. It made him wonder who she was defending—herself, or Irene?

"We have to trust we're being heard," she went on. "The same way that we trust God to hear us."

"Or that God trusts us to hear Him," Rudi said.

Daminca smiled, her expression a jumble of agreement and relief. "Yes. It's important we don't give up or lose faith—in God or in ourselves."

"I know." Rudi nodded. "But sometimes it's hard not to get discouraged."

"Don't worry." Daminca touched him lightly on the arm. "It will be okay."

"What?"

"Irene. Or whatever else is upsetting you." Her hand retreated as she busied herself with the next bowl.

"I'm not upset. Just worried."

"Is there anything I can do for you?" Sister Daminca hesitated. "I mean... do *you* need anything?"

"I'm fine."

"You seem anxious."

Rudi could see it in her eyes. She wondered if he was strung out. "I didn't sleep very well last night," he said.

"If you do need anything, let me know. All right?"

Sister Daminca seemed expectant. She was like that, one of those people who needed to be needed.

"Promise?" Her voice prodded.

Rudi forced a nod. The back of his neck prickled under her ardent sincerity.

That evening, he broadcast from the Costco parking lot near the homeless shelter, using Corinthians verse 7 as his starting point—"we walk by faith, not by sight"—and followed it with "Way Down in the Hole," by the Blind Boys of Alabama.

"Those boys are blind," he said, "but they can see. You know why they can see? I'll tell you why. They can see because they are filled with the Holy Ghost. The light that enters them comes not through their eyes but their hearts. When you see with your heart—with faith—you will never walk in darkness..."

He drummed his fingers on the Bible opened in front of him. "John tells us to 'walk while ye have the light, lest darkness come upon you.' But if the light comes from within, darkness will never come upon you. The world will always be brightly lit. The path ahead will always be clear, and you will always be able to find your way home."

Rudi wrapped up with another tune, "Motherless Child," from the same Blind Boys CD. He often felt motherless, friendless, and homeless—he wondered if Irene felt the same way.

He wasn't right—not with God and not with himself. He needed to set his house in order. After the accident, during the year-long recovery, the church had helped him do that. It had taken care of him when he couldn't take care of himself.

It had rearranged the furniture of his life so he knew where to sit, sleep, and eat. The storm had made a mess of that. Like the homes in Mobile, Fairhope, and Prichard, the floodwaters had coursed through him, undermining his foundation.

"After my head injury," he confessed, his voice dipping to a whisper, "I had no one to go home to, no place to rest. I was alone. I never knew my dad. My mother never told me his name. She was in jail, and my sister was gone. So were all the people I'd counted as friends. After the accident, I was left high and dry. My world was dark as the Valley of Death. I couldn't find my way out until I found Jesus. Jesus took me by the hand. He led me out of the darkness. He can do the same for you."

Talking to himself as much as anybody. Trying to find his way back again, as if mouthing the words would make them come true.

Irene wasn't in the doorway. She had moved on, migratory, foraging for food.

Hours later, around midnight, Rudi heard her humming to herself from behind a low wall sheltered by a row of red-flowered bottlebrush. She was bundled against the fog in a Salvation Army blanket ripe with the smell of cigarettes, naphthalene, and dried sweat. White plastic grocery bags hung off the sides of her shopping cart like saddlebags on a horse, sagging under the weight of aluminum cans, bottles, and articles of clothing that he couldn't identify.

"Tin Head," she said.

"You don't stay put very long, do you?" Rudi joked. "Who are you running from?"

She blinked, trying to bring him into bleary focus. "Who do you think?"

Her breath stank of wine. There was a weary droop to the wrinkles on her cheeks. "I don't know," he said.

She sniffed. "Same person as you, I reckon."

"The devil?"

"Myself." She spat on the hardpan. A streetlight spilled halogen glare onto the office building behind her, and the asphalt glittered with bits of mica and broken glass. She wore the same wool cap, sweater, and ankle-length skirt as the day before. Her cane rested next to her, within easy reach.

Rudi set his shoulder pack on the ground and plopped down next to her, his back against the rough white stucco. The headache was back. He shut his eyes, then opened them. "You hungry?"

"Depends."

"I got some leftover pizza." He pulled a foil-wrapped slice out of the pack. "It's cold but it's still good."

"What kind?"

"Pepperoni."

Her eyes narrowed. "You didn't jizz on it, or anything? Did you?"

Rudi blinked. Irene burst into a cackle, the laugh working its way back from the corners of her mouth to reveal bloody gums.

Rudi opened the crumpled foil and tore the slice in half, careful not to touch the food with his fingers. He took a bite from one half, then offered her the other.

She accepted the slice, but paused briefly to inspect the topping. "You can't be too careful," she said. "Nothin' personal."

Rudi scowled. "People really do that?"

"Some folks think it's funny to hurt people." Irene took a test bite. "Think we're stupid or deserve to be punished."

"For what?"

"They're the ones need help," Irene said. "Not me. I don't hurt no one. Mind my own business." She took another tentative bite, careful to avoid chewing on the right side of her mouth. "If you're smart you won't take nothing except cans, and no cans with any punctures or puffy tops."

The child seat on the shopping cart held her boom box. Rudi stood, retrieved the radio, and set it between them. He switched on the power, and the dial lit up. It wasn't tuned to the right place. She had it set to the local NPR affiliate.

"I did a broadcast a little while ago," he said. "I thought you might have listened, heard what I had to say."

"I ain't exactly the church-going type." Irene swallowed the last of her crust, then coughed at something deeper in her lungs.

"Maybe next time," Rudi said.

Her focus floundered. One hand flopped aimlessly. No promises, it seemed to say.

"How are your knees?" he asked.

"Been worse."

Rudi went to move the dial and the headache yawned, opening up just behind his eyes, splitting his head in two.

"Rudi?"

The voice reached down, like a hand, to pull him up, out of himself.

"You sick?"

"No."

"You can tell me."

Light pressed against his eyes. Rudi turned toward the brightness, blinking under the glare. The streetlight left a graffiti-bright scrawl.

"You're crying." Fingers brushed at the tears crawling down his cheeks, as if they were ants.

"You need me to go for help?" she said.

"No."

The headache was gone. Rudi looked up into Irene's face. He was stretched out flat on his back. Irene had pulled him onto her natty blanket. The front of his shirt was damp, Rorschach-stained.

"You threw up," Irene explained. "I used some water to wash it off. But it might not come out."

"It's funny," Rudi said.

"What?"

"I came to help you."

Irene snorted. "Can't nobody help me. Not you. Not Jesus. Not anybody. I'm beyond help."

"You don't really believe that."

The snort became a good-natured chuckle. "I don't believe in anything anymore."

"That's too bad."

"No, it's not. It's a blessing."

Past her backlit silhouette, through the clutching limbs of the bottle brush, he could see stars. "I should go." He started to sit up, but felt suddenly light-headed.

"It's all right," Irene said. She eased him back down. "You just need to get some rest. That's all. Don't worry. I ain't going anywhere. By the look of things, neither are you."

The offer, and how unthreatened he felt by it, caught him by surprise. "Just for a while," he said.

Irene took one of his hands and patted it, as if kneading dough. Under her strong fingers he could feel himself changing, being shaped into someone else.

2

San Francisco, Circa 1937

Benjamin Taupe lay on the hospital examination table, sipping careful breaths as he hoped for the best and prepared for the worst.

The room smelled of alcohol-dipped stainless steel, disinfected leather, and old paint. The off-white enamel walls were bare, and a steam radiator sat under the casement window at the far end of the room. It was sunny outside, unusual for nine o'clock in the morning. In the summer, San Francisco was often foggy until eleven or twelve. Today the thick glass panes let in bright, wavy light. In another room, scratchy laughter trickled from a console radio tuned to the latest episode of *Amos 'n' Andy*.

Despite himself, Benjamin allowed a faint smile.

"Just relax," the nurse said as she adjusted the X-ray machine. "You won't feel a thing. It'll be over with before you know it."

Moments earlier, an orderly had rolled him into place under the machine, carefully positioning him under the camera, if that's what it was called. The lens was attached to the end of a metal arm mounted to a support stand. The arm could be moved up and down, closer to his body or farther away. A second arm supported a tray or screen, which the nurse locked into place a few inches above his stomach. Thick electrical cables dangled from the machine, looping shadows onto the wall.

"You've done this before," Benjamin remarked, assuring himself. He hoped it didn't sound too much like a question.

"Lots of times." The nurse adjusted the camera, moving it right up against his head. "It's not as bad as it looks."

He focused on her instead of the machine. She was beautiful, angelic in her pure white uniform and creamy smooth skin. Dark tresses tumbled back from her forehead, held fast by a barrette on each side.

"I'll be right back," she said.

She moved out of his field of view. There was a barely audible hum and then she returned.

"One down," she said cheerily. "Five to go."

Dr. Keane had ordered the X-rays a week ago on Tuesday.

"The University of California has the best X-ray department in the San Francisco Bay area," Keane said during Benjamin's last visit. "No more fooling around."

For the last six months Benjamin's double vision, and the related headaches, had grown steadily worse. None of the physical therapy or drugs prescribed by Keane so far had helped. His condition had become debilitating. He couldn't read a topography map, peer through a transit, or enter stadia readings into a logbook.

His business partner, Zachary, had been understanding if not exactly sympathetic. But after six months, his patience was wearing thin.

"This can't continue," Zachary had said a month ago. "*I*

can't continue. Something has to change." He'd been putting in sixteen hours a day for months, doing the work of two. He couldn't keep the office running on his own. Already they were falling behind, losing business. If Benjamin couldn't hold up his end, Zachary would have to bring in someone else.

So Benjamin had gone to the doctor. Keane had a reputation around town for no-nonsense competence. Gruff, even. But Benjamin was looking for answers, not comfort. Keane had also been the only doctor who could see him that afternoon.

"You here for laudanum?" Keane had asked, peering at Benjamin over wire-frame spectacles and a large uncluttered desk. Plaques hung on the wall behind the doctor, the Latin on the diplomas unreadable.

Benjamin shifted on the hard seat of his chair. "Will that cure the headaches?"

Keane peered intently at him. "Probably not. But it'll help with the pain."

"For how long?"

"Until it kills you."

"The laudanum or the pain?" Benjamin said.

Keane's bloodshot eyes narrowed behind the circular lenses, deepening his crow's-feet.

"I want to get rid of the cause," Benjamin went on. "Not the symptom. If you are unable to do that, I'll find someone else."

Keane nodded. "Most people want me to hide their problems. Not tell them what they are."

"Thank you for your time." Benjamin stood, retrieved his jacket and hat from the stand, and prepared to leave.

"Not so fast." Keane rolled up the sleeves of his wrinkled white shirt and stepped from behind his desk. The dirty cotton exhaled the scent of perspiration and rich Havana tobacco. It was only two, but already he'd been drinking.

The nurse hummed quietly to herself as she rolled the examination table from under the X-ray machine. Benjamin kept his eyes closed and let the sound lull him.

Lately, Zachary's wife, Etta, had started humming in the same absent way whenever she came by the office and had to wait for Zachary. She had a lovely voice, and Benjamin found himself pausing to listen, lingering at Zach's door when she visited. Eight months ago, she had almost succumbed to an overdose of laudanum. A miscalculation, according to Zachary. Benjamin felt guilty for looking forward to her visits. It wasn't right, taking pleasure in his partner's wife. He had tried shutting her out. But it was no use. He couldn't....

The humming stopped. "You can get up now," the nurse said.

Benjamin sat up and blinked at the bright wash of light from the window. "What happens now?" he asked.

"Dr. Ritter will review the plates when they're done. After that, he'll contact Dr. Keane to discuss the results."

"Thank you," Benjamin said.

She smiled. "Good luck."

You're going to need it, Benjamin told himself, filling in the unspoken words he read between her peony red lips.

He put on his coat and hat and left the laboratory, unsure where to go next or what to do with himself. He felt unmoored.

He caught a trolley to Market Street. From there he headed toward Fisherman's Wharf. Streetcars from the Municipal Railway and the Market Street Railway rattled past one another in competing blasts of air. In the distance, he could make out the towers of the new Bay Bridge rising above the waterfront. The piers would be busy, bristling with its fleet of clipper-bowed Monterey fishing boats. Gone were the sprit-rigged crab boats and the fantail gasoline launches that had been prevalent in his youth.

Too busy, he decided. It would be easy to get lost in the bustle of the fish market, the boat-building shops, and the machine shop of Boicelli and Boss. He'd done it many times as a kid, watching the ships unload, fishing from the piers near the Ferry Building—or even taking one of the gigantic Southern Pacific ferries across the bay to Sausalito for the afternoon.

Now he wanted quiet. The frenzy made his head hurt; he could feel the familiar pressure squeezing his vision. Light splintered inside his head like shattered glass.

He pressed his fingers into his eyes, then headed back along Market toward 16th and Bryant and Seals Stadium, home of the San Francisco Seals, Lefty O'Doul, and Dom DiMaggio. The Mission District was more temperate than the wharf, usually free of wind and fog. The Seals were on a road trip, the stadium quiet except for the groundskeeper. Benjamin sat on the third-base line, the wooden planks hard but warm, and shut his eyes against the jagged splinters of light.

At thirty-two, it was the third inning of his life. The top of the third. The visiting team was at bat. He was playing infield, second or third. He couldn't let anything get by him, a groundball or pop-up.

He felt sick to his stomach, dizzy. To keep from throwing up, he lay down on the bench.

Focus, he told himself. *Don't think about anything else. You might be down, but you're not out.*

3

Orthinia, Design Space

Like most tears, the discontinuity started at a weak point and followed the path of least resistance. In just under a femtosecond it traveled over eighty million light-years and echoed across a lifetime like a half-remembered song. As the tear propagated, strings broke, branes chafed, and quantum foam boiled. A baryonic mist rose out of the rent, then settled like dust on the flimsy black lace of a moth-eaten funeral veil.

Perched in the center of a web of silk-fine wormholes that stretched across sixty light-years of globular cluster, the *Wings of Uriel* shuddered as the threadlike singularities tore. The swarm of nanocollectors that gathered and transmitted data to the ship along these threads ripped free and scattered leaflike in the cosmic gale. In the resulting discontinuity, time fractured and memory shattered into glassy shards. . . .

Olavo woke to a sharp stab of pain that extended from just behind his forehead to the back of his skull. He lay in bed on his back, his eyes wide open. Sweat cooled on his neck and brow. When he tried to turn his head, his neck refused to move. Likewise his arms, legs, hands, and fingers. All he could see of the room was the white plaster ceiling, textured with cumulus swirls, and rough-hewn marble walls veined with minerals, dank and varicose.

The corners of the room sweated shadows. With each beat of his heart, the gloom pulsed and his eyes rattled.

He shut his lids to quell the vibration. When he reopened them, the walls flickered in a sputter of spent neon and the room filled with ghosts. A tumultuous fresco of flattened, distorted faces appeared on the ceiling, pressing against the dull plaster and seeping through it in graffiti-bright stains. They peered down at him from anti de Sitter space with the chipped luminous expressions of Sistine Chapel cherubs.

Panic gripped him. A chalky, metallic taste filled his mouth. His heart raced as he gazed helplessly at the ceiling.

Then the room stabilized and the transients vanished.

Gingham-curtained windows gaped above his head. Pale moonlight rubbed gauzy shadows onto the blue-and-white checkered fabric. He could see the diffuse outline of a tree smudged on the concrete-cold wall across from the window.

Olavo fought to open his mouth, choked on half-formed words caught deep in his throat. He couldn't breathe. Slowly, as if drowning, he sank back into darkness, feeling it close around his head.

Where was he?

Who was he?

Footsteps in the hall outside the door.

Olavo blinked, opened his eyes. Gray, pre-dawn pallor had replaced the moonlight. The light was brighter, the shadows cast by the leaves darker. He shifted his head on the pillow, then one hand, followed by a leg.

Volition had returned, and with it recognition.

He wasn't aboard the *Wings of Uriel.* He wasn't even in hardspace. He was in a virtual construct, aboard one of the other nanoships in the Ferrer cluster. On the *Golden Fleece, Lulendo's Dream, Ignis Fatuus,* the *Green Jellaba,* or the *Swift Stitch,* somebody was testing a design thread, modifying an existing actuality or creating a new one.

This softspace upload had been more jarring than most. The back of his neck hurt. There was a persistent throb at the point where the vertebrae connected to the base of his skull. The flesh around the wound was tender. He prodded it gingerly, then checked the tip of his finger for blood.

Nothing.

Olavo sat up slowly. He took a moment to examine himself. The simunculus wore a green caftan over loose cotton leggings. The cloth hung in ample folds over some type of bulky white armor that sheathed his legs and forearms. A smooth-shelled helmet protected his head. Overlapping platelets, blood-dark, scabbed his chest, stomach, and the backs of his hands. The scabs itched.

Under the bedsheets, his hand brushed something sharp nestled in the folds of soft linen.

A mechanical insect, with a brass body and blown glass wings. One of the wings had snapped off in a crystalline shard. The remainder of the body was bent and flattened. He must have rolled onto it, crushing it while he slept.

He picked up the artifex. It resembled a moth, or a bee with large ungainly wings, and seemed to weigh nothing.

The footsteps drew near, then stopped outside his room. There was a firm tap on the door, more a warning than a knock.

Before Olavo could respond, the door swung open and Vania eased into the room.

He now knew where he was. The *Ignis Fatuus,* sometimes

referred to as the *Will o' the Wisp*. The ship was in orbit around Orthinia, thirty light-years from the *Wings of Uriel*, and another hundred and fifty from Earth.

Vania wore a clinical white dress. Barrettes, one on each side of her head behind the temple, held her hair in place. She sat next to him on the bed. "How are you feeling?" she said.

He ran his hands over the helmet. "My head hurts."

Vania rested a hand on his thigh. "I'm sorry. The upload didn't go as smoothly as planned. There were... complications."

Olavo nodded. He showed her the artificial insect, cradled in his palm. "I found this."

Vania removed her hand from his leg to collect the insect. "It's part of the latest evolutionary path I'm modeling."

"What does it do?"

"It carries lexomes—chemical instruction sets that modify the physiology of your body."

"Hormonally?" he said.

Vania nodded. "Or genetically. To deliver a lexome, they inject it into a socket on the back of your neck." She slipped the artificial insect into a loose pocket on the front of her dress.

Olavo rubbed his face, massaging bone. The contour of his cheeks and brow felt odd, misshapen.

"For example," Vania said, "a particular update might allow you to see a specific electromagnetic wavelength. Or taste a particular chemical."

"So it's a survival mechanism," Olavo said. "A way to quickly adapt to a rapidly changing environment."

"Yes."

Olavo accessed the ship's library for information about the planet. The last entry for Orthinia was several years old. According to the library, copies of him had been uploaded to this particular design space seven times before. Olavo queried the memory modules of his former simunculi. The softspace construct had been created thirty-eight years ago. Vania had updated the virtual design space a total of seven times. Each time, in response to new environmental data gathered by the swarm of collectors scouring the planet, his simunculus had modeled a different evolutionary path.

"I'm still in the process of updating the library with the latest datafeed from the collectors," she said.

She had incorporated familiar details into the softspace room of the building. The leafy shadow on the pink marble wall came from a magnolia tree. The shutters were Aegean blue. Vania was an incurable romantic. From the beginning there had been peonies, her favorite flower, and the chirp of crickets at night. Olavo remembered popcorn-yellow clouds in the sky. The centuries-gone memory of an August afternoon at Coney Island. As her knowledge of the world grew, these details would be gradually, systematically, overwritten. In time the magnolias and the peonies would disappear, replaced by softspace representations of the actual hardspace flesh and bone of the world. Meanwhile, unlike Ramunas and Uta who had severed all emotional ties to the past, Vania recapitulated what she loved.

It was the one trait about her that most endeared and concerned him. Memory, he knew, had a dangerous angle of repose. And it was always harder climbing out of a hole than falling in.

"When can I have a look around?" he said. In previous design spaces the room and building had been set atop a squat hill surrounded by greenhouses. The greenhouses were test beds filled with extrapolated or hypothetical plants he had been free to explore.

"I'm not sure. For a while you'll be confined to your assigned wing. I want to introduce you to outside stimuli slowly, in a controlled setting. Once we verify that your design path is stable, you'll be free to roam as you please."

Olavo nodded. He recalled a nice garden in the courtyard—peaceful—where she introduced simunculi to specific aspects of the environment. "Are the others awake yet?"

"They're in the courtyard. Would you like to visit them?"

Olavo stood. He followed Vania to the door, then out into the hall. It was wider than he remembered, and brighter. Glass panes, supported by iron joists, had replaced the marble ceiling. Doors, identical to his, lined the corridor on both sides. At the end of the hallway, a gated portico opened onto the courtyard.

White marble walls, veined with gray and punctuated with windows, enclosed the courtyard. Louvered awnings and second-floor balconies leaned over them. Moisture dripped from gutters on the rooftops. The pavement was damp. Mist boiled off the terra-cotta root and tendrils of fog clung to a pewter sky. To the east, the first glimmer of sun appeared, bright and keen as the edge of a sword.

Four simunculi materialized in the courtyard. The softspace apparitions drifted toward him along different evolutionary paths. First Uta, smiling in welcome, then Ramunas, his complexion darkened by a scowl, perpetually serious, followed by Jori and Hossein, engaged as usual in some ongoing argument. They resembled pale ghosts. The details of his softspace construct shone through them. Perhaps they were ghosts, unable to take form outside their quantum-linked ships and design spaces.

"Where's Acantha?" he said.

The simunculi glanced among themselves. "I'm afraid she's not here," Vania said.

"Why not?"

"Have you heard from her?" Uta said. "Since the burst?" The smile slipped to one side as her expression sobered.

"No." Olavo shook his head. "We haven't talked." Not in a while. Months. The exact number eluded him, or hadn't been included in the softspace version downloaded by his hardspace source. Other parts of him seemed to be missing, as well. Unsettling gaps. Either that information had been deleted, or it hadn't been provided in the first place.

"The AdS storm," Ramunas offered vaguely. "That might explain it." He avoided looking at Olavo and seemed to be talking to others.

"Probably," Uta said.

"What AdS storm?" Olavo asked, confused.

"There was an anomalous quark-gluon discontinuity in our region of anti de Sitter space," Ramunas said. "It appears to have collapsed all of the quantum wormholes linking us to home and the other simunculi."

"Those quantum links are the longest," Hossein said, "the weakest. Our local qinks took a hit, but the wormholes appear to be stabilizing as things calm down."

"Unfortunately you caught the brunt of a nearby gamma ray burst," Uta said.

"What happened to the *Wings of Uriel*?" he asked. All of the information he had collected and stored.

"We're still in the process of reconnecting to your ship," Uta said. "Recovering data and assessing the damage."

To the library, Olavo thought, and the hardspace copy of himself—both on the ship and Sand Mountain.

"The bottom line," Jori said, "is that we're cut off. We haven't been able to contact Earth or any of the other simunculi. We don't know if the discontinuity is permanent or not. If it is and we can't qink back, reestablish contact, then we need to start thinking about how we're going to survive."

"Long term," Ramunas said. "In the off chance help never arrives."

Hossein shifted his attention to Vania. Anxious, impatient. "What now?" he asked.

Vania sighed. "We might as well get started."

With that, the simunculi departed. Each of them eager to return to their particular design space.

Vania was the last to leave. "We'll start out slowly," she told him. "Nothing too complicated, and go from there based on your responses."

"You're afraid," he said, "aren't you?" That was why they were all in such a hurry to get going.

"We're worried," she admitted. "Before, we had time to figure out where we were going to settle. How we would live. Now we don't know how much time we have. It's resurrected a lot of old fears."

"Because of what happened to me?"

Vania averted her gaze. Nodded. "It could have happened to any of us."

"And you don't want to go through it again." The uncertainty. The end of one life and the piecing together of another one.

Vania shuddered. "Once was enough."

She departed then, leaving him with the long shadows of morning and the turbulent feeling that all was not entirely right with the world... or him.

4

Santa Cruz, September 14

Sister Daminca approached Rudi in the kitchen, where he was doling out bowls of minestrone soup for dinner. She touched him gently on the arm. "The police want to talk to you," she said, her voice barely audible over the clank of pots.

Rudi's stomach lurched. "What about?"

"They didn't say. Come on, they're waiting outside." She continued to hold him by the arm, supporting as much as guiding him. His knees felt weak, and oily sweat tickled his armpits.

Two downtown bicycle cops loitered on the sidewalk, chatting. Both wore shorts and helmets. He'd seen them around town before. One was a woman, taller than her male companion by several inches.

They were here for the stolen broadcast van. He was sure of it. Somehow, it had been identified by the local police. At least they had the decency not to arrest him inside, in full view of everyone.

"This is Rudi," Sister Daminca said.

"All right." The male officer gave a curt, dimly appreciative nod. "We'll take it from here."

Sister Daminca hesitated.

"We'll let you know if there's anything else you can do," the female officer added, dismissing her.

Sister Daminca gave Rudi's arm a quick squeeze, then headed back into the Veterans Memorial building.

Rudi waited, not trusting his voice. Out of the corner of his eye, he could see the van. It was parked half a block down the street and looked exactly the way he'd left it an hour ago.

"We're looking for someone," the male officer said. "We were told you might be able to help."

"Irene," the female officer said. "We understand you're friends with her."

"Not friends," he said.

"Okay. But you talk to her sometimes."

Rudi's skin itched. He resisted the urge to scratch.

"Have you seen her?" the male officer said.

Rudi shook his head, carefully vague. "Not for a while."

"How long's a while?"

"I don't know." His thoughts tumbled, tripping over themselves. "A few days, I guess."

"Where did you last see her?"

"Down on River Street. Why?" His voice strengthened as some of the tension in his lungs eased. "What's this about? Is she in some kind of trouble?"

"We're following up on a complaint filed by one of the store managers at Longs," the female officer said.

"About what?"

"Shoplifting," the male officer said. He watched Rudi closely for a second, then continued. "You know anything about that?"

"No." The itch in Rudi's crotch spread upward, encroaching on his stomach.

"You ever seen her steal anything?"

"No."

"We've got a security camera video," the female cop said. "It shows two people. One is a woman. The other's a man."

"I shared a piece of pizza with her," Rudi said. "That's all." Not that it seemed to change her opinion of him.

"Well," the male officer said, "if you see her let us know. All right?"

He found Irene camped behind a pile of wooden pallets that had been stacked next to a trio of garbage bins outside of Costco. She'd brought her shopping cart with her, still loaded with recyclables and clothes. She had hooked her cane on the side. The boom box was silent. Apparently, she only played it at night. Or when she'd had a few too many.

"The police are looking for you," Rudi said.

Irene squinted at him through a spliff-induced haze. "How do you know?"

"They talked to me. At the Veterans Memorial." Rudi looked down at her. He adjusted the aluminum foil under his cap. "They asked if I knew where you were."

Irene offered him a drag. When Rudi refused, she cackled and pinched the joint between cracked lips, sucking hard.

Rudi looked around. The marijuana was making him nervous. The stench of refuse wasn't quite strong enough to mask the pungent aroma of weed. Shoppers walking to their cars in the parking lot didn't seem to notice. Most wore expressions of practiced disregard. That was one advantage to being homeless—people turned a blind eye.

Rudi moved closer to Irene but remained standing, hoping to hide the stub of the joint pinched between her grimy fingers.

"I got a prescription," she said, catching his look. "Legal, from a doctor."

"That's not what they were asking about."

Irene took a final drag on the joint, pulling the hit deep into her lungs. She held her breath for several beats.

"Don't you want to know?" Rudi said.

She coughed out the smoke. The cough brought tears to her bloodshot eyes. "Not really." She tossed the butt onto the asphalt, where it disappeared into bits of broken glass, screw-top bottle caps, flattened scabs of gum, and dull cellophane wrappers.

"Shoplifting. At Longs drugstore."

Irene rubbed her nose with the back of one hand. The skin was swollen red and cut with fine wrinkles, as if years of dehydration had formed thousands of tiny cracks.

"How do they know it was me?"

"They got it on video."

"If they were asking, they don't know for sure. It could have been somebody else. The pictures on those cameras ain't too good."

Rudi eased himself into a crouch in front of her, next to a cardboard box she was using as a table. "What'd you take?"

"I s'pose you ain't never stole a thing in your life," Irene said. "A God-fearing Bible-thumper like you."

Rudi tensed, sensing a trap. "That's why I read the Bible," he said. " 'Cause I'm a sinner. There's no shame in admitting that."

"Reading the Bible don't give you the right to cast stones. If anything, it ought to make you more compassionate and understanding."

Rudi flushed. "Being compassionate doesn't mean you let people hurt themselves," he said. "Or others. 'For whom the Lord loveth he chasteneth.' "

"How do we know anybody's going to be able to listen when we get there?" Travis said.

"Yeah," Bethel said. Her breath fogged the side window. "It looks downright ugly out there."

The storm swelled like a black eye on the horizon. Torrential rain wept against the windshield.

"'Cause we'll be the only station transmitting," Jim Odette said. "Least for a while. We'll be the only voice they hear."

"But if there's no power," Travis said, "people won't be able to turn on their radios to hear us."

"Batteries," Rudi said. "Most radios can run off regular power and batteries. Even big boom boxes."

A rain-sodden gust slammed into the side of the van, wrenching the steering wheel in Jim Odette's hands. The van swerved, fishtailed when it hit a puddle, and then straightened when the tread caught pavement. Lightning pitchforked in the distance.

"Won't matter if the storm messes with the signal," Bethel said, her face white. She cut a mascara-veiled glance at Travis, who wet his lips and nodded. "Ain't no one going to hear us if we aren't transmitting."

"You got a point," Jim Odette agreed. Reluctance tugged at his voice. And when they finally crawled into Pascagoula, he pulled into a motel that was fast filling up with the first wave of evacuees.

"We can transmit from here," Bethel suggested. She stared nervously at the chaos around them. "Just look at all these people, up from the coast."

"It's not the same," Rudi said. "We need to get closer if we're going to be heard by the people most in need."

"Bethel's right," Marilee said. "This is where the biggest audience is. Where we can do the most good."

Rudi looked to Jim for support. Jim's gaze darted anxiously, caught between the hurricane and his wife. In the end, he chose the latter, leaving Rudi to fend for himself.

Irene cast him a heavy-lidded glance. The dope was hitting her hard and fast. "You holier-than-thou church people are all the same," she said. "You think if someone goes to church, that makes 'em a good person. And if they don't go to church, they a bad person. You automatically assume the worst."

The flush spread, and with it the itch. "That's not true," he said.

Irene sighed. Her head lolled, as if she were about to nod off. "I'm tired. I don't have the energy to put up with your nonsense."

"That's because you're stoned." Rudi stared at the still-smoldering butt of the joint. "What's wrong with you, anyway?"

"I'm dying."

"We're all dying," Rudi said.

"I'm doing it faster than most." She grabbed his left hand. "Here, feel this." She drew his hand in the direction of her ample breast.

"I don't think..." Rudi stammered. "This isn't..." He stiffened, resisting the pull.

"What are you afraid of?"

"Nothing. I just don't..."

She pressed his hand to her left breast. It gave way under his fingers, softer than he'd imagined.

"Go ahead," she said. "Squeeze it."

It didn't feel real. Horrified, Rudi jerked his hand back, uncertain what he'd just touched.

"You want to help people," she said, "you got to know what you're dealin' with. Then maybe you can do some good."

It took a moment for him to regain his composure. "Is it just the one?" he finally asked.

"So far. I don't miss it, if that's what you're wondering. The worst is the chemo. You don't know what sick is until you had that shit pumped into you. You'd be stoned, too. Pot is the only thing that helps cut the nausea. It ain't just some excuse to legalize weed, no matter what your prescription-addicted televangelists say."

"I almost died once," he said as she was readjusting her blouse. In the wide gap between the buttons, he caught a brief glimpse of something....

"Good for you," she said, noticing his gaze.

Ashamed, he shifted his attention from her chest to the street. "In a motorcycle accident."

Irene frowned. "Don't tell me. You weren't wearing a helmet. That's how come you're such a mess."

"I was in rehab for a while. A year. I think they did things to me there," he said.

"Therapy?"

"Other things. Inside my head." Rudi touched the brim of his cap, felt the faint crinkle of foil against his hair and scalp.

"Is that why you're all holier than thou?" she said. " 'Cause you had a near death experience?"

"The church helped me after I got out of the hospital. They welcomed me in and cared for me—cared *about* me."

"So you figure you owe 'em."

"No." Rudi shook his head. "I owe God. He saved me. Now He's protecting me."

"You don't have no family to look after you?"

"I have an older sister, up in Eugene. Linnea. I don't know where my mother is. She took off when I was little. When my grandmother died, I ended up in foster care."

"How come you went to church for help instead of your sister?"

Rudi thought for a moment. "I haven't talked to her in years. It didn't seem fair. Besides, she had her own problems."

"Maybe she's changed."

"Maybe," he allowed.

"If you've got family," Irene said, "you should find them."

Rudi shrugged and Irene let it go. She shut her eyes and leaned her head against one of the pallets. Rudi watched her for a few minutes, until she began to snore. Then he went back to the van, climbed in, and rested his forehead on the steering wheel.

After a couple of minutes, when his breathing slowed, he opened the glove compartment. Inside was a get well card from his sister. She had sent it while he was still rehabbing in Lakeshore, confined to a wheelchair, both of his arms in casts and a protective helmet on his head to prevent further trauma.

He removed the card from the envelope. The card was simple. The flower on front looked like it had been painted by a child. Ditto the brushstroke letters on the quote from the Buddha. "With our mind, we make the world." Inside the card was blank. Was she trying to tell him something? Or had she simply forgotten to sign it, in her typical drug-addled, forgetful way?

Rudi returned the card to the glove box, next to her joss sticks and the dog-eared copy of *The Blue Cliff Record* he'd been meaning to give back to her for years. Under the wan glow of the glove compartment light, he noticed the rash had spread to his forearm. Tea-rose pink and puffy, it bled when scratched.

5

San Francisco, Circa 1937

A week after the X-rays were taken, Benjamin Taupe received a call from Keane. "I have the results of the analysis," the doctor said.

"And?"

"How soon can you be here?"

Benjamin rubbed at the creases in his forehead. "Give me half an hour." That was the soonest he could catch a streetcar.

"Fine."

The doctor hung up. Benjamin lowered the handset into the cradle. His chest was tight, his heart pounding. He stared out the window of the second-floor office, not really seeing or hearing the bustle on the street below. The rumble of passing trucks; the clop of horse-drawn wagons delivering vegetables to the corner market; construction workers arguing politics at the corner newsstand—all had vanished. All he could hear was the roar of blood in his ears. Gone were the aromas of coffee, car exhaust, and fresh smelt from the Castagnola, Tarantino, and Alioto fisheries. All he could smell was the dank oily fear in his sweat.

"Well?" Zachary asked behind him.

Benjamin hadn't heard his partner enter the room. He turned from the window to face him over the maps and other paperwork spread out on his desk. "Keane has the test results. He wants to talk to me in person."

Zachary tugged on the handlebars of his mustache, coiling the ends around the end of his index fingers. "I see."

Benjamin forced a smile.

Zachary nodded, the glare from the window glossing the slick-combed waves of his hair. "Let me know how it goes."

"You have a tumor," Keane said. He held an X-ray up to the window in his office. The radiograph showed a skull in profile.

My skull, Benjamin thought. He was seeing himself, stripped bare of all pretense. As death would draw him, nothing but glowing white bone against a gray background.

Keane touched the tip of the pencil he was holding to a bright spot on the image. "You can see it visible here."

The lump, located about two inches behind the socket of his left eye, was roughly spherical in shape and the size of a large walnut. Around it Benjamin could see shadows, the vague outlines of arteries, veins, and other structures.

"That's what's causing the headaches?" he said.

"Yes." Keane lowered the X-ray. He set it on the desk, next to the others. "It's putting pressure on the surrounding tissue, including the optic nerve. Which is why your vision is blurred."

"Why didn't I notice any symptoms before?" A month ago? Six months ago? A year?

"Because it's growing. Before, when it was smaller, there was less pressure. Less trauma."

"How big will it get?"

"We don't know. Given the rapidity with which your symptoms have progressed in the last few months, it appears to be growing rapidly."

"So it should be removed as soon as possible," Benjamin said.

"Yes." Keane returned to the chair behind his desk. "Unfortunately, that's not an option."

Benjamin followed him, but didn't sit. "You can't operate?"

"The tumor is attached to an artery. There is no way to remove it without killing you. I'm sorry."

"What about treatment other than surgery?"

Keane folded his hands on the desk in front of him. "Radiation is an option. But there's a good chance it would kill you faster than the tumor."

"What do you suggest?"

Keane flipped open a pad of paper. He jotted something on one of the sheets and handed it to Benjamin.

A prescription for morphine.

"Get a second opinion," Zachary suggested. They sat in their office, surrounded by survey books, logs, and maps of the city. They'd been working on a proposal to do the topographical measurements for a projected expansion of Fisherman's Wharf.

Benjamin shook his head. "There's no point."

"Why not?"

"The tests are unequivocal. Any other diagnosis, or promise of a cure, will be an illusion. A lie."

"You don't know that." His partner tugged on his suspenders, running fingertips along the elastic.

"I'm certain there's no shortage of physicians out there

willing to tell me what I would like to hear in exchange for the appropriate fee."

"There may be another option." Zachary stood and began to pace, rubbing his chin. "It's rather unconventional. But Etta, God bless her, has been helped enormously by it these past few months."

"I hadn't noticed," Benjamin said. "I'm sorry."

Zachary waved off the apology. "She's even started going out on her own again."

"Out?"

"Shopping, short walks in the park. For a while, I thought her spirits would never improve."

"I'm glad," Benjamin said.

"She's been going to a teacher," Zachary said. "A spiritual healer she met in New York during her recovery. This woman studied for several months in Paris with a mystic named Gurdjieff. You may have heard of him. I understand he's quite famous in Europe. Ouspensky was one of his students, if that name means anything."

"I'm afraid not."

"A theosophist and a mystic who has written a number of seminal tracts, as well." Zachary tugged thoughtfully on his mustache. "In any case, the teachings of Gurdjieff, and to some extent Ouspensky, are reported to instill a certain restorative life force . . . a new way of growing beyond oneself and the world."

"And this healer can do the same for me," Benjamin said.

"It's worth a try. Of course, I can't vouch for it myself. But Etta's improvement under her tutelage has been nothing short of miraculous."

"Is it expensive?"

"Nothing is free, Ben. Least of all life. But I have Etta, and that's priceless. Worth every penny."

"It sounds like charlatanry to me. Occultism."

Zachary shrugged. "What can it hurt? If the diagnosis is correct, what have you got to lose?"

Benjamin left work early, took a streetcar to the Golden Gate Bridge, and walked under the massive cables to mid-span, where they sagged the deepest.

He looked down at the water, scalloped with light. There were no whitecaps, no feathery plumes of spray. It was one of those rare days when the breeze calmed and the waves quieted. Across the bay, south of Alcatraz, he could see the skeleton of the Bay Bridge, rising leviathan-like out of acrylic grays and greens.

The bay was shallower than it looked, and every so often when the light was just right, he thought he could see sand beneath the water, parodying the waves.

He gripped the railing. The steel was warm and salt-bitten, pocked where sea and fog had gnawed through thick red paint, leaving uneven tooth-marks of rust under the puckered tips of his fingers.

Jump, a voice urged.

He shivered. On the radiograph, the tumor had resembled a large pearl. Thick and round, it had built up in layers. It was almost as if his mind was reacting to an irritant, the way a clam instinctively tried to ease the discomfort of a grain of sand.

Maybe at its center, invisible to the X-rays, there was a dark mote—an uncomfortable feeling or memory—that his subconscious was trying to protect him from. Breaking him in the process of trying to keep him whole.

Behind him, traffic rattled in and out of the city. Smoke from a steamer drifted quietly. Twenty feet away, a couple of kids licking fresh peanut butter off wood spoons swatted at one another and laughed. Farther down, a little girl wearing a blue dress and holding a balloon tugged on her father's hand.

Benjamin shook his head. He couldn't do it.

Why not? What was wrong with him? His condition would only get worse. Better to end things now. But the moment had passed. He'd hesitated too long, and knew that it wasn't going to happen.

Not now. Not today.

An insect tickled the nape of his neck. He slapped at the bug. When he looked at his palm, it was smeared with blood. A moment later, his neck began to itch.

6

Aelon, Softspace

Monastiraki. Theklas Street. An old sandal-maker's shop filled with the scents of linseed oil and extinct leather.

That was where Olavo would find Acantha—where she inevitably took refuge when she sank into one of her unresponsive funks. She liked to wander the replica of the Acropolis she had hardspaced on the surface of Aelon, browse the flea market, or spend the afternoon perusing the poetry of the long-dead sandal maker as he cobbled together straps and soles.

If the AdS storm had caused Acantha to pull into herself, it would have had the same effect on Mee Won. They shared the same base personality. But instead of the hard-edged depression that plagued Acantha, Mee Won tended to withdraw into quiet contemplation. Easier to start with her. If he could get a feel for where Mee Won was at, it might give him a better idea of what to expect from Acantha.

Before qinking to the *Golden Fleece* and Aelon, Olavo opened a carved oak door on his ship and stepped through it, into the Pink Flamenco.

Sand Mountain crackled with the smell of ozone. Silicate-laden clouds glittered low over acid-etched streets bustling with pedestrians and gyrocarriages. Beneath the shifting vaporlight, origami awnings tattooed with carp, red dragons, and white cranes folded then refolded under the relentless, unforgiving nuances of globular flux.

As far as worlds went, Sand Mountain wasn't all that sandy or mountainous. It was mostly flat and wind-abraded. What it had that no other world he'd surveyed had was water. Not much, but enough to think about putting down roots. The UV was soft... yet still hard enough to strip all subtlety from the landscape. It was important, he felt, that any visitors—potential colonists—who qinked in for a day or night knew what they were getting. The light brought out every nuance in the face of the night waif sitting at the table next to him.

"There's an aurora on the way," Mee Won said. Her eyes flitted from Olavo to the dark horizon beyond the waist-high trellis girding the balcony.

Olavo followed her gaze to the flat-topped hill across the lake. From the terrace of the Pink Flamenco diner, forty-three levels above the ground, he had a clear view of the city. Two hundred years earlier, he had seeded the polis at the edge of a shallow, dust-filled depression shielded from the prevailing wind by a low mountain along one rim. He stared glumly at the hardspace scape. It hadn't taken shape the way he'd hoped. Nothing ever did. He wasn't exactly sure what he'd expected, or wanted for that matter.

Over the years, he had dispersed data collectors to several thousand potential worlds in the Ferrer cluster. The collectors were stripped-down Drexler machines that qinked back to his ship via the same anti de Sitter rabbit holes they followed to the most promising gravity wells. In three centuries, only a handful of his high-probability worlds had shown any promise. Most of the worlds cataloged by J.I.S.E.C., the Joint International Space Exploration Consortium, were dead, inhospitable lumps of rock. Unsuitable for pretty much anything. Sand Mountain was the best he could do.

"It's beautiful," Mee Won murmured. "Don't you think?"

"In its own way," Olavo said.

Above him the Ferrer cluster hung from the sky like a chandelier. Facets in the crystal canopy covering the balcony divided the sky into kaleidoscope petals. Below him: terraced mezzanines; gardens tented by yellow- and mauve-tinted cellophane; Puritanical spires; domed mosques. Beyond the limits of the city, exurban sprawl. Shantytowns had risen up around the blister pack grid of agriciles. Tesselated ceramix decorated the square roofs, glyphlike in the fickle skeins of light.

"Can you smell it?" she said. She breathed deeply. Her nostrils flared, drinking in the aroma of the beeswing flowers that had opened in sticky clumps on the railing.

The aurora formed suddenly. Without warning a curtain of chelate-hard raindrops sheeted down between the lake and the mountain. The curtain rippled. Driven by a microburst, it slammed into the tree-dotted slope of the mountain. Wire-thin limbs flexed and bent under the assault, twisting into new aesthetics. On the narrow suspension bridge that crossed the lake to hillside apartments on the far shore, pedestrians opened umbrellas or scrambled for refuge in parked gyrocarriages.

Mee Won fixed her gaze on the downpour and watched the precipitation lash the tall reeds that fringed the open space around the lake. Olavo thought she seemed less interested in the storm than avoiding the clientele of the Pink Flamenco. He knew the diner made her uncomfortable, with its retro fluorescent tubes, brushed chrome decor and greasy vinyl under limp-hanging ferns. It was always a revelation for him to see a reflection of his own fears mirrored in her crossed arms and averted eyes. Her excuses gave him a fleeting glimpse into himself—some feminine principle that had split off from him when he'd been genetically mapped, digitized, and grafted onto a molecular automata capable of surviving anti de Sitter space.

She was a classic night waif—albino white and brittle—datamapped with baseline personality tropes. Long white hair trailed from her scalp in cobwebs. The night waifs had been one of his earliest and most successful design threads. Thin-bundled bones, held together by a frail subcutaneous membrane, they didn't require much raw material to assemble in the city's parthenosynthesis tanks.

As quickly as it had begun, the aurora dispersed, leaving a fine mineral residue on the marsh.

Olavo turned to her. "Tell me—"

Mee Won touched a fingertip to pale pink lips. A spectral moan rose from the cane, wooing a flock of tallowtails to the hollow, flutelike reeds.

"That's my favorite part," she said when the moan sank to the lake bed, joining the wind-sculpted dunes that lapped the tourist beaches and parasol-shaded picnic areas along the shore.

"Tell me about the burst," he said. The collectors had recorded physiological responses in the simunculi to the gamma ray burst. What he hoped to learn from this visit were subjective reactions, psychological impressions.

"It was bright," she said. Her eyes glistened. "I could feel it shining through me, bright enough to see inside myself. But when I looked, there was only pure white light. I had disappeared. Even my shadow was gone."

"How long did it last?"

Her gaze seemed to shift inward. "I can still see it on the

back of my eyelids. Even when my eyes are open, like now, I can't get rid of the images. And I have a headache."

"What images?" he said.

She blinked. "The city looks different. Changed. People do, too."

"Changed in what way?"

"They're wearing different clothes." She shifted uncomfortably in her skin. She had never been completely comfortable with herself. "Plus, there's water in the lake. Blue. And the bridge is red, not black. It's like a dream I can't wake up from. I went to a doctor. To see what was wrong."

"What did the doctor say?"

"He said there's nothing he can do." Her eyelashes trembled under acetone-sharp light. "I don't know what's going on. I don't know who I am anymore. I don't feel like me."

"Who do you feel like?"

"I don't know." Her expression corroded around the edges. "Like I'm changing into someone else. Like I'm living in a dream. Or like I've been someone else all along, and didn't know it." Mee Won glanced up quickly, fearfully. "Am I going crazy?"

"You seem fine to me. A little scared, maybe. But that's to be expected under the circumstances."

She squirmed, trying to find a comfortable position. "It's not just me. A lot of other people are having problems, too."

"They feel the same way you do?"

"We held a prayer session," Mee Won said, caught up in herself. "The meditation calmed me."

"And the rest of the sisters? Did it help them?"

"I think so." The articulated bones of her shoulders finally realigned in a way that stopped them from twitching.

"How about the rest of the citizens?" he said. "How are they coping?"

"The doughmen have started gambling," she said. "They've opened parlors in the lower city."

"Where?"

"Sublevels two and four." Her nostrils pinched. "Near the bottom of the lightwell."

He frowned, unnerved. Gambling, along with prostitution, had been excluded from the simunculi's original personality maps.

"I went to visit them," she confessed, "out of curiosity. I wanted to see what it was like."

He looked around the diner. "What about the gnomen?" he asked. Short and squat, they were less ambiguous than the doughmen. Their taste tended toward charcoal pinstripe suits, purple stiff-brimmed hats, and a laconic efficiency in everything from business affairs to sex.

"I'm scared," Mee Won said.

He turned back to her. "Of the gnomen?"

A twitch yanked at the straps of her green cotton shift. "Of me, I think."

"You?"

"I'm not strong enough." Doubt occluded her eyes.

"Not strong enough for what?" he said. What couldn't she come right out and say?

She made a helpless gesture. A handkerchief fluttering of one delicate, pink-nailed hand. "For anything."

"Not alone, you aren't," he said. "None of us are, by ourselves."

"I'm weak," she said. "I don't trust myself. I'm afraid of what I might do." Thin lashes fell in a veil across her eyes.

He searched her downcast gaze. "Like what?"

"I don't know." The pale glassine eyelashes batted, flailing at tears. "That's what scares me. Anything seems possible. I don't know what to expect."

"From who?"

"From anybody."

Including herself. "I trust you," he said, doing his best to reassure her.

She bit her lower lip, leaving him unconvinced as well. There had always been an unsettled side of Acantha in her that had clung to her personality profile after he'd downloaded it into her simunculus. That connection was what had drawn him to her in the beginning, what made them *Nouveaux sapiens* sisters. With luck, Mee Won might be able to help him better understand Acantha. That was the hope. But today, she seemed more unsteady than usual.

"I have to go," he said.

Panic flared in her eyes. "Don't," she said.

Olavo stood, pushing back his chair. "You'll be fine," he said. "I know you will. You're stronger than you think."

"What if I'm not?"

"I'll be back," he said. "Soon. I promise."

He took her outstretched hand and gave it a reassuring squeeze before moving toward the exit. He didn't want her to see his fear. It would only add to her distress.

He stepped through the double glass doors into the softspace construct of his ship, unable to shake the feeling that he was the one who had been walked out on.

Abandoned.

Stepping back onto the *Wings of Uriel,* he felt disoriented, uncomfortable in the softspace living room of the ship. The walls were too bare, the floor too hard, the furniture too plain. He rescaped the construct with silver and gold striped wallpaper, thick-hanging curtains over wood frame windows that looked out on the globular cluster, plush carpeting, and overstuffed chairs.

He sat in the claw-footed chair and ran his hands over the

polished oak armrests and chintz cushion. He parted the green velour curtains, exposing old panes. The wavy glass, thicker at the bottom than the top, distorted the starlight from the Ferrer cluster and Sand Mountain's sun, Uriel prime.

Feeling a little calmer, Olavo took a moment to create a local library entry for the simunculus on the *Ignis Fatuus* and Orthinia. He was lucky. The gamma ray burst hadn't collapsed the micro-wormhole connecting him to the *Ignis Fatuus* and Orthinia; the tunnel was tenuous but stable.

For now.

Qinked to Vania's design space, the dataddress would track whatever happened to that particular version of himself. He initialized a non-sentient subroutine, running in the background, to monitor the qink real-time and update him if/when the simunculus changed, physically or psychologically. That way, he would know what was going on, even if the simunculus didn't. Next, Olavo queried the library for recent updates to his catalog of worlds.

When he had finished, he returned his attention to the window and Sand Mountain, framed in the imperfect glass. Just a few more minutes, he told himself. Then he would go. It felt good to sit. To breathe unencumbered.

Finally he stood—no more procrastinating—and headed down the hallway leading to the other ships and worlds that stretched across light-years. With each step, floorboards creaked and AdS space transients appeared, drawn by the sound. They floated in the shadows, peering in at him from the striped wallpaper as if from behind the bars of a cage.

Olavo did his best to ignore them, pretending they were bad memories, the tattered remnants of childhood nightmares. He stopped at the door that led to Aelon. Gripped the ivory knob set in blue-painted wood, twisted, and stepped through. . . .

The sun was abnormally large and red above the Acropolis, a blood-filled blister bulging against the sky. Unlike Vania's rosy romanticism, Acantha tended to the darker hues of nostalgia.

As expected, he found her in the sandal shop. She was naked, covered only in the piercings and tattoos she had worn before digital transcription. She sat on the scuffed floor tile, her thighs splayed wide. Her pubis was shaved, the labia hairless. She fingered herself, the tip of her index glistening, moist. Every now and then, she removed her finger to suck on it with childish innocence. Nipple rings glinted, halo bright. A zipper nestled in her belly button.

Olavo stood in the doorway for a second, his shadow darkening the floor, waiting for her to respond. When she didn't, he moved inside. His shadow stained her legs, and then the top of her head. Outside, the streets of Aelon bustled with simunculi from multiple design threads. Citizens coiffed in photovoltaic feathers walked side by side with loose-limbed multi-jointed anthromorths. Scooters bleated, street vendors shouted. More than anyone, Acantha mixed soft and hard, conflated the real with the imagined.

She had been a Suicide Angel in her previous life. Whatever that was. She hadn't elaborated. There were no references to them in the *Golden Fleece* library files he was authorized to access, and he had been afraid to ask. He wasn't sure he wanted to know.

"What's with the sun?" he said.

She touched the silhouette of his hand on the floor in front of her. "New collector data."

He sat on the empty chair next to her, the yellow plastic sun-faded and warped by heat. "From where?"

"The Okinoshi plume."

"You sent collectors there?"

"Before the AdS rupture," she said.

"Why?"

She shrugged. The tattoo on her left shoulder shuddered under indifference. "It's pretty. All that red and green plasma. I wanted a closer look."

"There's no point," he said. Statistically, the chances of finding a habitable world were low. It was a volatile region.

"That doesn't mean it's pointless," she said.

"It is if it's never going to be settled."

She shook her head. "Jesus. We don't even know if anyone else is still alive. In hardspace, I mean. We could exist only in softspace—nothing more than stored memories." Her mood was rapidly decaying into depressed histrionics. She reinserted her finger, the way she might a pacifier.

"So we should just give up," he said.

She bit her lower lip, stifling a gasp as she rubbed the labia pierce. "The data isn't normal."

"Of course it isn't. What did you expect?"

"The rupture left a hole," she said. "Some kind of diffuse Bose-Einstein bubble or singularity, and stuff is leaking out of it."

"What kind of stuff?"

She tugged on one of the nipple rings, and a new softspace construct replaced the sandal shop.

Olavo found himself in her second floor apartment. The room was tiny and a mess, as usual. Clothes were strewn across the floor and sofa. Dirty dishes were piled in the kitchen sink. The window next to the sofa was open. The gauzy curtain billowed under a fume-laden gust. Horns honked in the street below. A bus rumbled by, and brakes hissed. Somewhere a dog barked, then yelped. Athens was famous for its strays.

The reason Acantha fit in, he thought, felt at home among the dried turds. The city adopted anyone.

The television in the room came on. The Magnavox was old, the cathode ray tube heavy, the screen curved. It was like looking into an aquarium. The people on the screen could have been fish, living out their lives in a tank filled with static instead of water.

"It's the past," she said. She plopped down on the sofa, wearing lace panties and a black leather bra that squeezed her breasts.

Olavo focused on the TV set. "Whose?"

"I don't know yet. It came from the black hole. I think it's from an old broadcast that got trapped there."

"What are we doing here?" he said.

"Watch." She patted the Kanji-patterned seat cushion next to her. Her nails were bitten, the black polish chipped.

He sat in the puddle of an old stain. Tired foam exhaled under his weight, easing him into the sagging embrace of the couch. Her hand crawled onto his thigh, spiderlike, to crouch on his hand. Gathering his fingers in hers, she moved his hand to her lap. The thin lace of her panties was damp.

He stiffened. "What are you doing?"

"Getting comfortable."

She moved his hand lower and he squirmed. He'd always felt like a child when confronted with this side of her.

"This is wrong," he said.

"Why?"

"It's not normal."

Her lips yielded under the pressure of her fingers, suddenly moist and warm under his. "Who says?"

"Everyone." His own lips were dry.

"So what? It feels good."

"Not to me."

"In other words, I'm not normal."

"No."

"Just sick."

Slowly, carefully, he shook his head. "I didn't say that."

"Still, you think I need help. That's why you're here. To save me. Convince me I should undergo treatment because I've been corrupted, or some part of my personality was lost in translation, and I'm *not myself*."

Organic-to-inorganic transcription wasn't perfect. Some aspect of the original was always altered or degraded. Detached. The ship's library stored trillions of synapse firing patterns . . . memetic maps that could be integrated into the primary transcription to normalize it in the event a personality profile became unstable.

"I came because I was concerned about you. That's all."

"Did it ever occur to you that maybe you're the one who needs help, not me?"

"I'm not here to pressure you," he said. "Or tell you what to do. I didn't tell anyone I was coming. No one else knows I'm here. It's just us."

Acantha pouted, but stopped pressing his fingertips against the delicate lace of her panties. Instead, she brought her knees together in a slight concession to modesty. "Happy?"

He swallowed. Nodded. Ashamed of his desire.

She stroked his fingers absently. "Want to know what I think?"

"What's that?"

"I think the AdS rupture tore this part of the universe. I think it's bleeding out, or maybe another universe is bleeding in. That's why the hole is red."

"Bleeding how?"

The side of her cheek bulged under the tip of her tongue.

"Like air from a balloon. So our universe is either inflating or deflating. It doesn't matter. Either way, we're history." Her stare was vacant yet serious.

"Even if you're right," Olavo said, "it wouldn't happen right away; it would take a long time."

Her hand tightened around his as she turned to him. "We're already cut off. What difference does it make if it takes one year, or a billion years?"

He understood now. She'd already given up. No matter what happened, she had decided there was no going back. Not for her. Not for any of them.

She returned her attention to the Magnavox. "We'll only watch for a while," she promised. She undid her brassiere, exposing one nipple and accompanying aureole. The ring had a gargoyle's head on the bottom. She tugged on the face.

The channel changed, and with it the room.

7

Santa Cruz, September 24

The yarn was nutmeg brown, the color of skin freckled with specks of blue and green.

"What are you knitting?" Rudi said.

Irene paused. She frowned, either at him or the row of stitches she was coaxing into shape on her lap. "What's it look like?"

It didn't look like anything yet. "I don't know."

"Good." She sounded satisfied. "Ain't none of your business."

The knitting needles resumed their clatter, clicking and flashing under the harsh fluorescent glare of the Veterans Memorial lobby.

Some kind of bowl, he decided, or small bag. The swatch was circular, close to seven inches in diameter. It curled upward along the edges.

Irene looked comfortable in her new wheelchair. Not new. It was refurbished, a charitable donation from the Interfaith Cooperative. She had been limping a lot in the past couple of weeks, leaning heavily on her cane. Her wrist and shoulder had begun to ache under the strain. Tendonitis, according to Doctors on Duty. To bring down the inflammation, she was popping Motrin like candy. Between that and the drinking, Rudi worried she was going to trash her liver.

Irene scowled at him. "There must be someone else out there who needs saving, besides me."

"Where are you going to spend the night?" he said. It was almost ten. The Veterans Memorial would be closing soon.

"Not with you, that's for damn sure. That van of yours is about as comfortable as a church pew."

"You know what I mean."

"I'll be fine. Don't worry about me. I can take care of myself. I don't need you—or God."

"'Know ye not that a little leaven leaveneth the whole lump?'" Rudi said, citing Corinthians.

"I already got one lump," Irene said. "I don't need another. And I sure as hell don't need it leavened."

Rudi's face warmed. He'd been thinking about prayer and the bread of life, not cancer.

"You wanna raise my spirits," she said, "come to the dance tomorrow night. It might do you some good."

"What dance?"

"Right here. It starts at seven. If you really want to help people, you'll be there."

The hammering returned, louder and more insistent. It rattled the interior of the broadcast van and jangled the wiring in his head.

Disconnected, ripped from sleep, he rolled out of the sleeping bag and propped himself on one elbow.

The pounding stopped. "Hello?" A woman's polite voice. It came from behind the van. "Mr. Lauchman?"

There was a pause. Rudi imagined an inquisitive ear cupped to the back doors, a foot or so away.

When he didn't respond, the banging resumed, this time from the front driver side door of the van. Rudi groaned and clapped his hands to his head.

"I just want to talk," the woman said. "My name is Celia Truong. I'm a freelance journalist."

Rudi sat up, jackknifed by a palpitation that hit him, fist-hard, in the chest. "Just leave me alone!"

"I heard your show last night," the woman said. "I'd like to interview you for a piece I'm doing on the different ways people express their faith."

Rudi patted his head. The aluminum foil had slipped to the floor. He slapped it back into place, securing it with his cap.

"It would be a great chance to get the word out. Tell people what you're doing. Where they can tune in."

"Just a minute," Rudi said.

He stood up, stepped into his pants, and shrugged on the shirt he'd hung from the equipment rack next to him.

He opened the back doors. Blinding morning light flooded the van. He retreated from the glare. Below him, broken glass, pancake-flat bottle caps, and silvery wrappers glittered on the cracked asphalt.

A slight woman peered into the van. She was dressed in black denim jeans, a purple sweatshirt, and had a shock of black, wiry hair that refused to lay flat. She carried a Sony WX7000 iCam, hard-tethered to a smart phone that Rudi suspected was hubbed to the Net.

The woman whistled in admiration. "Nice setup you got there. State of the art."

Rudi lurched into the glare, climbing down to the tarmac of the parking lot. "Since when did reporters start carrying their own cameras?"

"I'm not a reporter. I'm a video journalist working on a documentary about the role of faith in society."

"How did you find me?"

Celia Truong stepped back, giving him room. "I talked to Irene, down at the Veterans Memorial. She told me where to look."

"When?"

"Last night."

Rudi's heart broke through the surface tension of his fatigue, rising up from murky depths. Irene had heard him. She was listening. He was getting through to her, baptizing her.

"Don't worry," the woman said quickly. "I won't give away your location. That's part of the intrigue."

"Intrigue?"

"The pirate radio preacher. I listened to your broadcast. That was some hard truth you laid down, let me tell you. I think a lot of people would be interested in hearing your story. Where you're coming from. Where you're headed. And what you hope to accomplish."

Rudi screwed his knuckles into his eyes. He couldn't remember what he had said, what he'd confessed.

"'For ye are like unto whited supulchres...'" Celia intoned, affecting a slight singsong.

Which appear beautiful outward, Rudy thought, *but are within full of dead men's bones.*

"Matthew," Rudi said. He recalled the passage, but nothing about the broadcast itself.

"That totally describes society," Celia said. "Don't you think? Beautiful on the outside. Dead on the inside."

"You don't sound like a journalist," he said.

"I like to keep things informal. I find it makes things easier for me and the people I'm chronicling."

The light on the camera blinked expectantly.

"We're all dead on the inside," Rudi said. "Most people just don't realize it, because they can't see their bones."

"We cover ourselves up," Celia said. "To hide the ugliness that lives inside us. Is that what you're saying?"

Rudi adjusted his cap. It gave him a chance to press his hands to his scalp—push his thoughts into shape.

"Until you strip away the flesh," he said, "and wear your bones on the outside, for all the world to see, you can't see the truth about yourself." He rubbed at his arms, which had begun to itch under the flannel sleeves.

"That's great." Celia grinned. "So that was what you did. What you're still doing, in effect. You sobered up, took all of your skeletons out of the closet, and put them on display for everyone to see."

Be sober, be vigilant; because your adversary the devil, as a roaring lion, walketh about seeking whom he may devour.

"Peter," Rudi said.

The camera leaned in. "What about him?"

"He said if you're not sober you can't be vigilant, and you will be devoured by the devil. I was devoured. The devil swallowed me . . . tried to digest me in order that I might feed and sustain him. The only way to deny the devil is to deny the flesh. Only then will you be free."

"And you want to spread the word. Right? Help prevent others from suffering the same fate."

"The devil's always hungry. I'm no different from anyone else. If it happened to me, it could happen to anyone."

"So that's why you're literally taking scripture to the streets? Using the gutter as a pulpit for your grassroots message?"

"According to Isaiah, 'All flesh is grass.' "

Celia Truong's head bobbed fervently. "Do you regard yourself as an example for others, based on personal experience? Is that what gives you the authority to speak about what people need to do to save themselves?"

Rudi's mind hiccupped. In the ensuing blank he scrambled

for a response, flipping frantically through the passages he'd memorized.

" 'For if any be a hearer of the word,' " Rudi said, " 'and not a doer, he is like unto a man, beholding his natural face in a glass: for he beholdeth himself and goeth his way and straightway forgetteth what manner of man he was."

"So"—Celia creased her brow—"what you're doing, in addition to helping others, is also a way of not forgetting who you are, where you've come from and what you've gone through."

The shriek of tearing metal screeched inside Rudi's head. It grated against bone, filed at the enamel on his teeth. He sat down hard on the back bumper of the van and slid sideways.

Celia caught him by the shoulders. "You look a little pale."

Rudi leaned his head back and sucked air.

"You need anything?" The woman leaned close. "Medication? You want me to call 911?"

Rudi swallowed. He started to shake his head, but stopped when nausea welled up, hot and bilious.

"When was the last time you ate?"

Rudi opened his mouth but couldn't speak... couldn't think through the whirlpool of dizziness. He felt his lips moving compulsively, soundlessly.

"Come on." Celia tugged Rudi to his feet, steadied him. "Let's grab a bite. Before you pass out."

Celia Truong studied him over the remains of a raspberry scone scattered between them on a table at The Buttery cafe. She'd placed the camera on the far edge of the table, the lens pointed directly at Rudi, but it was dead, the light off.

"You look better," she said.

Rudi nodded. He washed down his last bite of the scone with acidic, black coffee that ate through the sugar.

"You had me worried there for a second."

"I'm fine."

Celia seemed to accept this. She sipped at her latte. "So are you affiliated with any particular church?"

Rudi cleared his throat. "Not anymore."

"But you were, at one time."

"For a while."

"Where was that?"

"Alabama."

"So what brought you out here?"

She had long, delicate fingers. The nails were painted metallic pink. "I needed to get away," he said.

"From what?"

Rudi swished the oily surface of his coffee, watching it swirl under the halide lights.

"Were you looking for something?"

"Myself, I guess." That was who he had been running from. At the same time, it was who he hoped to find.

Celia nodded in the direction of the window. "So what happened to your van? It's pretty beat up."

"It was in an accident."

Truong laughed. "No shit." She twirled her paper cup absently for a time. "You said something about a storm."

Rudi forced his attention from the mesmerizing rhythm of her hands to her smooth-polished gaze.

"Back in the parking lot," she clarified. "You were mumbling under your breath. Talking to yourself."

Rudi gripped his coffee with both hands to keep from shaking. "What else did I say?"

The journalist gave a tiny shrug. "You only babbled for a few seconds. I couldn't make it out."

"'The Lord hath His way in the whirlwind and in the storm,'" Rudi said, reaching into the book of Nahum.

"I guess we all have our storms," Truong mused. "So how long you been on the road?"

Rudy blinked, his mind a blur.

Truong smiled. "That long, huh."

Too long, he thought. Not long enough. How many days since the accident, the initial crash that had set him on his way? He'd lost track.

"Any idea how long you'll be in town?" she asked.

"No."

She blinked rapidly. "My God," she said. "You're homeless, aren't you? That's why you're on the road, living out of a van. You're exactly like the people down at the Veterans Memorial."

"It's just for a while," he said.

"This is great!" She scooted closer. "This is exactly the kind of story I want to document."

"How's Irene?" he asked, hoping to redirect her enthusiasm. "What did she say when you talked to her?"

Celia Truong pursed her lips. Rudi could see her debating, trying to decide how much to tell him.

"She's doing all right. She's had a tough road. But I guess you know that."

Am I making a difference? That was what he wanted to ask. What he wanted to know, more than anything. *Am I doing any good?*

"One last question." Celia waited for his attention to wander back to her. "What's with the aluminum foil?"

8

San Francisco, Circa 1937

Madame Grurie considered Benjamin through horn-rimmed glasses. "You are a friend of Etta's?"

"I work with her husband. Zachary." Benjamin shifted on the hard wooden chair. "We're in business together." He handed her the letter of recommendation that Zachary had written on his behalf.

Madame Grurie accepted the proffered page, adjusted her glasses on the delicate bridge of her nose, and perused it.

The glasses, he decided, and sculpted Palladian eyebrows, added ten years to her age. He guessed she was in her late thirties or early forties. It seemed to be a conscious affectation on her part. As a spiritual teacher, she sought to cultivate an aura of physical detachment from the world. Her voluminous black hair was tightly wrapped and pinned, while her peacock green dress fell in Baroque, unrevealing layers. Despite this, she exuded a strong aura of femininity. Restrained, to be sure. Nothing about her flounced. But there was a ripeness in her eyes, a fullness to her tea-rose lips. The entire room was like that—thick, velvety, overstuffed. Bodice-tight drapes framed the window, leaving a soft cleavage of light. Silver and gold wallpaper striped the walls. The floor was carpeted, the ceiling scalloped.

Maybe he was simply projecting upon her some latent, long-repressed desire. He was dying, and the body naturally fought against that inevitability. It sought comfort in any form, no matter how unlikely. Was that what he'd been doing with Etta? No. He'd been drawn to her before he found out about the tumor. Still it was almost as if a part of him had known and had been reaching out . . . seeking something that was missing in his life. Where was Etta now? he wondered. At home? The Crystal Palace? A show, maybe, or a ferry ride to Sausalito?

Madame Grurie looked up and arched one fussily plucked brow. "You are unwell?"

"Yes."

"May I inquire as to the nature of your illness?"

Benjamin cleared his throat to cover his embarrassment. He wasn't in the habit of offering up the private details of his life.

"Come, now." Madame Grurie set the letter on the velvet folds overflowing from her lap. "If we are to work together, there must be no secrets between us. The first step on the path to healing is the truth."

"Of course." Benjamin tented his fingers under his chin. "I have a brain tumor. I'm told it's incurable."

"I see."

Benjamin waited for her to continue, to offer some expression of sympathy or pity. That was the normal reaction. Her silence unnerved him.

"Can you help?" he asked.

"The question is, can you help yourself."

"I don't understand."

"I teach self-help. Self-healing. It's not an easy path. But it's the only path. Not everyone is willing to do what is required."

"And what would that be?" he said.

"It shouldn't matter. That's the point."

"I need to be prepared to do whatever it takes," Benjamin said. "The particulars aren't important."

"Exactly." She smiled at him. "When you are willing to do anything, nothing is impossible."

Benjamin took a moment to consider this. "What if I don't know if I'm willing to do anything? If I tell you that I am, how do you know I'm not lying, to you or to myself? For that matter, how do I know I'm not lying?"

"Then you need to find out, don't you?"

Madame Grurie stood. She returned the letter to him, then drifted toward the door. Benjamin refolded the page. Was the interview over? He looked up. She stood at a small side table with a lamp. She seemed to be ignoring him, preoccupied. Was she waiting for him to leave? He couldn't tell.

As the moment dragged on, and she remained motionless, Benjamin found himself paralyzed. He didn't want to overstay his welcome. At the same time, he didn't want to disturb her by getting up.

"What are you waiting for?" she said. "Why are you still here?"

The sternness in her voice jerked him to his feet. "I'm sorry. I thought... I didn't want to..."

"You want me to tell you what to do, what you should do. Either by actions or by words."

It was true. He nodded, ashamed at how helpless he'd become in only a few days, dependent on the diagnoses and opinions of others.

"You are asleep," she said. "You must wake up. You must stop relying on others to tell you who you are. In the end, there is only your self. Only you can define your self. Only you can get in touch with your higher self."

"I haven't slept in days." He shook his head. "I can't sleep at all. I wish I could." He had lain awake for the past three nights, unable to stop his mind from racing. His thoughts refused to slow down. They gnawed at this worry or that, like gears in a crank shaft, compulsively, ceaselessly grinding.

"On the contrary," Madame Grurie said. "You can't wake up. That is your true problem. You proceed through life in a rigid, unvarying routine. You do exactly what is expected of you, by yourself and others. Always the same. You are like a machine—a marionette, if you will—content to go through the daily motions of life with no thoughts other than those you have been conditioned to have."

"I'm out of my element," he confessed. "I don't know what to do next with myself. I don't know where to turn."

"That's because you are a sleepwalker in this world. You think you are awake. But when you truly wake up, you will realize that what you thought was waking before was in actuality a kind of dream."

"How do I wake up, then?" Anything was better than the torment he'd endured since the X-ray results.

"Self-examination. You have recently gotten a brief glimpse of yourself, and you are afraid. You are like a child standing at the gate to a garden, captivated by what you see but too frightened to enter. Why are you frightened?"

"I don't want to die."

"Exactly. You want to conquer death. You want to create an immortal soul. But every rebirth requires a death."

"Surely you don't mean that literally?"

"Sometimes. But there are other ways to pass from this life to the next, from this world to the source world without permanent physical harm."

"Source world?"

"The dimension where the awake part of your self lives. It is a fourth dimension, a space beyond the three physical dimensions of height, length, and depth that we normally see around us." With a florid sweep, she indicated the drawing room around them. "Just because we can't see something," she said, as if anticipating his doubt, "doesn't mean it's not there. There are invisible worlds beyond our own."

"Heaven," he said.

"And hell," she added. "Among others."

Purgatory, he thought. How many other places like those might exist, beyond the pale of normal apprehension?

"You have gone through this process?" Benjamin said. "You have seen this other world with your own eyes?"

"I have walked through the gate, yes. I have entered the garden. I am in contact with my higher self, even as I speak to you from this self."

She had moved close enough for him to feel the heat of her body, inhale the soft, giddy scent of violets. "Zachary mentioned someone named Gurdjieff," Benjamin said. "And Ouspensky."

"Yes." She moved away, giving him room to breathe. "They were my teachers. Directly and indirectly."

"Here?"

"No. In London and New York. I first encountered them when I was living in Paris. A few years ago, during the summer of 1924 to be exact, I attended several seminars and workshops in New York. They helped me formulate the means to extend my life...to project myself in whatever manner I choose."

"Project yourself how?"

With both hands, she traced the hourglass of her torso. "What you see when you look at me is a shadow, projected from the fourth dimension onto the three-dimensional fabric of this reality. The same is true for you and everyone else you see." She held her hand behind the shade of the lamp sitting on the table beside her, casting a hazy shadow onto the wallpaper. "What you see is the simple silhouette of a more complex essence."

Which he could not, at least as yet, directly observe. "All right," he said.

She lowered her hand. The shadow faded. It slid from the wall, and he felt a part of him disappear with it.

"All right, what?" Hand at her side, she waited.

Jump, he thought. Don't wait. Or all was lost.

Benjamin took a deep breath—"I'll do whatever it takes"—and held it, imagining the water close over his head, as cold and black as the night sky.

9

Orthinia, Design Space

From the balustrade, Olavo stared out at a sea of clouds. Along the horizon, mist frothed against a shoreline of rocky mountains, sending up spumes of mist.

The design space had been modeled after the Greek-Orthodox monasteries found in Meteora. The building balanced precariously on one of several high rock out-croppings that rose two or three hundred meters above the surrounding plain. Dwarf trees and shrubs crowded the base of the spire. He could see no route down to the valley floor. The cliff face was sheer, worn smooth by wind and hard radiation showering down from the Ferrer cluster.

Olavo placed his hands against the stone balustrade that grew vertically from the edge of the cliff. The wall enclosed a small garden at the end of a narrow passageway off the main courtyard. The stone was rough-hewn and pitted, cracked by years of expansion and contraction.

He missed the greenhouses of previous scapes. The rolling hills. Real or not, they had offered the illusion of freedom. Here, the environment was closed. For some reason,

Vania had chosen a sealed microcosm for the softspace construct.

It was an effort to stand at the wall. The view down left him light-headed. His armor-encased arms were heavy. So was the helmet protecting his head. His entire body ached under the burden—too weak to support the weight of his unwieldy limbs.

"I wouldn't jump if I were you," a voice said behind him.

Olavo turned to Ramunas. "Why not?"

"It won't do any good."

Olavo turned back to the balustrade and the precipice. "Have you tried it?"

Ramunas joined him. "No point."

"Why not?"

Ramunas shrugged. "Even if you killed yourself—this copy of you, that is—you're backed up on your ship and wherever else you've made local copies. You'll still end up in the same situation in the long run."

"What situation is that?"

Ramunas stared at the mountains for a moment. "A simunculus. Halfway between dead and alive."

"Not exactly how you expected things to turn out, I take it."

"I didn't know what to expect. Or hope for. Not this, I guess. Still it's a damned sight better than the life I would have had if I hadn't signed up. Hell, it's probably better. Even if I hadn't had my head smashed in by a crowbar I'd have just pissed it away, drunk or what have you."

Olavo glanced at Ramunas's protective helmet. It was honeycombed in places but otherwise similar to his.

"Bar fight," Ramunas said. "I guess I can't complain. I got a second chance most people don't."

"Sounds like you had it pretty rough."

"Didn't seem like it at the time."

"Why not?"

"It was the way I was brought up. Beat, or get beat down. I didn't know any other life. You do what you have to do. Sometimes you make it, sometimes you don't. That's not being fatalistic. It's just the way it is."

Olavo let it go. Ramunas had made his decision. They both had. And if they had regrets, it didn't matter. There was no going back.

"So how are things on Lulendo's Dream?" he asked. Unlike the rest of them, Ramunas had given the world he'd decided to seed the same name as his ship.

Ramunas turned toward him. "As of my last update, I was putting a bubble around the planet, complete with air locks to maintain atmospheric pressure."

"Last I heard, you were planning to use surface domes."

"Yeah, well. What would be the fun in that? If you're going to create a world you might as well go balls out. All or nothing, that's always been my motto. And if it doesn't work out"—he waved a hand to take in the mountains—"there's always this. Right?" He stepped away from the balustrade and headed back across the courtyard to one of the narrow alleyways that led to his design space. "Not my cup of tea, exactly. Too fucking rustic, but it beats the alternative. You'd do well to keep that in mind."

"In case this is it, you mean? For me?"

"For all of us," Ramunas said over his shoulder.

When he was gone, Olavo moved from the balustrade to a stone bench and sat, his armor-encased legs splayed awkwardly in front of him.

The garden was beautiful, blooming with familiar and unfamiliar plants. Monkey bush, a pink-flowered dogwood, pawpaws, bottlebrush, and Chinese tallow. One or two artificial insects flitted about the foliage. They darted among the branches of the red bottlebrush and pink-leafed mimosas shading the flowerbeds. Sunlight sprayed off them. Iridescent fractals spun inside the glare.

Mesmerized, he stared. The pain in his limbs increased. It seeped into his spine, then up it, one vertebrae at a time.

He heard the insect before he felt it. A faint motorized whir, followed by a needle-sharp jab. He clapped a hand to his neck, but the insect was too quick. His fingers hit the socket, which had gone numb.

Vania materialized on the bench beside him. She wore the same antiseptic white dress as before. But now her hair swept back along the side of her head in black, white-streaked wings that hid her ears and the back of her neck.

"How do you feel?" she asked.

The numbness around the socket was spreading through him, systematically deadening the pain.

"Better," he admitted.

"Good. We don't want you to overtax yourself at this stage."

"What's going on? Why do I feel so weak?" It would be nice to know what particular adaptation he was supposed to be testing.

"You're still in the early stages of your recovery. It's going to take a while until you're fully rested."

He could see patches of blackish-green moss growing in the cracks between the marble paving stones beneath his feet. "Recovery from what?"

"How much do you remember," she said, "about your time here so far?"

"I remember waking up. Twice. The first time it was dark, and I couldn't move. The second time, you showed up and brought me out here with the others."

"How long ago was that?"

"Not long." A half an hour at the most. "Then you all left, and I came out here."

"That's all?"

"Yes." He frowned. How many times had this happened? They seemed to be going over old ground. "Has there been another update?"

"No." She smiled as she shook her head. "Your condition remains unchanged."

Olavo resisted the urge to pick at the back of his neck. "What kind of update did you just give me?"

"Something to help with the discomfort while you adjust."

"My arms and legs don't hurt as much." The pain was almost completely gone. Only a low-level ache remained. Background radiation, easily ignored.

"Good." Her smile seemed pasted in place. "I was worried. Do you think you might be up for answering a few questions?"

He lowered his hand from his neck. There was no blood on his fingers. But his palm itched. He rubbed it on the rough carapace encasing his right leg. "What kind of questions?"

"Cognitive perception."

A deck of cards appeared in her hands. The cards were about twice the size of regular playing cards. They had simple line drawings on one side of them. The other side was blank.

"What do you see?" Vania asked.

"I don't see any inkblots," he said.

"Sorry"—her tone picked up on his, half-joking—"no ink blots this time around. This is a different type of test."

"Maybe next time," he said.

"We'll see."

Olavo studied the drawing. "I see a man standing next to a car on the side of a road, with the hood up."

"Anything else?"

"No." There was nothing else. Just the man and the broken-down car.

"Okay." She moved on to the second card.

It depicted a woman kneeling in front of a gravestone. "A widow at a cemetery," Olavo said. The woman wore a long dress and a hat with a veil that fell across her face. She cupped one hand to her mouth.

There were ten cards in all. Each card depicted a person and an object. In each instance, only the object was familiar.

"What's the matter?" Vania said, noting his consternation.

Olavo pressed trembling fingers to the sides of his helmet. "I don't recognize any of these people. I don't know who they are. Am I supposed to?"

"Not necessarily, no."

"Then what do they test for?"

"Agnosia, for one. The ability to recognize or identify objects is an indicator for intact sensory function."

"How does this relate to the new design space?"

"If there are any areas where your perception is impaired, this will help identify them."

"What else?" He got the feeling she wasn't telling him everything.

Vania reshuffled the cards into a tidy deck. "I think that's probably enough for today."

He kept his fingers pressed to the side of his helmet. The pain was back, a diluted throb. "So what happens next?"

"Perhaps you should rest."

He looked up between his hands. "I meant with the program."

"That depends." She stood and smoothed the front of her dress with both hands. The cards were gone.

"It's complicated," he said. "Isn't it?"

"But not impossible," she said. "We just need to take

things slowly. For now. In time... well, let's just take it one day at a time, shall we?"

He nodded. "Can I stay here for a while?"

"Do you feel up to it?"

"It's peaceful." And he was too tired to move. He just wanted to sit alone for a while. At some point, he wanted to explore the narrow alleyways and streets that angled away from the courtyard. But not now.

"Don't overdo it," she said. "If you need anything, let me know."

Without looking up, he listened to her leave, footsteps scattering across the worn stone like windblown leaves.

More than anything, he wanted to talk to the others to find out what was happening to them. Were they experiencing the same complications? Ramunas hadn't said anything. At this point, their evolutionary trajectories couldn't be that different. Initially their design paths should be relatively similar to his, with slight differences in initial conditions tending them in one direction or another until one actuality emerged as more stable, more viable. Later, after a few thousand iterations, their paths would begin to diverge more wildly and rapidly. The differences between their simunculi would accelerate, becoming more pronounced.

A rustling in the leaves above him snagged his attention. He straightened on the bench and looked up, craning his neck. A small bird flitted between the uppermost branches of the locust tree. Leaves tittered in its wake. Twigs trembled, then stilled. He followed the zigzag descent until the bird alighted on a thick limb directly over his head. The bird studied him with one sequin-bright eye, and then pirouetted to reexamine him with the other. Instead of feathers, it appeared to be covered with iridescent threads of black, blue, and green silk.

With a twitch of its long, flowing tail, the bird hopped to

the ground a meter from the bench. When he didn't move, it approached carefully. The silky tufts on both sides of its tail curled up to keep from dragging on the stones. When it hopped onto the seat of the bench, the tufts unfurled like streamers on a kite.

Olavo reached out. The bird darted into the air, but not before his fingers closed around the body, gripping it tightly. He felt bones break.

10

Santa Cruz, September 25

"I'm so glad you came." Sister Daminca clasped Rudi's hands in hers and gave him a grateful squeeze.

"Why wouldn't I?" he said.

"Some people don't always do what... Never mind." A flustered Sister Daminca released him. "Forget I said anything."

Rudi scanned the Veterans Memorial auditorium. The collapsible dining tables had been neatly folded and stacked along one wall. Several rows of portable chairs had been set up in their place. A man with an accordion was setting up onstage. Rudi recognized him from downtown Santa Cruz. Accordion Man. He was a regular on the Pacific Avenue mall, famous for his elaborate, homemade costumes. Tonight, he had on a leopard-spotted stretch suit and a carved wood mask with silver tinsel for hair.

"Irene said this was a benefit dance." Several people, both in wheelchairs and out, had dressed up in costumes.

The nun looked around in a distracted tizzy. "It is."

"For what?"

"Victims of breast cancer. We're being joined by dancers

from the AXIS Dance Company. They're going to do a short program first. Then anybody who wants to will be free to participate."

Rudi blinked rapidly in a sudden panic. "No one said anything about wearing a costume."

"It's optional. Don't worry. You're fine." She patted him on the arm. "You can help me sell goodies, and collect contributions."

From beside the stage, a woman gestured at Sister Daminca, motioning frantically while mouthing a plea for help.

"I have to go." The nun bustled off.

"Well, well, look who made it!" Celia Truong said behind him.

Rudi's shoulders jerked as he turned. The reporter's iCam winked at him from eye level.

"What are you doing here?" he demanded.

"Making a documentary. Remember?"

"You're following me."

"Actually, Sister Daminca invited me," the journalist said. Then, "I'm surprised to see you here. I didn't think you danced. I have a hard time picturing it."

Rudi stared into the lens of the video camera, unable to escape his reflection. His baseball cap was askew, and he cringed at the unmistakable glimmer of foil.

"You don't have to be in a wheelchair," Celia Truong said. "Nondisabled people are encouraged to take part in the dance, too."

"I haven't decided."

"Come on." Celia turned up her smile. "It'll be fun. Besides, it's for a good cause." There was a gleeful prod behind the comment. Clearly she enjoyed making fun of him.

"I'm helping Sister Daminca with refreshments." It was a lame excuse. But he didn't care.

"I'm sure she'll let you take a break." The reporter winked. "Even God took a day off."

"Only when His work was done."

Celia looked around and tightened her lips into a tiny pink button. "It seems there's still a lot of work to do. At least when it comes to providing healthcare for people who can't afford it."

"He did His part. Now it's up to us to do ours."

"Do you think we're doing enough?"

"We can always do more."

" 'If there is a balm in Gilead,' " she quoted, " 'if there is a physician, there should be healing.' "

The verse, from Jeremiah, caught him off guard. It was the last thing he expected to hear from her. Was she making fun of him, slinging Scripture, or did she actually mean what the verse seemed to imply? Half the time, Rudi never knew why a particular passage leapt to mind. It came to him without conscious effort or forethought. He was nothing but a well, a vessel, from which to drink.

Celia Truong seemed anything but.

"I think they're getting ready to start," she said. She jutted her chin in the direction of the stage, where Accordion Man stood motionless on his box.

He reminded Rudi of a statue, or a figure in a wax museum. Around them, people were taking seats. Chairs scraped, clothing rustled. The auditorium had grown crowded and stuffy.

"Do you have any last thoughts on the evening, before we get started?"

Rudy turned back to Celia. The light on her camera was resolute, unremitting. " 'The race is not to the swift,' " he said, " 'nor the battle to the strong.' "

Irene always made him think of Ecclesiastes. Living on the street, she was forced to immerse herself in the simple pleasures and pains of everyday life. But her life was full of questions, without any real direction or meaning.

Celia Truong swung the iCam from him to the stage just as Accordion Man began to tune up. When the crowd had settled, Sister Daminca made her way onstage. She held a microphone.

"First, I want to thank you all for coming," she began. There was a reedy quaver to her voice. It started out frail, ready to break, but gained strength as she talked about money for research, the urgency of the battle, and the need to keep fighting. She spoke of courage and sacrifices, those already made by the dead and those still required of the living.

As she talked, Rudi retreated to the edge of the auditorium. He was ashamed, by both his ignorance and his lack of contribution. Her words were like a searchlight—under their glare, his shortcomings cast long, uncomfortable shadows.

His house was still a shambles. What he thought he'd straightened up was, in reality, a mess. He had kicked the boxes of his former life into the corners of his heart. He had replaced them with reams of Scripture and stacks of verse, piled high. But his current life was no tidier than his old one. It was disorganized and haphazard. Pointless.

Sister Daminca ended with a moment of silence, to be filled with prayer or any other thoughts people wanted to give. When she exited the stage, Accordion Man began to play, and the AXIS dancers appeared.

There were two men and four women, all dressed in black bodysuits. The women were confined to wheelchairs. They had wrapped their upper torsos in luminous white bandages, as if that part of their anatomy was mummified. They guided the chairs around each other with clockwork precision. Their movements were fluid, graceful. Not some pantomime of a traditional ballet, but an intricate, modern choreograph designed specifically, exclusively, for wheelchairs. None of the men were bandaged. They danced around the wheelchairs, occasionally making contact with the women. They seemed out of sync with the women, disconnected.

Then one woman took off her bandage, unraveling the single strip of gauze binding her breasts. The gauze swirled around her in a celebratory streamer. One by one the other women began to remove their bandages. The men joined in, awkwardly at first, then with more sensitivity and skill. What had been two dances became one.

"It's beautiful, isn't it?" Sister Daminca said.

Rudi, focused on the dance, hadn't felt her come up to him. He nodded, his throat squeezed tight on itself. Multicolored fabric had been sewn to the back side of the gauze strips. When they twirled, rainbow flashes of color arched between the dancers.

Three more wheelchairs came onstage. It took Rudi a moment to recognize Irene. Her chest was bandaged. But when the gauze was removed, he could see that one breast was gone.

He curled his fingers into his palm, away from the phantom softness of the breast she had pressed his hand to. It was the same breast, the left one. It had been there a few days ago. Now it was gone. Had it always been gone? Or had it recently been removed?

"My God," he said.

Sister Daminca cut a sharp glance at him. "You didn't know?"

Rudi's palm itched. The itch spread, traveling up his wrist and arm.

"She was in North Korea when Dolan was still President," Sister Daminca said. "She volunteered as a civilian nurse right after the joint stabilization force went in. Her brother was called up and she wanted to be there with him, in case he needed help."

Rudi swallowed at the tension in his throat. "What happened?"

"He died. She never had a chance to save him."

"To her, I mean."

"Hard to say. The North Koreans used a lot of depleted uranium for armor-piercing bullets, which can release tiny particles of uranium oxide. If these particles get in the lungs and other tissue, they end up exposing the person to alpha radiation."

"You think that's how she got cancer?"

"No one knows. That's why the VA refuses to treat her. There's no proof that's what gave her cancer."

"What else could it have been?"

"Her mother died of breast cancer. So she has the gene. At least that's what the Army is saying."

Rudi watched Irene on the stage. She lumbered in comparison to the AXIS dance troupe. But even that looked like it was planned, part of the routine. "If the Army's not treating her, who is?"

"She's gotten some help from state and county agencies that work with area hospitals."

"That's why she sometimes leaves town for a while."

"Right." Sister Daminca took Rudi by the hand. "Come on."

"Where are we going?"

"To dance." She tugged him in the direction of the stage.

"No."

The nun paused, but kept her hand firmly on his. "Why not?"

"I can't."

"Sure you can. All you have to do is move around a little. No one will know the difference."

"I have a headache." The itch had ignited a nauseous throb deep inside his head.

"You don't have to be up there long. A couple of minutes, at the most. It would mean the world to Irene."

Rudi trailed after her. "What about the concession stand?"

"We're not going to open that until the dance is over. That's why we need to go now. We need to be set up and ready when things wrap up."

There was a set of steps on the side of the stage. Sister Daminca led him up the stairs, into the brightness.

It was hot onstage. Spotlights glared down, half-blinding him. The dancers were ashen smudges in the light. They appeared singed, dark angels clinging to fragile white threads.

He could feel himself burning up. The radiance settled over him in an incendiary blanket. His eyes watered.

"Here." One of the dancers placed a bandage in his hands.

He clutched it. He held tightly to the thread and let himself be guided across the stage.

Like a blind man, he thought. Stumbling.

"You're doing fine," Irene said. Her hand found his left forearm and squeezed it in appreciation.

"I can't see."

"Grab hold of my chair."

"Where?"

"Here."

His hand brushed the side of her chair, then slipped off. He flailed for the sweat-slick chrome.

"Relax," Irene said. "Just take it easy. Let go."

Rudi let go. The gauze slithered from his fingers.

"That's better." She sounded farther away.

Rudi groped for her through the veil of light. The inside of his skull burned. He felt hollow. "Irene?" His tongue was a flame. He could taste smoke coming off his charred teeth.

"I'm here."

Head spinning, Rudi turned toward her voice. A petal of fire bloomed inside his mouth. Above him the spotlights tightened into a Coriolis spiral behind his eyes.

He vomited. Bile burned his lips. Accordion Man stopped playing, but the notes refused to be extinguished. They sifted down in embers, luminous white flakes out of a charcoal black sky that hardened as it cooled.

11

San Francisco, Circa 1937

Benjamin's first lesson with Madame Grurie turned out to be a group dance, held in a second floor room she had turned into a studio.

"We're going to be practicing Gurdjieff movements," she explained. The session was scheduled to begin in an hour. Madame Grurie had asked Benjamin to arrive earlier so she might prepare him.

They sat on plump-cushioned chairs, arranged at a forty-five-degree angle to the coffee table in front of them so they could comfortably talk and sip tea. A flower vase in the center of the table sprayed a fountain of white mums. The yellow glow from the floor lamps seemed to float in the room, not as shafts or beams but some buoyant luminous gas.

"These movements are intended to get in touch with your physical self," Madame Grurie went on. "You must inhabit your body, fully and completely."

"Why?"

"In order to provide balance. The human body is the alembic, the vessel for your ultimate transmutation."

"Healing," he said.

"Yes. The movements allow you to explore certain fundamental energies... to engage in the process of self-remembering."

"The way I was, you mean. When I was healthy."

"No. I mean sensing your self fully. Wholly and completely inhabiting your body, without reservation."

"To what end?"

"In time, this will lead to conscious suffering." She raised her teacup and sipped from the gold-leaf rim.

"I see."

She lowered her cup. "No, you don't. Not yet. Only through conscious suffering, by choosing to suffer, can we wake up. Only when we're awake can we begin to observe our true selves."

"Otherwise we see... what?" Benjamin glanced around the room. He caught a fleeting glimpse of their reflections, flat and distorted, on the polished silver curve of the samovar.

"Have you ever observed your self while you're asleep?"

Benjamin opened his mouth.

"Of course not," she said before he could make a fool of himself. "That is because you have been taught that the mind—like the body—cannot be in two places at once."

Benjamin felt his face color at the sudden image of her head on a pillow, dark tangles of hair coiled in filigrees.

"In addition to a physical awakening, you must also undergo an emotional as well as intellectual awakening. The three balance one another. Without that balance, you won't ever connect with your higher self; your soul will never develop to the point where it can be born and survive outside of the body."

Benjamin straightened. His hand jerked, sloshing tea on his pant legs. "The body gives birth to the soul?" he said, unnerved.

"The soul is conceived within the body. It is forged there. The body is to the spirit as the womb is to the body."

Benjamin sat in one corner of the second-floor room and watched Madame Grurie guide her students through a regimented series of bizarre but precisely choreographed and purposeful movements.

The tongue-and-groove floor creaked under the synchronized movement of the dancers. All were dressed in white silk tunics with different colored sashes—cobalt blue for the men, lavender or fuchsia for the women. All wore loose wraparound pants with a band at the ankle, and black leather-soled slippers.

Etta was among the dancers. Benjamin watched her out of the corner of his eye, careful not to stare. Her face was rapt, completely absorbed in the movements. There was no sign of strain, no physical or emotional discomfort. She seemed completely at ease. Even at the office, humming to herself, she had never seemed so relaxed. And the few times he'd visited Zachary at home, Etta had been muted. A haze had hung over her, a lifeless stupor that put him ill at ease. But now he realized the tranquility had been drug-induced. Here, she radiated a sense of quiet well-being.

Of peace, he thought.

Zachary wasn't present. Was he granting Etta a measure of privacy? Or was he too embarrassed to be associated with a known practitioner of the occult? It was one thing to have one's wife engaged in such activities; it was another to take part in them oneself. Zachary had always been concerned with appearances. Until a few days ago, Benjamin had been the same. As the owners of a business, they had to maintain a certain measure of respectability and conformity in the eyes of community leaders.

Those days were over, he realized. It was unlikely now that he would ever again be accepted as an equal in professional and social circles.

Zachary would cover for him as much as possible. Clients and business associates would be discreetly informed of the tumor. Part of that would be to protect Zachary . . . to disassociate him and the business from Benjamin's condition. If rumors arose concerning Benjamin's involvement with Madame Grurie, Zachary could intimate that Benjamin was not himself—not thinking clearly. As a victim of circumstance, his behavior wouldn't reflect poorly on Zachary. Benjamin's relationship with Madame Grurie would be forgiven. But from now on, whatever the outcome, there would always be doubt when it came to his faculties. He might not be treated as a leper. But he wouldn't be taken seriously, either. His abilities—his judgment—would be questioned. It would be better if Madame Grurie ran a brothel. That at least fell within the norm of acceptable, if not necessarily condonable, behavior.

Of the nine students, six were women. There were only two other men. One was elderly, on the downside of fifty and clearly in failing health. He had the congestive, bloodshot complexion of a heavy drinker. The other appeared to be in his early twenties, one of those wayward souls destined to end up in the gutter, jail, or Calcutta.

One decrepit, the other reckless and irresponsible. Benjamin didn't fit into either category.

What was he doing? He didn't belong here. He felt like a clown, dressed up in silk pajamas, attending to the gramophone. It was just as well Zachary wasn't here to see him. It saved them both from awkward discomfort.

Madame Grurie led the dance steps. The white silk tunic and pants flowed around her like windswept clouds, clinging here, trailing there, to reveal the subtle curves of her body, both imagined and real. Her movements were simultaneously fluid and precise, wild yet controlled. She seemed on the verge of flying apart or lapsing into mechanical repetition.

By contrast, the students looked clumsy. They stumbled to keep up with her. The result was less than artistic.

Madame Grurie had warned him about this ahead of time. "The point is to work on the movements, to feel one's way through them consciously. Not only externally, but also internally."

In time, she assured him, the movements would become effortless, second nature. They would imprint on him certain primordial patterns. These patterns would then heal him by restoring his body to its original nature.

The music stopped. As Benjamin lifted the needle from the platter and moved it to the outside edge of the disk, he caught Etta looking at him. Her gaze was clear and attentive, as if a fog had lifted and she was *seeing* him for the first time. She looked away quickly, busying herself with her clothing. Benjamin returned his attention to the phonograph. Before he could set the needle down and restart the music, Madame Grurie spoke. "Please join us."

Benjamin looked up.

She motioned for him with one hand. "Don't worry about the music. We shan't need it at this point."

Benjamin replaced the stylus, switched off the gramophone, and approached the sweaty group. Most of them were red-faced from exertion and breathing heavily, glad for the break.

"What do you think of the movements so far?" Madame Grurie asked him.

"Different," he replied cautiously. "Beautiful, in their own way."

"Is that all?"

Benjamin flushed under the question. His face and the back of his neck prickled.

Someone in the group chuckled. Madame Grurie smiled. "Let's go through that last sequence one more time," she said.

The dancers lined up in two rows. Madame Grurie stood behind Benjamin. "All right," she said. "First position."

Everyone shifted into a stance and held it, feet spread and arms raised. Benjamin imitated them as best he could.

Madame Grurie took hold of him from behind. She repostioned his hands and arms. Her breasts touched his back briefly, then retreated as her hands realigned his spine.

"Each position," she said, "has meaning. Symbolic content. It embodies a mode of vibration. A particular energy state that transforms us." He felt himself stiffen under the heat of her closeness. "Next position."

The dancers turned, taking up a new pose and holding it.

"This energy comes from without. It flows into us and through us from a higher dimension," she said.

The fourth dimension, Benjamin thought, trying to ignore the tickle of her breath against his neck.

"Each position in the movement resonates with, and indeed amplifies, a particular energy state. As we move through these different states, we progress upward. The disconnected aspects of our being—mind, body, and feeling—become integrated. In this way, discord is replaced with harmony. We become synchronized, more in tune, with the higher orders of our selves and the universe."

He was having trouble getting his body to perform as asked. He kept lapsing into positions that felt more comfortable, more natural.

"By learning to actively dance, we learn to actively live." Madame Grurie gently poked and prodded his limbs back into the proper position. "We free ourselves from the preprogrammed movements that are expected of us. If we shed all mechanistic behavior, we can shed mechanistic thought. New modes of thinking will open up to us, entire new modes of existence."

The position was becoming painful. Benjamin's arms and legs started to tremble. His muscles burned.

Out of the corner of his eye, he caught a glimpse of a man with a baby's face and soft down for hair staring at him from the far side of the room. The man's lips were moist and rubbery. His eyes glistened, glassy black marbles pressed into pale dough. His entire face seemed unformed, or perhaps formless.

Benjamin blinked. The salty sting in his eyes cleared and the man vanished, as if he had never been there.

"That's enough. Tonight was much better. However, I expect you to continue our work on your own in preparation for our next lesson."

Madame Grurie released him, and Benjamin sagged in both relief and exhaustion.

"We'll discuss your situation in more detail at another time," she informed him as they were walking out. "I'm afraid something's come up."

"I'm a student?" It wasn't clear to him if he had been officially accepted or not.

"You wouldn't be here if you weren't."

She had already made up her mind, then, during the first interview, when she'd invited him to the dance. She inclined her head slightly toward the red-faced man who appeared to be agitated and he trailed after Madame Grurie as she exited the room.

Etta avoided Benjamin. He didn't try to catch up with her when she scurried off with several other women to get changed. Clearly, she wasn't ready to talk with him. She might even think he was a spy, sent by Zachary to keep an eye on her and report back about her condition.

"Peter McGraff." The young man extended a hand.

Benjamin took it. The remaining members of the group introduced themselves to him in turn. Gerty. Neola. Beatrice. Myrtle. Eloise. The women were all in their bespectacled fifties or sixties, gray-haired and rheumy-eyed with crinkly wax-paper skin and the quaint eccentricities of devout widows.

"Welcome," the young man said.

"Thanks."

"So what brings you to our little gathering?"

One of the women, Eloise, waved a hand at him. "Don't scare him off, Peter. We can get personal later."

"What do you think so far?" Gerty said.

"It seems like a lot of work," Benjamin said. "What do you do when you're not dancing?"

"We meditate," Eloise said. "Or listen to music. Sometimes we talk to our other selves."

"Other selves?"

"Our unborn selves," Neola clarified.

Beatrice nodded. "In the future."

12

Aelon, Softspace

Olavo turned his attention to the television screen, where a team of paramedics was hustling a stretcher into a small auditorium. The auditorium was crowded. A cluster of onlookers gathered in front of a raised stage parted to allow the paramedics to pass. Bloodred lights strobed through the row of vertical windows on one wall.

The image jostled, then steadied. It panned from the crowd to the paramedics as they raced up the stairs on one side of the stage. Several of the people on the stage were seated in wheelchairs, forming a loose circle around a man on the stage. He lay unmoving on his back. A baseball cap lined with crumpled foil lay a meter or so away. A woman knelt down and leaned over him, both hands pressed to his chest.

The paramedics reached the stage and set the stretcher next to the man. One of them eased the woman aside. Another took her place.

Olavo turned to Acantha, seated on the sofa next to him. She nibbled at her nails, chipping the polish.

“Is there any sound?” he asked.

Her shoulder twitched in a shrug. "There might be. Or there might not. If there was, it might not have been transmitted. Or it might have gotten lost."

"You can't tell?"

A single shake of the head. On the screen, the paramedics were lifting the fallen man onto the stretcher. "I'm still trying to decode the signal and clean it up. This is all I have so far."

"Any idea why it's so dirty?"

Acantha dug a ragged nail into the narrow gap between two teeth. "How should I know? For one thing, the signal's nonstandard."

"In what way?"

"It looks like a regular low-density parity-check transmission. Kind of. It's way more compressed and efficient. I keep tweaking the standard LDPC decoders. But I'm still having trouble."

"The LDPC code isn't on file?"

"Nope. I can't find it anywhere in the library. So it must be something special. Proprietary shit. Military, probably."

"Maybe it's not LDPC," he said. "Maybe it's another format."

"The audio part?"

"Or anything else there might be. Maybe this is just a carrier wave for additional information."

"Embedded." Acantha inspected her nail. "I didn't think of that."

The paramedics were strapping the man down. Tightening the belts that held him secure.

"Where's the signal from?" he asked.

"Where's it look like?"

"The actual source of the transmission, I mean."

She sucked at her finger.

"I guess what I'm asking is if the transmission came from

one of our collectors or from somewhere, or something, else," he said.

"You don't have to get all pissy about it."

"I'm not."

"What difference does it make anyway?" she said. "Who cares? It's not like it's going to matter."

It might, he wanted to say.

Instead, he watched two of the paramedics lift the stretcher. The third cleared a path for them, forcing people back.

"You're probably right," he said, trying to let go of his frustration. She was so defeatist. It was hard to take sometimes. His first reaction was to lash out against it. But all that did was steel her against him. "I was just curious. That's all."

She inspected her finger again.

The broadcast ended with the paramedics loading the stretcher into an ambulance. The doors shut. A siren chirped as it raced off down a dim, grainy street into pixel static.

"Is that it?"

"Yeah." She retrieved a crumpled pack of Camels from the gap between her seat cushion and the side of the sofa. Lint and saltine crumbs clung to the wrinkly cellophane.

"What's a Suicide Angel?" Olavo asked, reading the delicate script tattooed on the inside of her left forearm. If he was going to understand and help her, he needed to step fully into the darkness—no matter how unsettling.

Acantha plucked a cigarette from the pack. Her fingers were shaking. It took her several tries. "It's an angel that kills itself."

"I thought angels were immortal."

"No." The denial was partially muffled by the cigarette pinched between her lips. "They can kill themselves."

"How?"

She lit the cigarette with a cheap plastic lighter. A halo of smoke formed around her head. "By coming down to Earth and hiding inside a person. If they do that, they're trapped. They can't get out."

"Then what?"

"They die, and you can see parts of them showing through the skin of the person."

"What parts?"

"It depends. Different stuff. Eyes. Wing feathers. Bones. Their bones look like lightning. They burn the person's skin, branding them from the inside out and leaving a black scar."

Acantha had wings across the top of her back, feathers spreading along the curve of her shoulders. A single lightning strike followed her spine, terminating at the small of her back.

"An angel committed suicide in you?" he said.

She rolled her eyes and pursed her lips around a jet of smoke. "Not literally. It's like when some part of you starts to rot, and something really beautiful is dying inside of you."

"You're beautiful. That part of you isn't dead."

"Yeah, it seems to be taking a long time." Acantha wiped at her nose with the back of her free hand. "Nothing ever happens as fast as you think."

"What about the part of you that isn't dying?" Olavo asked. "What happens to her after the angel part dies?"

"I'll carry her around with me. Her remains. It'll be like she's buried inside of me. Like I'm a coffin."

"Is there any way to stop her from dying?"

"Did she have a choice, you mean?" The cigarette dangled over the ankle she'd tucked on the cushion. "Did I have a choice?"

"Yeah. Who decided to commit suicide? You or her?"

Acantha jiggled the cigarette. Ashes settled on the couch, collecting there like gray dandruff. "I think I wanted her to die. That part of me, I mean."

"Why?"

She gave a diffident half-shrug, lifting the angel wing on her right shoulder and then letting it drop. "I wanted to change—for things the way they were to end—and this was the only way for that to happen. She's never been a big part of my life, anyway. And lately it seems like there's been less of her than usual."

Olavo stood. He went to the apartment window and looked out. Athens spread in all directions. It was getting dark, the night sky just starting to yawn wide to swallow the world.

Despite the low-slung sprawl of the cityscape, his thoughts turned to Mee Won. So different from Acantha in so many ways, and yet disconcertingly similar in others. They were like sisters, or two sides of the same person. Neither of them seemed whole. Both seemed lost, at odds with themselves and the world. Look inside Acantha, at the angel wings, and he saw Mee Won trying to take flight. Look into Mee Won, past the delicate ingenue, and he saw the bone-sketched shadow of Acantha.

The sun emerged from behind a smoky cloud, searing a red hole in the periwinkle sky. A bloody puncture wound, inflamed around the edges.

"The red hole," he said.

Acantha sniffed. "What about it?"

"Can you make the collector data available to the rest of us? So we can figure out what's going on? Even if you don't want to."

"Vania already has it. I sent it to her."

Olavo turned back to Acantha. "Is there any way to stop the angel part of you from dying? If you wanted to, I mean."

"I don't want to."

"But if you did. If you changed your mind."

"I don't think so."

"Why not?"

The sun dropped below the horizon, leaving her face in silhouette. "Because she's trapped inside of me. Like a bird in a cage."

Olavo nodded. "You don't have the key to open the lock. But could someone else help set her free?"

"Save her, you mean?"

"I guess."

Acantha stubbed the cigarette on the inside of her thigh, leaving an angry red sore. All the answer he needed.

13

Santa Cruz, September 25

Rudi woke to the digitized beep of his heart.

He was in a hospital, suffocating under the queasy odor of latex and disinfectant, the sibilant hiss of oxygen, and the squeak of nurses' shoes on waxed floor tile. It seemed as if he'd never left. Maybe he hadn't. What if his rehab and the storm had been one long dream, from which he was only now waking up?

Rudi blinked. Once. Twice.

Nothing happened. His eyes were gummed shut. His eyelashes clung to his lower lid. They refused to let go. Soft, mechanical susurrations whispered from several beds around him, filling the lungs of patients unable to breathe on their own.

He raised his right hand. Tubes tugged at his arm, restraining it. A chair scraped next to the bed. He raised his left hand to his face. Rubbed blurry light into his eyes.

"Hi there." The voice leaned close.

The light was bright. He cupped his hand over his brow.

"How do you feel?" Sister Daminca smiled down at him

out of the fluorescent glare. A blue privacy curtain, drawn around the bed on a ceiling track, hung behind her.

Not a dream after all. "What happened?"

Her face ballooned, then grew smaller, steadying as it shrank. "You gave us quite the scare."

He had a headache. He massaged his forehead. But the pain persisted, dull-edged. It felt like a piece of metal lodged deep in his skull—a leftover from the accident that had never been removed.

"My hat..." His hands floundered against his unprotected skull.

"I don't have it with me," Sister Daminca said. "I'm sorry. I forgot all about it in the confusion."

"They can see me," he said.

"Who?"

"Whoever's watching." Loose wisps of hair stirred under his fingertips. "Who has it?"

"I don't know. One of the dancers, I'm sure. Don't worry." She patted his hand. "I'll find it. Right now you have more immediate concerns. You're not out of the woods yet."

"I don't want them to know what's going on."

"You have an aneurysm." The nun sat, still holding his hand. "A blood vessel in your head is bulging."

"Bulging?"

"It hasn't ruptured. Not yet, thank God. But it's only a matter of time."

"How long?"

"The doctors don't know. It could happen anytime. The sooner they operate, the better."

He shook his head. "Here, I mean. How long?"

"You've been in intensive care for the past three hours. It's coming up on eleven o'clock."

The last few hours were a blank. He remembered being under bright lights, and then nothing.

The curtain parted and a woman entered, carrying a clipboard.

"Dr. Acker," she said by way of introduction. "I'm the neurosurgeon on duty tonight."

Rudi shook her hand. It was small-boned and reminded him of a precise, highly calibrated instrument.

"You've had a head injury before." The doctor withdrew her hand and flipped open the manila folder clipped to her board. "I'm seeing a lot of unusual lesions. Fairly extensive. Frankly, I'm at a loss to explain them. The damage is widespread."

"Motorcycle accident," Rudi said.

"How long ago?"

"Five years."

She clicked her tongue thoughtfully. "There was also some hydrocephalus," she said.

"Water on the brain?" Sister Daminca asked.

Dr. Acker nodded. "Persistent swelling. That's why they inserted a CSF shunt, to reduce the pressure."

"Shunt?" he asked.

"There's a tube in your head. It drains cerebral spinal fluid from the ventricles in the brain." She explored the bump on the top back of his skull. Rudi had always assumed the knot was a harmless remnant of the accident. Dr. Acker's fingers were cool against his scalp. "They didn't tell you about it?"

"No."

"It's possible you don't remember. Often, victims of severe head trauma have difficulty recalling the initial details of their recovery. It takes a while for the brain to fully wake up. Until then, some memory loss isn't unusual."

Dr. Acker took an X-ray from the folder and slipped it onto a portable light-screen next to the bed. She flipped a light switch, and an image of his head in profile appeared in stark black and white. Dr. Acker fished a pen from the front pocket of her smock. With the tip she indicated a straight line off to one side. It looked like a nail had been hammered into his head and left there.

"What's that, coming out the top?" Sister Daminca said.

"A permanent drain tube." The tip of the pen traced the tube to the base of Rudi's skull, where the image ended. "It tunnels just under the skin, and empties into the lining of your stomach."

Rudi swallowed. "What does it do?"

"Balances the fluid pressure in your spine and your brain. If there's fluid buildup, the excess fluid drains out the tube."

"Otherwise...?"

"The brain swells. You become progressively unresponsive and eventually lapse into a coma."

"Great."

"Typically, you wouldn't notice it." The doctor positioned an angiogram next to the first X-ray. She pointed to a root-like tangle of veins. "You can see the aneurysm"—tap, tap—"right here."

It looked like a bubble on the side of a bicycle tube, ready to pop.

"What caused the aneurysm?" Sister Daminca asked. "The accident?"

The doctor shook her head, freeing a strand of dishwater gray hair. "Most likely it's a weak spot in the blood vessel. These things tend to be congenital. They can show up at any time."

"So how do you get rid of it?" Rudi said.

"There are a couple of different options. We can go in and clip it off. Or we can use a process called endovascular coiling to block the flow of blood to the aneurysm and prevent it from rupturing."

"Coiling?" Sister Daminca said.

"We insert a catheter into the femoral artery in the leg. From there, we run microthreads of platinum into the head and the aneurysm. These threads are extremely flexible. They coil inside the aneurysm, blocking the flow of blood. Usually this embolization is all that's required."

"But not always," Rudi said.

Dr. Acker pursed her lips. "The success rate is very high."

"How high?" Sister Daminca asked.

"Every patient is different."

"But his chances are good."

"Statistically, yes. But statistics are meaningless when applied to an individual. They don't guarantee anything."

In other words she didn't want to get his hopes up. It had been the same at Lakeshore. Nurses smiled, but made no promises.

"You'll be lightly sedated throughout the procedure," the doctor was saying. "It isn't necessary to use a general anesthesia."

"When?" he said.

"I've scheduled the surgery for seven tomorrow morning."

"You can't do it now?" Sister Daminca said.

"I've had a long day," Dr. Acker said. "I want to be rested. *You* want me to be rested."

"What if it ruptures before then?" Sister Daminca said.

"I doubt that will happen." Dr. Acker adjusted a small control valve on the drip line feeding the IV needle taped to the back of his hand. "But if it does, we'll operate immediately. In the meantime try to get some sleep. Your chances for a full recovery are better if neither of us is tired."

"I'll be with you," Sister Daminca said, as soon as the doctor was gone. "I'm not going anywhere."

Rudi scanned the room for his Bible, thinking she might have brought it. "How's Irene?" he asked.

"She's fine. Don't worry about her. The most important thing is to take care of yourself."

"I want to help her." There was no sign of the Bible, which meant it must still be in the van.

"Right now, you need to help *you*."

"If anything happens to me..." His eyelids drooped, suddenly heavy. "If I don't make it—"

"Shh!" Her breath escaped harshly, like air from a tire valve. "Don't talk that way. Everything's going to be fine."

"If it's not..." He lifted his head, fighting to raise himself above the fatigue. "I want you to return..."

"Of course I will!"

"The van," he said.

"Don't worry about your van. It'll be fine. We'll take care of it for as long as we have to."

"The church," he said.

"What church?"

"Take it back."

"You're talking nonsense," Sister Daminca said.

Rudi tried to speak. But the words were stillborn in his mouth. His head settled back. It sank into the pillow, and continued to sink, smothered by the past....

"What are you reading?" Linnea asked. She tossed her backpack next to him on the couch.

Rudi started. His shoulders hunched and he closed the magazine on his lap.

"Let me see." From behind him, she reached over the back of the couch, making a half-hearted grab for it.

Rudi ducked his head and snatched the magazine away.

"Girlie mag," she said, taunting him with a rapacious grin. Her lips were black, her nails pink.

"You wish."

Linnea plopped herself beside him on the sofa. He relaxed. Today was one of her better days. She was up. Instead of dragging him down with her, he could ride her mood while it lasted.

"Come on," she chided. "I won't tell Grandma."

Rudi showed her the magazine. He almost wished it was a girlie mag. Playboy *or* Suicide Angel *would have been less embarrassing.*

"ION," she said. The title of the magazine seemed to wrinkle with her nose.

"Mr. Chin gave it to me."

She set the magazine on black fishnet thighs. "Who's Mr. Chin? Some perv you met?"

"He works down at the 7-Eleven."

"Right." She started flipping pages. "SpeculatION," she read. "ExperimentatION. MedicatION."

"They're science topics," he said.

"I don't see MasturbatION."

His cheeks warmed. "Very funny."

"That's a science," she said, matter of fact. "You'll see, when you're older. It can get highly technical."

Rudi made an effort to reclaim the magazine, but she swatted his hand. Maybe Linnea's being in a good mood wasn't such a good thing after all.

"What's this?" She bent her head closer to the text. Bleached, crimson-tinted hair fell in a white veil across the side of her face. Rudi couldn't read her expression. He turned his attention to the article on the page.

"Some researchers attached an artificial brain to a rat," he

said. "They were able to switch from the rat's real brain to the artificial one."

"Without killing it?"

"Yeah. It was even able to move around and do stuff. React to information stored in the artificial brain."

She brushed at the frizzed ends of her hair. "Like what could it do? With only the artificial brain?"

"Programmed behaviors that were copied from the real brain to the artificial brain," Rudi said. "It even remembered how to get through mazes it had been in before."

"Sort of like a robot," she said.

"I guess. Except the artificial brain was able to remember things that it had learned and the regular brain hadn't."

"What happened when they switched it back to its normal brain? Was it like normal and all?"

"Yeah. It went back to acting the way it did before."

She made a face. "Did it know it had been hooked up to an artificial brain?"

"I don't think so."

"That's sick." But she kept staring at the picture of the rat, the way she might a dead body on the street.

In the morning, a nurse moved Rudi out of intensive care to prep him for surgery. Sister Daminca had gone off to grab a cup of coffee and a quick bite to eat at the cafeteria. On the way, Rudi saw Celia Truong following his progress, camera in hand.

In the prep room, another nurse shaved his head and the inside of his thigh, then swabbed the bare skin liberally with iodine.

He thought of Jim and Marilee Odette—how calm they'd been when they visited him in rehab, how certain of his recovery. Their presence had been a source of strength—and comforted himself with Corinthians. *O death, where is thy sting? O grave, where is thy victory?*

The swabbed skin turned yellow and tickled as it cooled. Rudi shivered in the blue hospital gown as another nurse wheeled him into an operating room. "'Behold,'" he said aloud, "'now is the accepted time.'"

"You'll be back before you know it," the nurse said.

It sounded like something Marilee would say, and he imagined her patting his arm while Jim gave his hand a reassuring squeeze.

Dr. Acker and an anesthesiologist dressed in tie-dyed scrubs were waiting for him under ice-white lights.

Rudi switched to John. "'Let not your heart be troubled.'" Followed by Matthew. "'Be of good cheer: it is I; be not afraid.'"

"Ready?" Dr. Acker asked, checking a small television screen positioned next to her.

"Almost," the anesthesiologist said.

Rudi felt suddenly cut free. The rope holding him to the world had been cast off, allowing him to drift.

Dr. Acker turned to Rudi. "Can you feel this?"

"What?" He was sinking now—floating downward, toward the sandy bottom of consciousness.

"Okay," the doctor said. "Let's get started."

"'I know that my Redeemer liveth,'" Rudi told himself. "'Be thou faithful unto death.' 'He giveth his beloved sleep.'"

"We'll be waiting for you when you get out," Marilee said. "See you soon." What she always said at the end of a visit.

Rudi took comfort in her parting smile and wave. Maybe this time he would return unscathed from the belly of the whale, the same person he was before being swallowed, with the same life. He didn't want to lose who he was in the darkness. He didn't want to have to start over again when he woke up...didn't want to have to rediscover himself and God when he was finally vomited back into the world. One resurrection was enough. He wasn't sure he could survive another.

14

San Francisco, Circa 1937

Benjamin reeled in a giddy, half-intoxicated blur, his sense of inebriation heightened by the sway of the Number 22 streetcar. He couldn't shake the unreal quality of the last two hours. The feeling had settled in him, heavy as whiskey. He wanted to be someplace familiar, where his thoughts could sober and his body could condense back into the world.

A block from his stop on Fillmore, Benjamin spied Etta near the front of the trolley. Her back was to him as she stared out at the passing houses and shops, lost in thought. He pressed his fingers to his eyes. But when he looked again, she was still there. She wasn't an apparition. He'd simply missed seeing her in the crowd of passengers boarding the car.

Benjamin pinched the bridge of his nose. He had sunk deeper into himself than he realized. What he needed wasn't to be alone, but to talk, to reconnect with someone who shared, and hopefully understood, what he'd been through.

He let his stop pass, and instead stumbled drunkenly forward, working his way to her through the press of passengers.

Holding his hat in place with one hand, Benjamin tapped her lightly on the shoulder from behind, fingering the delicate weave of the gray woolen shawl she had drawn against the evening chill. "Etta?"

Gripping the rail with one hand, she turned, brown ringlets peeking out from under her blue bacolet.

"Mr. Taupe," she said, as though emerging from a dream. "What on earth are you doing here?"

He clutched the rail as the trolley pitched sideways. "Can we talk?"

Her pupils contracted. She withdrew from his hand, and would have taken a step back had she not been hemmed in. "Are you spying on me?" She spoke under her breath, softly but forcefully.

He glanced at the people huddled around them, wary of making a scene. "It's not what you think."

"You are, aren't you? That's why you attended tonight's session." She folded both arms across her stomach, straightjacket tight. "Zachary promised he wouldn't intrude. He said he trusted me."

"That's not why I was there tonight," Benjamin said, desperate to put her at ease. "As far as I'm concerned, the less Zachary knows, the better."

A new guardedness crept into her gaze. She yanked the shawl tighter, stretching the lace pattern where it cocooned her arms and knuckles.

"I'm sorry. I didn't mean to imply—" Benjamin shook his head, searching for a way to make his intentions clear. "Zachary didn't tell you about my . . . situation?"

"No. He never speaks of work. He seems to think I won't understand what he does."

"I . . . I'm not well." There was no point telling her that Zachary was the one who had suggested Madame Grurie to him.

"You look fine."

He touched a finger to his temple. "I have headaches. Problems with my vision. The doctors can't do anything."

"Why not?"

"It would do more harm than good to operate." Benjamin twisted his grimace into a smile. "The cure, as they say, is worse than the disease."

Her expression softened. Her grip on the shawl loosened, and some of the color returned to her knuckles. "What does that have to do with me? I'm sorry. I know that sounds callous, but I have my own situation to consider, as you put it."

Benjamin ducked his head. "I realize that. Still"—he let out a low sigh—"I was hoping you could take a moment to tell me what to expect." He forced himself to meet her gaze. "I have no idea what I've gotten myself into."

She gave a brittle laugh. "I'm not sure any of us do, Mr. Taupe."

"Zachary won't be worried about you?" Benjamin asked. He set his hat aside and blew on the petrol black surface of his coffee. The aroma eased the pain behind his eyes, but not the blurriness that haunted his vision.

Etta sniffed and cradled her cup of mint tea. "He's given up worrying, I believe. At this point, I expect he's more exasperated with me than anything."

They sat in a delicatessen, not far from Sutro Baths. He'd only gone swimming in the iron and glass canopied pool once. During the last few years, he couldn't seem to find the time. Now...

"He cares," Benjamin assured her. "It might not seem like it, sometimes. But he does. He speaks often of his concern."

"That's kind of you to say." She lowered her head to inhale the tendrils of steam rising from the tea.

"But you don't believe it."

"I believe that he says one thing and thinks another, without even knowing what his true feelings are."

"In other words, he won't admit them to you?"

"Or to himself."

"And that makes him a liar?"

"It's not his fault." Etta lifted her head. "It's what people do—what they've been conditioned to do. It doesn't bother me anymore."

"But it used to."

"I was asleep. Like everyone else, I was doing what I'd been taught, behaving and feeling the way I thought I should—the way people expected me to. At the time, it was the only way I knew how to express myself. The same is true for Zachary. It's not his fault."

"You seem at peace with your situation." The sullenness he remembered from his earlier encounters with her was gone. If Etta could undergo such a drastic transformation, did that mean there was hope for him as well?

She gave a modest shrug. "Madame Grurie is teaching me to see past this world to my true self."

"In the source world," Benjamin said tentatively. It sounded ridiculous coming from him, but she regarded him seriously.

"Yes. I feel as though I'm finally discovering who I really am."

"How?"

"The dance is one way. It helps you to make direct contact with the hidden aspects of your self." She pinched her lips. "I always feel as if I'm floundering around inside of an unfamiliar body that has several extra limbs. Like when one of your arms or legs falls asleep and you can't control it. Until the feeling returns, it's heavy and clumsy... dead weight."

She sipped her tea, watching him over the rim of the porcelain cup. "What was the dance like for you?"

"Awkward," he admitted. "In more ways than one."

She nodded, as if this made perfect sense. "It's supposed to be. If it wasn't, you wouldn't be making contact."

"How long does it take?"

"It's different for everyone. With some people it happens right away. With others it takes longer."

"How long did it take you?"

"A few weeks. Not until after the first séance I attended."

Benjamin frowned and shook his head. "Madame Grurie didn't mention anything to me about séances."

"She wouldn't. Not until you've attended several sessions."

"Why not?"

"I think it scares some people off. Several students have quit after taking part in a séance. Because of that she's become more careful about who she invites. She's learned to be discreet."

"How come you're telling me?"

"Is that a mistake?"

"No," he said quickly.

"The séances supplement the dances," she said. "They strengthen the connection to, and help unify, the different aspects of our selves."

"Different aspects?"

"They only feel that way, on this plane. In the fourth dimension they're integrated, part of a single body."

Benjamin winced. "I'm afraid I don't understand. I wonder if I ever will."

Etta unfolded a napkin in front of her. Next, she dipped the fingertips of her right hand into her tea and touched them briefly to the napkin, leaving five damp circles on the coarse brown paper.

"Pretend you're flat and lived on this napkin. You wouldn't have any height. You would just be wide and long."

He pictured it in his mind. "Like a cartoon figure," he said.

"Right. All you can see is what's printed on the surface of the napkin. You can't see anything above or below it."

"Okay."

"So when you get to one of these spots, all you see is a circle." She placed her fingertips back on the napkin. "Since you can't see up or down—only left or right—you can't see the hand that made the circles."

"What would I see if I walked up to your fingers while they were still touching the napkin?"

"A slice of my finger, as if it had been cut off."

It hurt to stare at the spots for any length of time. Benjamin blinked, leaving his eyelids closed for a beat as a balm against the blurriness. Nothing seemed real anymore—solid. He was gradually but inexorably losing touch with everything and everyone. Even Etta seemed dreamlike, a pale waif.

"The same thing applies to us," she continued. "When we look at our bodies, all we see is a slice of our fourth-dimensional bodies. We can't see the entire body, only the imprint it makes. The shadows."

"We're spots on the napkin," he said.

"Yes."

"Does that mean there are parts of our selves that are poking through into different parts of the world?"

"Madame Grurie believes so."

"Do you?"

"I believe that when you meet a person who looks like you or reminds you of your self, in terms of disposition or intellect, that that person is a different aspect of your higher body in this world."

Therefore, by logical extension—"We exist in different places in the world at the same time," he said.

"Or different times."

With an effort Benjamin refocused on the spots, trying to apprehend what she was saying.

"Our fourth-dimensional bodies exist outside the boundaries of time as we know it," she said. "This allows us to connect not only with our past selves, but our future selves as well."

"Have you?"

"Not yet. Soon, I hope. Maybe during the next séance."

"When is that?"

Etta smoothed the edges of the napkin. "I don't know. She never tells us ahead of time. We don't even find out if we're invited until the actual night."

"Not everyone gets to attend?"

"You have to have made progress in the dance and meditation sessions. Also, each séance tends to focus on awakening the consciousness of a particular person, and Madame Grurie selects students who she feels will best facilitate that."

"And you're hoping the next séance will focus on you."

"Yes."

Benjamin fingered the brim of his hat, tracing the soft curve of felt. "What happens when we die?" he said.

"According to Madame Grurie, that part of us returns to our higher self."

"In other words, the shadow disappears," Benjamin said, "but the object that cast it continues to exist."

"Yes. For now, all we can hope for is a glimpse of eternity."

Benjamin stared hard at his fingers. If Madame Grurie was correct, he could glimpse the future. And if he could see it, then he might be able to influence it, in the here and now.

15

Orthinia, Design Space

The bird had mutated overnight, like a cloud subtly reshaped by the wind while he wasn't looking. He had turned away briefly, and when he turned back it was gone, already replaced by a new shape.

The two long tendrils of the tail had braided together into a single tail that twitched randomly. The wings were smaller, and all of the remaining feathers had matted together into a rough nap. The talons had evolved into retractable claws.

"What's it turning into?" Olavo said. He watched the animal sun itself on the worn stones of the courtyard. The sun was hotter today, redder. Shadows from the bottlebrush tree and the Chinese tallow dappled the animal's back.

Vania sat with him on the bench in the garden. She seemed tense, as stiff as her resolutely creased uniform. More uptight than usual. But more determined as well.

More determined to do what? he wondered. Something had happened that firmed her resolve. She didn't seem any more sure of herself and what she was doing, just more committed.

"Do you miss the bird?" she finally asked.

Olavo frowned. He flexed his fingers around the remembered ache of breaking bones. Bile rose in his throat. He pressed his clenched knuckles to his forehead, leaned over, and dry-heaved.

Vania placed a steadying hand on his back. When the convulsion passed, he straightened, wiped his mouth with the back of his hand, and accepted the economically folded handkerchief she offered.

"Are you all right?"

He nodded. Swallowed. Started to unfold the handkerchief, then crumpled it in his fist. "What's wrong with me?"

"What do you think is wrong?"

He stared at the handkerchief, trying to sort through his feelings. But they were as tightly wadded as the white linen bunched in his fingers. "You know what I mean."

"Were you angry at the bird?" Vania asked when he failed to respond.

He dabbed the corners of his mouth. "No." There was nothing to be angry about. Why had he hurt it?

"Something else, then," she said.

Or someone else. Olavo shifted under her prodding. The skin beneath the armor sweated and itched.

"Are you in pain?" she said.

He looked up.

"Or scared?" Her expression was soft, forgiving.

"What do you mean?"

"Sometimes when we've been hurt—or are afraid of being hurt—we do things we normally wouldn't."

"Are you saying it's not my fault?"

"No."

Olavo avoided her gaze. It kept forcing him to look inward. Instead he squinted up at the blood-tinged sky. It appeared infected and inflamed. "What happened to the sun?" he asked.

Vania followed his gaze. "I had to replace it with a new one."

"What was wrong with the old one?"

"I received new information that required a change in the design space I had initially constructed."

"Something's happening to the original sun?" he said. "Is it changing as a result of the AdS discontinuity?"

She sighed. "Yes."

A sun didn't just change like that. It look billions of years. "What's going on?"

"I'm not sure," she said. "The information I have at this point is incomplete. More data needs to be collected."

He shifted uncomfortably. So the possible evolutionary paths she had plotted in the design space were no longer valid. They needed to be replaced with new paths, alternative threads of actuality, that took into account this new environmental pressure.

"How come nothing's happening to me?" Olavo said. If the environment had changed, shouldn't he have changed in response to the new conditions? But, as far as he could tell, he hadn't. He was the same. Whatever had changed the bird hadn't affected him. Armor still encased his arms and legs and a helmet still protected his skull.

"Patience," Vania said. She reached out to pat him on the leg, then caught herself. Withdrew her hand. "These things take time."

"How much time?"

"It depends." She folded her hands together in her lap, as if closing them in prayer.

"On what?"

Vania paused, her hands still. "Don't you like yourself the way you are?"

"No," he admitted.

"Why not?"

Olavo stared at his unwieldy, armor-clad arms. “It doesn’t feel right.” Or, more accurately, it felt wrong. Which wasn’t the same.

“You don’t feel comfortable with yourself?” she said.

“Not really. I feel . . . incomplete. Like something’s missing.”

“If you do change,” Vania said after a brief pause, “will you miss the person you are?”

Olavo frowned. “Who I am now, you mean? The *way* I am?”

“What if you like who you become even less than what—and who—you are now?” she said. “Will you regret the change? Will you want to change back?”

“No.”

She smiled at his certainty. “How can you be sure?”

He couldn’t. There were no guarantees where the design thread she had mapped would eventually lead.

“I have a favor to ask,” she said. Her hands twisted on her lap.

“What?”

“I want you to observe the daily changes in the animal.” An artificial insect emerged from the garden and flew toward him. “I’d like you to record everything that happens to it.”

The insect alighted on the back of his neck. His grip on the handkerchief tensed. “What good will that do?”

“It will provide a subjective record of how it evolves.”

“You don’t need me to keep track of that.” Softspace agents responsible for his design thread would do a much better job than he could.

“I also want you to think about how you feel about each change,” she said. “No matter how small or insignificant it might seem.”

“Think about it in what way?”

"Is it pleasant or unpleasant? Does it make you happy? Sad? Angry? Whatever feelings you have."

He watched the animal casually groom itself across the courtyard. "This is a test," he said. Everything was a test.

"What makes you say that?"

Olavo winced as the insect updated him with a new set of lexomes. "You want to monitor the reactions of my simunculus," he said. "Make sure it's adapting properly."

The animal was no different from the cognitive perception drawings she had shown him before. She was using him as feedback, to map the effects of the rupture.

"I want to know if your perception changes in response to any changes in the animal," Vania said. "And if so, how."

So he *was* evolving. Subliminally, in ways that weren't obvious . . . to either of them, apparently.

He licked the corner of his mouth, tasting salt. "You don't know what's going on," he said. "Do you?"

In her lap, her fingers plucked at the stiff fabric of her uniform. "These things take time."

"You've lost control, haven't you?"

She smoothed the creases she'd pinched into the fabric. "There's always an element of uncertainty in any evolutionary process. A certain latitude concerning the outcome."

"Whatever changed the sun is affecting everything around us—changing the world, and me, in ways you don't understand."

"We'll figure it out. There are always adjustments. You know that."

Olavo opened his fingers. The handkerchief uncrumpled in his palm, like a bruised flower. He offered it to her. "What if you don't figure it out?"

Vania clasped his fingers in hers, closing them around the handkerchief. "You'll come through this just fine. We all will.

Right now, it looks worse than it is. It always does in the beginning."

He raised the carapace on his free arm. "Are you telling me this is normal?"

She placed her hands back on her lap. "There is no normal. Everybody is different. Everybody progresses at a different pace."

His arm trembled under the weight. The sun was hot. Unbearable. He closed his eyes. But the image persisted, painful, entoptic. He could feel it burning inside his head, smoke rising where it formed a blackened, magnified spot on his thoughts.

Vania's dress rustled. A moment later he felt something soft on his lap. "Here," she said.

The animal. He opened his eyes. The creature crouched nervously on his legs, held in place by her petting.

"Why don't you try it?" she suggested.

Vania removed her hand, making room for his. The short nap was a lot softer than it looked. But the animal went limp under his fingers. Unresponsive.

His stomach tensed. "It's dead," he said. "I killed it."

There was no answer. A leaden numbness settled over him. When he turned toward Vania, she was gone. Assuming she'd ever been there. He had the feeling he'd been talking to a ghost all this time.

Or himself.

"Vania?" he called.

He lifted the animal from his lap, laid it on the bench beside him, and stood. Panic spun him around. He staggered in a tight circle, turning from the garden to the balustrade, to the narrow alleys and streets that meandered away under portico gates and overhanging balconies. The pink terracotta roofs overlooking the courtyard tilted at dizzy angles where they met the sky.

"Vania? Where are you?"

He lurched toward the first street. Like the walls, steps, and floors of the houses and shops, it was paved in pale-grained marble. The street rose gently, twisting and turning past side alleys, gated entries, and tunnels that emptied into residential courtyards. The doors leading to other ships and design spaces were all closed. He banged his fists against them, but they remained locked.

Hands bloodied, he gave up and followed the street to a small square shaded by an olive tree. A bicycle with a bent frame lay under the tree, the back wheel spinning. Music trickled from an open doorway at the top of a narrow flight of stairs. Olavo skidded to a stop. Something about the bike and the music was familiar. Had he been here before? He couldn't remember.

Hossein appeared on the steps. He sat there and stared down at the ruined bicycle, captivated by the spinning wheel.

"What are you doing?" Olavo asked.

"Waiting for the wheel to stop." Hossein kept his attention focused on the bicycle.

"And then what?"

"That part of my life will finally be over. But it keeps spinning. Forever, possibly." He forced a tortured laugh. "Maybe a watched wheel never stops."

"Whose bike is it?"

"Mine. I was riding it the day I was attacked."

"Attacked?"

"For being gay. I was riding to school one morning and two students leapt out and began to stone me."

"I had no idea," Olavo said.

"I don't know how they found out. I was very careful. I kept to myself, abstained, performed *salat* five times a day, and read the Qur'an and the Hadith. I believed that if I did those things, I would be cured."

"But it didn't work. You couldn't change who you were."

Hossein winced in shame. "I wasn't strong enough. For a while, I convinced myself I'd cleansed the stain from my soul—that I was no longer an abomination. But it was a lie. Deep down I knew I hadn't changed and Allah saw through me. In order to punish me, he allowed other people to see that I was still guilty of *liwat*."

"Even though God created you the way you were?"

Hossein shook his head. "Allah created me. But it's up to me to purify my soul. I failed. That's why I joined the J.I.S.E.C. mission."

"To change your sexual orientation?"

Hossein nodded. "Allah, in His infinite mercy, gave me another chance. After the stoning, I was in the hospital for months. My right side was completely paralyzed. I couldn't talk . . . couldn't feed myself. But I was still same-sex. They hadn't stoned that out of me."

"So you figured that with a new mind, you wouldn't have the same feelings."

Hossein nodded. "Rewired," he said. "It was the only way I could hope to become someone else. Even if that person was no longer me, it would at least be someone I could live with."

"And?" Olavo said.

Hossein returned his attention to the bent bicycle. "The wheel's still spinning," he noted. "Perhaps we can't all be who, or what, we want. Perhaps we have to accept our fate, that we might provide an example for others."

In other words, he was still waiting, still praying. Olavo frowned, watching the spokes rotate. When he looked back to the steps, a question on his lips, Hossein was gone, replaced by the music.

Olavo fled the courtyard, down a blind alley. Turned around and sprinted back to a different street. Up a flight of stairs, past a restaurant with umbrella-shaded tables. Breathless, his rib cage heaving, he stumbled onto the breezeway that led from his room to the garden.

“There you are,” Vania said. She was standing next to the door to his room. What took you so long? her expression seemed to say, as if she’d known where he was all along, and the only place he’d been lost was in his own mind.

16

Santa Cruz, September 27

The pain in Rudi's head had receded, leaving behind dehydrated lips and a parched lucidity. His entire body felt wrung out, as if he had just spent forty days in the desert and finally emerged, his thoughts clear, purged of delirium. The equipment in the ICU—monitors, tubes, IV stand—gleamed, hard-edged and sharp. Even the accordion creases in the powder blue privacy curtain seemed particularly crisp and well-defined in the morning light.

A miniature dachshund, twisted together out of red, green, and blue party balloons, stood on a table at the end of the bed, nibbling at a bouquet of pink carnations. There were also a handful of get well cards and a glossy red gift bag sealed shut with a bow of green and blue speckled yarn.

A shadow hunched against the wall, cast by the light of the equipment behind him.

"Linnea?" he said, turning his gaze from the cards, wondering how she'd found him.

Sister Daminca sat next to the bed. Her eyes were closed in prayer.

Rudi swallowed. "Sister," he said, forcing aside the disappointment lodged in his throat.

Her head bobbed. She'd been dozing, not praying. Her eyes started open and her chin lifted from her chest.

"Welcome back!" She half stood, then settled back onto the molded plastic chair. "How do you feel?"

Rudi wet his lips then touched his face, exploring his forehead and cheeks. "How do I look?"

"Fine."

"I'm not swollen?" At Lakeshore, post-operative puffiness had left his face a soft doughy mass, the consistency of risen bread.

"You look tired," she said.

"I'm thirsty."

"They're in the middle of a shift change, right now. So it might be a few minutes before someone comes by. Are you sure you're okay?"

Rudi nodded in the direction of the table. "Balloon Man was here?"

"No. But when he heard you were sick, he wanted to cheer you up."

Rudi had never spoken to Balloon Man, just as he'd never uttered a single word to Parasol Man or Accordion Man. On Pacific Avenue, he'd watched Balloon Man fashion pretzel-like animals for kids. Giraffes, birds, cats. It was amazing what he could do with just a few deft twists.

"How did he find out?" Rudi said.

"I don't know. He met me outside the Veterans Memorial last night, with the puppy, and asked me to take it to you."

"You don't know who told him?"

"I didn't think to ask. It wasn't any of my business."

There was a slow leak in the dachshund's tail. It was starting to deflate and sag a little between the hind legs.

"The police also came by, looking for you," the nun said. "They wanted to talk to you again."

The blood oxygen monitor clipped to his fingertip stuttered a beat. "What about?"

"They didn't say."

Rudi shifted under the sheets, closing a gap that was allowing a chill draft to slip under his hospital gown. "What did you tell them?"

"That you were in the hospital, recovering from brain surgery."

"What did they say?"

"They wanted to know how long that would take."

"I'm not surprised," Rudi said.

"I told them they'd have to check with the hospital," Sister Daminca said. Then she scooted her chair close. "Is there something you want to tell me, Rudi?"

"Like what?"

"You know what I mean. Is there anything you want to get off your chest?"

"You want me to confess?"

"I'm not a priest. Just a friend."

"My conscience is clear."

"I think they've been listening to your broadcasts," Sister Daminca said.

"You do?" He didn't know whether to feel elated or anxious.

"I think they're maybe worried you're going to end up disturbing the peace," she said. "Inciting a riot, or something like that."

"That's crazy. I'm trying to spread peace!" Rudi tried to sit, but fell back, held in place by the IV tubes and EEG wires dangling from his body.

"They don't see it that way."

"How can peace be a threat?"

"I know. It doesn't make sense. You think they'd welcome the change. But they don't. I think that like most people, they're probably scared of changes that aren't in their control."

"Are they going to ask me to stop?"

"They might. That's the way these things happen. People get talked to and then they quietly disappear."

"Leave town, you mean."

"Or dumped into the system."

Social workerese for getting thrown in jail.

"Can they do that?" he said.

"Not without probable cause," Sister Daminca said. "That's why I asked if you have anything you want to tell me."

Rudi shook his head. He wasn't going to involve her. "How's my van?" he said.

"It's fine."

"No tickets or anything?"

"I moved it to the church parking lot. Saint Jude's. I hope you don't mind being Catholic for a while." She said it jokingly, but he detected a flicker of worry behind her smile. "I didn't know what else to do and was afraid it might get vandalized if I left it downtown."

"You had it towed?" He couldn't imagine her hotwiring it.

"I took the keys when you first got to the hospital."

"Did the cops say anything about it?" he asked.

"Why would they?"

He shrugged. "You never know."

"Stop worrying." She leaned over and rummaged in the bag she had set on the floor. "I brought you this." She took out his baseball cap and straightened the brim. "I don't think you're allowed to wear it yet."

The aluminum foil was missing, but he might be able to find more in the cafeteria.

"Even if you can't wear it," Sister Daminca said, "I thought it would give you some peace of mind."

Rudi tried on the cap and was relieved to find that it still fit.

"Irene had it," she said. "One of the AXIS dancers found it on the stage after the ambulance took you away and gave it to her."

"Where is Irene?" He'd been listening for her all morning, hoping she would visit.

Sister Daminca shook her head. "Irene's gone, Rudi."

A bubble of panic formed in his stomach. "Gone?"

"She came by last night," the nun said. "She wanted to tell you good-bye. But you were unconscious and she couldn't stay."

"Why not?" The heart monitor behind him settled into its regular rhythm. "Where did she go?"

"To see another oncologist. In Portland, I think. She asked me to tell you she was sorry she didn't get to talk to you before she went. She left you this."

Sister Daminca retrieved the gift bag from the table and handed it to him. Rudi balanced the bag on his stomach. "What is it?"

"A surprise. She said you'd understand."

Rudi plucked at the knot of yarn holding the bag shut. It unraveled into a couple of loose strands, allowing the top to open. He reached in and felt his way past a wad of pink, crumpled tissue paper, until his fingers encountered a soft, round mound of...

He jerked his hand from the bag.

"What is it?" Sister Daminca leaned forward, curious.

"A ball of yarn."

"Let's see. Take it out."

"It's a joke," he said. His face heated. "That's all."

"She was very serious when she asked me to give it to you."

"It's no big deal." He set the bag aside.

"That's not the impression I got. I got the impression it meant quite a lot to her—something she wasn't doing lightly."

"Yeah . . . well."

"You don't have to show it to me, if you don't want." She sounded disappointed. "It's none of my business. I'm sorry if I embarrassed you."

Embarrassed at being embarrassed, he removed the knitted ball from the gift bag and examined it under the sterile lights. Dimpled by his fingers, it wasn't all that hard to imagine the mound filling one side of a bra.

"I had no idea," Sister Daminca said.

Rudi thought of Irene's hand on his, pressing it to her chest, the heart still beating under the scar the yarn tried to cover up. "I don't think it was something she advertised."

Sister Daminca nodded. "It makes sense, I guess. She knitted everything else she needed."

He stared at the improvised breast, uncertain what she expected him to do with it. Why him? He couldn't be the only friend she had. He stuffed the prosthetic back into the bag. "When is she coming back?" he said.

Sister Daminca polished the metal side-frame of the bed with chapped fingertips. "She might not."

Rudi searched her face, trying to read between the worry lines. "Why wouldn't she?"

"Even if the surgery is successful this time," the nun said, "and they get it all, she might have to stay in the hospital for a while."

"I thought she was getting chemo."

"She is." The muscles in the nun's neck tensed. "But the doctors found another lump. Last week."

In the breast that hadn't been removed. Queasiness washed over him. He broke into a cold sweat.

"Rudi!"

Sister Daminca leaned over the bed, her shadow spreading across him like a dark cloud.

When Rudi regained consciousness, Celia Truong sat in place of Sister Daminca.

". . . feel like I'm at my own wake," he rasped.

The journalist stood, iCam in hand. "You're not dead. You are not going to die."

Rudi wet his lips. His mouth felt gummy, his tongue flypaper sticky. He looked around. It was night. The windows above his bed were dark, littered with pale internal reflections.

Like me, he thought. "What time is it?"

Celia checked her wristwatch. "Almost nine-thirty. You've been out for most of the day."

"Where's Sister . . . ?" He swallowed thickly.

"She needed to get some food and rest. I told her I'd watch you until she came back."

"Watch me for what?"

Her eyebrows scrunched. "Signs of life."

He had a hard time focusing. His gaze pinballed around the room, bouncing from one flash of light to another, until it finally came to rest on her face. "What happened?" he said.

"According to the neurosurgeon, you had a vasospasm. Apparently, that's where the blood vessels, arteries, in your head suddenly constrict."

"I know." They'd worried about that at Lakeshore. One patient, a former Hells Angel, had lapsed into a coma one night. After the ambulance took him away, he hadn't come back.

"You're lucky," Celia said, "you could have died. The doctor thinks it was probably triggered by the surgery."

"No," he said, "spyware. That's what caused the spasm. Maybe now you believe me."

"You're talking about the invisible cameras you think they put inside you after the accident," she said, watching him for confirmation, "to map your thoughts and keep an eye on you."

"It's not just me," he said.

"Other people have them?"

The light on the iCam blinked on, anticipating his response. It didn't matter. He was tired of hiding. Maybe if more people knew about the machines, someone would do something about them. "Anyone can," he said.

"Even me?"

"Yes."

"But I've never had brain surgery."

"It doesn't matter. They're like viruses. They can infect anybody. No one is immune."

"So they're everywhere?"

"They didn't used to be. But they've escaped from people like me, and now they're spreading. Lots of people are being watched, having their thoughts mapped."

"By who? The government?"

"I don't know."

"If they're inside me, too, why don't I have vasospasms? Why don't a lot more people have spasms?"

"You get headaches, right?"

She made a face. "Everyone does. That doesn't prove anything."

Rudi shrugged.

"How come no one else has noticed them?" Celia Truong

persisted. "If they're all over, wouldn't someone have discovered them by now?"

"Not if they aren't looking for them. They're small. And they don't show up in normal tests." Rudi could tell she didn't believe him. That was all right. Most people turned a deaf ear to prophets.

"Okay. If they're so hard to spot, how do you know about them? How'd you find out?"

"They told me," he said.

She pinched her brow. "So you hear voices?" she asked, managing to maintain a straight face. She seemed determined to find out what made him tick—what he was afraid of and how it shaped his faith.

Rudi rubbed the dry, crusty corners of his mouth. He was tired, finding it hard to concentrate. "They said not to be afraid. They weren't going to hurt me."

She took a moment to absorb this. "Did you believe them, when they said they weren't going to hurt you?"

"No. Sometimes I hear music, too. That's how I know they're transmitting what I'm thinking."

"Or telling you what to think?" she said.

"Yeah." People were always telling him what to think. Even the Scion of Adam congregation. He hadn't realized it at the time. He'd been too caught up in the rush, the exhilaration of being part of something large and inevitable that could change the face of the world.

"Which is where the foil comes in," Celia said, "and the preaching. You want to get rid of them."

She seemed eager to put words in his mouth. "I don't want them to infect anyone else," he said.

"What do you think they're really doing?" she asked. "What's the real purpose of the maps they're making?"

Rudi shut his eyes. Counted to ten. Opened them. "I think that they're trying to preserve me."

"Preserve you?"

"That's what they said. But I think they meant save."

"Save you from what?"

"Not from," he said. "For. They want to save me for the future."

After Sister Daminca returned and Celia Truong left, the neurosurgeon came by, smiling. "The thrombosis appears intact. The microcoil is stable. So far, everything looks textbook."

Rudi followed the path the surgeon's finger traced on the latest X-ray.

"I'm going to transfer you out of intensive care first thing tomorrow morning. Get you in a regular room." She slipped the film from the light-screen, satisfied.

"When can I leave?" Rudi asked.

The doctor removed her reading glasses, and tucked them into a pocket inside her smock. "We want to keep a close eye on things for a couple days. If there are no further complications, you should be able to go home within the week."

A week. He couldn't wait that long.

Four hours later, when Sister Daminca had dozed off, and the on-duty nurses were defibrillating a stroke victim who had gone into cardiac arrest, Rudi yanked the IV needle from his hand, unclipped the oxygen monitor from the tip of his index finger, and slipped out of bed.

He didn't bother looking for his clothes or shoes. He had already determined his personal belongings weren't readily available. The pajamas Sister Daminca had brought him would have to do.

The keys to the van were another matter. He spent several

seconds debating if he should take the time to look for them in the nun's shoulder bag.

No. It wasn't worth the risk. He might wake her.

Wearing only his baseball cap, and under it, warm against his scalp, Irene's breast, he made his way out of the ICU and into the night.

17

San Francisco, Circa 1937

"What is the difference between essence and personality?" Madame Grurie asked.

Benjamin couldn't decide if the question was rhetorical or not. It was all he could do to hold the pose she had decided on for him, carefully positioning his arms and legs into what seemed the most uncomfortable arrangement possible. Around him, the other students in the session struggled to do the same, each frozen in their own physical torment.

Every session of the sacred dance movements for the past three weeks had involved the learning and maintaining of a specific position at the end of the dance. Each student was given a unique posture to hold, chosen by Madame Grurie according to the aspect of their being that the person needed most to develop.

The positions were inevitably awkward and painful. They left the group weak from exhaustion and seemed calculated to discourage any enjoyment the dance movement might otherwise have provided.

While they held their assigned poses, for upward of ten

minutes or more, Madame Grurie paraded between them, fine-tuning their stances and lecturing, forcing them to think and remain motionless at the same time, to balance the physical with the mental.

After five minutes, his legs burning, arms trembling, Benjamin found it nearly impossible to concentrate on what she was saying and absorb the lessons. His entire focus was confined to his physical discomfort.

"Essence is our natural state," Madame Grurie said. "It consists of the true feelings and emotions we are born with."

A few paces behind Benjamin, the red-faced gentleman, Charles Oxley, began to wheeze. His phlegmatic breath whistled in and out, shrill as a teapot. It was a wonder he didn't collapse... or quit. But he seemed determined to ride out the torments he was compelled to endure, driven by his own particular needs. Each of them had an overriding reason for staying. For Etta, it was freedom, from Zachary and the dark abyss that lay inside her. For Myrtle and Neola it was fear of death. Beatrice and Eloise were motivated by the desire to contact their lost husbands. Of all of them, Peter McGraff was perhaps the most sincere. He was on a spiritual quest. He wanted to discover the deeper meaning of life. Personal suffering was something he expected and willingly accepted. He actively sought it out. Putting himself through emotional, mental, and physical trials was a way of transcending this existence. So far, only Gerty had been unable to continue. She had dropped out a week ago, the sole casualty of the present group. But according to Etta, she wasn't the first. Nor would she in all likelihood be the last. Madame Grurie was a grueling and relentless taskmaster, uncompromising in her demands.

"Personality is what we are taught," Madame Grurie said, continuing her lecture. "What we learn. How we are conditioned to think, and behave, by society. Essence is interior—personality is exterior."

Benjamin felt Madame Grurie's hand pressing against the inside of his left thigh, forcing his knee into an even more strenuous bend.

"Both are necessary aspects of our being," she said very close behind him. "It is necessary to play the roles expected of us. To put on appearances." Her voice, and the violet aura of her presence, moved on. "To act and feel the way people expect us to, so that we are able to maintain the physical aspect of this life."

She had paused next to Peter McGraff, and seemed to be directing her comments explicitly at him.

"This is something that we must do consciously, through what is termed external considering. What we must not do is confuse this external machinery—our mechanized behavior—with our inner essence. We must not identify with the robotic movements of our personalities. If we do, then our lives become nothing more than those of actors in a play, following a script that has been laid out for us."

He had been doing that his entire life, Benjamin realized. As a boy, he had been obedient, respectful of his parents. His father was a firm disciplinarian, quick tempered, and just as quick with a belt. Rules had been hammered into him. At college he had studied architectural engineering instead of drawing because the former was more pragmatic, a solid profession.

The wheezing behind Benjamin sounded increasingly labored. The air in the tiny second-story studio was stuffy, redolent with sweat, perfume, and frail varnish. But Madame Grurie refused to open a window. It was important to inhale the same air, she maintained. To draw sustenance from one another.

"One way to avoid confusing our inner selves with our external actions," Madame Grurie said, "is to consciously suffer. Conscious suffering, intentional suffering, leads to internal considering, which in turn gives rise to conscience. In other words, awareness. And it is this awareness that allows us to transcend the realm of the three-dimensional world and make contact with our eternal soul."

He'd always taken the correct path, Benjamin realized, the cautious road. To do otherwise jeopardized his chances at an honest, respectable living. He should have married years ago, but work had prevented him from becoming suitably engaged. Now there was the tumor. Nothing he had been taught had made him happy. None of the lessons he had learned would help him now. They were useless. He was going to die without ever having lived.

The wheezing stopped. A soft thud ensued. Someone gasped, stifling a scream behind cupped fingers.

"Peter," Madame Grurie said, "please open the window."

Benjamin turned. Charles Oxley had collapsed on the floor. The women flocked around him, plucking at his silk pajamas like pigeons at a crust of bread, trying to loosen the fabric binding his chest.

"Roll him on his back," Eloise said.

"He's too heavy," Etta said with a grunt.

"Benjamin." Madame Grurie motioned for him. "We need your assistance."

Benjamin hastened to Oxley's side. The women scattered out of his way, making room for him. Benjamin rolled Oxley onto his back, trying not to further injure him.

"I'll call for a doctor," Myrtle said.

"In a moment," Madame Grurie said. "It may not be necessary."

"But he's not breathing!" Beatrice exclaimed.

"He's simply fainted." Madame Grurie unfolded a Japanese paper fan and began flapping it above the congested face.

Benjamin put his ear to Oxley's mouth and felt a soft tickle of air, warmer than the fan. He patted Oxley on the cheeks.

"A damp cloth," he said. "And some water."

"I've got it," Peter said. He hurried from the studio to the toilet at the end of the hallway.

Benjamin placed the damp cloth across Oxley's forehead. Next he dipped his fingers into the drinking glass Peter had set on the floor by them, and sprinkled water onto the insensible man's face and half-parted lips.

Myrtle clutched her wrinkled, liver-spotted hands. "He's not waking up."

Madame Grurie bent close to Oxley. "Charles," she whispered. Her mint-scented breath stirred the hair bristling in his ear. "Wake up, dear. You've been resting long enough."

Benjamin sprinkled more water over the man, flicking drops onto his veined eyelids.

Oxley coughed. His chest heaved, and his eyes fluttered open. He sat up, startled by the woman attending him.

"What happened?" he asked.

Madame Grurie sighed in relief. She folded her fan and stood up. "You pushed yourself to the limit, Charles. You took yourself to a place where you have never been before."

Beatrice leaned in, her eyes bright. "Did you see anything, Charles? Did anyone speak to you?"

Benjamin rose, encouraged by Madame Grurie's hand on his arm. She seemed a little shaky, her fingers in search of support.

"I'll be in my office," she murmured. "Please come by when you've finished attending to Mr. Oxley."

"You wanted to see me?" Benjamin stood in the doorway, uncertain whether she wanted him inside or not.

With her fan, Madame Grurie gestured for him to enter. "Close the door, please. And lock it."

Benjamin pulled the door shut and turned the key, leaving it in the latch to guard against prying eyes.

"How is Mr. Oxley?" she asked.

"Fine. As you say, he fainted from exertion."

She opened the fan and waved it briskly, displacing several strands of hair. "I'm glad it wasn't more serious. I'm afraid I might have pushed the poor man too hard."

"He seems no worse for the wear," Benjamin said. For some reason, he felt the need to reassure her.

"Still I feel responsible. I would hate for anything unfortunate to happen to him while he's in my care."

Benjamin said nothing.

"It's time we spoke privately," she said. "I need to instruct you on an individual basis. Please have a seat."

Benjamin sat. Madame Grurie remained standing, voluptuous in her silk pajamas.

"I spoke of essence tonight," she said, making a slow circuit of the room, forcing him to follow her with his gaze. "What I said is true for everyone. But it is particularly true for you, given your situation."

Benjamin waited for her to make herself clear.

"If what the doctors tell you is true, you don't have long in this world." Her path carried her behind the chair where he sat. "There's no way you can progress to the point where your soul can exist outside your body on its own."

Benjamin twisted in the chair. "What are you saying?"

She moved next to him and laid a comforting hand on his arm. "It takes years of study to discipline the mind and body."

"So it's hopeless?" He let his gaze fall from the porcelain smooth fingers on his arm to the lush vine-embroidered carpet.

"No," she said, trailing a finger down his arm. "Not necessarily."

Benjamin looked up as she moved to the chair across from him. "What?" His voice clotted with emotion.

"I can preserve your essence from this life," she said, seating herself. "I can carry it into the future for you."

"How?"

She fanned herself once more, exuding the fragrance of flowers stirred by a summer breeze. "By essence, I refer to the physical aspect of your present self that is the source of your future self."

Benjamin studied her face for clues. What, exactly, was she telling him? What proposal was she making?

"I'm offering myself as a vessel," she said. "A ship, laden with invaluable cargo, that can travel across the sea of time."

Benjamin frowned. "You're suggesting that I... that we...?"

"It's not something I do for everyone," she said. "In fact you're only the second person I've felt compelled to help in this way."

Embarrassment blazed in a firestorm across Benjamin's exposed flesh. Sweat prickled from every pore. He moistened his lips as he searched for an appropriate response.

"Why me?"

She remained composed, unperturbed by his discomfiture. "I see in you a unique soul. A purity of being that should not be allowed to fade from this plane of existence. That would be more criminal, more abject, than any physical consummation required to perpetuate it."

"Otherwise...?" he said.

"This aspect of your essence dies. Your shadow—cast in the here and now—fades from the walls of existence, along with everything you have learned and experienced. All that you are is lost, for all time."

Dead, Benjamin thought. Withered like a leaf in winter. His head ached. He buried his face in his hands and pressed the unyielding bone beneath his skin, wishing that he could reach in and pluck the rotten pith from his skull.

He lowered his hands and looked up. "What exactly will be required of me?" he asked.

"We can discuss that later." She stood, light rustling off the glossy fabric. "Think about it. You still have time."

But not much.

"There's going to be a séance tomorrow night," she told him. "I would like you to attend."

"What for?" he said after a moment.

"It might help you come to a decision," Madame Grurie said. "Either way, it will prove instructive."

He nodded, feeling bleak and trapped. "All right," he agreed. "What time shall I arrive?"

18

Aelon, Softspace

"I think you should go," Acantha said when the transmission ended. She switched off the Magnavox.

"That's it?" he asked.

"Yes." She continued to finger herself.

"Okay, then. If that's what you want." Olavo rose from the sofa, collected his jacket from the back of the couch, and headed for the door to the apartment.

"Not to get rid of you," she clarified. "To find out what's going on."

He stopped, his hand on the knob. "With the sun, you mean." Huge, blood-blister red, it remained suspended above the Athens-scape, stubbornly refusing to set.

She shrugged. The gargoyle hanging from her nipple shuddered. "Someone has to."

"And you think it should be me?"

"Aren't you curious?" she asked.

He nodded at the Magnavox. "I'm more curious about the transmission. Where it came from."

"Maybe they're related," she said.

"I doubt it."

She scraped her lower lip with her teeth. "What I said about there being less of the good part of me..."

"The Suicide Angel," he said.

"Yeah. I think that part of my synapse datamap—on the subconscious level—has detached from me and become quantum-linked with somebody else. That's why it feels like she's missing, and why the part that's left behind wants to kill herself." Acantha ran the tip of her tongue across the chapped indentations left by her teeth. "It happened right after the gamma ray burst."

"What?"

"I can feel the person," she continued. "I'm pretty sure part of her is now qinked to me."

"Who?"

"A hardspace simunculus, I think, on another world or ship. Somehow, the AdS storm jumbled and entangled us."

Olavo started to open his mouth, then closed it. He had the feeling that anything he said would do more harm than good.

"You think I'm imagining things, don't you? Hearing voices, hallucinating. But I'm not. You saw the transmission. Wherever it came from, it's real."

"I'm worried about you," he said.

Acantha gnawed on her bottom lip again, squeezing it to pulp between her teeth. "That's sweet."

"It's true."

She spread her legs wider, presenting herself to him. "How come you never try to fuck me? Ramunas does."

He had no answer for that. He simply shrugged.

Acantha played with the pierce in her labia, toying with him. "Don't you find me attractive?"

"No," he lied. It was easier than the truth, simpler, even if he didn't know what the truth was.

"I don't believe you." She sounded hurt. Petulant. But it

was just a game. She didn't really want anyone to find her attractive.

"Did you let him?" he said, for lack of anything better to say. He wasn't really curious. Didn't really want to know. More than anything he wanted to keep her talking. He wasn't sure why. It seemed important, for some reason, to keep her engaged.

"What do you think?" she said.

"I think it's your life. You're free to do what you want."

She pouted.

"Do you want me to?" he asked.

She ran the tip of her tongue across the bite marks on her lip. "I guess not." She sounded disappointed, more with herself than him.

"I wish I could help you," he said. "I wish I knew what to do."

She sighed, and brought her knees together. "It's not your fault. There's nothing anyone can do."

Back on the *Wings of Uriel* he found the coordinates for the red sun waiting for him. Acantha had sent them while they sat on the sofa, knowing that he would follow up on her suggestion.

It was the only way he knew to look after her, to try and care for her. She knew this, and took advantage of it.

He sat in the chair, with its overstuffed chintz, and stared out the window at Sand Mountain. He fingered the polished wood armrests. Watched dust slither across the scarred regolith of the lakebed, onto Silicon Beach, which was crowded with colorful benzene ring–shaped umbrellas. Overhead, dragon-winged kites gyred in the mica-bright sky, dipping and swooping to the laughter of beachgoers.

The waves hissed softly under the ablative susurrus of soft ultraviolet.

Part of him believed that Acantha was grateful. Another part knew he was being used. On some level, he'd taken on the role of enabler in whatever psychotic break she had fallen into. What Acantha needed was a new perspective, a new wardrobe of emotions. The old ones were useless, a threadbare raiment.

Much as he wanted, there was nothing he could do. He had his own problems—his own misplaced feelings of responsibility and guilt. He'd tried to leave all that behind when he signed up to become a simunculus. That had been the plan. Start life over, in a new place, in a new body, as far away from his old self as physically possible.

For him, it had been a way to be reborn.

For Acantha, *Nouveaux sapiens* had been a means of suicide. She had left home, never expecting to survive.

Olavo exhaled, felt the chair sigh under him. Neither of them, it seemed, would get their wish.

"What's wrong now?" Tenley demanded, sulking over a bowl of cold cereal.

"Nothing." He took his time chewing a forkful of sausage, hoping she would let it go.

They'd been living together in her off-campus apartment for nine months. It was the final semester of her senior year. Her father's short-haul trucking business had fallen on hard times and she needed help with the rent. He needed a place to stay while he tried to get back on his feet again, tried to scrape together enough money to enroll in community college and start classes himself.

That was the arrangement. But he'd been bouncing between odd jobs. Nothing seemed to work out. He kept having run-ins with coworkers and managers. He wasn't sure why. He sensed it had something to do with him, but couldn't put his finger on the problem.

It wasn't working with Tenley, either. Not the way he'd hoped when he moved in.

He caught her staring at the fresh cigarette burn on the crosshatch of razor-thin scars marring his wrists. At the beginning of his junior year in high school, the cuts had gotten him out of his foster home of six years into a Social Services group home. That wasn't much better. But at least it was a different kind of prison, one where the bullshit was honest.

"Is it me?" she asked. "Something I said, or didn't say? Did, or didn't do?" She had started blaming herself for everything, a passive-aggressive way of telling him their problems were his fault.

He swallowed. Stabbed another sausage. "No."

"What, then?"

The fork clattered on his plate. "I don't know."

"So there is something."

He slammed his hands on the table. "I don't know!"

All he knew was that this wasn't the way his life was supposed to go. It wasn't supposed to be this hard, this fucked up. Time was supposed to heal wounds, not make them worse. Every time he thought he'd hit bottom, the rug got pulled out from under him again and the bottom got deeper. There was no end to the deep; it went on for fucking ever.

"You're depressed again," Tenley said. "I think you should go back on your meds. Just for a while."

"No."

"That's the depression talking. Not you."

"Is that supposed to make me feel better?"

Tenley studied her limp cornflakes, then delivered her ultimatum. "If you don't go see a doctor, you can't stay here anymore."

"You're kicking me out?" He did his best to sound incredulous and hurt, but he wasn't all that surprised. He'd seen it coming for a while and hadn't done anything to stop it.

She stirred the flakes with her spoon. "It's your choice."

He watched the milk swirl in the bowl, forming laconic vortices and eddies and whorls. All around him, in the kitchen and the living room, he could feel her collection of stuffed animals watching him with accusing eyes. Dogs, cats, birds, even a few frogs. They were everywhere, on shelves, the top of the refrigerator, the TV. There was no escape. He said, "You told your mother about me, didn't you?"

"This doesn't have anything to do with my mother. This is about you getting the help you need."

Which was bullshit. "You can't do anything without your mother," he said, and was rewarded with an angry hiss of breath.

"That's not true."

"At least you have a mother."

She refused to take the bait. "Why do you keep hurting yourself?" she asked.

"Because it feels good." Which was true. The pain was cleansing, cathartic.

"Whenever you hurt yourself," Tenley stated, "you're also hurting someone else. It's how you get back at people."

"I never wanted to hurt you," he said.

"If that was true, you wouldn't burn yourself with cigarettes. You'd get back on your meds."

He stared at the half-eaten sausage on his plate. "Without you," he said, "I would never have made it this long." He didn't know for a fact this was true, but it sounded good. And on some vague level it felt right.

She didn't buy it. "You're just saying that."

How to explain? How to make her understand, when he didn't?

He couldn't help himself. Couldn't stop. Whatever was inside him, he couldn't get past it. Wherever he turned, there it was, staring him in the face like a high wall or a steep mountain he couldn't find a way over or around. If he could just do that—get to the other side—he'd be okay. Life would be different.

"Fine," he said. "If you want me to leave, I will." He stood and hurled the plate to the floor.

The *Wings of Uriel* was parked in a low-energy orbit around Sand Mountain, cruising one of the Lo-Marsden gravity tubes that crisscrossed the solar system between Lagrange points. This permitted the current probability phase of the ship to remain not only collapsed, but stable, while sitting in non-AdS space.

He decided not to check on the simunculus that Vania was fitting into her revised environmental model. It was too early for anything interesting to have emerged—only a few thousand years, subjectively speaking. Besides, if anything interesting did occur, he would be auto-notified.

Instead he plotted the AdS coordinates Acantha had given him for the sun. Olavo stared at the path etched in glass and framed by the drapes of the window. Because of the way d-3 coordinates mapped the d-2 surface of anti de Sitter space, it would require four separate jumps to and from the AdS boundary surface to arrive at the correct non-AdS coordinates.

Acantha hadn't sent collectors to the discontinuity. The mindless Drexler machines were capable of making only a single anti de Sitter jump from a source ship before qinking back. There was no way they had retrieved the information she had shown him.

No... Acantha had visited the rupture in person—

brought the transmission back with her on the *Golden Fleece.*

And now she wanted him to go to the discontinuity in person, as well.

Why?

Arms folded, Olavo paced in front of the window, where the chandelier of the Ferrer cluster shone through his reflection.

Because, he thought, she had seen or experienced something she wanted him to see or experience. Something that had sent her tripping down a rabbit hole, deep into herself. And the only way to help her was to follow her.

Giving him the coordinates was her way of reaching out. Calling for help. She had tried to seduce him into going. When that hadn't worked she'd begged. Pleaded.

She had said as much. Part of her was trapped. Dying. She couldn't free herself. By going to the red sun, seeing what she had seen, discovering what she had, he could free her.

Maybe.

Maybe she was just using him. Not to help her, but to hurt her, the same way he had hurt himself. He wasn't the only one who had been burned.

In anticipation of the AdS jump, conformal field transients had been drawn to flux changes in the Hawking radiation emitted by the micro black hole at the center of the ship. They fluttered around the room like a flock of angels, huddling in ceiling corners, clutching at the drapes, clinging to the polished arms of his chair.

Olavo shuddered. He rubbed his arms, trying to rid himself of the graveyard chill brought by the transients. During a jump they flicker-hovered, harmless auras limning the waveform of flattened, compressed three-dimensional objects. Normally they clung to particular objects in a ship. But occasionally they detached and drifted until the jump was over, at which point they vanished as abruptly as they appeared.

Most of the time.

Sometimes there were lingering psychological effects. . . .

Repressed memories. Nightmares, detached from the mind, that took on a life of their own in the nether regions of AdS space. Or a protracted, pervasive disquiet, filled with disconcerting whispers.

The whispers weren't in a language anyone understood. Leaves scraping against concrete; static from a radio; the wind moaning inside of glass jars. There was meaning, they intimated, hidden in the sounds. Secrets waiting to be revealed. Echoes of the past, embalmed in disembodied quark-gluon strings.

Maybe that was what Acantha was experiencing.

There was only one escape. Olavo cloned a softspace copy of himself and placed it in sleep mode for the jump.

Then he qinked down to the Pink Flamenco, synchronizing his softspace mind on the *Wings of Uriel* to the hardspace simunculus on Sand Mountain.

19

Santa Cruz, September 27

Rudi found a battered BMX behind the Dumpster of an Erik's Deli across the street from the hospital. The bike was too small for him, but he took it anyway, even though every turn of the pedals forced him to splay his knees to avoid hitting his elbows. It was faster than walking. Or running.

Still, it took him over ten minutes to ride the mile to the church. The night air was clammy, swirling with cotton-thick fog that reeked of brine and a skunk he had passed but hadn't seen.

Sister Daminca had parked the van at the back of the church lot, where it would be out of the way. The parking lot butted up against an apartment complex on one side and a wood fence along the back. A tall flat-topped hedge screened the ground-level apartments from the parking lot. An insomniac light burned quietly in one of the windows, pressing up against the leaves from behind. A salmon pink streetlight on the far side of the parking lot stuttered apprehensively.

Rudi leaned the mountain bike against the fence and

turned his attention to the parking lot, searching for a brick or rock, anything heavy he could use to break a window and crack open the ignition housing.

By now, the hospital and Sister Daminca would realize he was gone. They would search the building first—restrooms, cafeteria—thinking he had idly wandered off. Soon the search would expand outside, to the grounds and surrounding streets.

He didn't have much time.

He finally found a fist-sized chunk of concrete, and was walking up to the van, when a police car cruised by on the street in front of the church, slowed to a stop, and turned into the parking lot.

Just as the lights swept across the fence, Rudi ducked behind the van. A pair of beams, searchlight bright, illuminated the pavement. They angled toward the van, approaching cautiously.

Rudi scampered through a narrow gap where the hedge met the fence. Branches tore at his light cotton top, snagging and clutching. He stubbed a toe on a stone sticking out of the well-worn hardpan of a footpath.

The cruiser rolled to a stop several car lengths from the van, and the phosphor white glare of a high-intensity beam bathed the exterior. The air shattered into blinding noir-edged fragments of light and dark.

A car door opened. A radio crackled, brittle as old cellophane. A second light in the apartment complex winked on, roused by curiosity.

When nothing happened for a minute or more, Rudi risked a furtive peek from his blind of manicured leaves, shielding his eyes.

The van seemed to pulsate and glow, as if the paint were radioactive. After yet another pause, boots crunched on loose gravel. A tentative shadow stretched across the asphalt as the officer approached the driver's side door. He shined a flashlight under the van, into the cab, then came around to inspect the back doors.

Rudi retreated a step behind the fence. A dog barked and a second one answered. He listened to the officer approach the passenger side door. The radio crackled, a quick unintelligible burst.

The officer relaxed. Rudi could feel the tension drain out of his gait and, opening his mouth wide, Rudi exhaled noiselessly. A cricket chirped, fell silent. Chirped again as the officer's footsteps retreated to the far side of the van.

A couple of minutes later the searchlight snapped off, leaving only the headlights. The door closed, but the squad car continued to idle.

Rudi leaned his head against the fence, and gritted his teeth. He should just leave. Keep moving. Get as far away as he could. In the morning he would bum some clothes, hitch a ride.

The police cruiser backed away. Rudi forced himself to wait until he heard it pull onto the street. Then he pulled off the pajama top, wrapped it around the concrete block, and hurried to the van.

The sound of breaking glass revitalized the neighborhood dogs. A chorus of loud howls erupted, providing cover sound.

As he was preparing to break open the plastic casing on the ignition, a new pair of headlights barreled into the parking lot. One headlight was walleyed and dimmer, or at least dirtier, than the other. The engine sputtered as the car squealed to a stop next to the van. A car door creaked open, then groaned, emitting a hollow thud of anger as it slammed. The interior light stammered in protest before guttering out.

Sister Daminca stalked over to the van, her canvas bag

slung over one shoulder. "What in God's name do you think you're doing?"

Rudi waited for her to calm down. He set the chunk of concrete on the passenger seat, next to the cap and the stuffed ball of yarn beneath it.

"Well?" she demanded.

She looked older than she had yesterday, more homely, as if in twenty-four hours she had aged a decade. In reality, he understood he was seeing her now the way she truly was. For the first time in years he was seeing the world the way it really was... not the way he wanted to see it.

"I have to go," he said.

"That's crazy!" the nun sputtered. "You just had brain surgery!"

"If I don't go now, I never will."

"What in God's name are you talking about?"

"My sister," he said.

Sister Daminca's breath fogged the air between them. "Your sister can wait a few days, or weeks. I'm sure she's fine. The fact that you're here, busting into your van half-naked, proves you're not."

"I have to leave now," Rudi insisted.

"Why? What's so important that you have to go this very instant? What good is it going to do if you die on the way to see her?"

"I'll die if I don't go."

"Listen to yourself," she said. "You're not making any sense. You're not thinking clearly."

"Yes, I am. I finally know what I have to do."

"What about the people who have come to rely on you? You can't just leave them, without a word."

"You'll get along just fine without me," he said. "Someone will come along and take my place. In a few weeks, you'll forget all about me."

"You're an idiot," she said. "I can't let you do this." She turned from the van to go back to her car.

"Daminca," Rudi said. Without the Sister in front, her name sounded strange.

She pulled up short. Turned. Her nose was red. She wiped it with the back of her hand. Sniffed.

"What?" she said.

"If I don't do this now, I might not get another chance. I'm being called."

She stood there, the canvas straps of her shoulder bag digging into her shoulder.

"It can't wait," he said. "*I* can't wait. It feels like I'm finally waking up." And he didn't want to lose that. He wanted to take full advantage while he had the chance.

"You seem awake to me. If anything you need to settle down . . . take a deep breath and collect your thoughts."

"I feel like I've been sleepwalking for years," he said, "going through the motions. Acting like I'm alive, instead of being alive."

"Pretending," she said.

He nodded.

"Is that what the broadcasts were?" she said. "Your help at the Veterans Memorial? Was that pretending, too?"

"I'm not sure." That was one of the things he needed to figure out.

"How long has this been going on?"

"Since the motorcycle accident," he said. "I don't think I ever woke up from that. Not really."

"How do you know you're awake now? How do you know that your mind's not playing tricks on you again?"

"That's what I need to find out."

"By leaving? I don't see how that will let you know one way or another. What if you're just running?"

"Like before," he said.

She crossed her arms. "If that's what you were doing."

Was it? "Maybe," he admitted. "But it feels different, this time. More honest, if that makes sense."

"Yes." Her shoulder sagged under the weight of the bag. She walked back to the driver's window. "I think so."

"Thank you."

"For what?"

"Understanding."

"I don't understand. But that doesn't mean I have the right to stop you from doing what your heart is telling you."

Rudi smiled his gratitude. "For letting me go, then," he said. "What are you going to tell the hospital?"

She rested a hand on his bare arm. Her fingers were warm. "You're freezing. At least let me get you some clothes."

"I have a shirt and pants in back. An extra pair of shoes."

"All right." She fumbled in her shoulder bag. "Here." She held up the key to the van and his wallet. "You might need these."

Rudi squeezed her hand in gratitude then relaxed his grip, afraid of holding on too long or too hard.

Her fingers slid from his. "Are you sure you'll be all right?" Her gaze traveled to the broken window and the glass on the seat.

"Yes."

"Let me know."

"I will."

"Good luck. May God go with you."

"You, too."

Sister Daminca started to back away from the van. Paused. "What do you want me to tell people?" she said. "Someone's bound to ask. Not just at the hospital. But down at the Veterans Memorial, too."

"The truth," he said.

"Which one?"

"That I escaped. You tried to stop me, but you couldn't."

"And I don't know where you're going."

"You don't," he said, "not exactly. I'm not even sure where I'll end up. So it's not actually a lie."

Sister Daminca nodded. Swallowed. "Take care."

"You, too."

She turned and walked quickly, decisively, back to her Tercel. No going back, her measured steps seemed to say. He waited for her car to rattle to life and sputter out of the lot in a gout of exhaust.

Now it was his turn. Before the cops showed up, or he changed his mind.

He started the van, took a minute to cram the bike in back, then headed for the deli. After dropping the bike off where he'd found it, he opened the glove compartment and took out the get well card Linnea had sent to the Lakeshore Foundation while he was rehabbing. He still hadn't figured that out, how she'd known where he was and what had happened to him. One of the questions he planned to ask. She hadn't been as absent—as out of touch—as he thought.

He checked the return address on the envelope: 1145 Pineview. Eugene, Oregon.

Before he could change his mind, Rudi took Soquel Avenue to Highway 1. At the overpass he got on the freeway, heading north.

The only way he was ever going to move forward was to go back and clean up the past. Set things right with his sister. Maybe if he did that—if they helped one another—they could both move on, get past whatever was holding them back. He might not be able to save her. But together they might be able to save each other.

The music was back, an echo from years ago playing softly in his head. He hadn't been able to outrun it. It had followed him here. He wasn't sure he would ever be able to leave it behind.

To his right, a gibbous moon was rising over a tattered horizon of eucalyptus trees and date palms. Bright and bloodshot, it glared down at him, lighting his way.

20

San Francisco, Circa 1937

The séance was scheduled for nine. By eight forty-five, those students who had been asked to take part were gathered in Madame Grurie's study.

"Where are Charles and Peter?" Myrtle glanced at the clock on the table beside the door.

Benjamin had to squint to make out the time: six minutes before nine. His headache was acting up, exacerbated by the double vision, which had become considerably worse in the last day and a half. He felt sick to his stomach. Unable to bear the thought of food, he felt dizzy, light-headed with hunger.

"Apparently they weren't invited," Eloise said. "Along with Neola."

"I wonder why?" Myrtle said.

"Charles's health most likely precludes him," Beatrice said. "At his age one can't be too cautious."

Evidently, Charles Oxley was still recovering from the fainting spell he'd suffered during the movements.

"You're older than he is," Eloise reminded Beatrice.

"True," Beatrice said. "But I go to Sutro Baths for a daily restitution. It keeps me fit and vigorous."

"That doesn't explain Peter. Or Neola."

Beatrice flapped a hand. "Peter is young."

"What is that supposed to mean?" Eloise asked.

"Only that he's susceptible to distraction." Her hand descended to the arm of her chair. "Weren't you vulnerable to the temptations of youth at his age?"

"That doesn't mean he's irresponsible."

"Perhaps they've fallen out of favor," Myrtle said.

Beatrice snorted. "More likely she's trying to teach them a lesson."

In the past three weeks, Benjamin had learned that one of Madame Grurie's preferred teaching methods was to put students in situations or confront them with ideas that made them uncomfortable. It was a way of forcing people to face their fears, or disabuse them of certain long-held preconceptions in order to break down the patterns of thought that gave rise to machinelike behavior. At times it seemed heartless on her part, deliberately cruel. No one was immune—including Benjamin himself. If he was to survive, he would have to let go of his ideas of what was proper behavior; he would have to make himself think and act in ways that were antithetical to his nature. Only then would he be able to free himself from the world, connect with the higher aspects of his being.

Etta didn't partake in the idle patter. She looked distracted, nervous... even a little afraid. She stood off to one side, her hands folded in front of her. But when Benjamin tried to comfort her she withdrew further, became even more self-absorbed and agitated.

There was nothing he could do to help. So he did nothing. Anything else would simply make things worse.

"She'll be fine," Eloise said. In the corner, Beatrice and Myrtle continued to talk about Peter and Neola.

"I suppose it's normal to be nervous," he said.

"Of course. Fear of the unknown. You never know exactly what you're going to find on the other side."

"I didn't think there was another side." Benjamin thought of the dimpled circles Etta's fingertips had left on the napkin. There was flat space, contained within everyday space . . . but it was still the same space. "I thought it was just different projections of the same world."

"I know. It's just different ways of seeing the same reality." Eloise sighed, as if exasperated with herself. "But I can't seem to stop thinking of it as 'this side' and 'that side.' That's what it feels like. Life and afterlife, heaven and earth. Especially when the shades appear."

"Shades?"

"Shadows. The movements and the séances enhance our ability to see objects in higher space. Like seeing at night. The longer you stay out, the better you can see. It is simply a matter of giving yourself time to adjust and knowing what to look for."

"What kind of objects?" he said.

"Well"—her rouged cheeks indented—"the source objects which give rise to the world around us."

Benjamin nodded, feeling stupid. People would not be the only three-dimensional objects with a higher fourth-dimensional component. Every article—chairs, tables, and lamps—would naturally have a similar element.

"They look like barely visible ghosts," Eloise said. "That's because our eyes are limited. We can only catch a glimpse of the infinite."

"Have you had your own . . . session?" Benjamin couldn't bring himself to call what he'd agreed to take part in a séance.

A hand fluttered to her chest. "Not yet. I'm hardly ready. Besides, I'm afraid I would be terrified."

"Who has?"

"Beatrice. And Peter. Those are the only two so far. Etta will, obviously, be the third."

"What did you see?"

"Simunculi. That's what Madame Grurie called the fourth-dimensional aspects of Peter and Beatrice that we saw."

"What happened when these aspects showed up?"

"Beatrice heard a voice in her thoughts, talking in a strange language. Peter felt a hand touch him, from the inside."

"Did you hear or feel anything?"

"No. Only the person who the séance is being held for makes a direct connection, because they're part of the simunculus."

That made sense. "What do these simunculi look like?"

"It depends. With Peter they looked like strangely shaped people. Someone you might encounter at a circus. With Beatrice, they looked more like angels. They had wings."

"Like those in the Bible?"

Before Eloise could answer, Madame Grurie swept into the room with a flourish. "Follow me," she said.

They accompanied her down a dimly lit hallway to a plush room. Dark green drapes, floral-printed, hung from the walls. A chintz settee occupied one wall. A table another. On the table, three candles burned.

A circle of armless chairs occupied the center of the room. The chairs faced out, not in. Benjamin counted five chairs, arranged in a loose pentagram. Approximately two feet separated the back of each chair, leaving a gap large enough to walk through.

"Sit," Madame Grurie said.

Benjamin hesitated.

Eloise touched him on the arm. "Wherever feels most comfortable," she said in a whisper.

Benjamin nodded. What happened if two people chose the same chair? He migrated toward an empty chair that faced the settee. No one else seemed drawn to it. As though by mutual agreement, everyone seemed to have amicably settled on a location. Benjamin took his seat.

Behind him, Madame Grurie shut the door and turned off the electric light on the wall. Darkness rushed in, as if he'd plunged into water.

The hair stood up on his arms. Benjamin rubbed at the rash of goose bumps. It was an effort to breathe. The darkness pressed against his chest, filled his lungs like a viscous fluid.

A match flared. Sulfur stung his nose, followed by the scent of melting wax and French lavender. Around him, and in him, the darkness trembled.

"Don't move," Madame Grurie said. "No matter what you see or hear you are to remain in your current position."

Her dress rustled the semidarkness behind him. Then he felt her inside the circle formed by the chairs.

"Please take one another's hands," she said.

Benjamin groped in the darkness until his right hand caught Myrtle's, and his left found Etta. Myrtle's hand was dry and warm, Etta's clammy. He gave her moist palm a reassuring squeeze. In response, she tightened her grip.

"Close your eyes," Madame Grurie instructed. "Concentrate on self-remembering. Focus on your self. Sense your self physically."

She stood directly behind Etta. Through his fingers, he could feel the downward pressure of Madame Grurie's right hand on Etta's shoulder.

"This is how we ascend," Madame Grurie said. "By making a conscious effort to inhabit each moment—by turning our thoughts to the vibratory modes of our bodies—we cross the interval. We bridge the gap between shadow and being."

Etta gasped.

A moment later, Benjamin felt a faint tingle, as if an electric current was coursing into his fingertips. The charge originated from Etta, passed through him to Myrtle, who stiffened in response.

"Feel the vibration as it arises within you," Madame Grurie said. "Focus all your thoughts on it, to the exclusion of all else."

Benjamin could no longer distinguish the source of the vibration. Perhaps it had arisen in him after all—out of him.

"Give yourself over to the vibratory excitation within you," Madame Grurie said. "Become one with it. Allow yourself to be transformed by it."

Benjamin felt the current resonating deep within him. And felt himself letting go, content to be carried along. He no longer felt Etta's or Myrtle's hands. The pressure of their fingers no longer connected them. They were joined by an invisible force. Beside him, Myrtle began to hum, as if giving voice to the current.

"By allowing ourselves to be transformed," Madame Grurie said, "we progress. We pass from one stage of being to the next, one level of existence to the next. This is known as the Ray of Creation."

Benjamin found himself humming. Not just with Myrtle, but with the rest of the group. They were all humming, even Beatrice, each of them picking up the drone and adding to it—deepening it.

Change is possible, he thought. He could die and still live.

"We create ourselves in steps," Madame Grurie said. "We ascend one step at a time, moving in octaves up the scale of existence."

The sustained murmur, emanating from the center of his

being, both calmed and uplifted him. Benjamin felt buoyed by it, as if the sound was carrying him upward to a different plane of existence.

"And as we ascend," Madame Grurie said, "we arrive at different bodies. First, there is the physical body, the body we are born with. This is succeeded by the second body, known as the astral body. Next, we arrive at the third body, the mental body. Finally, there is the fourth body, the divine body. This is the body that exists in the fourth dimension—simultaneously in the past and the future."

Benjamin thought he felt something tickle the back of his neck. A finger? Or an insect? He quashed the impulse to recoil. The insect, if that's what it was, traced a line along the vertebrae of his spine. Hot as a struck match, it burned a hole in his neck and traveled along a single filament of pain into his head.

"During our passage to a higher-order body, the current of life circulates in and through us. It does so to lesser or greater degrees, depending where we happen to be located on the Ray of Creation."

Madame Grurie shifted her position, away from Etta to the opposite side of the circle.

"If we are to grow," she said, "we must permit the uninhibited flow of energies within us. We must be receptive to all aspects of our being... willing to accept whatever shape it takes."

Had he imagined the touch? Perhaps it had been a muscle spasm.

"Wake up!" Madame Grurie commanded. "Do not be afraid to look. The miraculous lives among us all the time. Just because we are asleep, with our eyes closed, doesn't mean it is not present."

Madame Grurie clapped her hands once. Startled by the sound, Benjamin's eyes jerked open.

A pale shadow wavered in front of him, unsteady as the candlelight. The smudge appeared to be vaguely human-shaped. It had thick arms and an amorphous, somewhat bulbous head.

A trick of the light? he wondered. Or simply a trick, perpetrated by the curtains and his mangled vision?

If so, how did he know what was real anymore?

Pain squeezed Benjamin's temples. He let go of the hands he was holding and pressed his fists to his eyes, crushing the light from them.

21

Orthinia, Design Space

During the night, the bird shed its wings.

Olavo found them on the covers when he woke, small and useless. Where they had detached from the shoulders, the matted nap was disfigured by a partially open wound that oozed white fluid. The seepage had clotted in the seams of the torn skin, oddly sponge-like and resilient under his exploratory touch. The tail had fallen off, too, and lay on the floor by the side of the bed, like the shed skin of a snake.

The creature seemed to be losing body parts as it evolved, changing from an animal that flew to one that walked. It had curled up near his feet. The talons were gone, as well, retracted into soft-padded paws. The animal sprawled with its eyes open, watching him. He hadn't killed it after all.

He searched the bedsheets. If he'd been updated by one of the tiny insects, it was gone now. He didn't feel any different. He blinked at his armor-clad arms, tapped the helmet on his head. Nothing about him had changed. Why would the creature evolve and not him? What was it responding to that he wasn't?

The sun was high. Crimson light smeared the wall opposite

the clerestory window above the bed. Olavo got out of bed. He picked up the discarded tail. It rested limply on his palm. Either rigor had yet to set in, or it had already passed. Olavo set the tail on the bed with the wings. Then he dressed, collected the floppy remains, and headed out of the room. In the courtyard, the sun had baked the tile red. He stood at the balustrade, staring across the valley floor to the rim of mountains. Footsteps scraped the paving stones behind him. He turned.

"How do you feel?" Vania said.

"Better," Olavo said. But the response was rote, what he knew she wanted to hear.

"That's good." A thin smile veiled practiced skepticism. Her gaze traveled to the tail and the wings he still held. "What are you doing?"

He looked at his hand. "I thought I would bury them."

"Where?"

He looked up. Squinted. "In the garden."

"Why do you want to bury them?"

He shrugged. It seemed like the right thing to do. "Do you want to help?"

"If you like," she said. "If you think it would make it easier."

He nodded. "I think so."

She followed him into the garden, letting him lead the way along a footpath to the base of the locust tree from which the animal had emerged the very first time it had visited him in the courtyard. The marble flagstones were damp. Dew glistened on the balustrade and pink terra-cotta roof tiles, dripped from the geraniums hanging from one of the iron railings visible down one of the side streets.

"Are things under control yet?" he asked.

"What do you mean?"

"Stable," he said, unable to think of another word to describe the unease that had taken root in his stomach.

"Not yet. But we're getting there. These things take time."

Olavo dropped to his knees. The ground was dry but soft, composed primarily of sand instead of clay. Vania joined him, careful to keep her dress from snagging on nearby twigs and thorns.

Olavo set the tail and wings between two roots. "What about the others?" he said. Jori. Uta. Ramunas. Hossein. "How are they doing?"

"They're coming along fine."

"Good."

"You're concerned about them?"

"I was just wondering."

"Their progress has nothing to do with yours," she said. "This isn't a competition. There are no losers. It's not fair to compare yourself to them. Or them to you."

Olavo said nothing. He began to dig with his bare hands, scraping out a hole in the sand. After a moment Vania pitched in, clearing away the sand before it could slide back into the shallow depression. When the grave was wide and deep enough to accommodate the wings and tail, Olavo arranged them carefully, respectfully.

"Would you like to say a few words?" Vania said, straightening.

"A prayer?" he asked.

"It doesn't have to be."

Olavo thought for a moment. "'A living dog is better than a dead lion,'" he finally said.

Vania pursed her lips, pressing the color from them. "I'm not sure I know what that means."

He wasn't, either. But under the circumstances it seemed appropriate. "It's from Ecclesiastes." He began to fill in the hole.

"Where did you hear that? At church?"

Olavo shook his head. Someplace else; he couldn't remember where exactly. He finished covering the dismembered body parts and tamping the soil in place.

"What does it mean to you?" Vania said.

Olavo paused. Dry dirt caked the ends of his fingernails. "It's better to be alive, even if you're not the strongest or most noble person in the world."

"Is that how you see yourself?"

He curled his nails into his dirty palms. "As a dog?"

"No. Glad to be alive."

"Sometimes," he said. "Not all the time." He went back to the grave, carefully smoothing the dirt into place.

"Do you think it would be easier to be the lion?"

He paused. Stared at his grit-covered hands, as if transfixed by the bits of mica glinting in the sunlight. "Maybe. How come I'm not changing? Everything around me seems to be."

"You are. Not so much on the outside. Not yet. But on the inside. You're making progress."

He brushed the dirt from his fingers. "It doesn't feel like it."

"Well, you are," Vania said. "Even if it's not obvious, or as fast as you might like. The important thing—the hardest thing—is not to give up."

"It's discouraging," he said.

Vania glossed her lips with the tip of her tongue. "There's somebody I would like you to meet."

She stood and he rose like a shadow by her side. "Who?"

"She's from a different design space. She'd like to ask you a few questions, if you don't mind."

"Is she a therapist?" he said.

"No, more like a mediator. She's with a special program. Would that be all right?"

"When?"

"Now. If you're not up for it at the moment, I understand. You can talk to her at another time."

Olavo glanced back down at the grave. If he had to talk to her, he might as well get it over with. "Talk about what?" he said.

"She didn't say."

Which meant that Vania didn't want him to know in advance what the person was going to ask him about. She didn't want him to have time to think about the questions or prepare answers.

"Where is she?"

"In another part of the facility."

"All right," he said.

Vania smiled, pleased. "Just a minute."

She faded out and the scape changed. A window appeared in place of the railing, framing the mountains in glass panes. The sky lowered and flattened into a white plaster ceiling. The garden became a collection of potted plants, scattered about the room. One found its way onto the desk that had formed out of the stone bench closest to him.

The simunculus that replaced Vania was short and slightly built. Ringlets clung to her brow, some of them curled into stiff question marks over olive-brown eyes and tight, diacritical lips.

"Hi, there." The visitor forced an upbeat smile. "How have you been?"

22

Eugene, October 4

From the sanctuary of his van, Rudi peered at the address next to the front door of the trailer home: 114—.

The metal numbers—tacked to the white aluminum siding—had faded from matte black to silver. In the gray overcast of the failing afternoon light, they were scarcely visible. The outline of the missing last number, dimly stenciled on the paint, was undecipherable. It might be a five.

He couldn't tell if the address matched the return address on the card. He didn't want to go up and check. Not yet. Not while it was still light.

Even if it did match, there was no guarantee Linnea still lived there. The card was five years old. As far as Rudi knew, she'd never lived in one place longer than six months... the time it took her to break up with whatever boyfriend she was living with. It had been that way for as long as he could remember, ever since she ran away, leaving him in the care of their grandmother. He was ten at the time, Linnea fourteen. Their mother had vanished six months earlier, freeing them from the endless cycle of booze, boyfriends, and police visits in the middle of the night.

Rudi had parked across the street from the dilapidated double-wide. It was an obvious rental, set on an otherwise unbuildable piece of land on the outskirts of town. Desiccated, mold-blackened leaves clogged the drainage ditch running along the gravel drive that pitched drunkenly up to the front steps. A narrow footpath from the driveway to the awning-protected porch had been trampled into the leaves. Moss grew in patches on the roof, scabbing the sheets of corrugated plastic that had been placed on top of the original roof.

No one appeared to be home. The windows were dark and nothing moved behind them. No life at all.

A breeze rustled the maple he had parked under. Leaves clattered, and branches scraped against the cardboard duct-taped over the broken window.

Rudi sat quietly and stared at the house. Watching. Listening. Remembering...

At night, Rudi's grandmother went to sleep with the clock radio whispering in her ear. And each morning she woke a little different, changed by the music she'd steeped in during the night.

That was the way it seemed.

Her hands shook more. Her eyes grew cloudier. She forgot another word, or couldn't get the words out. In the last month, it had gotten worse. Rudi had to speak for her, hear for her, remember for her.

And clean up after her. Yesterday she had dropped a teacup. The day before that she'd knocked over one of her favorite flower vases filled with dried, dusty flowers from the garden in the back.

Late at night, lying awake in his own bed across the hall, Rudi could hear the music. It trickled from her room into his. Rudi wanted to turn the radio off, but was afraid. What if she left with the music, disappeared like everyone else?

In the morning, before his grandmother awoke, he got up to heat water for the Lady Grey tea she liked to drink before breakfast.

The water in the kettle was just beginning to boil when Rudi heard a low moan from the house next door. The anxious sigh came from the backyard, stirred by a fitful breeze that scraped the leaves of the privet tree just outside the open window above the stove. The sound reminded him of the soft wheeze his grandmother sometimes made in her sleep. It was followed by the empty clink of glass on glass. Then the breeze died and with it the hollow whisper.

One of Tenley's spirit bottles.

Two months earlier, a few days before school ended, Tenley had moved into the house next door. A day after the moving van left, Rudi heard an eerie cry on the other side of the low fence between their yards. Peering through the bamboo hedge on her side of the fence, he'd seen Tenley tying bottles to a small dogwood tree. Different colored bottles dangled from the tree on strings. The bottles twirled like bright, misshapen fruit.

"What are those?" he asked.

She jerked and her dark pigtails swung from side to side. "They're called spirit bottles. They protect us from evil spirits that hurt people or make them sick." Her voice reminded him of lazy creek water.

Rudi climbed the fence, squeezed through a gap in the bamboo, and stood next to her. Her hair smelled of apricots. "How can a bottle protect you?"

Tenley picked up a perfume bottle. It was small and blue with a skinny neck. She put it to her lips and blew into the hollowness. "The spirits are attracted to the pretty colors. Like bees. Except after they go inside, they can't get out. They're trapped. So they can't hurt anyone."

Rudi squinted up at the limbs of the dogwood. "If the bottles don't have any tops, can't the spirits just leave?"

"Not unless a bottle breaks." She set the perfume bottle down, knotted a piece of string around the neck, and tied it to the tree. . . .

The teapot whistled. A moment later his grandmother shuffled into the kitchen. Her slippers scraped on the uneven linoleum. She clutched her flannel nightgown to her chest with one blue-veined hand. Her hair was a blizzard of gray cotton, her face cobwebbed with wrinkles.

"I thought I heard the kettle," she said. The kettle always woke her; it was the only thing that pulled her from the grip of the radio.

"Here." Rudi pulled out her chair at the end of the table and helped her sit.

She turned to peer at the clock on the microwave, her eyes bird-bright behind the thick lenses of her glasses. Varicose veins traced the tendons on the backs of her hands. Her clear skin reminded him of the tracing paper they used in school. "Shouldn't you be leaving for class?"

"School's out," he said. "Remember? It's summer vacation."

She pulled her nightgown tighter. "It doesn't feel like summer."

He carried the teacup to the table. "We're out of milk."

"That's fine." She reached up and patted his hand, bundling his fingers in hers.

He sat at the table with her while she sipped her tea.

"I wonder how Linnea is," he said after a while. She hadn't been home for three weeks, but he couldn't believe she was gone for good.

The fluted cup clattered on the saucer. She wrapped her hands around the gold-lipped rim to steady it. And herself.

"Rudi..."

"I know." He dropped his gaze and his voice. It was better if he didn't ask. Better if he didn't know. Or care. The same way it was better if he didn't know or care about his mother. But sometimes he couldn't help himself. Birds went somewhere secret when it rained and then suddenly came back, filling the sky. Maybe it would be like that with his sister. The rain would clear and she would show up out of nowhere.

"I wish she'd call," he said. "That's all."

"She will."

"When?"

The cup rattled again. This time his grandmother removed her hands to keep the tea from sloshing out. "When she's ready, Rudi."

Rudi's chest ached and his throat shut tight. If he hadn't been born, Linnea might have stayed with their grandmother. He knew that. He was a burden. She took drugs to get away from him. And when that didn't work, she left.

"I'm sorry," Rudi said. He was being selfish.

His grandmother dabbed at his arm with palsied fingers, caught his wrist and held it. "You don't have anything to apologize for. It's not your fault. Don't ever think that." Her hand trembled against his skin. "She'll be fine. So will we."

He swallowed. Nodded. "I'm going to get some milk," he said. Outside, the morning air was already starting to swelter and he drew the blinds on the window to cut the heat.

"Be careful," she said.

"I'll be back in a few minutes."

She didn't answer. Her back was hunched, her body curled over the teacup as she breathed in the warmth.

Rudi took a ten from the metal canister where she kept grocery money. On the way out, he switched on the television in case she wanted to watch The Price Is Right.

The 7-Eleven was three blocks away. Rudi locked his bike—

an old BMX with a torn seat and a scuffed, rust-pitted frame—to the bike rack out front and entered the store. As usual, Mr. Chin was behind the counter, humming softly as he worked.

"I haven't seen your grandma in a while," Mr. Chin said, looking up from the carton of cigarettes he was pricing. "How's she doing?"

Except for a wispy goatee, Mr. Chin didn't have much of a chin. Rudi wondered if that was how he got his name. A lack of something could be just as important as its presence—even more so, sometimes. What he did have was a splotch in the center of his forehead that looked a little bit like the pyramid eye on a one-dollar bill.

"I have the latest issue of ION *for you," Mr. Chin said, as he was ringing up Rudi's milk and Snickers. "It has an interesting article on branes."*

"Brains?"

"Membranes." Mr. Chin took the ten from Rudi. "Hidden dimensions that make up the universe." When Mr. Chin leaned forward to hand Rudi his change, the third eye seemed to blink under the bright fluorescent lights. "Sometimes, these membranes bump against each other and create new universes."

Rudi pocketed the change and looked up, careful not to let his gaze wander to the eye on Mr. Chin's forehead. He didn't want to be rude, but more than that, Rudi always felt like the eye belonged to someone or something else living inside Mr. Chin. Something that was watching him.

"If this theory is correct," Mr. Chin said, "then the world as we know it is nothing more than a shadow, a reflection of some deeper truth." He reached under the counter and handed the magazine to Rudi.

"Thanks."

"Each dimension is a parallel universe," Mr. Chin said. "These universes are flat. Like sheets of paper." He held his

hands up, palms facing each other but separated by half an inch.

"Cool." Rudi flipped through the magazine. A coffee stain on one edge wrinkled the pages, turned the address label brown.

Mr. Chin smiled, revealing uneven brown-stained teeth. "Tell your grandmother I said hello."

Rudi rolled the magazine into a tight cylinder. "I will."

"Let me know if you need any help, okay?"

Rudi pedaled home awkwardly, unbalanced by the white plastic grocery bag in one hand and the magazine in the other. A fitful breeze tugged at the locust trees and combed his hair from his face. The trees seemed to be waving their limbs frantically, trying to get his attention.

Passing Tenley's house, Rudi heard the sound of breaking glass. He turned onto her driveway. Hopping off his bike, he propped it against the bamboo hedge, then made his way through the side yard of her house to the backyard.

Tenley knelt on the ground at the base of the dogwood tree. One of the spirit bottles had fallen. Splinters of blue glass lay in a pile in front of her folded knees.

"What happened?" he said.

"I didn't tie this one tight enough." With tremulous fingers she prodded the jagged bits of glass.

"Are you okay?" he said.

"My mom's gonna whip me good."

He watched her scrabble among the shards. "If you're not careful, you're going to cut yourself."

Plucking at the shards, she started to pile the broken bottle in the loose folds of her skirt between her knees.

"Can't you just use another bottle?" he asked.

She shook her head. "It's too late. The spirit's got out. Besides, this was one of my mom's favorites. It's a family heirloom."

"Maybe you could glue it back together."

She cut him a sharp glance.

Rudi swallowed, felt himself grow small under her scrutiny. "Where will the spirit go?"

Tenley shrugged. The movement was languid, a catlike stretch. Rudi wanted to put a hand on her shoulder, feel the smooth supple skin under her top.

Tenley stood, cradling the broken glass in her skirt. "I have to go."

Before he could stop her, she hurried to the back door of the house and disappeared inside, swallowed up by white clapboard.

When she was gone, one of the bottles on the tree began to moan. "Wooo-deee," it seemed to say. "Rudi. Help meeee. . . ."

Rudi ran down the driveway, not bothering to stop for the milk and his bicycle. His grandmother wasn't in the living room. On the television screen Bob Barker smiled at him and the empty couch.

She wasn't in the kitchen, either. The teacup sat on the table, barely touched.

Rubbing his pant leg, Rudi made his way down the hall . . . slowly at first, then faster. Running, out of breath, he burst into the room.

She lay in bed under the covers, eyes closed. Light from the clock had turned her face green. The lenses of her glasses flickered, empty as Tenley's broken bottle.

"Grandma?"

He reached out a hand to wake her and stopped. His vision blurred, smeared by the watery light from the blinds. His face felt puffy, his eyes swollen. Outside the wind gusted and the spirit bottles wailed, not quite drowning out the sound of the radio.

It blinked balefully at him from the night table. Seconds ticked by as the tired music hissed out. Rudi lurched forward.

He turned off the radio, knocking it to the floor. The green readout died, but the music kept playing. One song followed another, even after he yanked the plug from the wall.

"Stop," he whispered. "Please?" He clapped his hands over his ears.

Instead of getting softer the music got louder, as if his fingers were holding it in. With each breath, he could hear his grandmother's voice, like the wind in one of Tenley's bottles, rising to a howl.

Rudi blinked, roused by a light switching on in a room at one end of the trailer. Dusk had fallen. The light glazing the window was sallow and a frail shadow sputtered on the jaundiced walls. The source of the movement was invisible. From where he was parked, Rudi had a limited view of the room. Through the window, he could make out a closed door and little else.

The gray flame on the wall sputtered and curled across the ceiling. It was coming from cigarette smoke, he realized, rising in front of a lamp.

Did Linnea smoke?

She hadn't when she'd left. She'd given it up, out of spite. *I hate Mom! I never want to be like her!*

But maybe she'd picked it up again. Old habits. Or one of those moth-eaten promises that becomes so tattered over the years it's no longer worth keeping.

The smoke dissipated, stubbed out.

Rudi imagined the person sitting on the edge of the bed, taking a few shaky puffs just to get moving. Their mother had done that. He would find the remains of partially smoked cigarettes in glasses, pots, pans, plates, and soap dishes, scattered about like the bones of a small animal that had been devoured in different parts of the house.

A shadow-puppet silhouette appeared on the wall. Then the top of a head, frizzy with blond hair. The door opened inward, and the woman stepped forward, flipping the switch on the way out.

Was it her? Or someone who resembled his memory of her? His mouth felt dry. The cigarette scar on his arm throbbed. A few minutes later, a light bloomed in a window at the other end of the trailer home.

There was only one way to find out.

As Rudi was about to open the door, a car turned onto the street and came toward him. He paused, his breath fogging the window while he waited for it to pass.

Instead it groped its way up the driveway to Linnea's trailer, tires crunching on the loose gravel. The headlights cut out and a figure stepped from the car. A man. He followed the path tromped into the leaves, up the steps, to the front door.

A moment later the door opened. The man slipped inside and the door shut behind him, leaving Rudi in darkness.

23

San Francisco, Circa 1937

Etta was lily-white when the lights came on. Benjamin stared at the side of her face. She seemed paralyzed, waxen with fear.

What had she seen, or felt?

Before he could take her hand, or stand up and move toward her, Madame Grurie intervened. The spiritualist gathered Etta up with a bustling flourish of hands and whisked her from the room. Benjamin was left with the animated chatter of the three elderly women and the strident electric blaze of the wall lamps.

"I heard Arthur," Beatrice said, "as clearly as if he was standing next to me." Tears dewed her eyes. "He kissed me on the hand." She looked at her fingers in wonder.

"I saw my grandmother," Eloise said. "I always knew she lived in me, exactly like Madame Grurie said. We're one soul. I'm just an extension of her." Relief and gratitude colored her voice.

Myrtle remained silent, introspective.

Feeling sick to his stomach, unable to endure the dagger-sharp glare of the incandescent lights any longer, Benjamin groped for the door.

"Benjamin," Eloise called, "are you all right? Where are you going? You haven't told us what you saw."

"Lavatory." Head throbbing, he made his escape. He stumbled from the room, then the house.

Fog embraced him, muffling the glare of the streetlamps in a downy glow. He pulled the brim of his hat low, kept his head down, and began walking. Gradually the pain subsided to a tolerable roar, like the sound of waves crashing against a distant shore. He no longer felt consumed by nausea. Dampened by mist, the thud of his heart dropped to a murmur.

What, or whom, had he seen? He didn't trust himself anymore to know what was real, and what was a product of his imagination. Who knew what effect the tumor would have as it grew? It was pressing against his optic nerve. He couldn't rely on his vision. The world he knew was being taken from him—decaying around him.

He stopped next to a dimly lighted store window to stare at his hands. His fingers shook in the wan glow. They seemed solid enough, but he couldn't stop them from trembling. They no longer felt like his fingers. They seemed to belong to somebody else, as if another man's hands had been grafted onto him. The dizzy sensation that he was in the process of becoming a different person washed over him. Over time, every aspect of him would be replaced, unrecognizable, foreign.

He curled his hands into fists, as if the trembling could be squeezed from them like excess water. When his hands continued to shake, he pressed them against the plate glass window. Behind the glass, confections sat in neat rows on delicate shelves. Fancy chocolates. Saltwater taffy.

It wasn't fair. He didn't deserve this. What had he done? He was a good person. Honest, hardworking. Why had God done this to him? He hammered the window with his clenched fists. Gently at first, then harder, the glass rattling. A faint crack brought him to a sudden halt. He blinked several times until the shelves and bins of candy came into dim focus.

What the hell was he doing? He couldn't think straight anymore, couldn't control his feelings let alone his movements.

He staggered back from the storefront, quickly glanced up and down the street to make sure no one had seen him, then—angry with himself now—stuffed his hands in his pockets and hurried on. Perhaps he was going insane, driven by doubt to uncertainty and madness. If he couldn't trust his senses to tell him what was true, then nothing was true. Nothing he felt, saw, tasted, or heard could be believed.

And yet the three women were convinced by what they had seen. They couldn't all be crazy. The figure could have been from the fourth dimension, appearing to him as a vivid waking dream. Maybe, as he began to wake up, he dreamed the world of his higher self into existence in this world.

Perhaps he should have stayed. There was still time to turn around, go back. The women would be comparing notes, arguing and chiding. Now that his headache had abated he felt calmer. He could tolerate the lights and their repartee, at least for a while. He might even get a chance to talk with Etta. But probably not alone. The other women would be anxious to question her. He might learn something vicariously, but he would have to wait to speak with her alone.

Benjamin heard footsteps behind him, quickening as they drew closer. He hadn't been paying attention. He was in a disreputable part of town. The street and buildings around him were dark. Seeking solitude, he had tended toward side streets, avoiding the well-lit clamor and safety of the main thoroughfares.

Too late, he yanked his still-clenched hands from his pants pockets and picked up his pace. A hand gripped him on the shoulder, preventing him from escaping.

Benjamin spun to face his assailant.

"Easy," the man said.

Peter stepped back, releasing his grip on Benjamin's jacket, and held up his hands, palms out.

"What are you doing here?" Benjamin demanded.

Peter chuckled, diffusing some of the tension. "I might ask you the same thing. I followed you from Madame Grurie's."

"Why?"

"To find out what happened."

Benjamin nodded. Peter had been excluded from the séance. Naturally, he'd be curious.

"I don't know how much I can tell you," Benjamin said. "I don't know if what I experienced was real or not."

"It's a sham," Peter told him.

Benjamin blinked, taken aback. "What?"

"Everything. It's all a charade. Illusions. I know you don't want to believe that. But it's true."

They were seated in a booth at a pub called the Black Seal. The bar was mercifully dark and hushed. Polished leather seatbacks and wainscoting absorbed any stray light and sound. A dense haze of cigar and pipe smoke mimicked the fog outside.

"How do you know she's a charlatan?" Benjamin said. "The others thought they saw something. Beatrice. Myrtle. Eloise."

Peter swirled his beer. "Of course they did. They're old. They want to believe. Like you. They don't have much time left, and they're frightened. That makes them vulnerable and gullible."

It was true. Benjamin might not believe; but he didn't want *not* to believe, either. That clouded his judgment.

"What about Etta and Charles?" Peter asked. "What did they see? Or think they saw?"

Benjamin watched the bubbles in his beer turn to foam. "Charles wasn't invited. For health reasons. Etta I don't know about. I didn't get a chance to talk with her after things ended."

Peter laughed. "Madame Grurie took her away before you got a chance, am I right?"

Benjamin looked up at him in surprise.

"She did the same with me," Peter explained. "That's what she does. Before anyone else has a chance to question you."

"Why?"

"To make sure you saw what you were meant to see. She helps you interpret any strange effects you experienced. And so she steers you into believing exactly what she wants you to believe."

"To what end?"

"Financing. If she hasn't approached you about that yet, she will. Trust me. It won't be long."

"The subject hasn't come up," Benjamin said.

Peter snorted and sipped his beer. "Has she offered herself to you?"

"No," Benjamin lied, glad of the dimness between them.

"She's a whore," Peter said. "Nothing more. She preys on people. Uses them. That's how she makes her living. By selling herself."

Peter was bitter, Benjamin thought. He'd been snubbed, was angry at not being invited to the session. Now he was taking revenge. What better way to hurt her than to attack her reputation?

"Am I to understand you have learned nothing from your involvement with her?" Benjamin said. "Gained no valuable knowledge about the world or yourself?"

"I've confirmed that people will believe anything," Peter said. "No matter how implausible or outrageous."

Benjamin stood. He'd had enough. He reached for his coat and hat.

"Don't be a fool," Peter said.

"Why should I believe you, any more than I should believe her?" Benjamin said. "It's your word against hers."

"Just because I can't disprove what she claims, doesn't mean that it's not false," Peter said. "A lie."

"What did she do to you?"

"Nothing I didn't expect."

"Then you have no reason to be disappointed or offended. No reason to attack or vilify."

"On the contrary." Peter smiled. "It's my job."

Benjamin shook his head. "To impugn people? Without proof?"

"To be a skeptic. To find the proof. The only way to do that is to ask questions. Doubt everything."

"You're a scientist, then?"

"A reporter." Peter sipped his beer. "I've investigated a dozen Madame Gruries over the last five years. They're all the same."

Benjamin sat. "You're writing a story on her?"

"The world needs to know." Peter spoke firmly, matter-of-factly. "People must be warned before they get hurt." The reporter let out a heavy sigh. "I realize it's probably too much to hope for. Desperate people are willfully blind to the facts. Not only do they blind themselves, they take comfort in that blindness. It's easier than confronting the truth. But if I can open the eyes of a few people, I'll have done the world a service."

"Who else have you told?" Benjamin asked.

"You're the first. I've been afraid to confront the others. It's too early."

"Why? If it's a sham, they should know."

The reporter hunched his shoulders. "Because they'll just go to Madame Grurie. You've heard them talk, they're completely loyal. They'll tell her I'm investigating her."

"How do you know I won't?"

"You're new to the group. You haven't been under her influence as long as the others. I'm hoping you might still be open to the truth."

"Suppose I do tell her?"

The reporter's expression soured. "She'll pack up and leave town. Set up shop someplace else. The people with her now will get hurt. Myrtle. Eloise. Beatrice."

"They're going to get hurt, anyway," Benjamin said. "Regardless of where they hear the news."

"Not if they see for themselves that she's a fraud. Otherwise, they'll just go on believing."

"What do you want from me?" The reporter was confiding in him for a reason. This wasn't just idle conversation.

"Your help."

"I don't see what I can do."

"Keep your eyes and your ears open. Poke around, if you get a chance. Look for anything suspicious."

"You want me to be a *snitch*?"

The reporter's gaze darted past him. But no one had turned to them. Benjamin's raised voice hadn't attracted attention. "If you do find something—"

"Like what?"

"Stage props. Recorded voices. Medicines that could be used to drug people or beguile their judgment."

"You can do that yourself. Far better than I ever could."

"She suspects me," the reporter said. "That's why I wasn't

invited to the séance tonight. I wouldn't be surprised if she kicks me out of the group altogether. If she does, I'll need to have someone there in my absence."

"Why?" Benjamin said.

"I just told you."

"No. Why are you doing this? If you want me to help you, I want to know what the reason is. Your reason."

"That's none of your business."

"Then the answer is no." Benjamin stood. Relieved, he began to slide out of the booth.

Peter caught him by the wrist. "Wait."

Benjamin paused.

"My sister," Peter said, his voice lowering.

Benjamin dropped with it, settling back to the leather seat. "What about her?" he asked. He wasn't sure he wanted to hear this. He hadn't thought the reporter—if that's what he was—would tell him. Now Benjamin felt he had no choice but to listen.

"When our grandmother died eleven years ago, our mother wasn't around. We were going to be put in an orphanage. I was nine at the time. She was thirteen. Instead, she ran away."

"With whom?" There was always someone. It was the only reason people left the people they loved—for someone they thought they loved more.

"A man she met, at a circus. He claimed to be clairvoyant. He had a show. She was going to become his assistant."

"But she didn't," Benjamin hazarded.

"I got one letter from her, three years after she left. Things were hard. The stock market had crashed and money was tight. He was using her to..." Peter's expression twisted. "When I wrote to her, I never heard back."

And he was still trying to find her. Trying to find out what happened. Or failing that, stop it from happening to someone else.

"She wasn't the first," Peter went on. "I found out later that this man had duped other women. They disappeared, too."

"Let me go," Benjamin said, extricating his wrist from the younger man's fingers. He'd heard enough.

"If you don't help me take her down," Peter said, "you're going to go down with her."

"Are you threatening me?"

"Make up your mind," Peter said. "Soon. I'm not going to let her get away with this. That, sir, is a promise. Not a threat."

24

Sand Mountain, Hardspace

The Pink Flamenco was bustling, crowded with gnomen and a few doughmen in blue maintenance overalls, salt-infested and smelling of brine. The waitress, Tamsin, was busy, juggling plates of food between tables. The place was undergoing a remodel. Drop-down LED bulbs had replaced the hanging plants. Pink marble flooring in lieu of black and white tile. Translucent green privacy screens, crawling with cryptic pictoglyphs, now separated booths and tables. In place of zydeco, threadbare static rasped from the jukebox.

Olavo sat at his usual table and waited for Mee Won to arrive.

Despite the reflective awning over the balcony, and a thin sheet of clouds pulled tight across the sky, the sun was hot. It beat down on his head. Every now and then, a cloud shifted, dissolved into lazy cigarette wisps of smoke. In those moments the stars of the Ferrer cluster emerged, suddenly, viciously, a clenched fist of light.

Five minutes passed. Ten.

Mee Won had never taken this long to meet him. Agitated, he gestured for Tamsin a few tables away. Flustered, she wiped stout hands on the front of her pink, grease-stained dress and hurried over.

"Sorry," she said. She brushed at a loose strand of hair. "New owner's making a mess of things."

"I can see that."

Her mouth puckered and a puff of air escaped from tight lips. "What can I mech for you?" she said.

"I'll have a Red Plasma," he said. It was the closest he could come to a daiquiri, based on the tweaked genes available to the agriciles.

She placed the order and a moment later a gleaming metal tumbler assembled in her hand. It filled with fizzing red condensate, viscous at the bottom and frothy on top. She set the tumbler on the table and stepped back, one brow pointed. "Can I mech you anything else?"

"As a matter of fact," he said, "I was hoping you could help me. I was supposed to meet someone here...."

"Your *nouveaux* sister?"

Olavo smiled, nodded. "If she shows up after I leave, could you tell her that I'll meet her at the prayer hall instead?"

The waitress's dark eyes narrowed and shifted focus. For an instant, as if peering through the lens of a microscope, Olavo could see in her expression a flicker of who she'd once been—the vestigial source code of humanity that had given rise to her—all of those tireless, efficient women who kept the world turning...spinning under the sheer weight of their determination. Without them, there would be no rest at the end of the day, no dawn to wake up to. Life would grind to a torturous, entropic halt.

"She was in the other day, with a stranger. Not a waif, mind you. A doughman."

"I see."

"Not a workman. No salt in his pores. More sticky-soft." Her nostrils wrinkled. "Had that wax about him."

Olavo nodded. As soon as Tamsin left, he stumbled out in a queasy rush, rancid with urgency. . . .

It was late, after eleven. He hadn't seen Tenley in a while. Months. He couldn't remember exactly how many. For years they'd been more than friends, less than lovers. Perhaps they still were.

That was the hope. That was what he needed to find out. The one thing he wanted to know, more than anything else.

They'd had a fight. He couldn't remember about what. Something stupid. It was always something small between them, some trivial quarrel about the garbage, unwashed plates in the sink, or dirty socks on the floor that intimated some deeper fault line.

His pulse vibrated to the high-pitched whine of his Kawasaki. His underarms were oily, slick with fear that she wouldn't want to see him.

Not now. Not ever. Not after the way he had walked out.

Did she still love him? Or had she moved on while he'd been scraping out the hopelessness that built up over time, like a heavy metal, in his system?

That was the question. He was racing to find out, taking the turns low and tight, a little too fast. Adrenaline-fueled. Trying to recapture lost time, make up for past mistakes, secure the future.

Did he still care for her?

That was another fear. Another question he needed to confront and answer, head-on. Maybe he'd never loved her.

He must . . . he was going back. He needed her. Was that a kind of love? Or was it simply desperation?

Did she need him? Had she ever needed him? She must

have, at one time. If he could convince her he was better, changed, she might again.

So many questions. Too many.

He had waited as long as he could, but agitation and uncertainty had finally caught up with him. He needed to know, one way or another, where they stood. And then he could rest. Then he could get better.

Trees rushed by. Sycamores, pine, and Chinese tallow reached for him with leafy fingers. Before they could touch him he was gone, one step ahead of the mounting dread that threatened to overtake him.

Don't stop, he told himself. Don't think. Just go.

And keep going. Head down, knees clamped tight, eyes focused on the center line of the road. The pavement unfolded in front of him in waves, gullies and hills, peaks and valleys rippling under the beam of the headlamp.

At some point, he no longer saw the road, or heard the scream of the engine, or felt the cool press of air against him. He was riding in a vacuum, cut free from space and time as he plummeted into the nebulous haze of the Opelika city lights a couple of miles ahead of him.

Falling. That's what he was doing. Into the gravity well of a diffuse sun.

In the fall, she would enter her first year of veterinary school at Auburn. She had always loved animals. Birds and cats were her favorite. She owned a parakeet named Campbell, and a cat named Ayane. Both hated him. He was better with dogs. But a dog needed more space than she had at the apartment. A dog would have to wait.

Like him. He would have to wait. For what, he wasn't sure. It wasn't clear. He suspected that Tenley herself wasn't sure. She was just buying time, putting off as many life decisions as she could.

He didn't want to be a life decision. She had made him that.

He just wanted to be with her, the way he had when his grandmother died. He didn't care about the future. The future could wait. He was simply trying to outdistance the past.

But it kept catching up to him. Anytime he paused, anytime he got comfortable, it found him. He would hear his grandmother's music, the music she was listening to the day she died. It was as if the clock radio next to her bed was embedded inside his head. Every now and then, for no reason, something jarred it and the music crackled to life, as loud and unintelligible as it had been the day he found her.

And he would panic, start running again. If there was no place to run to, the music brought him to a dead stop. He stopped going to classes. Stopped eating. Stopped taking showers.

Soon the photosphere of the town engulfed him. Streetlights burned his arms and the back of his neck.

Tenley's apartment was on the second floor. A light shown through the yellow curtain drawn across her living room. He was afraid that she wouldn't be home, that she had gone out with friends.

Or left completely, without telling him. No forwarding address. That was his big fear. That he'd never see her again.

Anything, no matter how small or fleeting, was better than nothing.

He sprinted up the stairs two at a time, afraid that if he took them any slower he would lose momentum. He wouldn't have enough energy to make it all the way to the top and he would fall to earth, sink back into the lightless depths of his depression.

At the door, he composed himself. He could hear voices inside, muffled, followed by laughter.

He knocked. Knocked again. Finally the door opened. Light, music, conversation spilled out, along with Tenley.

Her face opened in surprise, catching the glare from the

streetlights in the parking lot. Just as quickly it closed. The petals of her lips curled shut, her nostrils tightened, and the corners of her eyes sharpened.

"I need to talk to you," he said. It came out half gasp, half sob.

"Rudi . . ."

"It's important." His hands bunched.

"Rudi." She forced patience. Self-control—she was good at it. She had to be, in order to survive. He'd taught her, but she'd never taught him. He hadn't learned a thing from her.

"Please?" he said.

"I can't. Not now. I'm busy." She stood in the doorway, keeping him from going into the apartment. But also blocking him from view.

"Later," she said.

There would be no later. The steadiness in her face and voice gave her away. She always became expressionless when she lied. If he was going to talk to her, it would have to be now.

"No." He pushed past her.

A young man sat on the couch. The two of them had been watching a movie, While You Were Sleeping. *He'd paused it while she answered the door, freezing Sandra Bullock on the screen.*

Pictures of animals, clipped from out-of-date calendars, were tacked to the walls of the apartment. Textbooks covered the kitchen table. Ayane's cat condo still stood in one corner, claw marks scoring the exposed particleboard under the tattered carpet. He didn't see any of the stuffed animals Tenley normally kept around the apartment. They had been moved out of sight, probably onto her bed. The bedroom door was tightly closed, the menagerie of circus animals—lions, bears, giraffes—locked up in their cage.

A half-dozen spirit bottles decorated the room. One hung from the curtain rod over the room's only window. Another dangled from a hook screwed into the ceiling. She had used clear fishing line instead of string to hang the bottles, and they appeared to float in the air, defying gravity as they twirled and swayed in the breeze that wafted through the partly open door behind him.

Tenley had taken up knitting since he had last seen her. A pair of circular needles and a skein of black yarn sat on one of the cushions, joined in what appeared to be the rim of a wool cap. More yarn peeked from a bag under the coffee table.

The young man stood up to face him, all bravado, the remote clutched in his hand, a kind of weapon.

"Don't," Rudi warned. He pushed back the long sleeves of his shirt, exposing the road map of scars and cigarette burns on his wrists.

The parakeet fluttered nervously, despite the towel covering the cage. The cat was nowhere in sight. Evidently, it didn't like the new guy any better than him. Rudi smiled in satisfaction.

"Leave him alone." Tenley's voice knotted hard and tight, leaving the words bloodless and white with fury. "Leave me alone."

"All I want is a few minutes," Rudi said. "Then I'll go. I promise."

"That's what you always say."

"What's going on?" the young man asked.

"It's okay, Dylan."

"You sure?"

"Yeah. No problem."

Another student. Rudi recognized the type. He guessed that the young man was someone she'd met at a summer class while he recovered in the hospital.

"We went to school together," Tenley said.

"Yeah?" Dylan asked, laid-back but hoping for more information.

"When we were kids," Tenley said. No big deal, *her tone*

implied. It had the desired effect. Dylan relaxed and nodded in understanding. Rudi and Tenley were childhood friends. More like brother and sister. There was no need to feel threatened.

Tenley turned to the dude. "I'm sorry."

He offered a gallant shrug. "S'okay. I understand." With a sweep of one hand he combed the bangs from his forehead.

"Maybe you could go get some KFC?" she said.

"Sure." Dylan grinned. He was coming back. They were going to unfreeze Sandra Bullock and pick up where they'd left off. He still had a chance.

"All right," Tenley said when he was gone. She turned to Rudi, folded her arms, and tapped her tongue against the back of her teeth, counting out seconds.

Rudi listened to the roar of a muscle car rumbling out of the parking lot. Heat lightning flashed behind his eyes.

"Well," Tenley said. She shifted her weight, as if trying to decide between pity, anger, or something else neither of them could put a finger on. "What's so important?"

The polis had become strangely unfamiliar. Olavo had built it, conceived it at the level of blueprints, and assembled it from the ground up, one molecule at a time, until it was self-sufficient enough to support the first generation of simunculi to emerge from the parthenosynthesis tanks. But for all of the ways in which the polis had followed the design space plan, it had diverged/deviated in thousands more. Streets had been walled off, new levels added, reconfigured, or eliminated entirely. The polis was changing. If Olavo didn't change with it, he would be left behind—alienated, outcast.

From the tourist/restaurant level of the Pink Flamenco, he took one of the platform elevators down several floors to the commercial sector of the city, a three-level sprawl of multitiered malls, shopette-lined streets, and glass-walled gallerias that looked out on the hanging gardens in this part of the lightwell.

He started with the expensive interior gallerias and worked his way outward, through the enclosed shopping centers, modular shops, and mobile kiosks to the exposed outer terraces of each level.

Mee Won liked to lose herself here, in the makeshift bazaars, the flea market labyrinth of open-air stalls that spilled out onto these sections of the polis. Olavo missed the original public space the terraces had provided—the little parks, koi ponds, fountains, and walkways he had planned. Unlike Mee Won, he took little comfort in the anonymous bustle of shoppers . . . the endless rows of garment racks, bolts of programmable linen, and self-cleaning footwear. There was no pleasure, no sense of delight, in the sample fabrics that condensed out of the air, assembled on his hand or arm, then evaporated just as quickly and capriciously as they had formed, leaving a dataddress for the vendor/seller. For some reason, Mee Won enjoyed these sensory bon mots. The unexpected shudder of a new taste on her tongue, scent in her hair, or lotion on her fingers.

"They make me forget myself," she'd explained once. "I don't have to think about stuff."

"What stuff?"

She rolled her eyes, bubblegum pink under the LED fixture in her room and sticky with sarcasm. "You know."

Her job selling shoes; how broke she always was; how utterly pointless school had become. But what she wanted to forget, or leave behind, he wanted to fix.

If she had taken refuge, it was someplace unknown to him. He hit her usual shops, but no one had seen her.

"She hasn't been by in a while," an old gnowomen seamstress told him. "Not since the burst fried us." Intaglio patterns on her face lit up as she smiled, pulsing with the fiber optics she'd embroidered into her skin.

"Did she tell you where she might have gone?" he asked a gaunt night waif dotted with multicolored gems.

"I'm afraid," the girl said. Her eyes were mercurochrome pink behind coin-sized lenses, her teeth the color of tar.

"Afraid to tell me?" he said.

The girl shook her head, blue beads glinting on her lips. She seemed disappointed. In who, he wasn't sure.

"I'm worried about her," Olavo said, one level down, where the market consisted primarily of services rather than goods. He could have the salt concentration in his tears balanced, the veins on his eyes read, his sense of taste adjusted.

"I don't know what to tell you," a teenage doughman who hawked holograms said. Bone-white dice, faceted, engraved with red Chinese characters, rolled inside the orbs of his eyes.

"She was confused," Olavo said. "Scared."

The kid smiled, lapsed into the street patois of the doughman. "We're all confused. Scared. After the burst, changing. Forgetting. Becoming into someone else. All risking, chance taking."

"You're saying... what? She can't remember who she is, or she's trying to find out who she is?"

"Self losing," the kid said. The dice in his eyes tumbled again, revealing a different pair of characters. "Away running."

"Running where?"

The kid said nothing. The dice danced, taunting Olavo with endless possibilities.

25

Eugene, October 4

Rudi considered the situation. The man had knocked before Linnea, if that's who the woman was, let him into the mobile home. That meant he didn't live there. Otherwise, he would have opened the door and let himself in. He was a visitor, and sooner or later he would leave. When that happened, Rudi wanted to be ready.

Rudi removed the ball of yarn from his baseball cap. He snugged the cap onto his head, opened the glove box, took out the get well card, then locked the ball of yarn in the compartment.

The light at the right end of the trailer winked out. Another light winked on in the middle of the trailer. A red square glowed in the darkness.

Rudi stepped from the van onto loose gravel, then gently leaned against the door to close it behind him.

The night was quiet, cool. Crickets chirped. They fell silent as he made his way across the street. The chirping resumed as soon as he reached the driveway.

The red glow from the aluminum frame window came

from a wrinkled bedsheet hung behind it. The fabric was thin, the glass dirty.

He followed the path beaten into the dead leaves to the porch, but instead of taking the steps, he worked his way past them through waist-high grass and weeds to the end of the trailer.

The mobile home sat at the base of a gentle grade clogged with undergrowth and debris. Old tires, a rusted box spring, and several pieces of rubbish-infested cinder block huddled in the light from the small window a couple feet above his head. New Age music leaked from the window. Soothing, meditative, flutelike.

Rudi dragged one of the tires next to the trailer. Water sloshed inside the rubber, forlorn and hollow. He stacked a second tire on the first. Standing on his toes on the tires, Rudi peered through the window. He could just see into the darkened kitchen.

Beyond it, through an open doorway, he could see the man and the woman in the living room. The man lay on his back on the floor, his flannel shirt crumpled in a heap on the couch shoved against the back wall. The woman had on a nightgown. Rudi could see her silhouette through the sheer fabric, the curve of her hips, buttocks, and breasts when she squatted next to the man.

Her hair fell forward, concealing the side of her face. She opened a small leather pouch she was holding, reached in, and pulled something out.

A stone. Green.

She set it in the center of the man's chest. He inhaled deeply, ribs expanding and collapsing. The woman took another stone from the pouch. This stone was red. She set the stone on the man's navel. Each time she moved the nightgown drew tight against her skin and tattoos bloomed on the fabric.

Angel wings.

Rudi remembered the night she'd gotten them...

Linnea was watching something called Headbanger's Ball. *Crushing chords spilled from the TV, down the hallway to his grandmother's room, where Rudi had taken refuge.*

It was close to midnight. Linnea had invited a friend over. Rudi didn't know if the dude would spend the night or not. Sometimes her boyfriends did, and sometimes they didn't. He would know if he heard yelling. Or crying.

Rudi's grandmother sat in the chair next to her bed, humming to the music coming from the radio and knitting. Years ago, before his mother left, his grandmother had done needlepoint. She still had some of them on the wall. Landscapes and still lifes, mostly. Bethlehem at night, under desert palms and a single bright star. Daisies, bursting from a blue vase in yellow fireworks.

The music was harsh, his grandmother's humming tuneless. Every now and then she sang one of the lyrics, as if suddenly remembering the words, or reminded of how to pronounce them.

"What are you making?" Rudi asked.

"It's called a spencer," his grandmother replied.

Rudi wrinkled his nose. The beat of the heavy metal brought with it the stench of cigarettes. One night, a few months earlier, his grandmother had lost her sense of smell. The loss happened suddenly. That part of her mind hadn't woken up with the rest of her when she got up in the morning.

Over the past month, more little deaths had followed. Her eyesight started to fail. Then her words began to slur.

"She's getting worse," Linnea said one afternoon, when their grandmother was taking a nap. The corners of her mouth tightened, then turned down, the way they always did when she needed to face something unpleasant.

"Grandma will be okay," Rudi said. "She's just tired."

Linnea shook her head. "We should get her into assisted living. That's what some people I know did. Before it's too late."

"We can take care of her."

"No. We can't." Linnea spoke slowly, sharpening each word. "Not the way she needs. No way I'm cleaning up after her."

Rudi thought about what Linnea had said while he watched the stitches assemble into rows and a pattern of interweaved cables. "What's a spencer?" he asked.

"A small jacket."

"For who?"

"Linnea."

"How come all I get are socks?"

"Because you don't like the sweaters I make you."

"They're scratchy. They make me itch." And they never fit right. He felt like a retard whenever he wore them to school.

The knitting needles flashed. In the low light, they looked like an extra finger on each hand.

Like a spider weaving a web, he thought. His grandmother was trying to prevent Linnea from leaving. The yarn would snare her.

Suddenly, he had to pee.

"No television," his grandmother said.

"I won't."

He went down the hall to the bathroom. The smell of cigarettes was stronger. In the living room, he heard a muffled cry as the song ended.

Rudi crept to where he could see what was going on. Linnea was on her knees in front of the couch, her face buried in the cushions. She didn't have a blouse on. The man knelt behind her, hunched over her naked back. She moved against him. He pressed her into the cushions, hard. She moaned. Then the man straightened, pulling back from her, and stood.

Rudi blinked. A new tattoo of raw, black-feathered wings

bloodied her back. He eased away, but not before Linnea opened her eyes and caught him staring.

He fled down the hall. His grandmother had dozed off. So he went into his room and shut the door.

Half an hour later, Linnea knocked on the door, then let herself in. Rudi couldn't look at her. It was too painful.

Linnea sat on the side of the bed. "I'm all right," she said. "It looks worse than it is."

"He hurt you."

"No."

"Then why were you crying?"

"It's hard to explain."

"I saw him . . ." His voice broke.

"What?

Rudi curled harder around himself. He could smell beer on her breath. "Nothing."

"It's not what you think," she said. "Geoff doesn't like girls. That's why I go to him. He's safe."

"Then what was he doing?"

Her hand touched his shoulder, smoothed the hair around one ear. "Rubbing vitamin E on the tattoo, to help it heal faster. So it doesn't get infected."

Rudi could always tell when she was lying. He could see in her eyes that she had paid for the tattoo without money. He swallowed a thick glob of mucus. It didn't matter, he told himself. It didn't change who she was.

"So why do it?" he asked. "If it hurts, I mean."

She sighed. "Sometimes, you have to do things you don't want, to get what you want. You have to make sacrifices."

"What do you want?"

"To get out of here." The hand fluttered from his shoulder. "Away from all this. The wings will help me do that."

Rudi sniffed. "They can't make you fly."

"Yes, they can. Inside."

Rudi still couldn't look at her. He stared at the wall. Licked his lips. Tasted salt.

"I can take you with me, if you want," she said. "I won't leave you. Like Mom. I promise."

"When are you going?"

"Soon. I'm almost ready. I've been saving up. I have enough for both of us for a while."

"Where?"

"As far away from here as we can get. Seattle maybe. Or San Francisco. That's where Grandma used to live."

"We could take her with us," Rudi said hopefully.

"She'll never make it. She's too old."

"Do you have to leave?"

"Yes. So do you."

"No." His grandmother needed him. She'd looked after him. Now it was his turn to look after her. It was only fair. Who else would make her tea in the morning, if not him? Do the laundry? Go shopping? Especially if Linnea wasn't going to be around anymore.

Linnea's hand returned to his shoulder. She squeezed him. "You have to change," she said. "Grow up."

"Adapt," he said.

"It's the only way to survive," she said. "You know that. You're smart. I've seen the crap you read."

"I can change the environment," he said. "Make it better." For all of them. Then none of them would have to leave.

"You can't," Linnea said. "Not the way you want. You're not old enough. The only way to change things is to move. Go someplace else."

"We could try to change things."

"I already have. It won't work. I know."

Rudi thought of the spots of blood welling up on her back. "Would I have to get wings?"

"No." He felt her shake her head. "Mine are enough for both of us. I can carry you with me. Up, up, and away."

The weight of her hand on his shoulder lifted.

"Look at me," she said.

He shook his head.

"I'm totally fine," she said, "really. Come on." She tugged gently on him, urging him to uncurl.

He rolled onto his back, and looked up at her. She had put on her blouse. It was white in the light from the doorway. She smiled down at him with forced optimism, her mouth an exaggerated grin, pushing aside all doubt, shoving it to the corners of her face, where it would be less noticeable.

"What if the wings aren't enough?" he said.

"They will be."

"How do you know?"

"Don't worry. I have it all planned out." She stood. "Now go to sleep. I'm going to check on Grandma. Okay?"

She turned and walked to the door. Rudi looked for the wings, but he couldn't see them. There was no blood on the fabric. Linnea shut the door behind her, leaving it open a crack the way he always did, so he could listen to his sister and his grandmother breathing while they slept and know they were still there... that they hadn't left.

The man on the floor was older than Rudi first thought. The hair on his head was gray and thinning. His skin was wrinkled and slack over thin coat-hanger shoulders and a large paunch.

Not a boyfriend, Rudi thought. Someone who came to her for... what?

Rudi stared at the stones arranged on the man's torso, trying to make sense of the pattern they made. A white stone sat in the middle of his forehead. A purple gem sealed his lips. The green rock sat in the center of his chest.

The last stone was black. When she placed it a few inches below his belly button, the man trembled.

Linnea touched her fingers to his eyes, closing them. Then she unzipped his pants and straddled him.

Rudi stepped down from the tires. He staggered, placed one hand against the wall to steady himself, and forced slow breaths. It was none of his business. Who was he to judge? They'd both changed, in ways neither of them expected. He'd made his share of mistakes. He would make more.

He took the card from his shirt pocket and studied it. "With our mind, we make the world."

That was who she wanted to be, not who she was. The wings hadn't worked after all. She was still trying to escape the gravity of the past. But she was trapped in the well, unable to find the strength or direction to climb out.

Rudi climbed back onto the tires.

Linnea was no longer straddling the man. She was removing the stones, replacing them in the leather pouch. When she finished, the man stood. He retrieved his shirt from the sofa, pulled it on, and took out his wallet.

Rudi lowered his head and shut his eyes. He sank to his haunches on the tires, his back propped against the wall. After a few minutes, the door opened. There was a brief pause, whispered words. Then the door closed. A minute later the ignition squealed, the transmission thunked, and the Subaru coughed down the drive.

Rudi traced the flower on the front of the card. Then he slid it back in his shirt pocket, climbed down from the tires, and went up the leaf-covered steps to the screened door.

Linnea answered on the third knock. A breath of incense exhaled from the trailer. She had pulled on jeans and a sweatshirt.

"You're early," she said. "I said seven. I'm not ready yet. Come back in half an hour."

She started to close the door.

"Linnea?"

Her gaze hardened. "Who the hell are you? What do you want?"

A moth fluttered around the bare, fly-specked porch light, its wings cobwebbed and incandescent. He took the cap from his head, and the light scraped the shadow it cast from his face.

"Rudi?" She slumped against the doorframe and brushed back coiled tangles of hair. "Jesus. I thought you were still in a coma. Or dead. When I didn't hear back..." Her gaze skittered to the scars on his wrists and arms.

"It's all right," he said, "I'm okay." He smiled, returning the encouragement she'd given him, all those years ago. "Can I come in?" he asked.

26

San Francisco, Circa 1937

Benjamin walked in a fog down Van Ness Avenue.

The conversation with Peter had left him rattled. He felt disoriented. When he looked around, the streets were unfamiliar. They belonged to a different city, one that had been there all along, but which he had never visited. He seemed to be seeing this other city for the first time. It was much larger than the one he normally inhabited, filled with a maze of blind alleys populated by strange denizens. He came across a one-armed dwarf dressed in a tuxedo and a top hat.

"You're not from around here," the man observed.

Benjamin turned in a wide circle, searching for a street sign, couldn't find one, and staggered to keep from falling. "Where am I?"

"Go back," the man said. He produced a black iron-tipped cane with a gold handle and pointed it at Benjamin's chest. "You don't belong here, you're not one of us anymore."

"Go back where?" Benjamin asked.

But the little man lowered the cane and hurried on, tapping the cane on the cobbled street. Down another alley he encountered a tall albino woman dressed in a green kimono.

She had stick-thin arms, long white hair, and the pink furtive eyes of a rabbit.

"Lost," the woman hissed, managing to convey both sadness and resignation.

Before Benjamin could question her, she vanished from view, engulfed by a smoke-thick swirl of fog. Was this what Madame Grurie meant by waking up? Had he been sleepwalking all these years, unaware of the larger world around him? Had his perception been that narrow, that limited? Or was he simply hallucinating? None of this existed, except as a delusion.

He passed the baby-faced man he'd glimpsed at Madame Grurie's the other night. "Who are you?" Benjamin asked.

The man grinned. Chinese characters flashed in his eyes.

"Where are you from?"

A throaty laugh blubbered out of the man, hysterical, leaving a bubble of saliva on one corner of his mouth.

Perhaps the tumor was the source of the illusions. It contained them, the way his mind contained his thoughts and dreams. As it grew, it imposed itself on him. Over time, the tumor would replace his thoughts with other thoughts. He would become someone else.

An old woman dressed in black peered out of the fog. When Benjamin reached for her, she backed away on bowed legs.

Benjamin pressed his hands to his head. It wasn't a headache he had been feeling, but labor pains—the tumor growing inside the womb of his skull.

When it was born, would he die? Or would it continue to suckle at him, like a baby, feeding on the milk of his mind? At what point would he lose control? Would he know when it took over? Or, like an old man, would he simply sink into dementia and cease to exist?

A foghorn blared on the bay, long and deep, rising whale-like out of the depths of the mist.

What if Peter was right about Madame Grurie? Even if she couldn't save him as promised, did it matter? He was going to die, regardless, sooner rather than later. If she could help Etta and others cope, what difference did it make? Was the salvation promised by the Bible any more real? Just because people had believed in something for thousands of years didn't make it any more true. There was no guarantee that the Bible itself hadn't been assembled by charlatans, church leaders motivated by politics, wealth, and power.

Did their self-interest invalidate the teachings of Jesus? Several years ago he had come across a priest who no longer believed but continued to say Mass, continued to go through the motions of ritual. Did that make him a charlatan? Did his dishonesty invalidate the Gospels?

If there was truth in what Madame Grurie taught, that truth would remain whether she believed in it herself or not. The teachings didn't come from her. She was just using them.

I have nothing to lose, Benjamin thought.

The foghorn blared again, louder. A siren call. He had been drawn to it—following it unconsciously. The houses lining the street seemed familiar. He glanced around, craning his head. Overhead, a hole had opened up in the fog, like an expanding smoke ring from invisible lips. Stars shown in the puckered O, needle sharp.

He stood outside Zachary and Etta's house. Why? What in God's name had led him here? Had he come to question her? Or warn her? How much did she really know about Madame Grurie?

The house was unlit. Etta was either asleep or not yet home. He stared at the dark interior, disappointed that he wouldn't even catch a glimpse of her through the window.

Was that enough at this point—simply to see her? What was it about her that attracted him, like a moth to flame? Was he dreaming the light she offered? Could she really lead him out of the murk? Or was the light dreaming him?

It felt like that lately, as if he existed to complete Etta. No doubt he was projecting his own wishes and desires on her. In order to feel alive—real—Benjamin needed her to need him. Otherwise, if he ceased to matter, he would vanish, swallowed by the fog.

He should go home, he could find his way now. It was getting late. His temples ached. If he stayed out much longer, he was going to catch his death. He shivered, suddenly chilled. The fog had saturated his clothes. His hair was plastered to his scalp. Moisture dripped down his back. The night itself seemed to be perspiring, gripped by a cold sweat. He mopped his forehead with the sleeve of his jacket.

Just as he turned, a light came on in the front room. A shadow flitted behind the drapes.

Then the front door at the top of the steps opened a crack.

"Zachary?" Etta said. "Is that you?"

Benjamin thrust his hands into his pockets and hunched his shoulders against the chill and embarrassment. "It's me."

"Benjamin?" Trepidation, neatly folded, creased her voice. "What are you doing here?"

"I was out. Walking."

"Walking where?"

He shrugged. Nowhere. Everywhere.

"You followed me," Etta said. "Didn't you? To find out what happened tonight. What I saw, or didn't see."

He hunkered deeper into his shame. "I'm sorry."

"It's all right." She stood framed in the doorway, as if painted there by Vermeer, luminous yet forlorn, her lips glossed with candlelight, right cheek smudged with gloom. "You're shivering. Would you like some tea?"

He rubbed his arms. "Where's Zachary?"

"Working late, I assume. He doesn't tell me what he does or where he goes, and I don't ask. It's better for both of us."

"You don't want to know?"

"No." She shook her head. "If that's what you're here to tell me, I don't want to hear it."

"He doesn't tell me, either."

"But you can guess. We both can."

In the past month his former partner had taken to visiting certain establishments in the evening, now that Etta was incapacitated. It was hardly fair to her, but Zachary argued that it was better than leaving her, or having her committed. At least she still had a place where she could go and be alone, if that's what she wanted.

"I should go," Benjamin told her. It was a mistake to have come. It would be an even worse mistake to stay.

"Are you worried someone will see us?"

"It's late."

"I'm not. Worried, that is. People already think the worst of me. They expect me to be indiscreet. It's a side effect of my *condition*." The door eased wider, a passageway through the leviathan darkness.

"How's your head?" Etta asked. She touched him lightly on the shoulder, letting her fingers rest on the shawl she'd draped over him before setting the water to boil.

Benjamin stopped massaging his brow and looked up at her. The wool smelled of sandalwood, her fingers of lavender. With each heartbeat, his vision shook. "About the same."

"I'm sorry." She withdrew her hand and filled the fluted cup in front of him from a dainty teapot.

"I talked to Peter," he told her. "Earlier tonight."

She set the kettle on the stove and joined him at the table. "About the séance?"

"He says Madame Grurie is a fake."

"I'm not surprised." She spooned sugar into her tea and stirred. Silver clinked against the china, each tap a nail in his eardrums.

"Why do you say that?"

"She probably is."

It wasn't the answer Benjamin had expected. To cover his surprise, he picked up his cup and sipped.

Etta took the seat across from him. "I'm not a fool. It might look like it, but I'm not." She took her teacup from the saucer. "I know when the wool's being pulled over my eyes."

"Is it?" He cradled the cup in both hands, letting the warmth make its way into him through his palms.

Etta pursed her lips, not quite touching the gold-leaf rim of the cup. "Yes, and no."

"You're not sure?"

"I'm sure she's using me. Us. But there's something out there, too."

"What you told me about before?" Benjamin recalled her fingertips on the napkin.

"I don't know." She stared in consternation at her tea, brows knitted. "It's hard to explain."

"I saw someone," he said. "Felt something touch me. Not from the outside. But from the inside."

Etta nodded. "Zachary believes it's my imagination. He says whatever I experience—what any of us see or feel—isn't real."

"Then why did he recommend her to me?"

"According to him, imaginary problems require imaginary fixes."

Benjamin snorted. "It's nice to know where I stand."

She smiled. "Isn't it."

"Christ." Benjamin set his elbows on the table then clasped his hands around the back of his neck, threading his fingers together. "Peter says he's a reporter," he finally said.

"He's out to get her?"

Benjamin nodded and wrenched his mouth to one side. "He wants me to spy for him. Tell him what's going on."

"What do you want?" she said.

I want my old life back, he thought, but that wasn't true anymore. It would have been a few days ago.

"I don't want to go back," he said.

"But you don't know where you want to go."

"I don't think I have much time left," he said.

"Don't say that!"

"It's true." Like it or not.

Etta folded her hands in front of her. She had beautiful fingers, delicate as flower stems, but the nails were bitten. As if insects had been chewing on her.

"What do you think?" he said. "Really?"

Her hands twisted, then stilled. "I think there are forces in the world—perhaps in ourselves—that we don't yet fully understand. That doesn't mean they aren't real, and it doesn't mean that Madame Grurie is a charlatan."

"You're saying she doesn't understand, either."

"She's pretending to understand."

Which was different from simply pretending.

"She's interpreting things in a certain way," Etta said. "That doesn't mean there aren't other interpretations for the same phenomena."

"Such as?"

Etta thought for a moment. "When we first talked, she told me that we were all shadows of a more complex image."

"A simplification," Benjamin said. "Like a shadow of an object projected onto a wall."

"Right. But what if it's the other way around?" she said.

Benjamin waited for her to explain.

"What if we're the complex manifestation of something simpler? A solid object projected into the world from a flat surface, like a movie screen."

"Heaven?"

"If that's true, then God, the angels, and even the devil are illusions. We are the embodiment of them."

"You're saying they're the shadows? Not us?"

"Sort of." Etta blew on her tea. "Except we wouldn't exist without them. We're the form they take in the physical world."

"So you believe we're the higher dimension," Benjamin said. "Less than God and the angels—because they come together to create us—but at the same time greater."

"Right. And when one of those aspects in us gets sick, we have to find a way to heal it." She looked up from her tea. "Otherwise we start to disembody. We become less solid, less in touch with reality, as each of the lower-dimension aspects in us goes back to being a shadow . . . and we die."

27

Orthinia, Design Space

Vania left Olavo and his visitor alone, allowing them to speak in private.

"I'm sorry I didn't come earlier," the woman said. Apologetic, observing him for cues, she stood uncertainly beside the desk. The office and the desk might be hers, but then again maybe not. She looked even more uneasy than he felt in the unfamiliar room.

Olavo shrugged, affecting nonchalance to cover his own distress. He had seen her before, somewhere. He should know her, but couldn't place her. She was part of his life, or had been at one time . . . the surface expression of something deeper and more extensive.

"I would have come sooner." Wrestling with what to tell him. Some lame excuse or another. "But—"

"That's okay." He waved a hand. "Don't worry about it."

"You don't know who I am, do you?" she said. Pain shadowed her eyes. "You don't remember."

So he hadn't been able to hide his lack of recognition, after all. Either that, or she had access to thoughts of his that were beyond him.

"Tenley," she said. "Does that name ring a bell?"

He stared at the mixture of hope and fear twisted in her fingers. "You're not real," he said. "Are you? You're not really here."

Her expression crumpled, but quickly recovered. "That depends on what you mean by here."

"You're a memory," he said.

"I came," she said. "Didn't I? That's all that matters."

"Fine," he said. "Now that you're here, what do you want?"

She gathered herself, straightening the sleeves of her white cotton blouse, the cuffs of which had crept up her tanned and lightly freckled wrists. A delicate silver cross hung from her neck.

"So"—the woman took a deep breath—"how are you doing? Are they treating you all right?"

"How do I look?" he said.

"Good." She ignored the white armor-clad arms he held up and smiled through her apprehension. "Better than I expected."

He lowered his arms. "What did you expect?"

She fingered the cross. "I wasn't sure. That's one of the reasons I wanted to come. Not knowing was worse than knowing."

"Tell me about it." He walked to the window and looked out at the cloud-scabbed sky.

Tenley joined him, as if this would bring them closer, make it easier for them to talk. "I also wanted to tell you how sorry I am. I can't imagine how you must feel. This must be a nightmare for you. But at least you're alive."

"Am I?" Olavo still wasn't convinced. "I guess it all depends on what you mean by alive."

She winced. "It might not seem all that great right now, but it is."

"For who?"

"You. Everyone. You, most of all."

"Is that what you want to talk about? You're afraid I'll try to kill myself again?" He indicated the mountains. "Try to put an end to this."

"Do you want to?"

"Sometimes."

Olavo turned his attention from the mountains to the potted plants in the room, half expecting an insect to emerge from the foliage. Her gaze tracked him. "Are you going to update me?" he said.

"Update you?"

"You know. Give me something to make me feel better. To help me *cope* with the situation."

"I brought you a present," she said.

She went back to the desk. There, she bent over and picked up a paper bag from the floor. She set the bag on the desk, opened it, and took out a brown-tinted bottle, which she held up to the light. "Do you recognize it?" she asked, hopefully.

"Should I?"

"Here," she said.

She held out the bottle. Small clear bubbles were trapped in the glass, like the expectation on her face, wavy, riddled with imperfections.

"What's it for?" he asked.

"Lots of things," she said.

Flowers, he thought. Decoration. "Where did you get it?"

"I've had it for a while."

"What am I supposed to do with it?"

"Whatever you want. It's up to you."

"I don't want it." He had no use for it. "Thanks, anyway."

"Rudi . . ."

The name struck him, ruler-sharp. He stiffened. "Don't..."

"Rudi—"

"I'm not..." He balled his hands into fists.

Apprehension trembled on her lower lip. "I can see that. Not anymore. But you were. At one time."

"In a different design space?" he said.

"Yes."

"Rudi?"

The voice came from the shoulder of the road next to the drainage ditch. He glanced over his shoulder, shading his eyes against the mottled afternoon glare slanting through the sycamore trees.

"It's me." A girl on a bike waved, her blue dress flapping in the breeze.

Rudi returned his attention to the muddy bank of the ditch. If he ignored her, if he pretended he hadn't heard her or that he was somebody else, maybe she would go away and leave him alone. It took him a moment to relocate the small frog he'd been trying to catch. It hadn't moved, but it was well-concealed among the twigs and trash.

As he reached for the frog it hopped out of his grasp, heading toward a shopping cart poking up out of the water. He crept after it, past a half-buried tire, mud oozing up around the soles of his shoes. Behind him grass rustled, snagging in spokes and whispering against metal.

"Rudi?"

He heard her set her bike down in the grass higher on the bank. His hand cupped over the frog, trapping it, and he could feel it squirming against the cage of his fingers.

"What are you doing here?"

Rudi stood. He held out his hand. The frog's frantic efforts to escape tickled his palm. He grinned.

Tenley made her way toward him, picking through the quagmire of puddles and garbage. "What is it?"

"Look." He loosened his grip so she could peer through his fingers.

Her nose wrinkled. "What are you going to do with it?"

"Take it home."

She straightened, her expression serious. "You said you were going to visit. After you moved."

"Yeah, well." An insect whined near his ear. He swiped at it with his empty hand.

"I looked for you," she said. "At school."

"They put me with a foster family. I'm going to a different school now."

"You still could have come by."

He shook his head. She didn't understand. Between his social worker, court appearances, and therapist, there hadn't been time. He hadn't been able to do anything he wanted the last six months. Everything had been decided for him, every minute of his day scheduled.

"I'm sorry," Tenley said. "About your grandmother."

"Me, too."

"She was nice. I miss her. I bet you do, too."

"I'm used to it."

"What about your sister? Is she in a foster home, too?"

"I don't know."

"You don't?"

"I haven't seen her. I don't know where she is."

"She hasn't called?"

"I think she's afraid of getting caught and maybe ending up in jail. Like my mom."

"I thought you didn't know what happened to your mom."

"Where else would she be?"

Tenley was silent, unwilling to speculate. Her fingers picked at the white lace fringing the buttonholes of her dress. "So where do you live?"

He jutted his chin down the road. "Over by Denny's."

She smoothed the front of her dress, ironing the wrinkles with flat palms. "How is it? Are they nice?"

"They're all right. They have a dog."

Her face, already sticky with heat, brightened. "What kind?"

"A beagle, I think. It's pretty small." The dog, named Daytona, had the nasty habit of humping his leg.

"I want a cat," Tenley said. "But my dad hates cats. He says all they do is fight and claw things."

Pouting made her look older, more grown-up. She would be thirteen soon. Her posture seemed straighter, her chin higher. The pigtails from a couple of years ago were gone, replaced by shoulder-length hair that framed her face. A silver cross, bright as a new filling, glinted on her collarbone. Her parents were churchgoers. He imagined her flossing her thoughts with prayers every night before she went to bed, cleaning them of anything unpleasant that had gotten stuck there during the day. No nightmares for Tenley. Her thoughts were pure, her dreams as sweet and fluffy as cotton candy.

"Some people moved into your old house," she said.

Rudi's stomach pinched. He hadn't been back to look at the place. He'd avoided going past it on the way to the 7-Eleven. He didn't want to see anybody else living there. He wanted to remember it the way it had been.

"They're all right," Tenley said. "Except for Justin. He keeps throwing rocks at my mom's spirit bottles. He's broken three already."

"I bet your mom's pissed," he said, relieved they'd moved on to another subject.

"Yeah. If it happens again, she's going to call the police."

Rudi nodded. "Where's Mr. Chin?" he asked.

"Who?"

"The man who worked at the 7-Eleven."

"The one who used to give you magazines?"

Rudi nodded. The reason he'd come to this part of town was to visit Mr. Chin and see if he'd saved any copies of Science News, Discover, *or* ION. *Before coming to the ditch, he'd stopped by the 7-Eleven. Through the glass door, he thought he'd seen Mr. Chin working the counter. But there was a long line of customers, and Rudi decided to wait until things slowed down before going in.*

Just as he was turning away from the door, Rudi heard Mr. Chin's voice in his head. "You have a good spirit looking after you."

"What kind of spirit?" Rudi said.

"Ancestor," Mr. Chin said. "Someone from your past who has come back to guide you."

Except for his grandmother, Rudi didn't know who any of his ancestors were.

"They know you," Mr. Chin said. "I'm sure this spirit has much wisdom. All you have to do is listen. Keep your ears and your heart open, and when you are ready to hear, you will."

Rudi hung out until the last of the customers had left the store. But when he went in, Mr. Chin wasn't there. In his place was an acne-scarred teenager who had never heard of Mr. Chin and told him to get lost.

"Mr. Chin hasn't been there for a long time," Tenley said. "Three or four months."

"How come?"

"The store got robbed. He was in the hospital for a while. When he got better, he didn't come back."

"Oh." Rudi let his gaze slide past her.

"Stop it!" Tenley said, her voice sharp as glass.

"What?" His gaze panned back to her.

"Squeezing the frog." Her eyes had widened, distraught. "You're going to hurt it, if you don't quit."

Rudi followed her gaze to his hand. His fingers were clenched tight. He could no longer feel the frog breathing. With an effort, he forced his fingers to uncurl. The frog's eyes were dull. The body felt rubbery, slack against his palm.

"You killed it," Tenley said.

The accusation in her voice sucked the air from his chest. He shook his head no.

"It's not moving," she said.

He prodded the frog with his thumb. "It was an accident."

"No, it wasn't. You're mad about what happened to you, so you have to hurt other people or animals. Like Justin. He burns bugs with a magnifying glass. It's disgusting."

"It was an accident," he repeated.

"I don't believe you." She turned and climbed up the side of the ditch to where she had left her bike.

"Wait." He scrambled after her, the frog still clutched in his hand.

Tenley watched him, observing his reaction to the bottle and the scrap of attached memory.

"Stop it!" she said.

Olavo stared at his right hand. The frog was gone, but not the blood. His fingers were sticky. The socket on the back of his neck hurt. He reached around to prod the raw flesh around the opening.

"I'm going to call a nurse," the woman said. "Before you hurt yourself."

Olavo expected to feel the familiar needle-sharp jab. Instead a softspace download dissolved inside him. Lassitude spread.

"What do you want me to do?" he asked. "What do you want me to be? *Who* do you want me to be?"

"I want you to be yourself."

Meaning his old self. "I don't know who that is."

"I'm not sure I do, either." Tenley's face crinkled with sympathy. "I'm not sure I ever have. That's what scares me the most."

28

Eugene, October 4

Linnea led him to the couch shoved against the back wall. Joss sticks smoked on the coffee table in front of it. Under the smell of sandalwood, the carpet stank of mildew. "You look good," she said.

"So do you," Rudi said. A little skinny, he thought, and pale. But her hair looked clean, her eyes clear despite a faint penumbra of fatigue and the heavy pierces in her nose, lip, and left eyebrow.

She sat on the sofa, and he settled next to her into the uneasy embrace of the drink- and food-stained cushions.

"Really," she said. "You look great." Not surprisingly, she seemed to be having a hard time getting her bearings. Or sitting still. She itched her nose, tugged on her left earlobe, rubbed the back of her neck.

"I keep hearing that, so it must be true." He pulled the get well card from his shirt pocket.

She took the card from him, opened it with trembling fingers. The shadow from a cobweb clinging to the light fixture above them fell across the blank paper. "I couldn't think of what to write," she said.

"Sometimes there's nothing you can say. Sometimes the best thing to do is just let people fill things in on their own."

"Don't tell me," she said. "I can imagine what you must think of me."

"It made me feel good that you were thinking about me. It helped get me through."

"I'd like to think that was true," she said. "I used to."

"What happened?"

"It's tough." Linnea sniffed. "Sometimes what you imagine you want isn't all it's cracked up to be."

"Things don't always work out," he agreed.

She handed the card back to him. "I would have come to visit you. I wanted to. Lots of times, but . . ." Whatever defense she had in mind withered on her tongue, starved of conviction. "I tried to go back," she said. "A few times. But I couldn't stay. I didn't belong there anymore."

Rudi took a moment to inspect the sofa. The Magnavox crouching in one corner. The dishes and spoons in disarray on the beat-up tray table. They all looked like hand-me-downs, scavenged from The Salvation Army, yard sales, and the occasional Dumpster. "Do you like it here?"

She shrugged, resettling her shoulders. "It's okay."

"There's no place else you want to go?"

"There's lots of places I'd like to go. It just feels like there's no place else I *can* go. Like I don't belong anywhere."

It was like old times. Whispering to each other on the couch at night, the TV turned down low so as not to wake their grandmother. Rudi confessing his fears. Linnea confiding her hopes. Both of them wishing things were different, unable to agree on how to make that happen. Even now, they had the same shared dream, the same difference of opinion, that had always cleaved them.

"It was as far away as you could get," he said. As far as she could fly. "The wings worked."

She smiled. "I guess so. They got me this far, anyway." The smile slipped. "I'm sorry I left the way I did. When I did. I know it was hard on you. But I offered to take you with me. Remember?"

"Yes."

"I would have," she said.

She didn't want what had happened to him to be her fault. She didn't want it to be anyone's fault.

"I couldn't go," he said. "The same way you couldn't stay."

"You don't blame me?"

"No. You made your choice. I made mine. Simple as that."

Linnea let out a breath. "Did staying make any difference?"

"I don't know." He would probably never know. How could he? "But I couldn't leave. It would be giving up."

"On Grandma?"

"Yeah. But mostly on myself."

She frowned, not understanding.

"I'm not sure I can explain it." He'd wanted to face his fears. It felt important to confront them head-on. But he could think of no way to tell her that, without making her feel bad. Leaving out of hope and leaving out of fear were two different things.

"You did the right thing." She patted him awkwardly on the knee.

Before she could withdraw it, Rudi covered her chapped hand with his. "We both did."

A knock sounded on the door.

Linnea stiffened. He let her go. "Is that the person you were expecting," he asked, "instead of me?"

"I'll get rid of him." She stood.

"I can leave, if you want," Rudi said.

Come back later, he thought. Or not at all, if that was what she wanted.

"No. This won't take long." Linnea paused on her way to the door. "If you want, you can wait in back. There's a spare room across from the bathroom."

When Linnea called him out, she was buoyant. She microwaved chicken potpies and opened a couple of beers.

"Who was that guy?" Rudi asked around a mouthful of warm filling and crust. "A friend?"

"Client."

"The other one, too?"

She eyed him nervously over her fork.

"I saw him leaving, when I got here. And a little bit through the window, before he left."

She chewed slowly. "It's not what it looks like," she said. "I heal people."

"What kind of people?"

She swallowed. The food seemed to catch in her throat. She washed it down with a swig of beer. "Sick people. People who doctors can't help."

"By putting stones on them?"

"Crystals." She relaxed as she stepped onto more familiar ground. "They activate different wavelengths, and properties, of light. Focus the energy where it's needed."

"How?"

"By adding good energy. Releasing bad energy." She fussed with the label on her beer. "I know it doesn't sound very scientific."

"But it works?"

"People get better, more than if it was just a placebo effect. That's why they keep coming back."

Or maybe they just needed something beyond the conventional to believe in, to get them from one day to the next.

"It looks like you've done a lot of reading," he said. The

guest room doubled as a library. It was filled with books, stacks of papers, and magazines like *Psychology Today, Parabola,* and *Metaphysics.*

"Research," she said.

"How did you find out about the crystals in the first place?"

She stared hard into the mouth of her beer bottle. "Do you ever feel like you're being watched?"

"Sometimes." He thought about the aluminum foil, neatly folded and safely tucked in the van. He hadn't been able to throw it away. Half a dozen times he'd tried to crumple it into a ball. Each time, doubt held him back. He couldn't let go of his fear. He wasn't ready.

"That's because we *are* being watched," Linnea said. "That's why I had to leave."

"You thought Grandma was watching you?"

"Didn't you ever feel that way?"

"No."

Linnea looked up from her bottle. "I think Grandma was a Wanderer. Mom, too, maybe."

"What do you mean by a Wanderer?"

"A Wanderer is someone who's born here, on Earth, but is actually from another planet. I read about them, after I left. There's all sorts of books out there by people who went through a very painful process of awakening to their true nature, and the feeling of peace that this realization eventually brought them."

Rudi sipped his beer, the only response he felt capable of under the circumstances.

"When I went back to Grandma's," Linnea said, "that's what I was trying to find out."

Rudi swallowed. "If she was an alien, you mean?"

"Yeah. Or maybe an angel. After she was gone, I thought I might find something in the house—some artifact—that was from a different world. Something she'd kept hidden from us for years."

"Like what?" Beer foamed against the tightness in his throat.

Linnea rotated her bottle. "Evidence. Proof that she was different."

"Did you find anything?"

"Nothing conclusive. I'm still trying to find out who she really was, and where she came from. Who I am."

Rudi raised his beer for another sip. The bottle was perspiring; cold sweat beaded on the glass.

"That's where I got the crystals," Linnea said. "They were in a shoebox under her bed, along with the books on how to use them."

Rudi set the bottle back down. His grandmother had never said anything about the crystals.

"I don't think Grandma knew she wasn't human," Linnea said. "Most Wanderers don't."

Rudi forced a breath. "Why not?"

"When they come here, they lose their memory. They can't remember who they are, where they're from, or why they're here. That's so they can fully integrate into our human world, and not be tempted to go home before their work is done. It's sort of like amnesia."

"What kind of work?" he said.

"They're here to help us evolve. That's why they're watching us and gathering as much data as they can."

"Data about what?"

"Everything. They record whatever we say, think, and feel in order to analyze us, better understand us."

Rudi closed his eyes. He thought of the tiny cameras he had felt crawling around inside him at Lakeshore like termites in soft wood. Hollowing him out and dissecting his thoughts.

They must have talked about this at some point, when they were little. That was the only thing that made sense. He just didn't remember it.

"How many of these Wanderers are there?" he heard himself say. Not feeling his lips move.

"I don't know. No one knows."

He opened his eyes. "Do you think you're a Wanderer?" Was that was she was afraid of—what she had been running from all these years?

Her shoulders hunched. "You know what I said about not belonging?"

"Yeah." He felt that way sometimes. A lot of people did.

"Well," she said, "I feel that way all the time. I feel out of place, wherever I go. I'm always the outsider. I never fit in."

"Alienated," he said.

"Right."

The headache was back. It had been gone for days. But now he could feel it, an inversion layer of pressure slowly settling over him. He massaged the back of his neck, trying to rub the tension from his shoulders.

"It took me a long time to wake up to who I was," she said. "To accept the fact that I might be an alien soul. That's when I started wondering about Grandma and Mom, and if maybe I inherited something from them—something that made me different from everyone else."

"Like tiny cameras inside you, watching everything you do."

"Yeah. Or some genetic predisposition." She returned her gaze to the lip of the beer bottle. "I hear voices sometimes."

"Whose?"

"Other Wanderers. We're all connected somehow, resonating to the same mental frequency."

"What do these voices say?"

"Not much. It's not like they're telling me to do anything,

like go out and protest the war or shoot someone. They're more like telepathic urges and feelings. They aren't very focused."

"Like having the TV on in the background," he said.

"Yeah. Except you're listening to a bunch of different channels all at once." She peeled a strip from the label. "I was on pills for a while. It was the only way I could keep from freaking out. I was in denial. I didn't want to believe it was true."

"But now you do."

She pinched the damp piece of paper, crumpling it into a ball. "I know it sounds crazy. But it's the only thing that makes sense. My life finally makes sense. All of the puzzle pieces that were out of place fell into place. I understand now there's a reason I never fit in. There's a reason for all the pain and suffering I went through."

"And now you're at peace with yourself."

"For the most part. It's a process. The memory of who I was before I woke up—my old identity—is still there. It hasn't gone away. So I still have to deal with that. At least until I get called home. Which is what I think happened to Mom."

"The reason she left us, you mean."

"That's why she hasn't been back. Why we've never heard anything from her or about her. She's moved on."

His beer was gone and his mouth was dry. "Have you talked to any other people who feel this way?"

She looked up from the jagged ball of paper pinched between her fingers. "You mean like a support group?"

"Not necessarily."

"No." She let out a breath. "It's not the sort of thing you advertise."

"I guess not."

"It's not like being an alcoholic or a substance abuser. You can't go to rehab, or anything."

"I thought there might be a way to recognize them."

"Not really. I only learned about it after I found the crystals. Researching them—and how some Wanderers are attracted to crystal emanations—catalyzed certain feelings that led to my realization."

Rudi nodded, uncertain what to say or where to go next. He was exhausted. The beer and the discussion had worn him down.

"You could be one, too," she said suddenly, hopefully. "We come from the same family. You've gone through a lot of the same things I have."

"I guess."

"I'm just saying," she said. "It might not be true. But sometimes, just finding out about the possibility can trigger an awakening."

"I'm pretty tired," Rudi said. "I need some time to think, see how I feel." If he didn't extricate himself soon, put some distance between himself and what she had told him, he was going to be crushed by the headache. Already, he could feel its inexorable teeth digging into his skull, the jaws squeezing shut.

"You can sleep here." Linnea bounced to her feet. "I'll get you a blanket." She started into the living room.

"I can stay someplace else," Rudi offered. He could park the van a short distance down the road, give them both some breathing room.

Linnea waved off his concerns. "Forget it, you're staying with me. It's the least I can do."

"As long as I'm not in the way."

"You won't be." She gathered up their empties and stood them on the countertop next to the already overloaded kitchen sink. "Don't even think about it. I'd never forgive myself."

"You don't have another appointment?"

"Not until tomorrow afternoon. We'll go out for breakfast. There's a great place down the road. Peach pancakes. Omelets."

"All right, sounds good." He couldn't bring himself to dampen her enthusiasm. It seemed to mean a lot to her, to have something she could give him.

29

San Francisco, Circa 1937

After saying good night to Etta, Benjamin made his way to the deserted office of Taupe & Kohler. He felt more at home among the survey logs, topographic maps, and architectural renderings than the furnishings of his own home.

This was who he was. This was where he belonged.

And yet when he stared at a map on his drafting table, his eyes betrayed him. He might as well be looking at a child's scrawled drawing. The topo lines were a blurred, meaningless jumble. He could no more make sense of the landscape they described than he could the surface of the moon.

Still, it gave him time to think. He sat at his desk and, tracing a finger in the fine layer of dust silting the surface, went over what Peter and Etta had told him. There was a topology to their words, no different from the elevation lines and compass readings on a topographic map. All he had to do was read the contour of what had been presented to him. That would allow him to plot a course. Like any terrain, the topology of his life could be surveyed and the results interpreted. Make sense of what he'd seen and heard and, in theory, he would know how to proceed.

Etta believed—to a point. She didn't believe everything she had been told or shown by Madame Grurie. She believed that the simunculi came from within her—from within each person. Each one of them possessed a simunculus, an inner being or beings that gave shape and dimension to the outer being.

Peter, on the other hand, believed in nothing. He was an avowed skeptic, determined to cast Madame Grurie as a fraud, even if the teachings were not. He wasn't objective. Peter's perspective was even more distorted and less trustworthy than his own.

Where did that leave him?

What do I believe? That was the question. Did the dwarf with the purple top hat exist? The albino woman? The dough-faced man? If so, had he perceived them accurately? Or had his eyes and tumor reshaped them to fit the new reality that was mercilessly replacing his old one?

How much longer did he have? A month? A week? A day? It didn't matter—his days were numbered. What difference did a week or a month make? There was no point waiting. If he was going to do anything, it had to be soon.

Do what?

Benjamin couldn't forestall Peter forever. Soon the reporter would grow agitated, impatient. Benjamin wouldn't be surprised if he was already exploring other options for gathering incriminating information.

No, he had to—

The front door to the office rattled. A moment later it opened and the electric light in the front office glowed. Benjamin shaded his eyes against the glare slanting through his doorway and stood, chair scraping.

"Who's there?"

Keys rattled on a chain. A figure loomed, blocking the light.

"I thought I might find you here," Zachary said. He took out a gold pocket watch and squinted at the face.

"What time is it?" Benjamin said. He had no idea. The night stretched behind him forever.

"Etta wouldn't tell me where you'd gone," Zachary said heavily, his diction ponderous. Benjamin caught a whiff of whiskey on his breath. "When you weren't home, I knew this was where you'd be."

"What's going on?" Benjamin said.

Zachary swayed in front of him, moving in and out of focus. "You know." The cover on the pocket watch snapped shut.

"I'm afraid I don't. Is Etta okay?" As soon as the words left his mouth, he knew it was the wrong thing to ask.

The swaying stopped. "Did she seem all right to you?"

"Yes. But that was a couple of hours ago. And I was only there for a few minutes."

"I take it she wasn't packing."

Benjamin blinked in surprise. Etta was unhappy, but she hadn't said anything about leaving. Maybe she thought he would say something to Zachary. Evidently, with the help of Madame Grurie, she had discovered within herself the courage and strength she needed to survive without her husband.

"I'm sorry," he said. "I had no idea."

"What did you say to her?" Zachary demanded.

"Nothing."

"You must have done something." Zachary lurched forward. He caught himself with both hands against the front edge of the desk, shoving it back a few inches.

"You're drunk." The heady reek of whiskey intensified. Cigar smoke clung to his friend's clothes and hair.

"And you're a goddamn liar." Zachary's breathing was

labored, congested with fury. The air between them grew thick.

Benjamin shook his head. "You don't know what you're saying. Let's discuss this in the morning, when you're sober."

"I've never been more sober in my life!" Zachary hammered the desk with meaty fists. A drafting pencil leaped, rolled, and clattered to the floor. It was followed by several loose sheets of paper. "I thought I could trust you. That's why I recommended you see Madame Grurie."

So Zachary had intended to use him as a spy, as well. An informer, however indirect, on Etta.

"Nothing happened," Benjamin said. "She made tea. We discussed the séance for a while. Then I left."

"I thought you would look after her. Instead, you betrayed me. Turned her against me." Zachary lunged for him across the desk.

Benjamin lurched back, but Zachary caught him by the front of his shirt and hauled him onto the desk, scattering triangles, straight edges, and a handful of French curves.

"I had no idea she was thinking of leaving," Benjamin said through gritted teeth. "But I'm not surprised."

Zachary's eyes bulged. "Why not? What are you talking about?"

Expensive rosewater eau de cologne coiled under the tawdry patina of tobacco and alcohol. "You spend all your time at work... or out. You're not there for her. No wonder she's depressed."

Zachary hit him. The blow caught Benjamin on the side of the head and momentum carried them both sideways, off the desk and onto the hardwood floor.

Zachary hit the floor next to him, and spilled headfirst into the steam radiator under the window. The air whuffed out of him. He grunted in pain as the two of them foundered on the exposed piping.

Benjamin clutched Zachary by the coat. With his right hand, he lashed out. Benjamin couldn't control the blows. The hand wasn't his; it belonged to a stranger, another man living inside of him. He had no control over the punches. The hand swung blindly, mechanically, until something inside of him snapped and he slumped onto his side, utterly spent, emptied of rage.

"Son of a bitch!" Zachary said, cursing, his lips bubbling with foamy red spittle. Stunned, he crawled to his knees and, gasping for air, sagged against the wall next to the radiator.

Benjamin struggled to sit up through waves of actinic dizziness. His head throbbed. He leaned over, vomited, and straightened. The radiator was pleasantly warm. He gripped the top, pulled himself up, and rested his head against the metal tubes.

"She was miserable before," Zachary said after a time. "We both were. You have no idea what it was like, being suffocated by her. Some days, I couldn't breathe. It felt like my head was in a canvas bag. I had to get away."

Benjamin swallowed the bile coating the back of his tongue. "Or get her out of the way."

"That's ridiculous."

"Is it?"

"Listen to yourself. You're ranting."

"That's why you encouraged her to see Madame Grurie," Benjamin said. "To get rid of her."

"That's not true. I thought it was doing her some good. Instead, all it did was turn her against me."

"Madame Grurie didn't turn Etta against you," Benjamin said. "You managed that yourself. The only thing Madame Grurie did was show her a different path."

Zachary straightened unsteadily. He shifted a rumpled shoulder against the wall and dabbed at the side of his head. Blood streaked his hair. "Christ. What a mess."

"You treated Etta as an embarrassment," Benjamin went on. "You didn't want her condition to reflect poorly on you. Better for her to endure the humiliation and shame you felt."

"No." Zachary resettled his jacket on his shoulders. "I've always had her interests at heart. I never wanted to hurt her. I've always tried to do what's best for her. You may not believe that, but it's true. I love her. I always have."

"You just don't want to look after her."

"She needs to be someplace safe. Someplace where she won't present a danger to herself or others."

"Hospitalized, you mean."

Zachary straightened the collar of his jacket, then his cuffs, trying to regain his composure. "Is that what she told you?"

"No. But it's not hard to figure out. There aren't that many places people can go for treatment."

Zachary dabbed at the lump on his head again. He grimaced as his fingers came away sticky with blood. He rubbed them absently together. "What happened in there?" he said after his breathing had returned to normal.

"Tonight? With the séance?"

Zachary waved his hand. "With everything. I never asked her. I didn't want to pry. I wanted her to feel I trusted her."

"Even if you didn't?"

"The last thing I wanted to do was push her away."

Sparks of light prickled Benjamin's vision. He adjusted the position of his head on the radiator.

"She wants to move into the institute," Zachary went on. "That's what she told me. She's going over there tonight."

"She's going to stay with Madame Grurie?"

"I guess there's a spare room in her house."

"She's afraid of being committed."

"No." Zachary let out a breath. He clasped his knees to his chest and rested his head on his arms. "She hasn't been interested in me in a while." He rocked his head from side to side. "I think something's going on between them."

"That's crazy."

"Is it?" Zachary wiped sweat and blood from his forehead with the sleeve of his jacket. "You were there. You saw them together. What were they like? Were they . . . close?"

Benjamin shook his head. "I never saw anything like that."

"Would you tell me, if you did?"

"I wouldn't lie to you."

"It'd be easier if the two of you were having an affair," Zachary said. "If she left me for another man. Any man. I think I'd prefer that. At least then, I'd know how to react. What to do."

"You don't know for a fact that's what's going on."

Zachary laughed, as if he found the entire situation absurdly comic. "It's pretty damn clear, if you ask me."

"What are you going to do?"

Zachary lifted his head to appraise him with a bleary squint. "Is there anything I can do?"

"To get her back?"

"Or to let her go."

"Talk to her," Benjamin said. "Don't run away. Don't let her run away without telling you the truth."

"It's too late. She's made up her mind. She doesn't want to talk. As far as she's concerned, it's over."

Benjamin nodded. He knew what he had to do.

30

Sand Mountain, Hardspace

Calle Paloma. Blaustrasse. Rue 24.

Mee Won lived in a residential district, where the three streets met at right angles in a blast of hot-vented air and the stench of methane from one of the polis's underground bio recyclers.

The district was a honeycomb arrangement of apartments clustered on the east face of the level. From the streets, the housing complex comprised three terraced sublevels set back on an incline. Olavo crossed Calle Paloma, filled with public transit gyrocars, to one of the short-run lifts that accessed the comb. He rode the platform up to the second level, and stepped out onto the street-facing promenade, with its cafés, salons, and kiosks lit by overhead LED panels. From there it was a short trip through soporific, heat-dulled foot traffic to one of the interconnecting walkways. Partitioned off by a latticework of privacy screens and garlanded trellises, these walkways led into the awning-shaded, heat-exchanger-cooled microclime of the apartment cluster.

Down an LED-illuminated substreet, he passed several doughmen casting dice in a corner. With each toss, the dice clattered like loose teeth against the yellow crysteel walls. Each die made a different sound when it hit, chattering to the players.

Squatting around the dice, they paused at his approach. Dull-eyed and slack-faced. As soon as he had moved on, the clatter resumed. In his wake, silent laughter eddied and pooled, agitated by invisible currents. The wraithlike suspicion of the doughmen clung to him with incorporeal fingers, plucking out a chord of disquiet on taut, catgut nerves.

He turned right, down an alley shielded from the afternoon sun by a barrel vault of spun diamond foam, and mounted the flight of steps that ended in the carved jade door to Mee Won's apartment. The laboratory jade was pale green—nearly white in places—and depicted a pine-covered cliff. A crane stood in a pond at the foot of the mountain. A trio of monkeys leaped between branches.

He reached for the access pad . . . and paused, his hand suspended. Caught between lives, somewhere in the middle of coming and going. . . .

The sound of the muscle car faded. He turned.

Tenley stood, hands on her hips. Impatient? Expectant? Her lower lip trembled, as though something was about to emerge from her—some long-imprisoned rancor, rising up like the smell of sewage from a manhole.

He held his breath, turned his face to one side, and moved farther into the apartment.

Tenley slammed the door on the droning of cicadas and the electric buzz of the bug zapper outside the door. "Well?" she demanded. "What are you doing here?"

"I want to talk." He took up a position by the television.

"I can see that."

"About us."

"There is no us."

"In what sense?"

"In any sense." Tenley walked to the couch, picked up the ball of black yarn and circular knitting needles tucked in one corner.

"Please," he said.

"There's nothing to talk about." She plopped on the couch and, doing her best to ignore him, began to knit.

He clasped both hands behind his head and paced under Sandra Bullock's pained gaze, chiseled in pixels.

"Who is that guy?"

"A friend."

"Boyfriend?"

She didn't answer. The needles clicked. Firmly, resolutely. Stitching a new life, one that didn't include him. He could see it taking shape in her hands—row by row—a new pattern emerging.

"When did you start knitting?"

She took a moment to respond. "At the start of the semester."

"You taking a class?"

"No. It gives my hands something to do," she explained. "Helps me concentrate better."

At the moment, it seemed more of a distraction. "What are you making?"

"A hat."

"For who?"

"No one. I'm just practicing."

The black watchman's cap was for her friend, he knew. Tenley hated black. "Will you make me one?" he asked.

"No." She refused to look up from the yarn. She pretended to give the cap her undivided attention.

"Why not?"

"Stop it," she said.

"What?"

"I'm tired of playing games with you. No more games."

"Just tell me."

Her expression soured. The needles paused. "You wouldn't appreciate it. You never appreciate anything I do for you."

"Like what?" She only spoke in generalities when she had something specific in mind she was trying to hide.

"It doesn't matter." She pursed her lips at the yarn, feigning deliberation. "Not anymore."

"But it did," he said.

"It was a long time ago," she said. The needles resumed, picking up where they had left off, adding another round to the pattern. . . .

They stood on the muddy shore of a small pond, skipping rocks across placid sun-drenched water.

"I saw your sister the other day," Tenley said in between throws.

He paused in mid-toss. "My sister?"

Tenley flung a stone, watched it skip erratically before it sank with a plunk beneath the mossy surface. "Two nights ago. She was here."

He didn't believe it. "Where?"

"At your old house."

"It must have been someone else," he said. If Linnea had come back, he would've heard from her.

"It was her," Tenley insisted. "You don't know what I saw. You weren't there."

He threw his stone. Anger whipped it low and hard and fast. "How'd you know it was her? It could have been someone who looked like her." Probably was, he thought to himself.

"Because I talked to her. She was in a car, watching the house. When she saw me she waved me over."

Tenley liked to hurt him with facts. It didn't help that he did the same to her, small jabs calculated to let the prim air out of her better-than-thou snootiness.

"She asked where you were," Tenley said. "She wanted to know how you were doing."

"What'd you say?"

"I told her I didn't know. I said she'd have to ask you herself, it wasn't any of my business."

"What'd she say?"

"That it was good to see me. She couldn't believe how pretty and grown-up I'd gotten since she left."

"Where is she now?"

"Gone. She said she was leaving that night. She didn't say where she was going or when she was coming back."

Rudi picked another rock from the edge of the pond. "That's not true. She just said that in case someone asked you about her."

"Who?"

"The cops, maybe. Or someone from Social Services. That way they'd think she was gone."

"What if you're wrong?"

"She's still here. She wouldn't leave again without talking with me."

"She might if she couldn't find you. If she didn't know where you were living or anything."

"She'd find a way."

"People change. They grow up and they aren't the same person they used to be. They're different."

It sounded like something her mother would say. She was always repeating little phrases her mother told her, trying them out to see how they fit.

Rudi shook his head. "Not always."

"There's nothing you can do to stop it," Tenley continued. "It just happens."

"Not to everyone," he said. It didn't have to. Not to him, or Linnea. They were different. They'd always been different.

"You have to let go," Tenley was saying.

He blinked. The hypnotic movement of her hands had stopped. The needles lay motionless on her lap. "Let go of what?"

"Us. That's the problem. You don't want to move on. You don't want anybody else to move on."

"I need you," he said. "What's wrong with that?"

"I can't be there for you anymore. Not the way you want."

"Don't you want to be needed?"

"Not that way."

"What way?"

"We're not kids anymore. We've changed. I've changed. But you want us to be exactly like we were."

"We were there for each other when other people weren't. There's no reason we can't still be friends."

She stared at the half-formed watchman's cap. "We stopped being friends a long time ago."

He ran his fingers through his hair, pulling it back from his forehead. "How can you say that?"

"You want me to be someone I'm not, you always have. I didn't realize it until a little while ago."

"Who told you that?" He moved toward the couch, but didn't take a seat. She remained hunched, as if backed into a corner.

She looked up. "I've been seeing a therapist. I think you should consider seeing one, too. I think it would help. I think it would be good for you to talk to someone you don't know."

"About what?"

"Your feelings."

"For you?" That was why she was seeing a therapist: to figure out how she felt about him.

"Not just me. Your mother. And your sister. I think they're all mixed up inside you. I think you're in denial about a lot of stuff. Confused."

"So what are you saying? Just cut the crap and get to the point!"

Tenley inhaled... more a sob than a breath. "We shouldn't see each other anymore. We need some time apart."

"How much time?"

"I don't know." She went back to the cap, idly fiddling with the needles and the yarn. "A while. Until I get things figured out."

"Is that your idea, or your therapist's?"

"What difference does it make?"

"A lot. It's the difference between what you want to do, and what someone else wants you to do," he said.

"In that case, I want you to go." She lifted her chin and met his gaze, holding her ground.

"When?"

"Now. I'm not going to do what you want anymore. You don't really care about me. You're only looking out for yourself. Which is what you've always done."

"Tenley—"

"Just get out." She gripped the circular knitting needles tight and closed her eyes. "Leave me alone. Please?"

He left while her eyes were still closed, refusing to look at him. The last image he had of her. Defiant but pleading.

He revved the motorcycle to a high-pitched howl, leaving a rooster tail of exhaust and gravel as he roared out of the parking lot.

Streetlights contracted in front of him. Time slowed as his thoughts sped up. Behind him, the city lights retreated and red-

shifted. Ride hard enough, fast enough, and he would break all connection to the past. Nothing would catch up with him.

Not Tenley, not his sister, not his mother.

They would become vanishingly small, unimportant. Eventually, their grip on him would loosen.

He passed beyond the event horizon of the city. Nothing but darkness ahead. The night sky gaped wide, sinuous and muscular.

His vision tunneled, contracted to a wormhole of pavement. The white lines at its center narrowed into a single tight beam.

An Ariadne's thread of elementary particles, electrons, and photons, leading out of the labyrinth.

He rounded a turn, one knee scraping pitted asphalt.

And the beam diverged.

He felt the bike start to slide out from under him. Tried to hold on. A horn blared and brakes squealed.

A scream escaped him. All of the pent-up frustration and rage he'd been holding in clawed his throat, tore at his lungs.

Then he was falling.

Tumbling into a circle of bloodred light.

The door opened under Olavo's touch and swung aside. He stepped forward, into tomb-still air and origami folds of dust.

31

Eugene, October 4

Rudi couldn't sleep. He lay on the couch in the living room, listening to the trailer tick as it cooled.

The way a coffin must cool, he thought. Once it had been lowered into the ground.

Slowly, reluctantly.

After a couple of hours, when the light down the hall from under Linnea's door had been snuffed out and no more sound came from her room, Rudi eased from under the spare blanket she had found for him. Taking the blanket with him, he crept down the hallway. He didn't want to wake her. Just as importantly, he wanted time to himself. He wanted to be alone, not just to think, but to go through some of the books and magazines he'd seen in her study—to try to understand the journey she'd been on.

Dirty moonlight filtered through the room's only window, which faced the overgrown slope behind the trailer. The window was partly open, veined with spider silk that seemed to cling to the sky. Brisk night air carried the chirp of crickets and the faint smell of a skunk.

He shut the door quietly, tucked the blanket in the gap along the floor, and flipped the light switch.

A rectangle of light flooded the undergrowth outside the window. A pair of eyes glowed luminous pink in the brush, then waddled off. A moth batted against the grime-streaked glass, desperate to immolate itself.

Linnea used an old wooden table as a desk. White plastic trays lined the back and sides of the desk. The trays were divided into compartments filled with different types of rock, stone, or crystal. Quartz, garnet, pyrite. There were dozens more that he didn't recognize. Green stones and purple crystals. Shards of polished glass, smooth bone, and ivory. In the empty space between the organizers, diagrams had been taped to the water-stained veneer. One of the diagrams showed a human body with chakra points. Another depicted a numbered enneagram, marked with octaves and intervals. Several Chinese drawings appeared to indicate acupuncture points and holistic medians.

He turned his attention to the bookshelves and the stacks of magazines, sitting in groups on the floor. There were dozens of books about crystal healing, multiple personality disorder, hypnotic regression, UFOs, past lives, and interdimensional communication. One book, called *The RA Material*, appeared well-read. A companion title, *The Law of One*, consisted of three volumes of information that had apparently been telepathically received from an entity calling itself RA. In addition to the mainstream psychology and spiritual publications he'd noticed earlier, he found several years' worth of back issues of magazines called *Sage Woman*, *Shambhala Sun*, and *Permaculture*.

Her seeking had taken her all over the map. There was no way to know where, exactly, the journey had begun, or what course it had taken over the years. He knew only where it had brought her.

He scanned the shelves for a copy of the Bible, or any other books relating to angels. Genesis, 6:2 in particular, recorded how fallen angels had come down to Earth and bred with the attractive daughters of men: . . . *they took them wives of all that they chose.* But breeding was different from possession or soul exchange. Next to the Bible, he found a dog-eared copy of *Chariots of the Gods.*

In her mind, had she conflated angels with aliens? Had the angel wings tattooed on her back translated into possession by a being from another world? And when the angel wings finally failed her—could carry her no farther—had she fallen to Earth as a Wanderer? If so, that still didn't answer the question of his grandmother. Who she was, and who Linnea thought she was.

It took another half hour of digging to find what he was looking for. The papers Linnea said she had found under their grandmother's bed were in a scrapbook in a small closet. Several short articles, preserved in plastic, that had been clipped from the *San Francisco Examiner, Chronicle,* and *Call-Bulletin.* The paper was yellowed and crinkled, the type faded.

One of the storylines read "Metaphysics or Occult?" The article, written by Peter McGraff, was a short exploration of the teachings of a school run by one Madame Grurie. The Somnambulist Institute had been ostensibly set up to further the philosophical teachings of G. I. Gurdjieff and P. D. Ouspensky. But questions about the school's mistress, her background, and how the institute raised its funds, cast a pall of suspicion over the school.

Who was Madame Grurie? Where had she come from?

The article was short on facts and long on supposition. Its sole purpose seemed to be to raise doubts. It mentioned séances, during which a ghost, referred to as a simunculus, appeared to one or more of the participants. According to

Madame Grurie's teachings, these simunculi were apparitions from the fourth dimension and alleged to be the embodiment of a person's soul on a higher plane of existence and an extrasensory source of knowledge.

The next article, "Somnambulist Falls Ill," quoted Madame Grurie directly: "My goal is awakening. Most people are somnambulists. They sleepwalk through life." Later, she went on to say, "I awaken people by shocking them."

The implication was that students submitted themselves to experimentation, like test animals in a lab. According to McGraff, one of Madame Grurie's students had been forced to seek medical attention as a result of her techniques.

More vitriol spilled from the third article, "Somnambulist Missing."

> Etta P. Kohl, wife of Zachary Kohl and a student at the Somnambulist Institute, was reported missing yesterday by her husband. According to Mr. Kohl, his wife had been undergoing treatment for melancholy at Madame Grurie's school. Mrs. Kohl had been a full-time student at the Institute for three months. During this period, she was often required to attend classes in the evening. As a result, she frequently returned home late at night. The last time Mr. Kohl saw his wife was Thursday night. Earlier that evening, Mrs. Kohl had attended a séance at the Institute. When questioned, Madame Grurie refused to comment on Mrs. Kohl, her mysterious disappearance, or the occult tutelage that seems to have triggered it. Anyone with information as to the whereabouts or condition of Mrs. Kohl is asked to contact police as soon as possible. "We need to wake up to what is happening at the Institute," Mr. Kohl said. "Before it's too late."

At the bottom of the article, there were photographs of Madame Grurie, and Etta and Zachary Kohl, set side by side. Zachary Kohl was heavyset, with a handlebar mustache, a round face, and wavy hair parted in the middle. Etta Kohl was thinner than her husband, almost delicate, while Madame Grurie appeared to be several years older and heavier. Voluptuous, judging by the fullness of her lips. The photos were grainy and faded, the details blurred. But Rudi could see that one woman had a flower fastened above her right ear . . .

His grandmother tucked a tiny pink rose into her hair, then handed Rudi a bobby pin. He fumbled awkwardly, the pin slipping on the brittle waves of her wispy, gray hair.

"Take your time," his grandmother said. "There's no hurry." She kept her head steady, gazing out at the yard from the back porch, where they were drinking lemonade.

Rudi finally slid the pin over the soft stem, pinching it in place. He could see her scalp through the hair, turnip pale and spotted with age.

"How do I look?" she said when he was done.

"Pretty."

She smiled and patted the pale rose with trembling fingers. "I used to have such beautiful hair." She sighed and lowered her hand to her lap. "But that was a long time ago. And nothing lasts."

He sat on the chaise next to her. "Except for you," he said. She was the only thing that had *lasted, now that Linnea was gone.*

The sigh broke apart into a phlegm-choked cough. "I've lived far longer than I have any right to, Rudi. I'm old. I was old when your mother was born."

"How old?"

"Old for my time. Old enough to be a grandmother." She cleared her throat, then swallowed. "I won't last forever," she

went on. "I'm winding down. Every day, I feel a little more tired. Sometimes it's all I can do to keep my eyes open."

"But you get lots of sleep."

She went to bed before him and woke up after him. In the afternoon she always took a long nap. How could she be tired?

"It's not enough," she told him. "Not anymore. I've reached the point in my life where ghosts keep me awake."

"You see ghosts?"

"Just before I go to sleep," she said. "That's when they usually come out. Just when I think they won't show up, they do."

"Where?" In her bedroom? He had never gone in after shutting her door for the night and going to watch television or read.

"Don't worry. They're not going to hurt you." She patted him on one leg. But the reassurance seemed a frail afterthought. "I'm the only person they can do anything to."

"How do you know?"

She smiled at the concern on his face. "Because they aren't the kind of ghosts you read about, or watch on TV, or see in the movies."

"What kind are they?"

She tapped her forehead. "They're the kind that come from inside a person. They start out small. Sometimes you don't even know they're there... but they grow inside you over time."

"Where do they come from?"

"Lots of places. All of the people you ever wanted to be, or could have been, but never were for whatever reason. All of the dreams that never came true. And all of the regrets that did. Each one has a different personality."

"I don't want you to turn into a ghost," Rudi said.

"There's nothing you can do," she said. "It just happens. It's part of life, just like dying."

"You're not going to die," he said.

"Everything dies, Rudi. We all go back to our original self. The person we were before we were born."

"In heaven?"

"Heaven is all around us, Rudi. We're wrapped up inside it. It surrounds us, and sustains us, even though it's invisible to us."

"Like the Big Bang," he said. "Our universe was born out of another universe we can't see."

She nodded. "Sometimes people see it, but they have to know how to look. They have to wake up."

"I'm awake."

"No. You just think you are."

He squinted out at the yard, at the rose arbor, and the butterfly bush, and the foxgloves that had come up in sudden, unexpected places. He didn't see any difference. It looked the same as it always did.

"How do you wake up?"

"It's not easy. It takes a lot of time and practice."

"Are you awake?"

"Yes. But like I said it's getting harder to stay awake. It takes a lot of energy that I don't have." She stared off into the yard.

"Can you teach me?"

"I've been trying," she said.

"You have?"

But she wasn't listening. "I tried with your mother, too. But she refused to wake up. She did everything she could to stay asleep."

Getting drunk, Rudi thought. Or stoned. She always went to sleep after smoking pot.

His grandmother had become silent and settled into herself, especially around the mouth, which was dry and puckered as an old cantaloupe. The rest of her seemed to be hanging by a thread. Trembling. Any second, she would detach from the world.

"Tell me about Grandpa Frank," Rudi said. If he let her

go—if he allowed her to keep sinking—she might never come back.

She blinked and straightened on the chaise. "There's not much to tell." One of her standard lines.

"Where did you meet him?" Rudi persisted.

"In Denver. That's where I was born and where I grew up. Mother moved there from San Francisco. I was thirty-five when I met him, an old maid in those days. I never thought I'd marry."

"Why not?"

"Mother didn't want me to. She was very protective. She didn't want me to get hurt the way she had been hurt."

"By who?"

"My father."

"Was he a loser?" His mother's boyfriends had all been losers. Constantly on the lookout for the cops. In and out of jail. Shouting. Breaking glasses or furniture, getting into fights and burning people with cigarettes... Presumably his father had been no different.

"No." A vein in his grandmother's temple pulsed. "But I never knew him. Mother never talked about him."

The same way his grandmother never talked about Grandpa Frank and his mother never talked about his father. "Why not? Did he leave?"

She nodded. A gentle breeze stirred the pause between them, tousling the flower clipped to her hair.

"What was his name?" Rudi said.

Her head jerked, like a fish on a line. She had drifted off again. "Benjamin," she said. "Benjamin Taupe. He had a brain tumor the doctors couldn't cure."

"He died?"

"There was an obituary in the local newspaper. But according to Mother, only his shadow died."

"His shadow?"

"The part of him that was projected into the world."

"How can a person be a shadow?"

"The same way a square shadow on a piece of paper can be used to create a solid cube."

Rudi considered for a moment. "By moving it in a straight line through space, or time."

She nodded and patted him on the knee.

"So what about Grandpa Frank?" Rudi said, getting back to his original question. "What happened to him?"

His grandmother blinked. The owlish lenses of her glasses flashed in the sunlight, bright with memories. "He died in the war. Vietnam. Your mother had just turned four. The war was almost over. He was a photographer there. We'd gotten a letter from him, promising he'd be home soon. When he didn't come back she blamed me. I'd promised her a life that never came true. I think that's when part of her went to sleep forever. She didn't want to go through the pain of that loss again. To make certain that didn't happen, she never let herself get close enough to anyone to get hurt."

So instead, she had a lot of boyfriends. And when one of them got too close, she moved on to the next one. And when he and Linnea got to be too much for her to handle, she moved on.

Her shadow disappeared, swallowed by night.

"I haven't been able to find your magazines," his grandmother said after a while. "I'm sorry. I don't know where I put them."

He had left them out a few weeks ago, in the kitchen. When he came home from school they were gone.

"That's all right," he said. She had probably thrown them out by mistake. It was his fault. He knew better. Other things had disappeared from the house. A vase, an old ceramic teapot. Broken, he assumed. By accident.

"I'll keep looking," she said. "I'll find them."

"I don't need them," he said.

"Are you sure?"

"Yes."

It was time to move on.

With the newspaper articles on the Somnambulist Institute, Rudi found an obituary for Benjamin Taupe. Business partner of Zachary Kohl. Died December 10, 1939, at the age of thirty-four, after being diagnosed with a brain tumor two years earlier. Following the closure of the Somnambulist Institute, Benjamin Taupe had moved to Sausalito, where he made his living as a clairvoyant. There was a picture with the obituary. It showed a clean-shaven young man with short straight hair, parted on the side. He seemed haunted in the picture, already hollowed to a ghost by the cancer.

Rudi had the feeling that he was looking into a mirror, or at a grainy picture of himself.

His head began to throb. He pressed his fingers to his eyes. When he was able to focus again, Rudi continued through the documents.

Photocopies of police and court records relating to Benjamin Taupe, as well as a number of handwritten letters and printed e-mails Linnea had written to people who claimed to have known Taupe personally or could provide information about him secondhand. In all these correspondences, Linnea had used Benjamin Taupe's last name and her middle name, Acantha. It seemed that for whatever reason, she had wanted to keep her identity secret—at least for the time being.

Finally, at the bottom of the stack, he came across a handwritten diary. The pages were yellow with age, the ink from a fountain pen or possibly a drafting pen. The writing was small and precise, the entries exacting. Rudi thumbed through the pages. They covered the period from 1937 to 1939 and described in detail the last two years in the life of Benjamin Taupe.

32

San Francisco, Circa 1937

An electric light glowed pale green behind the curtains in an upstairs window of Madame Grurie's house, as if the room were being consumed by Saint Elmo's fire.

Was Etta here now? Benjamin wondered. She must be. If so, would he get a chance to see her, speak to her?

His hand shook as he rang the bell and waited on the stoop. Soon, footsteps creaked on the hardwood floor inside. The white lace veil behind the window parted briefly, then settled back into place. The lock turned, the door opened.

Madame Grurie stood in the doorway, dressed in a blue silk kimono. Her hair was down. Long and glossy, it fell in luxuriant ripples to her waist. In her left hand she held a hairbrush.

"Benjamin," she said. "I didn't expect to see you so soon."

"I'm sorry," he said.

"There's no need to apologize."

"I know it's late. But I need to speak with you. It's urgent."

"Please come in." She stood aside, ushering him into the house. When he started past her, the kimono fell open. She wasn't wearing undergarments. Full breasts swayed against the kimono.

Benjamin averted his gaze. He removed his hat, using it as a prop to conceal the color rising in his cheeks. He edged quickly past her, into the dimly illuminated hallway, where the gloom offered a refuge of decency.

"Can I get you something?" she said, leading him into the sitting room where they had first met. "Water? Tea?"

He swallowed. "I'm fine."

"You don't look fine." She eased onto one of the stuffed chairs, drawing the blue kimono tight with one hand. In the light, it had a repeating pattern of birds and blossoms. "You look upset."

Benjamin cleared his throat, then concentrated on his black-polished shoes. "This isn't about me. That's not why I'm here."

"Isn't it?"

"Etta," he said.

"What about her?"

Benjamin looked up. The paisley carpet was making him dizzy. "Is she all right?"

"Isn't that a question her husband should be asking?"

"I'm here on his behalf. He thought—"

"That since we know one another, I would be more disposed to speak with you in confidence."

Benjamin swallowed. His upper lip was wet, salty with sweat, his underarms hot and damp.

"You're not well." Madame Grurie leaned forward. Her hair was still damp, recently washed, and smelled of roses.

"I'm fine."

"If you can't tell the truth to yourself, who can you tell it to?"

Benjamin said nothing.

Madame Grurie rose. When she approached him, he held

his ground. When she allowed her kimono to fall open, he kept his gaze fixed on her eyes.

She placed a hand on his forehead, and then his cheek. "You're warm," she said, her voice barely a whisper.

"I'm worried about Etta," he said.

"Is that the real reason you've come?" Madame Grurie let her hand slide along his jaw. "Or is that simply an excuse... what you told yourself to get you here for some other reason?"

Benjamin looked at the brush clutched in Madame Grurie's free hand. "I'd just like to know if she arrived safely."

Madame Grurie stepped back. Turned. Took a few contemplative steps, and then pirouetted to face him. "Why wouldn't she?"

"I don't know."

"Is there some reason to think she might be ill or in danger?"

"The séance," he said.

"What about it?"

"Etta saw or felt something." Benjamin groped for the words.

"I take it you've already spoken to her about it." Apparently Etta had neglected to tell Madame Grurie they had talked.

"A few hours ago," he admitted. There was no sense hiding the truth. "I went to check on her at home."

"Because you were concerned."

"Yes."

"And naturally you wanted to know what was revealed to her. You wanted to compare it with what was revealed to you."

"Yes." It was getting harder to focus his eyes. His vision kept sliding off objects. Blurring them. The sitting room was a smear of wallpaper, carpet, crystal lamp shades, and chintz upholstery.

"What, if I might inquire, did she tell you about the experience?" Madame Grurie said.

"It persuaded her to leave her husband." Etta hadn't come right out and said the séance was responsible.

"I very much doubt that. I'm sure Mr. Kohl had a hand in matters."

"Still," Benjamin said. "Without the séance that would not have happened. She would not have come to the decision."

"My God," Madame Grurie said. "I don't know why I didn't see it sooner. How could I have missed it?"

He stared at the mild amusement on her face.

"You're in love with her," Madame Grurie said. "That's why you're looking for her. You see an opportunity."

"No." Benjamin started to shake his head, but stopped when he felt the floor wobble and tilt under his feet.

"Another lie. But understandable, under the circumstances. No wonder you're so terribly unhappy. You can't face the truth about who you are, or what you want. In that way, you and Etta are alike."

The merry-go-round spin of the room slowed, but it refused to come to a complete stop.

"I suppose you want to talk to her," Madame Grurie said. "It's not enough to hear that she's safe."

"If possible."

"In private, I assume."

"If she'll see me."

"Let's find out, shall we?" Madame Grurie headed for the door, her kimono sashaying from side to side.

He took a step, stumbled, and fell down hard. He lay on his back on the carpet, staring up at the unhurried rotation of the ceiling, circling like the night sky, around a single point of light.

Madame Grurie bent over him. "Don't move," she said. "I'll be right back."

Sometime later, he woke to semidarkness. He lay in bed. A yellow incandescent lamp glowed on a dresser at the foot of the bed. The lamp shade was stained-glass. Art nouveau daffodils burned from the inside.

He attempted to raise his head and look around.

"Don't try to get up," Etta said from the side of the bed. She pressed a cool, moist towel to his forehead, forcing his head back onto the pillow. She wore a nightgown, and when she bent over the collar opened to reveal a dusting of cinnamon freckles.

"Where am I?"

"One of the guest rooms."

"How long?"

"A couple of hours. It's late and you need to rest. Do you want us to call for a doctor?"

"There's no point. It won't do any good."

"Don't be so fatalistic."

"I'm not. There's nothing they can do for me."

"You're delirious," she said, but made no move to go for help. "You were talking in your sleep."

Uneasiness tightened his stomach. He searched her face for a clue. "What did I say?"

"You were arguing."

"With who?"

A shadow detached itself from the murky folds of the curtains drawn across the window. "With Peter," Madame Grurie said.

Benjamin watched her approach the bed. The tip of a long cigarette caught and sparked.

"He's a reporter," Benjamin said. "He wanted me to spy on you for him. He implied I was being duped, and that the only thing you were interested in was money."

"I know." Madame Grurie removed the black cigarette holder from between pursed lips, then exhaled. "Etta already warned me."

"I had to," Etta said. "I couldn't let him get away with it."

Benjamin nodded and turned to Madame Grurie. "He thinks you're a..."

"Fraud," Madame Grurie finished.

"He also implied that you were running a brothel, behind the scenes. As a way to fund the school."

"I imagine he wishes that were the case," Madame Grurie said.

Etta turned to her. "I still don't understand what prompted him to go after you in the first place."

Madame Grurie removed the cigarette from its ebony holder and stubbed it out in a silver ashtray on the night table. "He was looking for his missing sister," she finally said. "That was why he came to me."

"He thought that she was a student here?" Etta said, frowning. "Or had been, at one time?"

"No. He wanted me to locate her."

"During a meditation session?" Etta said.

"Yes."

"You agreed?" Benjamin said.

Madame Grurie let out a heavy sigh. "I thought that I might be able to help. In retrospect, it was a mistake. When his sister failed to manifest, he was upset. He grew angry. He blamed me, rather than his own shortcomings. Now, it appears, he harbors a deep and abiding resentment."

"He intends to create a scandal," Benjamin said. "To besmirch you in any way he can."

Madame Grurie tapped the end of the empty cigarette holder on her lower lip. "I wonder who else our dear Peter approached."

"He didn't say," Benjamin said.

"He wouldn't." She turned from the bed and made her way to the window sash. She parted the drapes and peered out for a time. "Do as he wishes." She turned decisively back toward the bed. "Give him whatever information he wants. I have nothing to hide and nothing to be ashamed of."

"I didn't agree to anything," Benjamin said.

"I expect he arranged to contact you again?"

"No. We didn't agree to meet."

"He didn't give you an address or phone number?"

"Nothing."

Madame Grurie went quickly toward the door. "I'm sure he'll be in touch with you soon enough."

"What should I tell him?"

She opened the door, and paused next to the jamb. "The truth." She shut the door behind her.

Etta removed the damp washcloth from his forehead. He'd forgotten it was there. Cool air tickled his skin.

"Thank—"

She touched a finger to his lips. "Don't talk."

Etta folded the cloth and set it on the night table. Then she lay down beside him, resting her head on the pillow.

Benjamin stiffened under the sheets. "What are you doing?"

"Shhh," she said. "We don't have much time."

"This isn't right," he said. "Zach—"

Etta touched a fingertip to his lips, silencing him. "Zachary had his chance." The fierceness in her voice startled him. "Now, I want mine."

33

Orthinia, Design Space

"I have to go," Tenley said. She wrung her hands. "But I'll come back. If you want."

Olavo nodded. He watched her fingers fidget against the front of her shirt.

"If you don't want me to come back," she said, "I'll understand. But I want you to tell me. The truth."

"All right."

"Promise?"

"Yes." The movement of her fingers mesmerized him. Any moment, he expected the skin to peel from them in soft, bruised rinds.

"I don't want there to be any lies between us," she said.

"Me neither."

"I want us to be honest with each other from now on. So if you don't want me to visit, just say so."

Her fingers stopped. They sought purchase on the lace edging of her blouse, like birds' feet on a clothesline. Her gaze glanced off the armor encasing his arms, too hard to look at for more than an instant.

"You, too," he said. "If you don't want to see me."

"I do." Her smile brimmed with encouragement.

"But you might not. You might change your mind."

The smile lapsed and some of the enthusiasm it contained spilled from one corner. "If I do, I'll tell you."

"No hard feelings," he said.

"That's right." She nodded earnestly. "No expectations, either. It's better that way, in the long run."

"When will you be back?" he said.

"I don't know." She started to shrug, caught herself. "As soon as I can get some more time off. Do you want me to call and leave a message? I can do that. If you want."

"No."

That way he wouldn't be waiting to hear back from her. And she wouldn't feel obligated, or guilty, if it took her a long time to call. Or if she never called. It was possible, after leaving, that she would decide not to come back. Perhaps, in retrospect, she had accomplished everything she'd come to do, gotten answers to her questions. There was no need for a follow-up visit.

"I'll see you." She moved from behind the desk, but seemed uncertain what to do next, with herself or him. "Take care," she finally said.

"You, too."

She turned and walked to the door, fading as she neared it, thinning and dimming.

When she was gone, the room began to fade as well. The floor, walls, and ceiling evaporated. Soon he found himself back in the garden. The only aspect of the room that remained was the bottle. She had left it on the desk. Now it sat on the stone bench to his right. He picked it up . . .

The brown bottle was round, almost circular, with a flat bottom and a short neck. Tenley had brought it with her when she came to look at the latest Science News *Mr. Chin had given him earlier that afternoon. This issue had an article on sea turtles that she was interested in reading. Lately she had begun collecting stuffed turtles, adding them to the growing menagerie of stuffed rabbits, birds, and frogs that had gradually taking over her room since she'd moved in. Rudi couldn't believe it had only been a month. It felt like they'd been friends for years.*

Tenley had peeled the label from the bottle and washed the glass. But he could still smell the scotch she'd poured out of it, as if she'd been in too much of a hurry to rinse it thoroughly.

They sat in the shade of the dogwood tree in his backyard. It was hot and humid. Inside his grandmother was napping in front of the television, lulled to sleep by whatever show she had been watching. Linnea was taking a shower. He'd heard her come home a few hours before dawn. His grandmother never seemed to notice. If she did, she didn't mind. Most of the time she didn't seem to care. It was as if she had decided that there was nothing to be done, nothing she could do. She had given up on Linnea in a way that she hadn't given up on him.

"You sure this is okay with your mom?" Rudi asked.

"She doesn't want it in the house anymore," Tenley said.

"Why not?"

"She told my dad he's drinking too much."

"How come she doesn't want it for your tree?"

"She says it would just make my dad mad. Instead of protecting us from the bad spirits trying to take over his soul, it would bring more of them to the house."

Why it wouldn't do the same to Rudi's house was unclear. But much about the way that the bottles worked was unclear. The colors, shapes, where and when to hang them. It all seemed arbitrary. If there were rules, they weren't obvious to him. In the end, there was nothing to do but trust her.

"What now?" he asked.

"You tie a string around the neck." Tenley said.

She handed him a piece of nylon kite string, frayed at both ends. He looped the string around the neck and tied it in a noose. When he was done, he was left with a foot-long length of string. He lifted the bottle by the string, testing the knot.

"Okay." Tenley stood. She shaded her eyes against the afternoon sun and squinted into the branches of the dogwood.

"Where does it go?" Rudi said. The bottle was heavier than he first thought. The string bit into his fingers.

"There." Tenley pointed to a thick branch, midway up the tree, that looked strong enough to support the weight of the bottle. "Have you got a ladder?"

Rudi shook his head.

"Then you'll have to climb," Tenley said.

Rudi could shimmy up. But once he was in the tree, there would be no way to get the bottle up to him, short of throwing it.

"I'll be right back," he said, handing her the bottle.

"Where are you going?"

"To get a chair."

He ran inside and grabbed a chair from the kitchen table. Linnea walked in, her hair in wet tangles, just as he was hauling it out the sliding glass door.

"What are you doing?"

"Making a spirit tree with Tenley."

Linnea frowned. Before his sister could say anything, Rudi carried the chair across the yard. He set it at the base of the tree, stepped up, and climbed into the lowest branches.

"Now you," Rudi said.

Tenley crawled onto the chair and carefully straightened, holding the bottle up to him like a lantern. The tree swayed under his weight and leaves shook when he reached down to take it from her.

"You're crazy," Linnea said, walking toward them. "Both of

you." She had a Pop-Tart in one hand and a glass of orange juice in the other. Her eyes looked bruised, but that could just be makeup that hadn't washed off. It was hard to tell with her. Sometimes her lips were red, but not from gloss. Other times they were black, and it was from gloss. He could no longer remember what her hair looked like. Each week, it was a different color, just like her fingernails.

Holding the bottle by the neck with one hand, Rudi crawled along the branch to the point where he planned to hang the bottle.

"The limb's going to break," Linnea said. She took a bite of Pop-Tart, then swigged the orange juice.

"That's good," Tenley said to Rudi. She stepped down from the chair and positioned herself under him, ready to catch the bottle if it fell.

Linnea took a step back, out of the way.

Rudi stopped crawling. The limb was beginning to sag. He tucked the bottle under his stomach and threaded the string between his fingers.

"You think it will do any good?" Linnea said. "Keep Mom's ghost from bugging us?"

Was that what he was doing? Trying to keep their mother from haunting them—from coming back and hurting them? He hadn't been thinking about his mother when Tenley showed up with the bottle. He had agreed to hang it as a way of helping her out, because she asked him to.

"It might help," Tenley said. "If she goes inside it."

Linnea snorted. "She never could find her way out of a bottle."

"Then she'll be trapped," Tenley said.

Rudi tied the loose end of the string around the branch. He knotted it four times to make sure it was secure, and then lowered the bottle. It hung below him like a ripe, oddly shaped fruit.

"I'm more worried about one of her old boyfriends showing up," Linnea said. She frowned at the twisting, turning bottle. "If they see one hanging around, they might come looking for another."

"Not if it's empty," Tenley said.

Linnea sniffed. "An empty's just a trophy. An invitation for some people. Where there's an empty, there's a party."

Rudi worked his way back down the branch, to the trunk, then cautiously lowered himself to the chair.

Tenley steadied it for him until he hopped to the ground. The bottle dangled two or three feet above his head, filled with a mixture of light and shadow.

That night, lying awake in bed, he heard the bottle moan. A sick, belly-deep groan, full of pain and discomfort. The crickets grew silent as the complaint grew louder. It went on for hours. Then, suddenly, it stopped.

In the morning, the bottle was gone. The string had been cut. The frayed end dangled from the branch, barely stirring in the still air.

Olavo stared at the bottle in his hand. It was the same bottle that Tenley had given to him in the memory. Was the memory real, or was it artificial—downloaded into him to see how he would respond?

He walked to the balustrade and stood at the stone railing, bottle in hand. If he hurled it over the edge, what would happen? Not to the bottle, but to him. Would the act alter his evolutionary trajectory? What path would his development take as a result of his action?

He knew what would happen to the bottle. It would arc out into space, and appear to fall. Softspace physics would simulate hardspace physics. The same equations would determine its trajectory.

What equations determined his trajectory? Were his thoughts capable of altering the path he took? If he made different choices, could he influence the final outcome of his life? Or was he a slave to the environment he'd found himself in?

"Do you think it will do any good?" a voice said behind him.

Olavo turned. Uta stood at the entrance to one of the alley-wide streets that angled away from the courtyard. She wore blue spandex leggings and a loose white sweatshirt.

"Will what do any good?" he said.

"Getting rid of the bottle." She crossed the courtyard, joining him at the balustrade.

"It's not real," he said. "It won't really break."

"That's not what I meant."

Olavo lowered his arm. It was too heavy to hold up for any length of time. He set the bottle on the railing. "What are you doing here?"

"What do you think?"

He squinted at her tiny upturned face. Russet-colored light shone on gold freckles and pixy-short hair. "Checking up on me."

"For Vania?"

"No one else seems to give a shit."

"You aren't yourself," she said. "You're not thinking clearly." She turned and walked from the balustrade to the edge of the garden.

He turned, but didn't follow her. He said, "If I'm not myself, then who am I?"

"You're not alone." She reached up and plucked a scarlet bottlebrush flower from a low-hanging branch. "You're not the only person to go through this. We all have." She twirled the long, fuzzy blossom under her nose.

Olavo had no idea what she was talking about. He wasn't

sure he'd ever known. He moved from the balustrade into the shade of the bottlebrush tree. "Is that supposed to make me feel better?"

"I was a type 1 diabetic." She stepped onto the ceramic tile footpath that ambled through clumps of foxglove, agapanthus, and purple heather. "I was diagnosed when I was twelve. Ever since I was a teenager, I had to take insulin. First the shots, then the inhaler. This was before islet cell transplants and gene replacement."

Olavo watched her bend down to crush the heather and rub it between her fingers. A cloud of mayflies formed around the fragrance.

She straightened, idly picking a bottlebrush flower. "I hated the shots. It wasn't sticking myself with a needle. You get used to that. The worst part was figuring out how to do it so people didn't know. Or, if they did know, didn't have to watch." She moved from the heather to a cluster of purple chrysanthemums. "Anyway, as a way of coping with—denying—my condition, I did a lot of stupid things. One of those things was having a kid with someone I shouldn't have. I knew it was a bad idea at the time. But I did it anyway. To prove I could, I guess—that I could have a normal life. Of course, after Nailah was born, it didn't work out. We barely lasted two years. When it was over, he wanted custody. He argued the diabetes made me an unfit mother. But there was no way I was going to give up my little girl."

She ran the bottlebrush in her hand over the top of the chrysanthemums, stirring the pompons.

"Anyway, things got nasty. When it was all said and done, I got custody. I thought that would be the end of it. Stupid me. As part of the settlement, he got visiting rights. Two weekends a month. But he wanted more. One day, he took me out to dinner to talk about it. He sounded reasonable. I thought, what the hell, maybe he'll start paying his child support on time. Instead he slipped me something, I don't know what. I woke up in a motel room, with him demanding to know who I'd left Nailah with. He'd tied me to the bed. I was going to stay there, he said, until I told him what he wanted to know."

"Did you?" Olavo said.

"No. I told him I needed my insulin. I said I wasn't going to tell him anything until then. What I didn't realize was that he never intended to give me the insulin."

"He brought you there to kill you."

She nodded. "And blame it on the diabetes. Even if I didn't die, he would still get custody."

"What happened?"

"I slipped into a diabetic coma. Luckily, someone found me before I died. But the damage was done. I'm told there were complications, maybe from the drugs he gave me, that affected the brainstem. You know the rest."

"What happened to your daughter?"

Uta stared at the red bottlebrush in her hand. "I never saw my baby again. I have no idea where he took her or what became of her. I looked, after the surgery and rehab. Even went to the cops. But by then almost a year had passed, and the police didn't have much to go on."

"I'm sorry."

"The point is"—she dropped the bottlebrush flower to the ground—"all of us have something in our past. Drive-by shooting. Bacterial meningitis. Broken baseball bat to the head during a company softball game. That's why we're here, that's what makes us who we are. All of us have had to pick up the pieces, put our lives back together, and start over again at some point."

"So I should just forget the past? Put everything behind me? It doesn't matter. Is that what you're saying?"

"No." She looked up from where she'd dropped the flower

and met his gaze. "If you don't want to go on, you don't have to. No one's forcing you. You can change your mind. You decided once to keep going. You don't have to make the same decision again. Sometimes, staying put is the best way to survive."

Olavo removed the bottle from the railing. He traced the outline of the neck. The smooth circumference of the body. He placed the mouth of the bottle close to his ear and listened.

Softspace modeled hardspace. It mapped design threads, followed possibilities. It extrapolated the effect of environmental influences and introduced mutations to cope with those pressures. If he was going to bend the path of his own design thread, he needed to change the environment he was responding to... alter it so that it affected him differently. Control the stimulus, and he controlled his adaptation. That was what the bird had been doing when it shed its wings and tail. It had been evolving in response to him. *He* was the environmental pressure that it had been adapting to.

He thought of Tenley, in the dream, and Linnea. Tenley had brought him the bottle to hang in his own tree. As what? Protection against his mother, as Linnea seemed to think? Or was there another, less obvious, factor?

He turned to the garden. The tree where he'd buried the shed wings and tail of the bird was still there. He carried the bottle to it. Instead of burying the bottle in the ground, he reached up and wedged it tightly in the cleft between a limb and the trunk. When the bottle was secure, he stepped back and looked at the shape of the glass. He stared into the space it contained—a cavity waiting to be filled, empty of everything except possibility.

34

Eugene, October 5

It was getting light when Rudi uncovered the magazines, buried under a pile of unrelated periodicals.

Science News. Discover. Scientific American. ION. All of the old back issues Mr. Chin had given him. They hadn't been lost by his grandmother, after all, or accidentally tossed out with the garbage. Linnea must have hidden them before she left, then taken them with her. One magazine in particular, the first *ION* he'd shown her, with the article about the artificial rat brain, was well-worn, creased along the spine. Another equally worn issue fell open to an article about junk DNA and certain chemical and neurological transients that led to feelings of supernatural possession in some people, the sense that they were inhabited by another person or being.

Why? What possible use could she have for the magazines? And why all of them? He could see her taking one, if it had an article she was interested in. But all of them?

To keep them from him, Rudi decided, although he could think of no logical reason why. Out of spite? Had she wanted to hurt him? Was she jealous of the time he'd spent reading? Or was she trying to protect him? If so, from what? Or who?

There was only one way to find out.

The door to Linnea's room was still closed, the light off. He put his ear to the thin, hollow core wood but heard nothing. She was sound asleep. He went down the hall to the kitchen. In one of the cupboards he found a can of instant coffee. A kettle sat on the stove. He filled the kettle with water from the tap and turned on the burner. While the water was heating, he went out to the van for a fresh pair of pants and shirt.

His headache was gone, and Rudi couldn't remember the last time his arms had itched. Not since leaving Santa Cruz for Eugene. The scratches were healing, the scabs beginning to flake off like old paint.

He sat in the van for a moment, surrounded by broadcast equipment. He no longer felt the need to speak out, for or against anything. The pressure was gone, relieved when the aneurysm had been repaired. That part of his mind was at peace, as if it had all been the bulging blood vessel pressing against his brain, bearing down on his thoughts.

He hadn't been thinking clearly. Not for a long time. Years. Before the accident, even. Could the aneurysm have been there that long? Slow-growing, the equivalent of a tumor?

He would have to take the van back, he realized. Go back. It was time. Now that he was at peace with himself, it felt possible to make peace with everything and everyone else in his life.

He changed into clean clothes, fished Linnea's copy of *The Blue Cliff Record* from the glove box, then went back into the trailer. He set the book on the coffee table, where it seemed to fit right in with the spent joss sticks. The kettle was just reaching a boil, hissing and spitting. He put two coffee cups on the countertop, spooned in coffee, and poured hot water over the dark crystals.

Letting the coffee cool, he went back to Linnea's room and knocked lightly on the door. . . .

"Linnea?" Rudi said. He cupped his hands over his mouth and spoke in a whisper, afraid of waking his grandmother in the room across the hall. When she didn't answer, he rapped lightly on the door.

The door swung open under his knuckles. A gust of sage incense escaped from the bedroom.

Linnea groaned. The covers shifted as she rolled onto her back. An arm appeared from under the sheet, followed by a face.

Rudi slipped into the room, then eased the door shut behind him. Light blurred the razor-thin gaps in the green plastic venetian blinds snapped shut over her window.

He went to the side of the bed and stood over her.

"What is it?" she said. She rested one arm across her forehead, hiding her face in the crook of her elbow.

"I need to talk to you."

"Now?"

"It's important."

"Is Grandma okay?"

"I think so." She wasn't up yet, but he'd heard her snoring when he passed by her room.

"Then it can wait." Linnea scratched the part in her hair, then yawned. Her black painted lips stretched wide, inner-tube thin.

"What happened to the bottle?" Rudi said.

Linnea lowered her arm from her forehead. Mascara gummed her lashes. Crow's-feet radiated from her lower eyelids where her lashes had pressed into the puffy red skin.

"It's missing," he said.

She rolled onto her side and gathered the pillow against her face. "What are you talking about?" Her voice was muffled.

"The spirit bottle Tenley gave me. Someone took it."

"When?"

"Last night."

She twisted her face on the pillow to blink at him. "How do you know somebody took it?"

"The string was cut."

"Maybe it was an animal," she said. "It could've been a squirrel or a coon. They have sharp teeth."

"The cut was clean."

Linnea let out an exasperated breath. "All right," she admitted, "I did it. But you already knew that, didn't you?"

"Why?"

"It was driving me crazy. I couldn't sleep."

"Is that the real reason? Or is that just an excuse you're making up?"

Linnea sat up. The covers bunched around her waist. Her skin looked pale against her black tank top. "You're right. It's not the real reason. The real reason is you need to let go. Once and for all."

"Let go of what?"

"Mom. She's gone, all right? She's not coming back. Nothing you do is going to bring her back."

"How do you know?"

"Because she's either dead or in jail. Okay?"

"You don't want her to come back," Rudi said. "Do you?"

"Damn right, I don't. Neither should you."

"I didn't put the bottle up there to bring her back," Rudi said. "I put it up there to protect us."

"A bottle isn't going to protect us from anything. It's just a superstition. You're smart enough to know that. Just because Tenley thinks something doesn't mean it's true. You don't have to believe in it just because she does."

"Nothing bad happens to her."

"That's because her parents aren't shithead losers, like Mom. There's nothing scientific about it."

"Sometimes science isn't enough," Rudi said. "It can't do everything. Sometimes you need more."

"Then what good is it? Why do you read all those science magazines if you're still going to believe in the supernatural?"

"A lot of scientists believe in God."

"Even though they can't prove He exists?"

"Just because you can't prove something doesn't mean it doesn't exist. The only thing it means is we don't have the tools to measure it."

"I'm too tired for this, Rudi." She rubbed her face, the way she always did when she made a mistake. "Look. I'm sorry I took your bottle. If you want, we can put up another one."

"Where is it?" he said. "What'd you do with it?"

"I threw it over the fence."

There was a street behind the fence, half asphalt and half gravel where the asphalt had crumbled and washed away.

"Did it break?"

"I don't know. What difference does it make what bottle you use? We'll get you another one."

He shook his head and went to look for the bottle. He found it in the weeds on the side of the road. Pieces of it, anyway, like the ones Tenley had been cleaning up the first time he met her.

That afternoon, while Linnea was out, he went through her stuff, looking for some way to hurt her—something personal he could take or destroy that would make up for the pain she had caused him. . . .

Rudi tried the bedroom door. It was unlocked. He pushed it open. The air inside smelled oddly stale and fetid.

"Linnea?"

She lay on her back in bed. She had pulled the sheets to

her chin. The plain white linen looked gray in the cloudy half-light.

So did her face.

She wasn't breathing. No movement at all, under the shroud of sheets. He could see the outlines of her thighs, hips, and breasts mapped out in wrinkles and creases. In addition to smoothing the sheets, she had combed her hair. Even in the dim light it was lustrous. Clear glassy light winked on her forehead, where she had placed a single quartz crystal. Another crystal, pink, gleamed in the hollow of her throat.

Rudi forced himself to take a step into the room. And then another.

"Lin," he said. He hadn't called her that for twenty years, or more. Not since he was a little kid, and couldn't string the syllables of her name together into a single word. "Say something."

He touched the side of her face. The skin was cold. "Wake up." He pinched her. Once lightly, harder the second time. He checked her neck for a pulse. When he couldn't find one, he carefully removed the sheets from her upper body, afraid to see what she had done to herself, and afraid not to.

She had covered her body in stones and crystals. The stones—mostly clear, pink, and red—were arranged in starburst patterns. They radiated out from her sternum, solar plexus, and abdomen. A single gold-orange stone nestled in her belly button.

She was gone. She'd been gone for hours, slipping away while he was just across the hall.

He stood up, his lungs shrink-wrapped. What now? Call 911. He looked around for a phone. The room was oddly tidy. He would have expected a mess, like the rest of the trailer. But everything was neatly arranged and in order. Dresser drawers closed. Shoes lined up at the foot of the bed.

Clothes folded or on hangers. As if by imposing order on this room she could somehow mitigate the mess she'd made of everything else.

He didn't see a phone. Under the lamp on the night table beside the bed, his gaze settled on an uncapped pill bottle and a mostly empty glass of water. The plastic bottle was empty of whatever drug it had contained. She'd placed it on a flower-speckled memo pad, as if using it as a paperweight.

A digital clock on the floor blinked at him, splashing light the color of blood on the wall. He expected to hear music, no different from when he'd found his grandmother. But this time the clock was quiet, almost mocking in its silence.

He moved the water glass aside, revealing a handwritten note. It took a moment for the blurred squiggles to resolve.

Dear Rudi,

I'm sorry to leave you this way. Truly. I didn't expect to be called home so soon, and not in this way. I expected to be around for a long time. Don't we all. It's not like I've been planning this for a long time. Believe it or not, I still had a lot of things I wanted to do in this life. Seeing you again, explaining myself, and apologizing to you for all the grief I put you through was one of them. In a way, your presence here has released me (the way it did back when Grandma was alive). Maybe that's why I got the call when I did. I've done all I needed to in this world, accomplished everything I came here to do. I still don't know exactly what that was. I'll find out soon. When I do, I wish I could tell you. Unfortunately, that will have to wait. There's nothing I can do now, except tell you that I love you. I always have, even though I didn't always say it or show it.

This is the second time I've left you. Both times, it's you who has given me the strength to leave. I know that probably sounds strange, but it's true. I don't want you to think that you caused me to leave. That's different from making it possible for me to go. I hope you understand that. I never meant to hurt you. That wasn't my intention then, and it isn't now. The first time I left you, I was trying to find my calling in life. I know how selfish and lame that must sound. But I was being called to leave then, the way I am now, by a higher power. And I wouldn't have left unless I knew that you would be all right without me. Better, maybe. I think that was one of the hidden purposes of my going off—to help you grow in ways you couldn't with me around.

I realize I've probably left you with more questions than answers at this point. Just like before. I seem to be good at doing that—not just with you but with myself. There's a lot I still don't understand, about who I am and where I come from. Where *we* come from. You're just like me. I say that because I believe it's true. I believe that, eventually, all this will make sense. I believe that we'll meet again, though I don't know when or where. Maybe not as we see ourselves now, but in a different form. Our true form.

Love always,
Lin

Rudi set the pad down. He turned to look at his sister. Her face was statuesque, her expression contemplative, inwardly serene. She seemed weighted down by the crystals and at the same time uplifted by them. A gap between the pillow and mattress revealed one side of her neck and part of her back.

There, he could see the outermost tips of the angel wings that spread from her spine to the sharp joints of her shoulders.

The night she'd gotten the tattoo, Rudi thought she'd sold herself—exchanged one part of her anatomy for another. Even if she had, what difference did it make? She knew what she wanted, what was important to her. A lot of people didn't. They were afraid to do what it took to break free, especially if it hurt.

And it always did.

It didn't look like her death had hurt. She'd slipped into it peacefully, the way she might a warm bath. She had let the water grow still around her, cooling as it cooled, until equilibrium had been achieved, balance restored.

The feathers weren't as clean and sharp as he remembered. They had blurred over time. Now they were smudged, soft-edged as melted wax. She had never been able to go as high or far as she wanted in this world. No wonder she had decided to end it here, now. It was the only way to keep going, to continue the journey. She'd come as far as she could. They both had. He couldn't go any farther, either.

"I don't blame you," he said. "I did. But I don't anymore."

All that was left to do now was see her on her way. Rudi bent over her, kissed her on the forehead, and straightened.

There was nothing more he could do for her here. The only question was whether he took her with him or left her.

"What do you think?" he asked her. "Do you want to stay, or do you want to come with me?"

In the end, there was nothing for him to decide. She had made the decision for him when she went on ahead without him. She had already tried to go back home once. There was no point forcing her to do it again.

Except for the note, and the newspaper articles on Benjamin Taupe, the letters to his relatives, and diary, Rudi left everything exactly as it was, including the magazines. No one knew who he was. The van could belong to any one of her clients. He was no one. He had never been here. He had already buried her a long time ago. One funeral was enough. It had been a long one. Now it was finally over.

35

San Francisco, Circa 1937

"Wake up!" Etta said in a rough whisper.

Benjamin stirred, dimly aware of muffled pounding. The thudding came from downstairs and reverberated through the plaster walls of the house.

"What?" He jerked blearily upright. "What's going on?"

Etta was already sitting next to him, half-dressed. She scrambled out of bed, just as Madame Grurie barged in.

"You have to leave," she said to both of them. "Now."

Benjamin located his pants under the covers at the end of the bed. He crammed his feet into the legs at the same time he pulled them to his waist.

"Who is it?" Etta said. She sat on the chair next to the window and pulled on a pair of leather shoes over bare feet.

"The police. You won't be able to leave through the back door. I'm afraid they've cordoned that off. You'll have to use the tunnel in the basement."

Clutching the bedding to his midsection, Benjamin reached for the shirt and coat draped on the back of the chair. "What do they want?"

"It's not hard to imagine," Madame Grurie said. "Our friend Peter has been sowing the seeds of discontent."

"Or Zachary," Etta said, buttoning a spencer jacket over her nightgown. "It's the sort of petty reprisal he would make."

Benjamin squirmed into his shirt, kicked free of the covers. He swung his legs over the edge of the bed and bent over, fumbling for his shoes.

"Police!" a voice called from the street. "Open up!" Several more thuds rattled the walls.

Benjamin stomped into his shoes, then stood up. His suspenders were tangled. He managed to sling one over his shoulder, but the second one was too twisted and knotted to stay in place.

"The tunnel entrance is behind the wine rack." Madame Grurie stood with her back pressed to the door, holding it open for them.

Benjamin peeked out the window as he hurried past. The street below was slick with condensation and saturated with glare, as if the predawn glisten of streetlamps and lanterns had precipitated as mist out of the night.

"This way," Madame Grurie said. She led them downstairs to a nondescript door under the main staircase. The door had been papered to match the wall. Only a latch and the faint outline of a rectangle was visible.

The door opened outward to reveal a set of narrow steps that plunged into a cellar filled with cool, musty air.

The hammering on the front door grew more adamant. At any moment, Benjamin expected to hear wood splinter or one of the Tiffany glass panes shatter. He turned back to the cellar steps.

"At the bottom, you will find the wine rack to your right," Madame Grurie said. She handed Benjamin the lantern she held.

"Where does the tunnel lead?" Benjamin asked.

"To an antique store across the street. There's an alley in back. You should be able to escape unseen from there."

Benjamin started down the stairs.

Etta hesitated behind him, caught in breathless uncertainty. "What about you?" she said to Madame Grurie. "Aren't you coming with us?"

"Not right now. Don't worry about me." She patted her French twist. "I'll be just fine."

"You can't know that."

Madame Grurie shooed off her protestations with an airy wave of her hand. "There is nothing the police can do to me. Particularly if they don't find anyone else inside of the house."

Benjamin seized Etta by the wrist and began their descent.

Etta looked back. "When will we see you again?"

"Soon," Madame Grurie said. She closed the door firmly and turned the key in the lock. The sound of the police dropped to a murmur.

"Let's go," Etta said.

Benjamin placed his right hand on the brick wall next to him. Holding the lantern in his left hand, he groped his way down. Shadows scurried out of their way, pushed back by the lantern's halo.

The wall ended at the foot of the stairs. The cellar floor was uneven brick. Above them, Benjamin heard the muffled thump of footsteps, the slamming of doors.

"They're searching the house," Etta said.

"Shh," Benjamin said.

He turned right. To their left, lined up along the wall, were six dining room chairs. Next to them, stacked against the wall and partly covered by sheets, were several large oil paintings with gold-embossed frames. A sailing ship graced one. Snow-capped mountains another. Fifteen feet ahead of them, dusty wine bottles gleamed in dusty rows on a floor-to-ceiling rack.

"That must be it," Benjamin said.

Etta peered into the unsteady gloom. "I don't see anything obvious. But I imagine that's the point."

"It doesn't look like it's been used in a long time," Benjamin said. "I hope it hasn't collapsed or been sealed off." He scanned the wine rack, searching for a way to move it.

"She wouldn't have sent us down here if that was the case."

"Let's hope so."

"I wonder why someone built a tunnel between this house and the store," Etta said.

"Bootleggers," Benjamin said. He handed Etta the lantern and approached the wine rack. There was no obvious mechanism to move it. He tugged on the rack. Joints groaned and bottles rattled, but the rack refused to move.

"Try moving it sideways," Etta suggested.

Above them, something crashed to the floor. Grit sifted down from the floor joists overhead. Benjamin pulled on the rack. Nothing happened. The door at the head of the cellar stairs rattled.

"Hurry!" Etta said. The lantern swayed and the halo of light wobbled around them like an off-kilter top.

He tried pulling in the opposite direction. The rack shifted slightly, then grated to a stop. "It's stuck," Benjamin said.

Etta set the lantern on the floor. Something hard struck the door to the cellar. Once. Twice.

Etta grabbed the rack. Together, they rolled it aside on coasters stiff with rust and disuse, exposing a narrow doorway less than three and a half feet wide and slightly over five feet tall. The entrance was sealed with a panel of wainscoting that had been wedged in place. The insert prevented the tunnel from being seen in between the rows of wine bottles. There were no hinges that he could see. No doorknob.

Benjamin tapped the panel. "Hollow," he said. "This is it."

While Benjamin looked for a way to move the panel, Etta retrieved the lantern. Another blow echoed from the cellar door. This time wood cracked and a splinter of light slanted down the stairs.

"Down here," a voice said. "Got us a wine cellar."

Etta came up beside him. Two brass handles, positioned on either side of the panel, glinted. They were positioned about halfway up. Benjamin gripped them and pulled. The veneer popped free, revealing the cramped interior of the tunnel.

"There's someone down here," the voice at the top of the cellar stairs said. "I can hear him."

"Come out of there now," a second voice called down. "It'll go easier if you don't make us come down."

"Go," Benjamin whispered. He moved aside and ushered Etta into the tunnel. She ducked her head and held the lantern in front of her. The walls of the tunnel were pickax-rough. Solid oak posts and beams supported the ceiling.

"Are you coming?" Etta said. The tunnel deepened with each step she took, growing longer and narrower.

Benjamin grabbed the handles on the thin panel. Instead of slipping into the tunnel behind her, he began to fit it back into place. "I'll catch up with you later," he whispered.

She twisted her head. But the shaft was too narrow and low for her to turn around fully. "What are you talking about?"

"They'll be down here in a few moments. There isn't time to move the rack back into place from the tunnel."

"I'm not leaving without you." She began to back up.

"They know one person is down here," Benjamin said. He

fitted the panel against the beams, leaving an inch-wide gap on one side. "Not two. If I stay, they won't look for you."

She paused, her head half-turned, an ivory cameo in the moth-gray light. "But you'll be arrested!"

"If you're caught, Zachary will have you committed. There's nothing they can do to me."

"They can put you in jail."

Benjamin shrugged. "I'm dying." Already dead, he thought. "They won't send a sick man to jail. What's the point?"

"What about Madame Grurie?"

"My being here won't make any difference."

"How will I find you?"

The cellar door squealed open. The gloom behind him ebbed, replaced by a mote-dappled luminescence.

"There's a Seals game tomorrow night," Benjamin whispered. "Look for me there."

Before she could respond, he shoved the panel into place and grasped the wine rack. It moved more easily now that the wheels had been loosened.

Footsteps clomped down the cellar stairs. They descended quickly at first, and then more cautiously.

A shadow stretched across the floor. Paused.

"Take it easy," a voice said. It was the same voice that had ordered him out of the cellar. "We don't want any trouble."

Benjamin pulled a bottle of wine from the rack. He broke the neck against the wall, sat down in front of the rack, and poured wine into his upturned mouth.

The shadow shifted. A policeman stepped into view.

Benjamin shaded his eyes against the glare of the man's lantern. He tilted his head back and splashed another drink onto his face and the front of his shirt.

"I'll be damned," the cop said. "What have we got here?"

36

Sand Mountain, Hardspace

Ghosts haunted the shadows of Mee Won's room.

They clung to the bedposts and the black lacquered dresser with its white lace runner, huddled in the closet and congregated in the shuttered lightwell like conformal field transients trapped in anti de Sitter space. The shadows themselves were like fabric, as smooth as the neatly tucked bedspread.

Mee Won had set her room in order.

Banshee wails scathed Olavo's thoughts. Interstitial auditory hallucinations whispered to him across dimensions.

Gone, the ghosts muttered, disconsolate, lamenting among themselves. *Not coming back.* Their voices taunted. They irritated, dry as desiccated leaves scratching at the panes of an unopened window.

He went to the window and parted the venetian blinds. The window looked out on the dune-filled lakebed, the bubble-domed agriciles ringing the polis, and the colorful benzene-ring umbrellas planted in rows on Silicon Beach.

The sun hung like a lantern over the suspension bridge, a gibbous red bulge pressing against the brown haze....

He lay on the side of the road, partway down an embankment cushioned with soft tufts of grass, prickly undergrowth, and rampant kudzu. The vines had stopped him, prevented him from being thrown even farther down the embankment. His legs and arms were tangled in the stuff, bound to the soggy ground by hundreds of Lilliputian snarls and snags.

Above him, a bright glare filled the sky.

The light was intense, painful to look at, but he couldn't close his eyes. Couldn't move. The faceplate of his helmet was cracked. Jagged fracture lines veined the plastic.

His head hurt. So did his arms. He could feel bone sticking out, pressing against wet fabric the way tent posts pulled and stretched wet nylon.

Every now and then, his arms and legs shuddered. The palsied spasm sloshed up and down him, jerking his limbs.

In between the sloshing, his body was inert. Paralyzed.

"Down here!" a voice above him called. The voice rang inside the glare, as if the radiance was a bell. Deep, resonant, full of authority.

More voices reverberated within the light. Soon he heard boots slipping toward him, scrabbling through the undergrowth in a barely controlled fall.

"Jesus." The man squatted next to him. "Can you hear me?"

Rudi opened his mouth, but vomit gurgled up, violently and unexpectedly.

"He's alive," the man called up the embankment. "But we got head trauma, and probably neck injury, too. Helmet's messed up and I'm not getting any response when I squeeze his hands."

The man hadn't squeezed his hands. Rudi could feel his hands. They were right next to him.

"I got two broken arms," the man went on. "Maybe a leg."

Rudi felt sick again. This time the puke boiled over, as hot and bitter as battery acid. It burned his tongue, scalded his lips.

"Shit," the man said. "He's choking. I'm gonna have to turn his head. Son of a bitch!"

Rudi couldn't breathe. Not only that, he was freezing. Dry ice frigid. The chill went soul deep, immersing him in blackness.

Later, he felt himself being lifted up, out of the darkness and into the sun-intense glare. It was a slow tortuous ascent, fraught with stumbling.

Hang on, *he told himself. Just get to the top of the hill and everything would be all right. He would live.*

More than that, he would be reborn.

An ambulance waited at the top. Red lights flashing. A tractor-trailer had jackknifed across the road. Some of its load had spilled onto the roadway. Enormous sections of concrete pipe crisscrossed the road like pick-up sticks.

Just before the paramedics loaded him into the back of the ambulance, he saw a mangled piece of metal, almost unrecognizable but not quite.

His motorcycle.

It had been crushed under the semi. The asphalt near it was chewed up. Deep gouges scored the surface of the road. One of the tires was missing, the other was flat. Glass sparkled in the strobe lights. It was a miracle he'd survived. He hadn't exactly walked away from the head-on collision. But he shouldn't have lived.

Lying in the ambulance, listening to the siren carve a path through the night, Rudi understood that he'd been given a second chance... an opportunity to make something of himself and his life.

After several minutes, Olavo turned from the window to the room. He checked the dresser first. He started with the top drawer and worked his way down, scavenging for an old touch-screen address pad or memory chip. For the most part, the drawers were empty. She had taken most of her belongings—socks, panties, bras, and thin-strapped camisoles, along with her makeup and jewelry. In the bottom drawer he found a loose gargoyle earring and a tube of crayon-black lipstick, worn to a nub.

Next he checked the bed, searching the crevices of the spun microfilament mattress and magnetic support frame. The frame was carved with erotic Japanese ukiyo-e woodcuts. The sheets were a tapestry of Edo period *shunga* prints, the fornication as colorful as it was animated.

Mee Won had changed. Without his realizing it, she had become another person, a version of Acantha he barely recognized. Perhaps he'd never known her, or seen only the person he wanted to see.

Feeling sick to his stomach, he turned from the woodcuts. It was happening again. First Linnea, then Tenley, and now Acantha and Mee Won. What was the matter with him? Why did he keep ruining everything, and everyone, he cared most about? Why couldn't he get anything right?

A Japanese scroll hung on the wall behind the bed, spare gray-and-black brushstrokes in the shape of a fisherman casting a net. He turned the scroll to another view, phosphor-etched on what appeared to be a curved glass screen...

...where an ambulance sat in the gravel driveway leading to a house. Not really a house, but a trailer with aluminum siding and a temporary awning erected over an equally makeshift porch.

It looked like the ambulance had been there a while. The emergency light on top was turned off and paramedics lounged next to a stretcher, waiting. The front door to the house was open, watched over by a deputy with a wide-brimmed hat. Through the main window on the front of the trailer, activity was visible. Figures moved about inside, measuring, collecting, photographing.

The picture cut to a woman holding a microphone close to her mouth. The reporter's lips moved, soundlessly documenting the scene behind her.

The camera switched back to the house. A plainclothes detective descended the stairs. The paramedics stood up, pulled a stretcher from the back of the ambulance, and carried it into the mobile home.

The camera zoomed in on the main door to the trailer. Presently, the paramedics reappeared, carrying a zipped body bag on the stretcher. In the background a second deputy walked down from the embankment behind the trailer. The camera cut back to the reporter. She raised the microphone...

...and evaporated into a cloud of static.

The ghosts had grown eerily somber. They gathered near the scroll as if standing vigil over a coffin.

Olavo turned from the scroll to the closet. The sliding doors were plain, white silk set in black-lacquered frames. They moved aside to reveal linen shelves and a few clothes on hangers, including a man's suit. There was also a collection of veils, which Olavo had seen for sale around the polis. The veils clipped to headlaces with decorative art nouveau and art deco clasps. When the silver or gold chains were fitted around the crown of the head, the veils hung down, replacing the face of the wearer with a stylized, digitized mask. Olavo traced the gossamer-thin fabric. The veils came alive under his touch, activated by bioelectrics. Faces bloomed and twisted on their chains. Most were women. But one was a man's face, clean-shaven with short straight hair, parted on the side.

Olavo shuddered. He felt the ghosts behind him, peering over his shoulder. What was Mee Won doing with a man's mask and clothing in her closet?

He shifted his attention from the veils to the suit. It was brown and appeared to be made of worsted wool, woven in a houndstooth pattern. The slacks were patternless, shiny, and hard against his fingertips. Tucked inside the jacket was a blue pinstripe shirt. There was a felt hat on one of the shelves. Beneath the hat, he discovered a small, tightly rolled scrollette.

Behind him the ghosts howled. They gusted about the room, ghoulish hands clapped to the sides of their heads.

Olavo removed the suit and veil from the closet. He laid them on the bed, removed his own clothes, and put on the suit. He fastened the headlace, felt the veil caress his face, and fitted the hat into place. Then he mirrored the scroll on the wall and looked at himself.

The veil appeared to be transparent. But instead of seeing his own face through the fabric, he saw the silkscreen image of a man who might have been himself, in another place at another time.

He ripped the veil from his head and flung it to the floor. Breathing heavily, he sat on the side of the bed. When he caught his breath, he picked up the scrollette and unrolled the vellum with trembling fingers.

He expected a note from Mee Won, explaining the veils, the suit. What he got was a diary. The entries, written in a cursive that had been outmoded for centuries, were dated 1937 to 1939.

37

Prattville, October 10

The house was robin's egg blue instead of sunflower yellow; red trim had replaced the white. There were other small differences. But overall the little three-bedroom clapboard hadn't changed much. If anything it looked better. The house was in good repair, the yard neat—newly landscaped with flower beds and ornamental fruit trees. Whoever was living there now kept the place well maintained.

Quaint, Rudi thought. That was the word. A lot of care and attention to detail had gone into upgrading the place. It wasn't the eyesore it had once been. The yard was mowed, the trees pruned. Even the bamboo hedge had been trimmed and a coat of fresh paint applied to the fence separating his house from Tenley's.

Her parents had moved out a long time ago, shortly after she'd gone off to college. The spirit tree was gone, cut down and replaced with a red and yellow plastic playset complete with swings and a slide.

No more spirits. That seemed like the biggest loss of all. No glass bottles—with their stems of twine—hanging in fruitlike clusters. He missed the sounds they made. The low, mournful notes that seemed to rise up out of nothing. Those spirits, trapped in their bottles, had spoken to him. They gave a voice to his own emptiness, and in that way filled it.

Rudi stepped out of the broadcast van. Shoulders hunched, feeling like an interloper in the neighborhood he'd once called home, he made his way quickly past Tenley's house until he stood in front of the one he had grown up in. That was what it felt like. His childhood had ended the day he was taken into custody. From that point forward, he'd been on his own. He'd lived with a foster family and in a group home, but his life was elsewhere. The problem was, he didn't know where. He kept waiting for his life to start over. But it never had. It hadn't gone anywhere.

It was mid-afternoon. The street was quiet, the curtains drawn. No one appeared to be home. He went up the walk from the driveway to the front door. He paused a moment. If somebody answered, he had no idea what he would say—what excuse he would make. Mainly he just wanted to see the person who lived there now. He wanted to put a face to the tidy yard and new paint—wanted to know into whose hands its upkeep had fallen. Then, he could let go.

He rang the bell. Rang it again. There was no answer.

Rudi glanced around. An old rusted Jeep passed by on the street and turned at the intersection half a block down. No curious neighbors had stepped outside to ogle him. Rudi retraced his steps to the driveway and made his way around the side of the house. He paused at the gate to the backyard, listening. When he didn't hear a dog, he undid the latch on the gate and eased it open.

The backyard had been landscaped like the front. A low wood deck, with square planter boxes, covered the old concrete patio. A sand path ran next to the bamboo hedge. From there, it followed the back fence to a pond. The pond, surrounded on all sides with flat stone, gurgled near the dogwood tree. Water lilies floated on the surface, and black and orange speckled koi drifted contentedly between the stems. They moved peacefully, gracefully, perfectly at ease in their small world in a way he'd never been in his. With the death of his grandmother and the disappearance of Linnea, his world had shrunk. It had closed in, rules and restrictions growing increasingly tighter and claustrophobic.

Like Linnea, his only escape had been the sky....

Rudi lay on his back in the drainage ditch behind the backyard, and imagined that he was falling into the cumulus clouds above him.

If he flip-flopped things in his head, sometimes he could make the clouds look like mountains and valleys. The blue sky was water: lakes, rivers, the sea. It was like looking down onto a different world.

A different planet, even.

He traced the outline of a coastal island. On this world, the environment would be different. Strange. Hostile. In order to survive there, he would be forced to change. He would have to adapt to the new conditions, evolve into a different form of life. After a while, he would no longer be human. But that would be all right. He would be smarter, stronger, capable of surviving on his own. He would be free of the constraints of the past. Free to determine who, or what, he would be.

And if one design didn't work, he would try another. He could change as much as he wanted, as many times as he wanted.

Like Linnea, with her wings and tattoos. But he would change from the inside out, instead of the outside in. He would start at the level of his cells and he would grow a new body.

On one world, his limbs hardened into sticks, capable of withstanding drought and sandstorms. On another planet, he excreted a thick, protective coating of armor over his arms and legs, the way a clam formed a hard pearl to protect itself from further injury.

There was no limit to who he could become. After a while he lost track of himself. He forgot who he was and, more importantly, where he was. The world in his mind became more real than the one he left behind. Maybe it was. There was no reason that it couldn't be. Perhaps the world he thought was real was actually imagined. He didn't really belong here. His true self existed on one of those other worlds, and the one where he lived with a foster family and a surrogate mother was a fever dream or a drug-induced nightmare or cybernetic hallucination.

He was all of these people. At the same time, he was none of them.

"Rudi?" his foster mother called. "Where are you?"

Rudi felt gravity lose its grip. Felt himself start to float upward, faster and faster, until his perspective flipped and he was falling.

"I know you're out there," Bethlyn said. "It's time for our counseling session. We have to leave, honey. We don't want to keep Miss Parkins waiting."

Yanked back to where he was lying on the grass, Rudi couldn't answer. Couldn't breathe. Above him the clouds spun, delirious. They were no longer gateways to different worlds. They were nothing special. Neither was he. Hopelessness settled over him like a heavy stone, crushing him to the ground.

"Can I help you?" The voice, a man's, came from the deck.

Rudi looked up from the pond. He had been staring at the koi, captivated by the hypnotic motion of light across their scales and fins. How long had he been gazing into the pool?

Seconds? Minutes? Longer . . . ?

"What are you doing here?" the man said, his face dappled by the shade of a small peach tree.

"I'm sorry." Rudi shook his head. "I knocked. But there was no answer." Which was hardly an excuse. It wasn't even a very good explanation for why he had entered the man's yard.

"What do you want?" the man asked. He seemed uneasy... agitated. Poised on the verge of calling for help.

"I didn't mean to trespass," Rudi said. "I was just in the neighborhood and I knew someone who used to live here."

He started toward the gate.

"Rudi?" The voice stepped toward him. "Is that you?"

Rudi hesitated in mid-step, then kept moving, his eyes downcast. The last thing he wanted was for anyone from the old neighborhood to know he was here... that he'd come back looking for himself.

"It's me," the man said, walking across the lawn toward him. "Mr. Chin."

Rudi stopped. Blinked at the grass, trying to bring the clipped blades into sharper focus.

"I didn't recognize you," Mr. Chin said. The man was peering at him, hands held out as both a greeting and an offering.

Rudi took them, accepting the gift the way he'd accepted the magazines, greedily and thankfully.

"I'm sorry," Mr. Chin said. "It's been so long. I never expected to see you again."

"Me, neither," Rudi said.

"Please, come in." Mr. Chin led him to the house. "Let me fix you something to drink. I have lemonade. And I just put on some water for tea. What a surprise, after all these years."

"It's true," Mr. Chin said. "I quit the store. A man struck me in the head with a gun. That day, he didn't pull the trigger. But I knew one day, he would. Not that man maybe, but another man."

"I looked for you." Rudi sipped green tea from a cup. "A few months after my grandmother died."

"I didn't know where to find you," Mr. Chin said. "Social Services wouldn't tell me. Then I went to live with my sister for a while."

"They put me with a foster family," Rudi said. "On the other side of town."

"I would have looked after you," Mr. Chin said. "You could have lived with me." He chuckled, both amused and wistful. "We could have taught each other many things."

Rudi set his empty cup down. "What could I teach you?"

"What it's like to be a father. I never had any children. I would have liked a son. Someone I could share all my crazy ideas with. But maybe it's not too late for that now. Eh? It's never too late. You're older, but so am I. All things are still equal."

Rudi finished his tea and set the ceramic cup on the placemat in front of him. "Where are you working now?"

"Down at the hardware store. I mix paint. It keeps my life colorful, not too dull." He laughed at his own joke, one he'd obviously told many times.

"The place looks great," Rudi said. The interior had been remodeled. White pine floors, skylights, new doors and windows.

"So," Mr. Chin said. "You're coming back now. I suppose I'm going to have to move after all these years. Find another place to live, now that I've gotten comfortable."

"What do you mean?"

"When I moved into this place, your sister said you might come back. I knew I might have to leave."

"You're renting it?"

"Not exactly." Mr. Chin dropped his gaze, sheepish. "She said I could live here, rent free, if I looked after the place. Kept it up."

"I had no idea," Rudi said.

"She didn't tell you?" Mr. Chin said.

Rudi stared into the empty cup. "She didn't say anything the last time I talked to her."

"About five years ago," Mr. Chin said, "I ran into your sister at the supermarket. I asked about you, but she said she didn't know where you were. She wanted to know if I knew anyone who needed a place to stay. I had just been given thirty days' notice on the place I was living. The owner had a newly married daughter who wanted to move in. When I showed up here the house was a disaster, a complete mess." Mr. Chin wrinkled his nose in disgust. "Whoever was staying here hadn't taken very good care of the place. It needed a lot of work."

"She didn't say who'd been living here?"

Mr. Chin shrugged. "No. It was none of my business, so I didn't ask. When she said you might be coming back I was happy to help. Plus it was free. Except for the cost of the repairs."

"I had no idea who owned the place," Rudi said.

Their grandmother must have willed it to Linnea. When she turned eighteen, the house would have become hers. She must have been planning to tell him at some point. Otherwise, why would she tell Mr. Chin that he might be coming back?

"I haven't talked to your sister in a while," Mr. Chin said. "I have a number she gave me, but it's disconnected."

"She's dead," Rudi said. "She passed away a few days ago."

"I'm sorry." Mr. Chin shook his head, sadly, regretfully. "I know how much she meant to you. I always wanted the best for her."

"She died peacefully," Rudi said.

"That's good." Mr. Chin nodded to himself. "She looked so hard for peace. I'm glad she finally found it."

"You think that's what she was looking for?" Rudi said. "Peace?"

Mr. Chin considered. "That's what it seemed like. To me.

The bird that struggles the most in its cage is the least content. Every time I saw your sister, I got the impression she was struggling."

"Against what?"

"Not against," Mr. Chin said. "For."

"Is there a difference?" Rudi asked.

Mr. Chin frowned. "It's easy to fight against something. You see your enemy, and the sight of your opponent reminds you of what, or who, you're fighting against. It's harder to struggle for something. Especially if what you're fighting for isn't clear in your mind. It's easy to lose your way."

"You don't think Linnea knew what she wanted?"

"I think she wanted to fly away," Mr. Chin said. "But I don't think she knew where she wanted to fly to."

"Like me," Rudi said.

"And now you're back." Mr. Chin beamed. He seemed genuinely pleased to see Rudi, even if his sudden appearance meant the man might have to move again.

"I don't know for how long," Rudi said.

"For as long as it takes," Mr. Chin said, equable. "After all, this is your house."

Mr. Chin put him up in his old room. It wasn't as bad as he thought. Like the rest of the house, it had been remodeled. Rudi lay awake for a time, listening to the night, but no voices spoke to him. No music played from inside his head. The darkness was filled with the chirp of crickets and the serene trickle of the pond.

And when he finally drifted off, there were no nightmares, despite what lay ahead.

38

San Francisco, Circa 1937

Day never came for Benjamin. Morning dawned, with its usual clatter of streetcars, truck engines, and whistles. But it was murky and gray. Fog swirled over his sight.

The walls of the jail cell were indistinct, more apparition than stone except when he touched them. Under his fingertips, they became hard and cold, and conjured a shiver that tingled through him like an electric current. The tingling remained with him as the morning lengthened. It ate at him, eroding his equilibrium and the strength in his left arm and leg. By mid-morning, when Zachary arrived to bail him out, he could no longer stand.

"Get up," a policeman ordered.

Benjamin shifted on the floor where he'd collapsed. Dimly, he saw two figures in the door.

One of the figures charged toward him, enraged as a bull. "I said get up!"

"He's sick," Zachary said.

"Drunk is more like it."

"No," Benjamin said. His head quivered in denial, almost of its own volition.

"He needs to see a doctor," Zachary said. "He has a tumor. In his head. If you know what a tumor is."

"I know what he's got in his head," the cop growled. "Christ, he's gone and pissed on the floor."

"I'll take care of him," Zachary said.

"Just get him outta here before he stinks up the whole place. Goddamn drunks."

One of the figures left. The other knelt down beside him. Benjamin felt a hand on his arm. "I can't see," he said. The edges of the words were fuzzy, eraser-smeared.

"Not at all?"

"A little."

"You're saying you're blind?"

"I can't stand up on my own, either. You're going to have to help me."

"All right." Zachary draped Benjamin's right arm over his neck, grasped him tightly, and helped him to his feet. Benjamin leaned unsteadily against him, and together they made their way out of the jailhouse.

"What the hell happened to you last night?" Zachary said when they reached the street.

"I was fine when they put me in here. But when I woke up, my vision was cloudy and I couldn't lift my left arm."

"The police said they arrested you and Madame Grurie. They're charging her with prostitution."

"They have no proof."

"They have you."

Benjamin choked on a laugh. "Look at me. I can't even stand. Nothing happened between us." Or anyone else, he almost added. But the lie gummed on his tongue.

Zachary nodded. "What do you want to do?"

"Sit down. I could use a bite to eat, too. They didn't feed me anything, in there. I guess they figured I'd just throw it up."

Zachary took him down the street to a breakfast café with a steam table. Benjamin smelled sausages, beef stew, potato pancakes, and Spanish tripe. Zachary found a table at the back, away from the window, and loaded up food trays for both of them.

Benjamin ate slowly. He couldn't hold a fork, so he ate the pancakes using his fingers, then turned his attention to the bowl of beef stew.

"What are you going to do now?" Zachary said. He had stopped eating to stare at him.

"I don't know. Not much I can do." Benjamin raised the steaming bowl to his lips and slurped.

"You want me to take you to the hospital?"

Benjamin set the bowl down gently, careful not to splash. With a napkin, he wiped stew from his chin. "The office," he said.

"The office?"

He didn't want to spend whatever time he had left in a hospital. At least at the office, he could pretend his life wasn't over. "After that," he said, "the Seals game."

"You're crazy."

"It might be the last one I get a chance to see."

"You won't be able to see it at all," Zachary said. "What's the point in going?"

"I'll be there," Benjamin said. "That's the point." He had to talk to Etta, if he could. It might not be possible, with Zachary at his side, but he had to try. He couldn't not show up.

"All right," Zachary said. "If that's what you want." He played with his hash for a moment. "Was Etta there last night?" he finally asked. "Did you see her at the institute?"

"Yes."

The breath hissed out of Zachary, loud and hot as steam from a boiler.

"She got out, just before the police arrived," Benjamin said. "They didn't see her. They don't even know she was there."

Zachary sucked air between his teeth. "Did you talk to her?"

Benjamin swallowed at the lump of guilt in his throat. "Briefly." It was true; they hadn't talked much.

"What did she say?"

About me. The unspoken words hovered in the air between them, tenuous as the vapor rising from their plates.

Benjamin located his spoon again, let the heat of the stew-warmed metal enter his fingertips. "She wants the chance to live her own life."

"I see." Zachary's voice dropped to the tray in front of him.

"I don't know for how long," Benjamin said. "She didn't say what her plans are."

"Do you know where she is now?" Zachary asked.

"No."

"She didn't say anything about what she planned to do next? Or where she might be going?"

"If she did, she didn't tell me," Benjamin said. "She might have told Madame Grurie."

A short pause filled with the clatter of trays, silverware, and the scrape of chair legs on the floor tile. "A reporter approached me," Zachary said.

"Peter McGraff?" Benjamin said.

"Yes. His sister disappeared a while ago. He claims Madame Grurie kidnapped her. He wanted to know if I could tell him anything about their relationship or what I might know about the institute."

"He told me his sister had disappeared earlier and that he'd gone to Madame Grurie for help in locating her."

"You don't believe him?"

"Things didn't work out the way he wanted. Madame Grurie was unable to locate her, and now he's out for revenge."

"What about Etta? Is Madame Grurie holding her against her will?"

"I don't think Madame Grurie could force Etta to do something she didn't want to," Benjamin said.

"You're certain?"

"I know you don't want to believe Etta chose to leave," Benjamin said, "but it's true. I have no reason to think otherwise."

"So it's over," Zachary said. His figure shrank somewhat, hunching into itself. "She's gone."

"For now," Benjamin agreed.

"Forever," Zachary said. A resigned fatalism settled over him, which he wrapped around himself like a heavy blanket.

"What about you?" Benjamin said. "What are you going to do?" He stared at Zachary's outline, unable to read the indistinct smudge of his face. He was like a charcoal drawing, sketched onto the air.

"Not much I can do."

"Meaning... what? You're going to let her go?"

Zachary's figure continued to slacken, slumping even deeper and more miserably into his chair. "If that's what she wants."

"Just like that? You're not going to go after her? Try to find her?"

"Like Peter, you mean?" Benjamin pictured Zachary's eyebrows rising a fraction, not quite amused.

"I'm sure he would help you," Benjamin said. "If nothing else it would give him a chance to pursue his grudge against Madame Grurie."

Zachary shrugged. "What good would it do? If Madame Grurie can't force Etta to do something, then neither can I. If

I try, I won't get her back. I'll only make matters worse. Push her farther away."

"What about the office?" Benjamin asked. "Are you going to find someone to take my place?"

The outline of Zachary's head turned back toward him. He had looked away without Benjamin realizing it. "What do you think?"

"I think it's your decision. You need to do what's best for you."

"I don't know what I want to do." He sounded overwhelmed, disconsolate.

"You'll be fine," Benjamin said. "There's no rush. Give yourself time to consider your options."

Zachary lifted both hands, where they disappeared into the indecipherable blur of his expression.

"What?" Benjamin said, watching Zachary rub the dark hollows of his face.

"Here you are, worried about me. Helping cheer me up, when I should be the one encouraging you."

"That's because you're the one who's got to carry on," Benjamin said. "Not me."

"Madame Grurie wasn't able to help you at all?" Zachary said. "You didn't learn, or discover, anything useful?"

"About what?"

Zachary waved a hand. "Anything, I guess."

Benjamin thought of Etta and the last hours he'd spent with her. "I found out I'm not the person I thought I was," he said. "None of us are."

39

Orthinia, Design Space

Olavo didn't remember returning to his room after wedging the spirit bottle in the tree. Neither did he remember going to sleep. Was it possible he'd been asleep all along, and only dreamed he'd placed the bottle in the tree? Perhaps Tenley had been a dream, as well.

And the armor. The thick, protective shell was gone from his arms. They now seemed stick-thin on the bedsheets, little more than bird-light bones. When he raised them, they felt hollow.

A line from Psalms rang in his head. *Oh, that I had wings like a dove!*

The helmet was gone, too. He touched exploratory fingers to his scalp. Instead of hair, he encountered stubble. Farther down, on the back of his neck, his fingers encountered smooth skin instead of the socket. The aperture had completely healed. No tenderness remained. If he had been visited by one of the little glass-winged insects in his sleep, it had sealed the opening like a surgeon when it departed.

He sat up. The room looked different. There were windows in the wall next to the bed in place of gray featureless stone. The new windows looked out on a lake surrounded by trees. The lake was gray, as smooth as puddled lead. Above the trees, dawn was seeping through the night sky. It cast a furnace red glow on the molten surface of the lake.

Olavo slid from under the covers. The cat, which had been curled up near the end of the bed, tumbled to the floor. It lay there unmoving. The cat wasn't alive. It wasn't a real cat. It was a stuffed animal. The tail had been ripped off. White stuffing bulged out the open hole. The ears were missing, too, torn off at the seams.

He picked up the toy. In his delirium, he had imagined that it was a bird. He had dreamed it was mutating.

He looked around, examining the new design space.

Linoleum tile had replaced the marble floor. The ceiling was lower. Acoustic tile, supported by a suspended ceiling, hid the rafters. Curtains framed the windows. The softspace construct was filling in. Details he hadn't noticed before—or was incapable of seeing—were emerging, becoming visible.

The design space was changing. Finally, he, too, seemed to be changing. Evolving.

"Welcome back," Vania said.

Olavo turned. Vania—her nurse's uniform radiant in the starched light—stood inside the door, as if she had just entered the room, though the door was closed. She was accompanied by the others. Ramunas and Uta on one side. Jori and Hossein on the other. Acantha was still absent. But the rest of them appeared more solid, less ghostlike than they had the last time he had been visited by them.

"So how do you feel?" Uta asked, forcing aside the apprehension in her eyes with a broad smile.

"Changed," he said.

Ramunas scowled under bushy brows. "For better, or worse?"

"Better," Olavo said. "I feel like I've rejoined the living."

"I'm glad," Uta said.

"How would he know whether he was better or not?" Jori turned to Ramunas. "If he's not himself—if his thoughts are still jumbled—then he can't be trusted. His opinion means nothing."

"Objectively you may be right. But subjectively it provides valuable insight into his current state of mind."

"Well, you sound and look better," Uta said reassuringly. "More like your old self."

"What happened?" Olavo said. He still wasn't exactly sure where he was, or why he was here.

"You were involved in an accident," Jori said.

He nodded, recalling the AdS rupture. The gamma ray burst.

"We had to do quite a bit of reconstructive surgery," Vania said. "For a while, it was touch and go."

"We didn't know if you'd make it," Jori said.

"And if you did," Ramunas added, "how much of you we'd be able to recover. Who you would be."

"We're still not sure," Hossein said.

"Neither am I," Olavo admitted. He still didn't feel one hundred percent. "I feel as if... something's still missing."

"It may take some time," Uta cautioned. "You've gone through a lot. A period of realignment is normal as the various aspects of your memory cohere."

"You're lucky," Hossein said. "We were able to ghost and reconstruct most of your personality profile via data superposition."

"But not all?"

"No," Uta said. "We're still in the process of recovering some of the synapse maps wiped out by the gamma ray burst, and integrating them into a stable resonant state."

"What about my hardspace source?" Olavo said. The molecular automaton on the *Wings of Uriel* provided kinesthetic feedback to the softspace construct. "What happened to it?"

"We don't know," Uta said. "We've lost contact with your ship. We've been unable to re-qink to it or Sand Mountain."

Vania stepped forward and the others moved aside for her. "Exactly how much do you remember? Just before you woke up here?"

Olavo shuddered at the first image that leapt to mind. "I was riding a motorcycle. It was late at night. I was upset. Angry."

"About what?"

"Tenley," he said.

"Who's Tenley?" Jori asked.

"A friend. We had an argument. I wanted to get away from her, from everything." Most of all himself. "I wasn't paying attention. I came around a turn, and . . ." He shook his head. She was gone, centuries dead by now.

"What?" Uta prompted.

"There was a bright light. Blinding."

"The gamma ray burst," Hossein said.

"Headlights," Olavo said. "I tried to swerve, but . . ." He squeezed his eyes against the remembered glare.

Vania winced in sympathy. "A crucial aspect of the reconstruction process involves threading in memories. Not all of them comfortable, I'm afraid."

"But necessary," Ramunas said. "An important ingredient in determining not only who we are, but who we will be."

"That's the reason you're in this particular design space," Vania said. "To help you remember."

Olavo looked out at the lake. "Rehabilitation," he said. More than anything else, Lakeshore had forced him to take life one day at a time. To forget the failures of the past, no matter how small or large, and move on.

"The crash injured you severely," Vania said. "Part of your

psychological healing involved physical healing. I've tried to simulate that here."

The softspace design thread she had created mirrored the one he had followed as a pre-simunculus. Her reasoning made sense. That thread of actuality had already survived once. There was a good chance it would survive again.

Olavo looked from the lake to the stuffed animal he still held in his hands.

"Part of the therapy process," Uta said.

"I don't remember what I did the first time around—or why." He had needed the animal once. To survive, he needed it again.

"You harbored a lot of anger," Uta said. "Frustration."

And he had taken it out on the stuffed animal.

"It made it possible for you to express yourself," Uta said. "It kept you from harming yourself or someone else."

He remembered wanting to kill himself. But the plaster casts on his arms and the crash helmet on his head had made that impossible. There was nothing he could do to himself. There was nothing he could do to Tenley, Linnea, or anyone else he might want to lash out at.

He'd been trapped, forced to find a coping mechanism. First he'd turned to the animal. When that didn't work, he found religion.

He set the mutilated cat on the bed. "Now what?" he said. "Where do we go from here?"

"Burn-in," Jori said.

Vania nodded. "We wait to see if the current datamapping of your mind settles into a stable structure."

"And if it doesn't?"

"It will," Uta said.

"If not," Ramunas said, "you might still be okay. Your mind could organize into a new pattern."

"You'd be different," Hossein said. "But at least you'd be alive."

"No," Olavo said. He would be permanently damaged. Part of him would always be missing. "You have to keep looking," he said.

"We've looked everywhere," Vania said.

"Then look someplace else." Olavo reached for the cat.

Uta put a calming hand on his arm. "We'll keep looking," she said.

They began to fade. Except that it was him vanishing, not them, as he sank back into himself.

40

Prattville, October 11

Rudi parked the van in the strip mall lot. He turned off the engine, let out a breath, and sat for a moment. Last night, he'd emptied the van of his belongings. There wasn't much. A couple changes of clothes and some toiletries. Except for his Bible, the clothes on his back, and the articles he'd taken from Linnea, he donated everything to the Salvation Army, leaving it in a paper sack by the back door. The only other item he kept was Irene's surrogate breast. He zipped the knitted ball in an inside pocket of the windbreaker, where the soft lump pressed against his rib cage.

In the side mirror, Rudi could see the front entrance and sign for the Scion of Adam church. At seven o'clock on a Thursday morning, the church was closed, the interior dark.

He slid the keys from the ignition and wiped down the steering wheel with one of Mr. Chin's dish towels. Bible in hand, he got out of the van, locked it, then turned toward the church. The first time he'd seen the converted storefront, it had been dark outside and bright inside. . . .

"That's the way the world is." Jim Odette said. "Darkness all around. You have to carry the light inside of you."

"Like a flame," Marilee Odette said, "burning all the time."

"You have to light the way for yourself and others," Jim Odette said. "You got to give people shelter from the darkness."

When they pulled into the parking lot, light and music were already spilling from the display windows and double doors. The music mixed heavy metal guitar with tambourine shaking, foot stomping, and hand clapping.

Travis and Bethel had picked the three of them up at the Odettes', where Rudi was renting a room after completing his rehab. Jim and Marilee had visited him at Lakeshore. They'd laid hands on him and prayed for his recovery. Except for a visit from Tenley, to give him one of her spirit bottles, the Odettes had been his only visitors. They came once a week, and gave him something to look forward to.

"First time?" Bethel asked him sweetly, the way she might a virgin. Her face was thin, feverish with repentance. Behind the sweaty fervor, he could see the life she'd lived poking through, a history bruised by alcohol and abuse.

Rudi nodded.

"Right on!" Travis exclaimed. He clapped Rudi energetically on one shoulder and gave him a shake. "Things are always livelier when we got a convert in the midst."

"I don't know," Rudi said. He laughed nervously.

"You will," Bethel said. "You'll see. You can't walk into a house of the Lord and not be moved."

Travis nudged Rudi in the ribs. "You ever held a rattlesnake?" he said over the din.

Rudi shook his head.

"It ain't for everybody," Bethel said. "You have to feel the Spirit. You have to be strong in your faith. If you aren't, the serpent will know."

"The devil always knows." Jim Odette turned in his seat.

"He can sense fear and weakness. If there's any doubt in your heart, he will strike."

Rudi swallowed but nodded, solidifying his resolve. He needed to be here. He needed a place to go and people to hold him up. Maybe with their help, and the help of the Holy Ghost, he could learn to stand on his own.

Inside the empty retail space, chairs had been set up in rows. Rudi counted twelve rows, with ten chairs in each row. About half the chairs at the back were empty. A wide aisle between the chairs led up to a square kitchen table that was being used as an altar. A pine box, flanked by beeswax candles, sat on the table. A guitarist and a drummer had set up next to the table. The tambourines were being played by the congregation.

"Things is just gettin' warmed up," Travis said, leading him to a seat along the aisle. A woman next to him smiled. She held her hands over her head and clapped. Rudi did the same. It was awkward at first. And not just because he was a few weeks out of rehab and his coordination hadn't fully returned. He'd never had a sense of rhythm. Not that it mattered. No one cared if he kept time or not. It was the act of participation, of getting involved, that mattered. But he couldn't let go of himself.

"Relax," Bethel said. "Close your eyes."

That helped. Rudi stopped comparing himself to what he saw around him. Then the music worked its way into him, sinuous chords that wound around his bones, pulling them this way and that.

"Now you're gettin' into the Spirit," Bethel said. "No different from what they got up on Sand Mountain. You ever been up there?"

Rudi shook his head.

"One of these days, we'll have to take you. If that don't fill a person with the Holy Ghost, nothin' will."

Even Jim and Marilee, normally straightlaced and serious, were animated. Marilee tossed her head, long hair whipping like a horse's tail. Jim stomped his feet, pounding and grinding away with manic frenzy.

A couple of the songs he recognized. "I Saw the Light," and "Ring of Fire," which Travis played, much to the delight of Bethel.

After a while, someone got up to preach. Rudi's ears continued to ring in the quiet. Sweat tickled his forehead, trickled down his sides. The air was stuffy, thick with perspiration, perfume, and hairspray. But inside he felt cleansed. Each breath he exhaled carried toxins out of him; each breath he took in changed the composition of his body. He could feel himself being remade.

Toward the end of the sermon a visiting preacher, a snake handler from Scottsboro and Sand Mountain, held a Bible up over his head.

"Unshutter your windows!" the preacher cried. He was a small man with a balding head and thick glasses. He didn't look like the kind of person who would pick up a poisonous rattlesnake. "Open your house up and receive *the Holy Ghost. Allow the Holy Ghost into you. Like a hurricane it will descend and the devil will flee before the force of its onslaught!"*

His voice grew hoarse from shouting. Rudi's own throat ached, scraped raw by all the singing. Without realizing it, he'd been shouting with the others. He'd stepped out of himself and become one of them—one with *them. In the process, he'd become somebody else. This person didn't have a past. There was only the present and the future. The past had dissolved in the music, like salt in water.*

The music, singing, foot stomping, and hand clapping formed the connective tissue, the muscle, tendons, and ligaments that joined them in a single body with a unified purpose. They were one person, and many people, at the same time.

Tears wet his cheeks. Rudi tasted the salt of the past, weeping out of him.

Bethel touched a finger to his face. "You feel it," she said. "You feel the salvation of Jesus. Praise the Lord!"

Later, after more singing, the bald preacher removed the lid from the serpent box and reached in to pull out a fat, diamond-backed snake. He held it up to the congregation, the way he held the Bible. The snaked draped around his forearm and flicked its tongue. For a brief moment, its tail buzzed. But the rattle seemed an extension of the tambourines—part of the lunatic music.

Then the preacher walked down the aisle, the snake rattling and flicking and coiling between them. People reached out for it. They pressed against Rudi from behind, surging forward.

Panic gripped him. He resisted the tide of bodies and elation rising up around him, but the surge swept over him. It carried him out of his chair and into the aisle. There was no backing up. Hands arched over his shoulders to touch the snake. Against his will, he felt his hand reach out. Felt the muscular brush of smooth, oily scales slither and contract. The touch left him faint. His knees buckled. Hands gripped him under the arms, hauled him out of the way, and sat him down to make room for someone else.

He didn't hold a snake that night. No one did. The preacher placed the snake back in the pine box.

And that was it.

Standing outside, in the parking lot, Travis said, "We're going to spread the Lord's word tomorrow. You wanna come with us?"

"Where?"

"All over," Bethel said. "But tomorrow we're going after illegal immigrants." She made a face. "That part of town."

"How?" Rudi said. Sweat was cooling on him, tightening his skin and the certainty that this was where he belonged.

"We're renting a broadcast van," Travis said. "We send out the Scripture over the airwaves."

"There's a station plays Mexican music," Bethel explained. "We're going to jam it with Jesus."

Travis grinned. "Jammin' with Jesus," he said. "Got a nice ring to it, if you ask me."

"Sure," Rudi said. He answered the grin with one of his own, feeling it stretch his mouth into an unfamiliar but pleasant shape.

To hell with Tenley and her spirits. He didn't need her or her bottles to protect him. He'd laid hands on a serpent, and the poison hadn't entered him. He'd found a strength she didn't have and couldn't offer. From now on, he would look after himself.

Rudi blinked. He stared through the glass doors and his reflection to the chairs set in their even rows. Someone had brought in two potted palms, and put them in the corners behind the altar. For a moment, he thought he heard music. Thought he could feel the sweat and the heat and Brother Dewey's words howling through him, tearing at the covetousness, anger, and vindictiveness that had built up inside him like trash on a roadside fence.

Rudi's head spun, and he pressed the palm of his left hand to the glass.

When the spirit caught you, he thought, it was supposed to lift you up. You might collapse, fall to your knees, but inside you were raised up. Once you had been lifted, the spirit wasn't supposed to let you down. It wasn't supposed to die, the way wind died in the eye of a storm. It was supposed to keep blowing through you, and carry you with it to salvation. They hadn't warned him that the wind could die at any moment as fast as it had risen. They hadn't told him that to keep the wind blowing he would have to touch the serpent again and again. Or that after a certain point, the only way to keep the Spirit alive would be to hold the snake in his own hands; and when that wasn't enough, he would have to hold the serpent inches from his face—kiss the devil on the lips to prove his faith.

They didn't tell him he would have to keep proving it, to himself and the entire congregation, lest he be condemned.

They didn't tell him that people had died, trying to prove themselves, and that this was seen as a failure on their part and held up as an example to others.

That's what he'd realized in the hurricane. Trapped in the fury of the storm, he could see that if he kept shooting up the Holy Ghost it would kill him, no different from heroin. Eventually he'd shoot up one time too many, and the serpent would strike. God would spite him, judge his motives for what they were, and let the devil sink its teeth into him.

Faith, he realized, wasn't all that different from love. It could be passionate, filled with giddy one-night stands. Or it could be quiet and lasting, the result of steady, mindful work.

Rudi slipped the keys to the van into the mail slot in the door. They jangled to the floor, impossible to miss by Brother Dewey, or whoever unlocked the church. He leaned the Bible against the door. Then he turned back to the parking lot and the bus stop on the sidewalk.

Halfway across the lot, a red sedan eased in and parked in the open space next to the van. The door opened and Celia Truong stepped out.

Rudi's joints seized. His knees ground to a halt, leaving him stranded on the glass-littered, oil-stained expanse of blacktop.

"You just going to stand there?" she said.

Rudi teetered. "What are you doing here?"

"I followed you." She stood behind the open car door, one hand resting on the top edge.

"How?"

"The same way I did before." She snapped her fingers. "I have amazing powers of prestidigitation."

Rudi glanced at the van, wondering if she'd hidden a cell phone or a GPS locator in it. He returned his attention to her. "What do you want?"

"To talk."

"About what?"

"Your sister, for starters."

Rudi blinked. The dawn sky seemed to spin above him, leaving a diffuse, concentric trace of stars. "I didn't have anything to do with that."

"I didn't say you did. But you were there. You know what happened."

"No I don't."

"I think you know more than you're letting on."

He shook his head.

"We can help each other," she said.

"I have nothing to say." Rudi turned and started to walk away. He didn't want to deal with her. He just wanted to be left alone—allowed to move on without complications.

"If you want," she said, "I can give you a ride."

Rudi kept his gaze fixed on the asphalt. "Some other time."

"Lakeshore," she said. "Right?"

Rudi paused. He stared at the blacktop for a few beats before looking up. "What gave you that idea?"

"Get in." She tipped her head toward the passenger side. "I'll tell you."

Rudi shut his eyes wearily. He was tired. Tired of running away, tired of playing games, tired of answering questions. Tired of not knowing the answers to questions that had no answers.

"You want a lift or not?" she asked.

Rudi stared at the crushed remains of a beer bottle ground into the cracks in the asphalt and wondered what spirit it had held—what evil it had trapped, what fear it had dulled.

"It'll be easier," she said. "You'll get where you're going that much quicker."

He got the feeling she wasn't just talking about Lakeshore.

"Unless you want me to wait for you there," she said.

"No."

He stepped toward her, thinking maybe she hadn't been following him all this time—that she'd been leading him, and he was about to find out where.

41

San Francisco, Circa 1937

Benjamin clutched the Seals cap in his lap, afraid that if he put it on Etta wouldn't recognize him. He gripped the cap tightly, hoping to quell the shaking in his hands. Any moment, it seemed the quavering would seize his entire body. If he could just see Etta, talk to her, the trembling would abate. Then he could stop fighting. He could let go. He could let the tremor rattle through him and lay down and rest.

The stadium was a blur around him, all the sounds and smells he loved merging into a single stream. The basso roar of the crowd, the sudden thunderclap of hands that washed over him in waves, rising and falling with each pitch, each swing of the bat that whiffed or cracked a ball past the infield. The aroma of roasted peanuts, cigars, and beer. The afternoon sun beating down on him, wringing sweat from his forehead as if his skin were a fog-dampened rag twisted over his bones.

Etta wasn't going to come. She couldn't. Not with Zachary sitting next to him. There was no way he could go look for her. He'd tripped several times on the way to their seats. He could feel people's eyes on him, pitying and disgusted, thinking he was inebriated. They'd steered clear of him, leaving several empty seats on the wooden plank to his left.

"How you doing?" Zachary said. His voice loomed at the corner of Benjamin's vision, a watery ripple that expanded in concentric rings. "You okay?"

Benjamin willed a steady nod. "Yes." He cringed at the slur his tongue made of the word. What difference did it make what people thought? It was Etta he was worried about. She didn't know how quickly he had deteriorated. Like everyone else all she would see was a drunk.

"We can go, if you want," Zachary said. "Anytime." He seemed anxious for the day to end.

"Not yet."

"Just let me know."

Benjamin nodded. Better not to speak at all. He hunkered down in his seat and curled his fingers around the cap. He traced the emblem, following the outline of the stitching. Once. Twice. Again, compulsively.

Even Zachary was embarrassed to be seen with him. Ashamed, worried people would get the wrong idea about him. He'd already mumbled apologies, excuses, to several of the fans Benjamin had bumped into.

Blind. Not well. Recovering.

All true. But it was also a way for Zachary to disassociate himself. He was in the process of letting go, distancing himself from Benjamin so he could move on.

A roar crested around him, brought people to their feet. Brought him back to the game. He could sense the anticipation, the collective held breath, of the crowd.

The crowd sagged. A long fly ball, Benjamin thought, caught at the wall, the batter robbed.

"DiMaggio almost hit one out," Zachary said. He hadn't settled back into his seat yet. "Listen," he said, bending next to him, "I need to take a leak. Will you be okay for a few minutes?"

Benjamin bobbed his head. "Sure."

"What about you? Do you need to go?"

"I'm fine."

"I won't be long," Zachary said.

"Take your time," Benjamin said. He let the sentence slosh around in his mouth, like warm beer, foamy and tasteless.

It was easier with Zachary gone. He didn't have to worry about the palsied restlessness of his hands or holding his back straight. There was no pretense of keeping up appearances. It was a relief.

Sooner than expected, Zachary returned. A fuzzy-edged and washed-out smear of blue, unrecognizable, solidified next to him out of the tumult. A hand took his; soft fingers stroked his knuckles. Benjamin stifled the urge to jerk away.

"I can't stay long," Etta whispered, so close her breath tickled his cheek. "What is it?" she asked, suddenly aware of the tremor in his hands. "What's wrong?"

"Can't see," he said.

"My God!" The exclamation tightened her grip on him. "What happened to you?"

"Not drunk," he said. That wasn't how he wanted her to remember him . . . besotted, wallowing in self-pity.

"Dear God," she said. "We need to get you to a hospital." She started to raise her hand, but he clasped it to his leg.

"No." His head wobbled from side to side, loopy, circuitous. He trained his gaze on her, and in the milk-white haze pictured a blue jay perched on a park bench, skittish, the collar of her dress fluttering nervously in the stadium breeze. "Go." He spoke slowly, laboriously imposing clarity on the words. "Before Zach—"

"I can't leave you."

"You have to."

"I could never forgive myself."

"I forgive you."

"Don't say that." Her hair shook loose, pulling free of the bonnet she wore against the breeze.

"It's true."

"What's going to happen to you?"

"I'll go back," he said. "To my original self."

Her fretfulness stilled. Her breathing regained its measured composure, its steady determination.

"I'll see you then," he said, believing for a moment it might be true. That somehow, somewhere, they would find one another again.

"All right," she said. Abruptly she kissed him on the forehead. Then she was gone, taking flight from the bench into another world or part of the world.

A spasm shuddered through him. Benjamin couldn't sit up any longer. He lay down on his side on the plank. He drew his knees up to his elbows. He felt the sun and the roar of the crowd grow distant and amniotic. It pulsed over him, as regular and comforting as a shared heartbeat.

He thought the kiss would cool as it dried. Instead it burned, as hot as the flame of a votive candle.

42

Sand Mountain, Hardspace

Bonpane's. The café was a murky hole-in-the-wall place on Karstrasse, in a sector of the polis where ad hoc businesses had sprung up in the underground catacombs fringing the original construction site. Some of these spaces were little more than caves, excavated one atom at a time by replicators hungry for raw material.

The establishment occupied a cluster of three interconnected chambers. Subterranean sprawl. The chambers hadn't been joined originally. The café's owners had bored a series of holes in the walls dividing the cavities to create access tunnels. Like the parabolic vaults in the main chambers, these passageways were arched, supported by load-bearing walls and columns. Despite the vaulting, and colorful tile mosaics, the café felt cramped. The ceilings were low, the light from the suspended LED panels and neon tubes even lower. Thick pillars crowded the room, shoving tables together. The claustrophobic pall of cigarette smoke and back-room dealings hung over everything. Curtains, both bead and cloth, hung across the doorways between rooms.

It was early, the clientele sparse, the mood desultory.

Olavo took a stool at the bar, under a purple LED panel and one of the low-hanging long-leafed plants that dangled from the gloom, spiderlike, on invisible monomol.

Faces—hunched over cups of kaffe, self-absorbed, some of them concealed behind veils—turned to look at him. Most were doughmen, shrivel-skinned in the dry air. But he spotted a smattering of gnomen, hunkered down under fedoras, and even a couple of night waifs, white hair and translucent skin tinted yellow, blue, green by the neon tubes.

A barkeep appeared from a curtained doorway behind the counter. He was a large heavyset doughman, fully hydrated, with almost no wrinkles showing on his smooth, puffy skin.

"Get you, what?" he grunted.

"Kaffe," Olavo said.

The barkeep turned on a screen hanging against the back wall. The scroll flickered as it picked up a latent synapse pattern in Olavo's microvilli, mapping it to an old romantic comedy called *While You Were Sleeping*.

The barkeep picked up a shot glass, which filled with steaming sludge, and set it on the counter.

"Seen them, haven't," the barkeep said. "Etta. Linnea. Been in haven't, since last you looking."

Etta was a name from the diary Mee Won had scanned in.

Before Olavo could question him about Linnea, the bartender slipped behind the blue-curtained doorway behind the counter.

"You don't belong here," a veiled night waif a few stools down from him said. Her skin shifted from mauve to red as she stood up, moved, and sat down beside him, smelling vaguely of spicewood. She wore a dark green sari that offset her pink eyes and Cleopatra-cut hair.

"I'm looking for someone," he said. "Mee Won?" If she was a regular, maybe the name would ring a bell.

"She's not here."

"Do you know where I can find her?"

"Lost." The night waif tilted a bottle of oily pearlescent liqueur to pallid lips. "We all are."

"But you've seen her here before? You know who she is?"

The night waif grinned, swallowed, and tossed back her head. A laugh foamed out of the grin, sickly sweet, mocking. The laugh chafed, under his collar and in the pits of his arms. Olavo tightened his grip on his kaffe cup.

"I don't think you want to find her," the waif said. "Not really. You don't want to discover that part of yourself." Her nostrils flared with disdain. "Then you'd have to see yourself as you really are."

"What part are you talking about?" he said.

"She's gone. She doesn't want to see you. The sooner you accept that, the better off you'll be."

"She told you that?"

"Leave us alone." The waif lowered the bottle from her lips and slid off the stool. "All of us. Stop pretending you're someone you aren't. Stop living someone else's remembered lives . . . or their imagined ones. That's why she left. Now it's time for you to leave, too."

Olavo stared at the waif, afraid that if he took his gaze from her she would vanish and he would be left with nothing, not even questions. "Who are you?"

The waif raised an eyebrow in the pause between them. "Who do you think?" Her mouth twisted around a smirk.

Mee Won. Etta. Tenley. Linnea. Even Acantha. The names crowded together in his head. Olavo could no longer tell them apart. He no longer knew where one ended and the others began. They had become the same person.

"I'm you," the waif said, as if in confirmation. "We all are, more or less."

"Not just me." He had used other memories, other psychological profiles, for each type of simunculus.

The waif shrugged. "We don't want to be human anymore. Human voices woke us, but that's not who we are. We want to forget we were human. We want to wake up to our own future. Not drown in the past."

She held his gaze for a beat longer, then made her way past him. The conversation in the café had died, and a new voice crackled from the screen behind the bar, cobwebbed with electrons.

"... coming to you live..." an announcer said. Then, "... that brings the count to two balls and two strikes..."

"Wait," Olavo said, yanking his attention back to the woman.

But the night waif had moved on, her face and hair orange under the next LED panel as she made her way from the café.

Behind him a crowd roared, nearly drowning out the excited voice of the announcer.

"... DiMaggio has given the Seals a one-run lead over the Portland Beavers in the bottom of the eighth. Up next..."

Olavo felt lost, gripped by the urge to run. But there was no place to go—not when he was running from himself.

43

Birmingham, October 11

Celia Truong pulled into a visitor parking space outside the front entrance to the Lakeshore Foundation. Set among thick trees held in check by tidy lawns and flower beds, the sprawling concrete-and-glass facility looked more like an exclusive health club than a rehabilitation center. There was an aquatic center with an Olympic-sized pool, tennis, bocci ball, and basketball courts, a field house, fully equipped fitness center, and even a shooting range.

"How'd you know this is where I was going?" he said. She didn't look as smug as he expected. If anything, more thoughtful.

"Eventually we all come back to where we started, Rudi. We have to. It's the only way we can move on."

"Pop psychology," he said.

She shrugged off his sarcasm. He shifted his attention to the main lobby, ablaze in fluorescent lights. As far as he knew it was always brightly lit, always staffed, always busy. The Lakeshore Foundation diagnosed and treated everything from fibromyalgia and Parkinson's disease to spinal cord injuries, arthritis, MS, cerebral palsy, amputation, stroke, and visual impairment.

"What makes you think I want to move on?"

"Simple. You don't want to end up like your sister."

The words stung. His face hardened. "If I was going to off myself I would've done it a long time ago."

"That's not what I'm talking about."

"You don't know anything about it."

She pursed her lips. "I know your sister ran away before your grandmother died. I know that it took her years to come to terms with her identity and her place in the world. I know it wasn't easy for her, the same way that it hasn't been easy for you."

He rubbed at the ache clenching his jaw. "No different from a lot of people."

"But you *are* different. You might not want to admit it, but it's true. You're special, in ways most people aren't."

Rudi shook his head.

"You survived," she said. "You went through a shitty childhood and a severe head injury and you came through more or less intact."

"It doesn't feel like it."

"But you don't want to be crazy," she went on. "You don't want to go through the same thing she did. That's why you're here."

Shoulders hunched, he stared at the main entrance. "I'm not looking for help."

"I know. You're looking for answers. You want to know if it runs in the family . . . if you're going to end up in the same place she did."

He pushed his head back against the headrest and turned to face her. "You seem to know a lot more about it than me."

"It's my job."

"In addition to being a journalist?"

Celia nodded toward the sliding double doors. "Are you going to see this to the end, or not?" she said.

The floors squeaked under the rubber soles of his shoes. He could see his reflection in the glass-smooth wax as he walked past the front desk. Celia followed a few steps behind. She hadn't asked to join him; both of them seemed to accept her presence as a necessary part of the process.

"Can I help?" the receptionist said.

Rudi kept walking.

"Are you here to see someone?" The receptionist stood. "Wait! You can't just walk in like this!"

The hallways were spacious and sterile. Many of them were walled on one side with windows that looked out on verdant thickets of Appalachian foliage, giving the facility the feel of a summer camp or isolated mountain retreat.

It didn't take him long to find the room he was looking for. The route seemed Pavlovian, part of his nervous system. It wasn't a room, but a small secluded waiting area furnished with pastel-cushioned couches and chairs, low tables stacked with magazines. A window looked out on an impenetrable wall of vegetation. A potted plant stood in one corner. The leaves were large and rubbery, the trunk spindly, the stems waxy. The ceramic pot was large and glazed, the color of sandstone at sunset. Grassy mulch coiled around the base of the plant, like long strands of matted hair caught in a bathtub drain.

"Your room was near here?" Celia asked.

"Close enough."

Usually, he'd visited the lounge at night. He slipped out of his room after midnight, in between nurses' rounds. It was peaceful here. He could sit in one of the couches and stare out the window at the trees, awash in exterior lights. Sometimes the moon shone through branches.

Rudi went over to the pot, dropped to his knees beside it, and scooped a handful of mulch onto the carpet. He cleared all the mulch from the base of the plant, exposing loose topsoil.

"What are you looking for?" Celia asked.

"You tell me."

She stood behind him, peering over his shoulder. When she didn't respond, Rudi dug his fingers into the soil. He felt sick, filled with anticipation and dread. He was afraid of what he would find. At the same time, he was afraid that what he was looking for wouldn't be there. He wasn't sure which outcome would prove he was crazy.

"Where's your iCam?" he asked.

"I didn't bring it with me."

"Why not?" Rudi hauled out a handful of moist dirt and dumped it onto the carpet. "Aren't you afraid you're going to miss something?"

"I have a good memory."

"Unlike me."

"Would you like me to get it? Would that make what you find any more—or less—real?"

Rudi turned a deaf ear to her. He shut his eyes and continued to dig. The deeper he dug, the drier the soil became and the harder his panic.

He'd dreamed the burial. It had never happened. What else hadn't happened? What other realities had he imagined? Maybe the plant had been repotted. The old soil would have been dumped, replaced with new soil. No, it was the same container. If the plant had been repotted, the container would be different. Larger.

His fingers scrabbled at tightly bound roots, twisting and tearing knot after tangled knot.

It wasn't there. He began to sweat under his light jacket. He rested his forehead against the rim of the pot. Felt Irene's wool breast squash against his side, ungainly and ponderous.

"Rudi." Celia's voice stabbed through his haze. "That's enough."

He pawed more dirt from the ceramic pot, then began to bang his head on the blunt edge.

"Stop it!" she said. "You're going to hurt yourself."

Rudi's fingers encountered something soft. Softer than the surrounding dirt, but not as soft as he expected or remembered. The fur was matted, clumped with soil. He lifted his head and peered in, inhaling the tang of old peat moss and loam. He excavated around grime-crusted fur, exposing a half-decomposed tail.

"What's going on here?" a voice said behind him.

Rudi turned his head. A nurse, backed by two beefy orderlies, stood in the entrance to the lounge.

"Have to ask him," Celia said. She took a step back from the plant and the orderlies. They carried themselves like bouncers, more comfortable with rowdy drunks than invalids.

Rudi turned his attention to the half-empty pot. Without much soil around the root-ball, the plant was starting to list. Leaves flailed about his head. He gripped the stem and pulled, uprooting the plant.

"Rudi?" The nurse's shoes shushed toward him.

Rudi scraped clods of dirt from the tail and gently pulled it free, exposing a pair of ears.

The nurse stepped forward. She stopped next to him as he unearthed the ears and set them beside the tail. "What in God's name are you doing here?"

Rudi looked up at her. Tears blurred his eyes. "I knew it wasn't a real kitten." He held up the foam-filled tail.

"It's all right," the nurse said.

It took Rudi a moment to realize that the nurse was speaking not to him but the two orderlies.

"You sure?" one of them asked.

"If I need help," the nurse said, "I'll let you know. Meanwhile, why don't you find a custodian to clean this up?"

The toneless carpet lightened as the male nurses departed, taking their shadows with them. Rudi hadn't realized they'd been that close.

The nurse knelt on the rug next to him. "You care to tell me what's going on? Why are you here?"

Rudi sat splay-legged on the rug, the tail and the ears in his lap. "I was afraid it was real," he said.

"The cat?"

He nodded.

Celia disengaged herself from the chair she was leaning against. "This isn't something we should discuss here."

The nurse looked past him to the journalist. "Who are you?"

"I'm with the program. I've been keeping an eye on him, since he was discharged."

The nurse nodded. She returned her focus to Rudi and offered him a hand. "I think we should go someplace private," she said, "where the three of us can talk. How does that sound?"

Clutching the tail and the ears in one hand, Rudi took her hand with his free one and let her help him up. Her face was a blur, muddled by relief and tears. But when she turned to lead him away, he caught a clear glimpse of the rectangular nameplate pinned to the front of her uniform.

VANIA.

He hadn't recognized her. She had changed. No, he

thought. She was exactly the same. For better or worse, he was the one who was different.

He remembered her as a reflection. That was what she felt like, caught in his mind. She always came at night. She checked his vitals. Adjusted the drip on his IV or the angle of his bed. She was like the red lights that blinked in the window. Not really there, and not really not there. They were part of the netherworld he lived in somewhere between waking and sleep.

Sometimes, she leaned over the bed and tapped the thick casts on his arms. Or the soft-cushioned helmet he wore in case he fell during physical therapy.

She was like one of the machines hooked up to him. She didn't seem human. She kept her distance—never allowed herself to get too close. If he'd wanted to make contact, he couldn't.

It occurred to him now that she'd treated him as if *he* were the machine. Something to be serviced, looked after, but not really cared for as a person. More like a mechanical device, a turbine or a pump. All she had to do was monitor pressure and check fluid flow, make sure everything was within the normal range. Routine maintenance. Beyond that, he didn't exist for her.

"You could have told me you were coming," Vania said.

They sat in a white-walled office devoid of decoration. She could have been talking to either of them. She paced, arms tightly folded across her chest. Clearly, she hadn't been expecting them, didn't know what to do with herself now that they were here.

"I didn't know we would be here," Celia said. "I only hooked up with him a couple of hours ago. It just happened."

"Still," the nurse said. "A little warning would have been nice."

"There wasn't time."

"What's going on?" Rudi said. He tore his gaze from the half-rotted tail and ears on the desk and looked to Vania. "How do you know each other?"

"We've never met," Vania said.

"I don't believe you."

"It's true," Celia said. "Not in person."

"All right." Fine, if that's the way they wanted to play it. "Why do you need to keep an eye on me?"

Vania paused. Her arms tightened over her chest. She turned to Celia. "How much have you told him?"

"Nothing."

"He has no idea who he is? What he is?"

"He thinks he's being watched," Celia said. "That's all he remembers, as far as I can tell."

"I was afraid this would happen," the nurse said. "It was too soon. We should have waited."

"If we'd waited, it would have been too late. We wouldn't have mapped a complete profile."

"Still." She made a face. "What about the others?"

"Has anyone else been back?"

Vania massaged her upper arms through the sleeves of her uniform. "Not yet. He's the first."

They seemed to have forgotten he was in the room. He'd become an object—little more than a piece of furniture.

"Frankly," Vania said, "I'm surprised he's here at all."

"Why's that?"

"I didn't think any of them would make it back."

"You didn't think the program would succeed?"

"Let's just say I had my doubts."

"You never wanted to be part of it."

"No."

"Then why did you sign up?"

"Someone had to. If it was going to happen, then those poor souls deserved at least a fighting chance."

"And it paid off," Celia said.

Vania scoffed. "I wouldn't call one person a success. What about the others? How are they doing?"

"If one made it," Celia said evenly, "others might. We know it's possible. That's the important thing to keep in mind."

"I don't know who to thank for that," Vania said. "God or the devil."

"What's possible?" Rudi said, feeling the need to assert his presence.

Vania's lips quivered.

"You did something to me," he said. "What?"

Vania pressed her lips tight. She shot a glance at Celia, turning the question over to her.

The woman took a moment to collect her thoughts. "You were dying, Rudi. After the accident, the doctors did everything they could to save you. They relieved the pressure on your brain . . . got you stabilized. But you weren't going to make it. Three days after you were brought in you slipped into a coma. Your condition continued to deteriorate. We had no choice, we couldn't wait. If something wasn't done quickly, you'd be brain-dead. You wouldn't be here now."

"What did you do?" he repeated.

"We enabled you to recover. We gave you back your life."

"Tell him everything," Vania said. "The truth. He deserves to know."

The vertical crease in the center of Celia's brow deepened. "We gave you a new brain," she said. "Artificial nerves, composed of nanotube microvilli, were introduced using a genetically modified virus. These CNT-based nerves replicated along your existing neurons and synapses, mapping them. Mirroring them."

Rudi stared at the stuffed tail and ears. He felt nothing—neither anger or surprise—and wondered if that numbness was part of who he was now.

"For a while," Celia Truong went on, "you had two brains, one on top of the other. Running in parallel, so to speak. When your natural brain died, the artificial one remained, taking its place."

"What do you mean, died?"

"Ceased to function," Celia said.

Decayed, he thought. Rotted out, like flesh from bone.

"By then," she said, "all your neural activity had been transferred to the artificial nerves. We kept you from dying."

"Who's we?"

Celia hesitated. "The agency I work for."

"J.I.S.E.C.," Vania said. "The Joint International Space Exploration Consortium."

"The government," Rudi said.

"Not just ours," Celia Truong said. "It's part of an international effort to develop long-term space travel and survival in hostile environments. Including Earth, if we ever get to that point."

"So that's why you've been watching me," Rudi said. "To see if I continued not to die."

He wasn't sure he could call what he'd been doing living. Or even if he was alive, for that matter.

"We needed to record your progress," she said. "We needed to figure out the best way to help you become fully functional."

"The messages," Rudi said. "The music I couldn't keep out of my head, even with the aluminum foil."

"They were a way to stimulate certain memories. Microvilli that weren't showing optimal activity."

"I'll be right back," Vania said.

"Where are you going?" Celia demanded.

The nurse hesitated in the doorway. "To get some personal effects." She shut the door softly.

No wonder Vania had treated him like a machine. "I'm not alive," he said. "Were you ever going to tell me?"

"You're who you always were," she said. "Different, yes. But you would've been different after the accident even if you had recovered from the coma. In fact, more of you would have died if we hadn't made a copy of you. You're more alive now than you would have been."

Rudi leaned his head back. He stared up at the ceiling tiles, hunting for a pattern in the dots, some hidden constellation to guide him. "You could've told me." His neck started to hurt and he lowered his gaze.

"No. It was important that you didn't think about yourself any differently after the accident than you had before."

"You had no right," he said. "I didn't ask for this."

"Maybe not. But your sister did."

"Linnea?"

"She was in town. When she heard about the accident, she came to the hospital where you were being treated. When the doctors started to lose you, she signed the consent form authorizing the procedure."

Maybe Linnea hadn't taken the magazines when she first left. Maybe she'd taken them after the surgery. That might explain why the *ION* article about artificial neurons in rats appeared so well read.

Vania returned. She held a spirit bottle in one hand and the stuffed cat in the other. "These are yours, if you want." She laid them on her desk. "I kept them. Just in case . . ."

"I remember Tenley coming," he said.

"We asked her," Celia said. "It was early in the rehabilitation process. We hoped she would speed up your development."

Rudi reached for the spirit bottle.

"You left it in the plant," Vania said. "I should have guessed that's where you put the tail and ears."

Rudi nodded. He ran his fingers over the smooth outline of the glass and watched them change color through it.

"I called her," Vania said. "But she didn't want either one of them back. She said they were yours. It didn't seem right to throw them out."

"How many others are there?" he asked. "Like me?"

Celia shook her head. "I can't tell you that, Rudi. I wish I could."

"It's classified, I guess."

"Yes. But I really don't know how many others there are. None of us do. They're everywhere, all around the world."

And nowhere, Rudi thought "What happens now?" he said.

"That's up to you," Celia said. "It's your life, Rudi. I'm just along for the ride."

"You're saying I can walk out of here? You'd let me do that? You aren't going to try and stop me?"

"If that's what you want."

"All right." He stood up, then collected the spirit bottle and the remains of the cat. "Let's go."

44

San Francisco, Circa 1937

Benjamin lay in bed on his back, and listened to the nurse fling open the curtains on a window a few feet to the right of his bed. The room brightened, from black to milky gray.

"Good morning," she said cheerily.

Her voice turned toward him as she spoke. He followed the approach of her feet across the room, heard her stop by the side of the bed. Felt the swish of air as her dress stirred the faint tang of alcohol.

"Who won?" he asked.

"Won what, honey?"

"The Seals game."

"I wouldn't know anything about that," she said. She bent over him. "How're you feeling? Are you hungry?"

"No." Last night, after Zachary had brought him in, he had vomited up the handful of salted peanuts he'd had at the game. Now the thought of food repulsed him.

"Well, you got to eat something to get your strength up." She gripped his left arm, pressing and prodding for a vein. "This should help."

The smell of alcohol sharpened. She swabbed the inside

of his arm near the elbow. The flesh tingled as it cooled. His hand shook, but he was unable to lift it from the bed.

"Now, just relax," the nurse said. "This won't hurt but a bit." She tapped his arm lightly in several places, as if tapping a wall for a stud. "Can you make a fist?"

Benjamin concentrated on curling his fingers into a tight ball. His hand shook. "Sorry." The word that passed his lips bore no resemblance to the one he heard in his mind.

"That's all right, honey. Don't you fret."

Undaunted, she squeezed his wrist tightly. The syringe stung briefly, then numbed. She pressed a damp swatch of gauze to his arm and taped it in place. A pleasant veil settled over him, muting the pain. The nausea hovering at the edges of his stomach retreated. The shaking in his hands calmed. "What did you give me?" he asked.

She patted his shoulder and pulled the sheets up over his chest. "Now you just rest a while."

She left. Benjamin slipped a little farther from the world, like a boat being carried imperceptibly out to sea.

Morphine, he thought.

He willed himself toward the horizon he sensed in the distance. It drew closer but he couldn't will himself over the edge. He didn't have the strength to force himself from one world to the next and the current had petered out. It would have been better if he'd died on the bench. Easier. That was what he'd wanted . . . expected, really, when he'd laid down in the top of the eighth.

I should have waited until the bottom of the ninth, he thought with bitter amusement. That had been his mistake. The game hadn't been over. As if his life were connected to the outcome. He still had an inning left, maybe more if the game went into extra innings. It would help if he knew what the score was. Maybe the next injection would push him closer to the edge. Near enough to fall off.

Sometime later—minutes or hours—a needle of pain slipped through the base of his neck and into his skull. For a moment he wondered if the nurse had returned to give him another shot, this time to his head. But then the pain withdrew, leaving a small puncture in his thoughts. The kind of opening left by a drill bit. Gradually, the hole expanded. The opening enlarged, forming the round entrance to a tunnel. His mind conjured the image of the underground passage Etta had escaped into, low-ceilinged and narrow-walled, barely large enough for a single person. Relief and gratitude washed over him. Finally! A way out. The end was in sight.

He moved toward the entrance. But when he got closer, he discovered that there was already someone in the tunnel, filling it, leaving no space for him. He would have to wait his turn. Slowly, the figure grew larger. It came toward him, hesitantly, tentatively feeling its way along the passage.

"Etta?" he called.

The figure paused. Faceless, featureless. It seemed momentarily uncertain, lost, almost as if it had arrived at the wrong address.

Not Etta, Benjamin decided, but the grim reaper, come at last.

Benjamin waited for the figure to beckon. He looked for the glint of a scythe, and steeled himself for the foul stench of catacombs rising to embalm his lungs. When the figure moved forward once again, with more certainty, Benjamin felt his perspective flip. He found himself staring out of the tunnel, into a cavelike room filled with exotic plants and music from an old phonograph.

The music scratched his ears, needle-sharp. But it also tantalized, luring and teasing him from one world to another.

45

Sand Mountain, Hardspace

Olavo found Mee Won at the center span of the bridge. It looked as if she'd been there a while—as if she couldn't decide what to do with herself. She wore a casual afternoon frock, light blue, with a scoop collar and black lace trim accessorized by a black doily cap and matching leather shoes. A blue umbrella stirred restlessly at her feet, tossing fitfully in the breeze whistling through the suspension cables.

He joined her at the rail. Together they gazed out over the inlet. The polis loomed to their right. Sand Mountain rose to their left, with its exurban jumble of domicile blocs and shanties clustered at the foot of the slope. Dust rippled across the dry lake bed beneath the bridge, piling up in low dunes on Silicon Beach. Above them, a gust of superheated particles from one of the suns in the Ferrer cluster buffeted the atmosphere, turning the sky blood-orange.

"What are you doing out here?" he said.

Her hair reflected the glow of the sky and her face flushed in the candle-soft flicker of the ion squall. "I haven't decided."

Olavo rested his elbows against the railing. Despite the

chaotic jostling of other pedestrians on the bridge, the solar-powered whir and buzz of gyrocarriages weaving back and forth under aerodynamic sunshades, he felt anonymous and alone with her. "Would it help to talk . . . ?"

Mee Won stared into the distance. "After the burst, the world looked different. For a while, I thought I was dreaming. You know, when you think you're awake but you're really asleep? Pretty soon, I couldn't tell the difference between the dream and what was real. I thought maybe I was awake, but hallucinating. Then I thought maybe the world really had changed, and I had changed, too."

"Changed how?"

The blush on her face and arms dulled as the howl of the storm faded to a whimper. "Like a part of who I was had been stripped away, exposing a different person underneath. A person I couldn't remember."

"A kind of amnesia," he suggested.

Her brow pinched. "More like a past life. Somebody I'd been once, but forgotten about. Repressed, maybe."

"Did this person have a name?"

"Yeah. Sometimes it was Acantha. Other times it was Linnea. But I think it was really the same person with two names, and each name represented certain aspects of the person. That's what it felt like."

Olavo repositioned his arms on the railing. "Why were you looking for Etta?"

Mee Won thought for a moment. "I remembered her . . . or imagined that I remembered her. I remembered seeing her name in a diary. I was even able to write parts of the diary from memory, and I thought maybe she could tell me something about myself. Who I was, and where I belong."

"So you thought you were the person who wrote the diary? Benjamin?"

She nodded. "In another life. But I was wrong. A memory

can't tell you who you are. It can't even tell you who you were."

That was why she'd dressed the way she had. First in a mid-twentieth-century suit, now in a dress from the same period. "And now you think you might be Etta?"

"I don't know. I don't think I'm anybody now. I was somebody once. But I'm not anymore."

Above them, radiation lightning crackled across the sky. "That doesn't mean you can't be."

"I feel trapped." She massaged her arms. Pale, bloodless skin left by the ion storm sloughed off in flakes, leaving pink undamaged skin.

He stared down at the six-sided flakes, as white as newly fallen snow. "Trapped by what?" he said. "Me?"

She shook her head. "Between worlds. Lives."

A breeze, glittering with sharp-edged motes of mica, scattered the dead flesh at his feet. "Which ones?"

"This one, and the one I can't remember. I don't know which one I belong in. I don't know how to go from one to the other. I don't know if I should go forward, or try to go back."

"I'm sorry," he said.

Her lips cracked under a wan smile, radiation-blasted skin splitting to reveal the ripe pulp of healthy underlying flesh. "It's not your fault."

But it was. She was one of the original simunculi—part of the initial seed population for the polis—he'd gestated in the parthenosynthesis tanks. Olavo had selected her at random. During inception, he'd datamapped her with an incomplete set of his sister's synapse patterns and memories... not the profiles he had optimized in design space. He wanted to see how the memes they contained would survive—if they *could* survive—on Sand Mountain.

And this was his answer. In the face of adversity, this was

what had persisted. The imprint of a life Linnea had read about and a man she had never met except through a diary and a few newspaper articles. Why? In some way that life had been more real, more important than the events that had happened in her own life. Something about it demanded to be lived—to carry on in spite of, or maybe because of, everything. The same was true for Acantha. She was the sister he had never had. The sister who still lived in his memory and dreams. But she was also the sister who'd volunteered for the J.I.S.E.C. project while he was in rehab, and then ended her life before the datamap was complete. He had wanted to make peace with her, to undo the past and start over. Maybe she'd wanted that as well. Maybe that was the reason she, too, had signed up to become a simunculus. And when the design space simulation on Aelon didn't go as hoped, he'd started over with Mee Won. Maybe on a different world, under different initial conditions, they could have the life they had missed out on.

As usual, things hadn't gone as planned.

"Are you going to jump?" Olavo asked.

"I was thinking about it. But it's such a beautiful afternoon. I hate to ruin it for all these people."

He stared across the lake bed. "Where will you go? Back to the city?"

"I don't know." The focus of her gaze shortened to her pink fingernails on the rail. "Is there anything to go back to?"

"That depends."

"On what?"

"You."

Mee Won turned. She rested the small of her back against the rail to look past the levee of hills that shielded the polis from the brunt of thermal storms roiling off the dune-studded plain. After a moment, she sat down next to her umbrella, settling herself against the thick structural supports.

Olavo joined her. He picked up the umbrella and held it over them. "I can help if you want."

"Can you?"

"I can take you from this world to another. It will be different. I can't promise it will be better."

"But there's a chance."

"When you wake up," he said, "you never know what kind of day it's going to be."

"Just that it will be different," she said.

He nodded.

"All right." She closed her eyes and went to sleep in the silken, blue-tinged shade.

46

Selma, October 11

"This is the place," Celia said. She cut the engine but continued to grip the steering wheel with both hands. To Rudi, she seemed reluctant to be here. She couldn't wait to leave.

The West Highland Veterinary Clinic was a relatively new cinder-block building next to an Exxon hydrogen fuel cell station and a yarn shop called the Golden Fleece. The cinder block was painted beige. Two glass doors, placed side by side, occupied the center of the otherwise featureless façade. The door on the right had a picture of a dog stenciled on the glass. The door on the left was for cats. A green pickup truck crouched in front of it.

"How's Tenley doing?" Rudi asked.

"I couldn't tell you."

"You haven't talked to her?"

"No, Rudi, I haven't." She sounded weary, bored almost, as if they were covering old ground.

For some reason, Rudi assumed they'd been in contact. Not on a regular basis, maybe, but from time to time. Not because Tenley cared about him—that was too much to hope for—but because Celia needed her for information about his past, things he'd done or what he'd been like. But maybe that wasn't important anymore. Maybe Celia had already gotten all the information she needed.

A rust-spotted station wagon pulled into the space next to them. The driver, an overweight woman with unkempt gray hair, eased out. A black Lab retriever panted in the passenger seat, looking enervated and desultory. It took the woman four determined yanks to open the passenger door.

The dog hopped out dutifully, favoring a hind leg. The fur was crusted with blood, dried and matted despite attempts to cleanse the wound. It looked like the dog had gotten into a fight, most likely with a raccoon, and come out worse for the wear. Together, they hobbled into the vet.

Rudi picked up the cardboard box at his feet. The box contained the remains of the stuffed cat. He had tried to wipe off most of the dirt, but the fake fur had started to come out in places and in the end he'd given up. "I won't be long," he said, and pushed open the door.

"Good luck."

"You're not coming with me?"

"Not this time, Rudi. You're on your own."

"You don't want to record the event for posterity, or whatever?"

"No. I don't think that would be a good idea. I think this is something you need to do yourself."

Besides, her expression seemed to imply, whatever happened would be recorded by the data collectors in his head.

"Right," he said, "I'll see you." He closed the door and made his way to the cat side of the office.

"Can I help you?" the receptionist said, smacking spearmint gum.

"I have a sick cat." He pointed to the box he'd left on one of the plastic chairs in the waiting room.

"Dr. Ferrer is with another patient right now. Have you been in before?"

"No."

"Here." The woman handed him a clipboard with an information sheet and a pen. "Why don't you go ahead and fill this out and have a seat, and she'll be with you as soon as possible."

Rudi sat down with the clipboard. He stared at the information sheet. What was he going to tell her? About the cat? About himself? What did he expect her to say? They had said it all, the night of the accident. The only thing left was for him to apologize to her, to free her of any guilt, obligation, or worry she felt. Other than that, it was time for them to move on. He thought he could explain himself. But there was nothing to explain. About the cat or anything else.

After that it was easy to complete the sheet. Under name he wrote, "Uriel." For home address, he used the veterinary clinic. Under description of symptoms he wrote, "Evil spirit. I'm sorry for the harm I caused. It won't happen again."

He set the clipboard inside of the box, on top of the stuffed cat and the spirit bottle. "I'll be right back," he told the receptionist on his way out. "I forgot something in the car."

"That was quick," Celia said when he got back in the sedan. "How did it go? Is everything all right?"

"Fine," he said. "Better than I expected."

"I'm glad."

"Me, too." He fastened his seat belt.

Celia tightened her grip on the steering wheel. "What now?" she said.

"Let's go."

Celia turned the key in the ignition, backed away from the clinic, and pulled up to the shoulder of the blacktop. "What's next, Rudi? Have you come to a decision?"

"Do I have a choice?" he asked.

"You don't have to stay with the project." She sighed. "It's up to you. If you don't stay, someone else will. There will be others."

"What happens if I agree to participate?"

"You go on living your life. We continue to datamap your mind, filling in the details until we have a complete profile." She gazed out the windshield at the road. "Then, at some point, we ghost it—make an image of it—to see if you can exist independent of your physical body."

"Exist how?"

"Eventually you're going to die, Rudi. Like everyone else, you're only going to live for so long. We need to find out if the datamap can survive in another medium. After your body dies."

"Digitally, you mean?"

"It's the only way."

"For how long? What kind of life expectancy are we talking?" he asked. "If things work out?"

Celia shrugged. "Hundreds of years. Thousands. Maybe tens of thousands. It's hard to say. The universe is a huge place. Unless we can figure out how to bypass the speed of light, it's going to take a long time to get anywhere."

Rudi considered for a moment. "If I agree to be part of the program, I'd be the first. Right?"

"Yes." She tensed, waiting for the next shoe to drop.

"The first what?" he asked.

She shifted her grip on the leather steering wheel cover. "I'm not sure I follow you."

"What will I be called?" he said. "If I'm not going to be myself anymore—objectively or subjectively—what will I be?"

"I don't know, Rudi. There's a lot we don't know yet. This is just the beginning, the first step. A lot of questions still need to be answered. Who do you want to be? *What* do you want to be?"

"A simunculus," he said.

"A..." She frowned. "Simulated... homunculus?"

Rudi shrugged. "Have you got a better name?"

Celia repeated the name silently, trying it out. "We'll see, Rudi. It's not my decision." She squinted down the road. "So what's it going to be? Where do we go from here?"

47

Prattville, October 11

Rudi set the bouquet on the grass, then stepped back from the grave, his eyes dry. He had expected to cry, perhaps because that's what people expected and what he had therefore come to expect from himself.

Celia didn't seem to have any expectations of him, at least not when it came to the way he grieved. In this case, her journalistic indifference was a relief. There was no judgment on her part. He was able to be himself, and say good-bye in his own way without fear of embarrassing himself or disappointing her.

It helped that he didn't care what she thought.

"Satisfied now?" she said after a respectful moment of silence.

"Yes."

"So is this it? The last stop?" She seemed anxious to get going.

"I can't think of any others," he said.

"Not even Mr. Chin?"

Rudi shook his head. He had to give her credit; she wanted his break to be clean. No regrets. "Some other time."

"You sure?"

He nodded. But when Celia turned to go back down the hill to where she'd parked, he hesitated.

"What?" she said.

"Linnea," he said.

Sensing a complication, Celia's eyes narrowed. "What about her?"

"Is she part of the J.I.S.E.C. project?"

"I don't know, Rudi."

"Don't know, or won't say?"

"She could be. If she is, I haven't been told. Why?"

"Something she said, before she died."

"What was that?"

"She promised that she'd see me in the future."

"I honestly don't know, Rudi." Celia's sigh fell just short of exasperation. "That could mean a lot of things to a lot of people."

"I guess."

"You're holding on to something. What is it?"

"Memories," Rudi said, surprised by the admission. Until that moment, he hadn't known what was bothering him.

"What about them?"

"That's all it feels like I am. Something reconstructed, brought back to life from a hodgepodge of recollections."

"That's all any of us are," Celia said. "Even the future—as soon as we imagine it—becomes a kind of memory. No more real, but no less real."

"Is this real?" Rudi said. "Are you real? Or am I still in a coma, dreaming all this?"

"Some philosophers and religious thinkers maintain that the only true reality is the one contained inside of us, and that everything else is unreal."

Hardly the reassurance he was hoping for. "What about the artificial neurons, are they real?"

"As opposed to what?"

"I don't know." He threw his hands up in the air. "A reason for me to feel okay about myself, even though I'm not normal and never will be."

"A coping mechanism, you mean."

"Well?" he said.

She wet her lips and, for an instant, looked past him. "Reality is what we make it, Rudi. What we want and need it to be. Everything man-made you see around you was a dream at one point." Then her gaze returned, and he knew that she'd been talking about herself as well as him. "Sometimes we imagine things—events and people—because we have to. We pretend they exist to get us through. And for us, they do exist."

"Like the mother or father we never had? Or the people we wished we could have known." Like Benjamin Taupe, he thought. Who wanted not just to live, but to go beyond life to a different kind of life, in whatever form it took.

"It's the only reality that matters, Rudi. The one inside us. Even the objective world, if there is such a thing, is subjective. Different people can look at the same cloud and see something completely different. So who's to say which reality is real? They all are, and none of them are."

"All right," Rudi said. Like most things it sounded a lot more complicated than it probably was. Peace—and if not that, then acceptance—lay in knowing not only what to hold on to and what to let go of, but when. Timing was everything.

He followed her down the hill. When they were both in the car, he said, "I know what I want to do next."

"What's that, Rudi?"

He touched the soft lump of the wool tucked inside his windbreaker, unzipped the pocket, and pulled the prosthetic out. He studied it for a moment, then turned his gaze to the storefront of the Golden Fleece. "Learn to knit."

Celia turned to look at the breast. "From Irene?" she said.

"That's what I was thinking. If she's all right."

Celia's gaze shifted to his face. "She's doing fine, Rudi. From what I heard, the latest test results were positive, better than expected."

"Are you sure?"

"She doesn't need you to save her, Rudi. You can let go."

Maybe it was time. Maybe he'd done everything he could. "All right," he said after a moment. "I'm ready."

"Good." She pulled onto the gravel shoulder of the road. A dust-covered pickup passed by, leaving the road empty in both directions. "This is it," she said. "No looking back."

"No looking back," he agreed. "Let's put everything behind us."

She turned her head from the road to look at him. "It will catch up with you, Rudi. There's no escape. There's only so far, and so fast, you can go."

"I know. But it will buy us some time. We'll be free for a while." That was all he wanted, a little breathing room.

Celia nodded. "We can try, Rudi. A little something is better than a lot of nothing."

She eased onto the two-lane blacktop, then accelerated toward the vanishing point where the road met the sky.

48

San Francisco, Softspace

Blindness allowed Benjamin to see the world anew.

It was as if he had a second pair of eyes behind those going blind. As his vision failed, he began to see the world through different eyes. Each day, the world he had always known became slightly more obscure, while another world taking shape in its place became slightly more detailed.

The change occurred slowly. Some days he barely noticed any difference between the two worlds: a door where there used to be an alley, a new car or style of dress. Other days, the change was more noticeable: city streets moved... buildings changed shape, were replaced by different buildings, or vanished altogether.

The change affected not only his vision but his body. Over a period of months his strength improved and with it his balance, allowing him to wander the city in brief forays.

Was this what it felt like, he wondered, to wake up? A little bit at a time? Some days he couldn't remember what had come first—what had always been there, and what had replaced it.

To help him remember, he carried a diary with him

wherever he went. On the days when his vision was clear enough to read, he wrote as much as he could. He recorded not only where he went but what he thought. He described his activities and feelings in anthropological detail. The diary was as much a scientific log as it was a memoir of his personal transformation. Occasionally he composed letters to Etta. He had no one else to talk to about what was happening. Of the few people he knew, she seemed most likely to not only understand but to care.

The medical establishment was of little help. Follow-up X-rays taken at UCSF Radiological Laboratory showed a decrease in the size of his tumor.

"I can't explain it," Dr. Keane said. Perplexed, he held the radiograph up to a window and shook his head yet again.

The tumor was dissolving. On the X-ray it looked faded, diffuse—more imagined than real.

Two or three times a week, if the weather was decent, he made his way out to the Golden Gate Bridge and stood at mid-span. He gripped the cool railing and braced himself against the stiff breeze coming off the ocean behind him. He remembered a voice urging him to *jump.* But it was faraway. Somewhere in the distant past. Or possibly the distant future. Maybe someday he would jump. But not today. Today, with the breeze tightening his skin, he felt the world itself start to change around him, not just the city.

Looking down, he could see through the deepest water to the sand beneath. As he watched, the waves thinned to a spectral translucence and vanished, revealing scalloped ripples of sand blowing across irregular stone. Color rinsed from the air, like paint washed from a canvas, to reveal a different landscape underneath. Above the ocean, the deep blue tint in the sky evaporated, leaving a pale brown haze illuminated by a bright cluster of stars. Under his fingers, the thick red paint dissolved to black unblemished steel.

Benjamin whirled, light-headed. And found himself surrounded by a group of white-haired albinos, a doughy, expressionless man, and a family of short gnomes wearing purple hats.

The sky spun. Dizzy, Benjamin stepped back from the railing and turned.

The bay had vanished. In its place he saw a shallow lake. A beach populated with multicolored umbrellas. Clumps of tall reeds that sang to him with siren voices. He sat on the side of the bridge and stared at the rock outcropping on the far shore of the lake. Sand Mountain. He looked from the escarpment to his hands. They were albino white, the fingers long and delicate, tipped with pink. He couldn't remember what they'd looked like before. Had there been a before?

A shadow fell over him, blue-tinged. He closed his eyes and leaned his head back against one of the bridge supports.

All this time, he'd been wrong. The simunculi he'd seen at the séance, and on the streets, hadn't been a dream. They had been real all along. Everything else was a dream. Including him...

"Mee Won?"

She blinked, startled by the voice next to her, and turned. For a moment, she had the queasy sensation she was looking into a mirror, at a human with hollow eyes and short hair parted on one side. But the moment, and the disorientation, passed as quickly as it had come.

"How do you feel?" Olavo said.

"Tired. Like I just woke up." She frowned at the dress she was wearing. "What happened?"

"There was an ion storm. You fainted."

"Did I?" Her cheeks felt warm, powdered with the dry flakes left by soft radiation. "For how long?"

"A few minutes."

"I had a dream. A nightmare," she corrected. "In it, I dreamed I was a human. In the past. I had a tumor, and to keep from dying I needed to wake up."

"But you couldn't?"

"No, I was trapped inside the dream. It wouldn't let go. I knew there was another world beyond the dream. Every now and then I would catch glimpses of it, but I couldn't get to it."

"Well, you're awake now." Olavo lowered the umbrella, stood, and offered her a hand. "Do you think you can get up?"

Mee Won nodded. She took his hand, and pulled herself to her feet. "I've never passed out like that before. Do you think there's something wrong? Maybe I should go see a doctor."

"I think it's been a long day," Olavo said. "I think you've been working too hard and with a little rest, everything will be fine."

49

Orthinia, Softspace

"It's time," Vania said.

Olavo looked up from the climbing rosebush he was threading onto a wooden trellis. She waited at the edge of the garden, her expression as starched as her uniform. A dervish cloud of glass-winged insects hung in the air between them. He finished weaving a thorny stem through the white-plaited lattice and, dispersing the insects with a brisk hand-wave, went to join her.

"We've done everything we can," she said.

"What does that mean?" he asked. "Everything we can?" It didn't sound good.

Her jaw tightened, her lips pinched. "It means that you're as ready as you're going to be."

A note of apology continued to vibrate within the words. Olavo kept expecting her to say she was sorry.

Uta entered the courtyard from a side street, followed shortly by Ramunas, Jori, and Hossein.

"I don't feel ready." He wiped his hands on his pants. The tip of his right index finger stung, pricked by a thorn that had caught in the fabric. He sucked at the pain, tasting dirt and uncertainty.

"That's normal," Vania said. "You've gotten comfortable here. You're afraid you won't make it on your own. It will be difficult at first. But you'll be fine."

"You're giving up?"

"There's nothing more I can do for you," Vania said. "We've done everything we can . . . recovered all the synapse profiles and memories we could from Sand Mountain and your ship's library."

Panic fluttered, moth-wing soft against the inside of his chest. "I'm not whole, am I?" And never would be. That's what they were telling him.

"Not completely," Uta admitted. "Not to the extent we hoped. But there's enough for you to start over."

"What if it's not enough?" he said.

"Then you won't make it," Ramunas said. "We all knew that was possible."

"Of course," Jori said, "none of us thinks it will be us. Each of us believes that our design thread will survive."

"We've got a hardspace simunculus prepared for you," Uta said, trying to sound as optimistic as possible, given the circumstances.

"Whose ship would I be in?" he asked.

"You won't be on a ship," Hossein said. "You'll be on Orthinia with the rest of us."

Olavo scowled. "The surface?"

"We've decided that's where we're going to start over," Jori explained. "It's time. Before something comes along that we can't recover from."

"What about Sand Mountain?" he asked.

"Orthinia provides the best chance of survival," Hossein said. "This is it. The end of the road, so to speak. No more qinks." He forced a laugh.

"You're already down there, aren't you?" Olavo said. "You've been on the surface the whole time I've been recovering."

"Before bringing you down we needed to be certain that you could adapt to the new environment," Vania said. "We had to be sure you were functional."

"What would you have done if I wasn't? Left me on the ship forever, in softspace?"

"Yes," Ramunas said.

"What about Acantha?" he demanded, driven by a kind of feral consternation. "You can't just leave her."

"Your sister's gone," Uta said, choosing her tone carefully. "I'm afraid she's been gone for a long time."

"What do you mean? Dead?"

Uta glanced at Vania, who nodded in confirmation. "We were afraid to tell you any sooner. We wanted to wait until we were sure you could handle it."

"I don't believe you," he said.

"She left a note," Hossein said. "We ran across it in the process of recompiling your memories."

"What kind of note?"

Ramunas activated a pointer to the synapse pattern, making the memory available to him.

Dear Rudi,

I'm sorry to leave you this way. Truly. I didn't expect to be called home so soon, and not in this way. I expected to be around for a long time. Don't we all. It's not like I've been planning this for a long time. Believe it or not, I still had a lot of things I wanted to do in this life. Seeing you again, explaining myself, and apologizing to you for all the grief I put you through was one of them. . . .

He stopped reading. His head throbbed.

"She clearly felt guilty for what happened to you," Hossein said. "For leaving you the way she did."

"For being selfish," Jori amplified.

Olavo pressed his fingers to his temples. He remembered now why he'd wanted to be someone else.

"You were fragmented," Uta said. "You weren't thinking clearly."

"She was real," he insisted.

"She was," Uta said, "back on Earth. Three hundred years ago. But not here, not now."

"I'm sure she *seemed* real," Vania said. "I suppose, in a way, to the disconnected part of your mind that didn't want to forget her, didn't want to let go, she was real. But it was a projection."

"A hallucination," he said.

"No. More like a virtual memory. A softspace reimaging that existed, for a time, outside of any larger context."

"Because there was nothing to contradict it," Hossein said. "Nothing to call it into question."

"What about the *Golden Fleece* and Aelon?" he said. "The collectors she sent out, and the transmission I watched? Are you telling me I imagined that, as well?"

"They all came from you," Ramunas said. "Or rather, different parts of you, in the process of attempting to reintegrate."

"I'm sorry," Vania said. "I know how much she meant to you, and how much you wanted to keep her alive."

And Acantha had been born out of that desire. Who else had he created out of the softspace fragments of his mind?

Olavo inhaled, his ribs rigid as the brass bars of a cage. "How much of me is missing?" he asked.

"We're not sure," Vania said. "Pointers in your ship's library qink to several design space simunculi."

"But we don't know how fragmented or intact these local clones are," Hossein said. "We don't know how much damage they sustained."

"We made copies of those clones here," Jori said, "then integrated them as best we could into several stable, functional wholes."

Olavo's gaze flitted between them. "There's more than one?"

"We thought the pieces of you that we were assembling would fit together into one image," Hossein said. "A single picture."

"Unfortunately that didn't happen," Vania said. "What we ended up with were the pieces to three different pictures, jumbled together."

"Because of the data loss from the gamma ray burst," Uta said, "there was no way to combine the three images into a single image."

"I don't understand," Olavo said. "You're saying there will be three of me . . . three different personality profiles?"

"No," Vania said. "I'm afraid you have to choose one. You have to decide which version of yourself you want to save. Which life you want to live from this point forward."

In other words, which memories he wanted to keep . . . and which ones would fall by the wayside.

"Good luck," Uta said, smiling feebly.

Hossein nodded. "We'll be waiting for you."

"Whatever you decide is fine," Jori said. "Do what's best for you. What you feel is right."

Together, the four of them turned and strode back across the courtyard to the street with the doors that qinked to their respective ships and worlds. Except now there was only one world—Orthinia—they would call home.

Vania remained behind. Her softspace image was frozen. It clung to the air in front of him like an AdS transient.

Through her, in the smooth marble wall across the courtyard he saw three identical iron-gated doorways. The gates were arched, with heavy hinges. The corridors they gave access to were shadowed. Even when he approached the doorways, he could see no more than a few meters into the passageways. Beyond that, they remained shrouded in darkness.

For no particular reason, he gravitated to the window farthest from the balustrade. The iron clasp was unlocked. He lifted the latch, pulled the gate open, and took a tentative step into the tunnel. . . .

Rudi looked for Linnea at the funeral, but she wasn't there. She didn't know their grandmother had died. How could she? How could she not?

He stood next to the grave, and listened to the man from the funeral home read a passage from the Bible. When the funeral director was done, he watched the casket sink into the earth.

"It's my fault," Rudi said when the casket was out of sight.

The court-appointed counselor next to him, a short woman in a blue dress, looked down at him. "What's your fault?"

"That she's dead. I killed her." The confession burned his lips.

The counselor, Miss Parkins, knelt on the soggy grass. She glanced at the funeral director, who nodded and then quickly hurried off, leaving them alone. "Why do you say that?" she asked.

Rudi stared at the backhoe a short distance away, waiting to pounce. "I wasn't in the house when she died."

"Where were you?" Miss Parkins said.

"Next door."

"What were you doing next door?"

"Helping Tenley clean up a broken spirit bottle."

The woman pursed her lips. "Do you think that if you had been in the house, your grandmother would still be alive? Do you think that by being in the house, you were keeping her alive?"

Rudi nodded.

Miss Parkins let out a breath. "That's not true, Rudi."

"Yes, it is." He refused to look at her. Refused to take his eyes from the rectangle in the ground. It looked like an open door, leading down. As soon as he looked away the door would close. It would shut, and lock forever.

"Listen to me," the counselor said. "Your being there, or not being there, made no difference. Your grandmother was old. God called her home. You didn't have any say. We don't have that much power. As much as we'd like to think that we do, we just don't. We have control over a lot of things in our lives. But death's not one of them, Rudi. When our time is up, we got to go home no matter what anyone says or does."

The words and her tone were meant to absolve him. Instead, they left him with a greater sense of loss. He could feel the grave inside of him, a dank, dark hole cut into his chest, smelling of rotting grass and faded perfume. He thought he could hear music rising out of the emptiness, cold fingers reaching for his heart.

"There's someone I'd like you to meet," Miss Parkins said. A woman stood a few feet away. He hadn't noticed her earlier, during the funeral. But he hadn't seen her show up afterward, either.

"Hi, Rudi." The woman smiled, revealing lipstick-stained teeth as falsely uniform and white as her nails. "I'm terribly sorry for your loss."

"This is Bethlyn Samet," Miss Parkins said. "Starting first thing tomorrow, she's going to be your foster mother."

"Cecil and I feel so blessed you're going to come live with us," Bethlyn Samet gushed, smiling. "I hope we can provide as warm a home for you as your grandmother did."

An engine rumbled to life. When Rudi looked back to the grave the backhoe was filling in the hole, leaving a flowerless scab....

Olavo backed out of the passage, into the courtyard. The memory faded. He shut the gate with a soft clang. The tunnel was dark again. A few meters of dully lit stone and then tomb-cold blackness.

He rubbed at the goose bumps on his arms. After a few moments, he moved to the next gate. Again the interior was dark beyond a few meters. When he raised the latch the iron was cool against his fingers and faintly damp....

Fog shrouded the street in front of the row house. Heavy as damp cotton, it muted the clatter of engines and the normally bright bell of the Number 22 streetcar. Under it, the afternoon sun fizzled to an ember, dousing Benjamin's already frail vision.

He sat in a chair next to a tall double-hung window. A gray fog descended over the room, dimming the floral moldings, polished oak floors, and paisley wallpaper. He turned on the light next to the chair. Electric glow spilled onto the diary open on his lap. He could no longer see the words on the page, a letter to Etta, which he continued to write in his head.

> *...I don't think I have much longer. I don't know why. Maybe because my vision is improving and, in some perverse way, I can see more clearly what awaits me.*
>
> *Friday night, October 13, I went to the War Memorial Opera House for the first time. I've never been to an opera, and thought I should attend one while*

I still have the chance. Since curtain call was at 8:00, I took my cane, even though I've gotten quite good at stumbling my way around town in a permanent fog. This is in large part due to memory. That, at least, has yet to fail. If anything, it's sharper than ever.

The opera was Manon. *It starred Bidú Sayão as Manon Lescaut, Tito Schipa as Chevalier des Grieux, and Norman Cordon as Count des Grieux. The composer was Jules Massenet, the conductor Gaetano Merola. I was seated too far from the stage to discern much in the way of details. The costumes and action were a blur. The voices however were beautiful. Throughout the performance, I kept thinking of you. I heard your voice in all the solos. At the end, I left feeling uplifted and hopeful. I think you're my Manon—or at least my memory of you. That is what keeps me going. If I'm ever going to be saved, that is what will be my salvation.*

Benjamin laid the pen he was holding in the crease of the diary, closed the pages, and set the book on the table next to the chair. In the kitchen, a radio was playing. He'd forgotten he'd turned it on.

He sat listening. The music was soft, a pleasant whisper. He couldn't quite make out the words. It didn't matter. Like water, the sound flowed over and around him, open to interpretation. He could hear whatever he wanted in the current. He sat in the chair, in the fog, and let it baptize him . . . .

Olavo stepped back. As soon as he shut the gate the music faded, leaving a residue of melancholy.

He looked around. Vania's simunculus remained frozen behind him. Still waiting, he realized, for his decision.

He moved toward the third gate, set a few feet from the balustrade. He paused for a moment to stare out at the shoreline of mountains in the distance. Clouds lapped against them, sloshed up valleys and ravines, and retreated, drawn back to the plain by an invisible undertow.

The third gate was warm and dry, the hinges squeaked. Stepping into the passage, Olavo felt a breath of moist, garden-scented air against his face....

The backyard of the villa was shaded by wire-limbed trees draped with translucent skeins that shimmered like cellophane in the breeze. They reminded him of papier-mâché ornaments, ripped and torn to expose the underlying framework of wire. A flagstone path led through the orchard to a large rectangular pool. Fumes boiled from the surface of the pool, which was filled with some sort of oily sublimate held in place by a semi-permeable membrane. This silver condensate was home to a species of genetically flattened fish, or worm, that conjured the squirming, vertiginous image of a water-filled casket awash with drowned maggots.

Olavo moved on to the low stucco wall at the back of the garden. The villa sat at the top of a gentle slope overlooking a valley with other villas. In the distance, mountains rose above the nascent town. The sun—burgundy red in a chalice-gold sky—no longer seemed on the verge of bursting. His eyes, like his exomer-sheathed arms, were hard and impervious.

Roads, lined with the wire-frame trees and thickets of braided grass, connected the villas. Pontoon-buoyed sleds glided along the gently rolling lanes, kicking up clouds of crystalline grime. A few chitin-helmeted children rollicked in the bucolic fields. Like him, they wore wire-embroidered robes or jellabas. The electroconductive fabric rippled under the placid magnetic currents seething up from Orthinia's core.

Olavo turned back to the...

...Garden? Cemetery? Was there a difference? Plants and animals died. New life took hold, rising up out of the old to drink the blood of the sun....

Vania met him as he stepped back, out of the passage, and shut the gate. She had changed into a blue and green robe that resembled a kimono, smooth as satin and stitched with intricate floral designs in yellow and red.

"That's it?" he asked. "Those are my options?"

"The most stable ones. The personalities and memories most likely to succeed, in the long term."

"What about the unstable ones?"

"I'm sorry." She sighed and slipped her hands inside the generous sleeves of her robe. "I was hoping you wouldn't be disappointed."

"But part of a life is better than none," he said. "Right?"

"We should be grateful for what we have," the softspace agent concurred.

It wasn't a statement the original Vania would have made. He remembered her as more fatalistic. But the finer nuances of her personality had been lost in the transcription that now stood before him.

"How much time do I have to decide?" he asked.

"The sooner you decide, the sooner you can leave here."

"So I guess it's time to make the jump," Olavo said. "The leap of faith."

"You've done it before," Vania said. "That's why you're here now—why you're part of the J.I.S.E.C. mission. You adapted. You knew when it was time to let go. And you survived."

The implication being that he could do it again.

"That doesn't make it any easier," he said. "That doesn't mean it isn't going to be hard."

"It all boils down to trust," Vania said.

"In who?"

"Yourself, mostly."

"Okay." Olavo turned, considering the three options laid out in front of him. "I've made up my mind. Like you said, it's time to let go."

Vania looked relieved. Relief turned to surprise, then horror, as he walked to the balustrade, climbed onto the railing, and stepped off the edge.

50

Sand Mountain, Hardspace

When one door closed, another opened.

Olavo couldn't remember where he'd first heard that particular proverb—or when, for that matter. The exact origin eluded him. It was Spanish, or possibly Greek. Maybe it was both... but perhaps neither. Old world, in any case. It had been around for a long time.

And like many old things, the proverb sometimes led to something unexpected—or new. Often by choice, but more often out of necessity.

Olavo heard the door shut, not with a wall-rattling slam but the sudden cessation of data from the simunculus on the *Ignis Fatuus*. The qink to that particular softspace version of himself fell eerily silent. The change was enough to trigger the softspace daemon, running dutifully on the *Wings of Uriel*, to save the datamap of the simunculus it had been monitoring and alert Olavo of the change in status.

He paused on the bridge, brought up short by the daemon's unobtrusive mind-of-his-mind whisper.

"What's wrong?" Mee Won asked. They were nearly to the

other shore of the lake. Sand Mountain reflected on the pink, fear-filled curve of her eyes.

"Nothing," he said. Hoping it was true.

"You look worried."

Shaken was closer to the truth. He instructed the daemon to reestablish the qink to the simunculus. But the umbilical connecting it to the ship and him had been severed, and along with it his only wormhole to the *Ignis Fatuus* and the other simunculi.

Mee Won placed a hand on his arm, more to steady herself, he suspected, than him. "Are you all right?"

"I think so."

She looked doubtful, mirroring his doubt. "What happened?"

"I'm not sure yet."

Whatever had happened, he was alone. He still had the *Wings of Uriel.* And the local copy of the ship's library with all the design space information from the dead simunculus. But he had lost all contact with the others. He was cut off... free for the first time in—

"Bad news?" she asked, still trying to find a name for the anxiety eating at him.

Olavo blinked, turning the question over in his mind. "I don't think so," he finally said. "I did at first." He caught himself smiling. "Now I think it might turn out for the best. In the long run."

Her grip on his arm relaxed. "What do you mean, in the long run?"

"I have a feeling I'm going to be here for a while. Longer than I thought."

Her brow wrinkled. "How long?"

"We'll see," he said. He took her by the hand. "Come on. Let's go home."

ABOUT THE AUTHOR

MARK BUDZ is the author of *Idolon*, *Crache*, and *Clade*. The latter won a Norton Award. He lives with his wife in the Santa Cruz Mountains of northern California.